Praise for Anthony Bidulka's previous books:

"Quant...makes for a riveting hero...the kind of friend you want to have—unless you're a killer." *Mystery Scene Magazine (New York)*

"Few...could match [Russell Quant's] over-the-top cleverness with words or archness of observation." *Canadian Book Review Annual*

"Bidulka is clear evidence that writing in the mystery genre does not automatically preclude character development or emotional connection with the reader." *Wayves (Halifax)*

"The best thing about Bidulka's mysteries is the cast of by now well-developed, endearing chracters." *Quill & Quire (Toronto)*

"...a novel that entertains and broadens horizons; something...all literature should do." *New Winnipeg (Winnipeg)*

"If you've missed the previous...novels set in Saskatoon and featuring gay sleuth Russell Quant, you'll want them first." *Globe & Mail (Toronto)*

"Bidulka is skilled at juggling a number of balls, keeping the plot and subplots spinning until the end, prompting the greedy reader to demand: 'Where's the next one?'." *Lavender Magazine (Minnesota)*

"Anthony Bidulka paints the Prairies a lighter shade of noir...." *The Georgia Straight (Vancouver)*

"Bidulka treats the reader to enough red herrings to open a fish-market and more than one writer's fair share of keen observations and appealing *bons mots*." *Outlooks (Calgary)*

"...the pages turn at frantic speed, each suspenseful chapter a chaser for the preceding." *Swerve (Winnipeg)*

"...Quant is a delight to spend time with..." *StarPhoenix (Saskatoon)*

"Between Quant's quips and hard-boiled comments and the colourful cast that includes enough suspicious characters to fill a rogues' gallery, readers will find that Detective Russell Quant is a fun guy..." *tobe (Ottawa)*

"...just about everything's right with Anthony Bidulka's fledgling series..." *The Free Press (London)*

"Bidulka manages to spin a compelling detective story with colourful characters, hilarious situations, and touching relationships." *Midwest Book Review*

"Bidulka gives Quant an exceptional voice in crime fiction, not only distinct but distinctly Canadian." *BooksnBytes*

"...a Russell Quant tale is highly entertaining, from strange beginning to amusing, twisted end." *The Edmonton Journal (Edmonton)*

"...carries the reader along on an exuberant joy ride of action with sporadic pit stops for mayhem, menace and occasional romance." *Wayves (Halifax)*

"One of the book's most enjoyable aspects is its lively descriptions of foreign places...it is clear that Bidulka has traveled there himself and his novel captures the flavor of those travels quite vividly." *Altar Magazine (Brooklyn, NY)*

"...Bidulka's Quant mysteries always crackle with action, suspense, intricate plotting..." *Planet S (Saskatoon)*

Sundowner Ubuntu

Also by the author

Amuse Bouche
Flight of Aquavit
Tapas on the Ramblas
Stain of the Berry

Sundowner
Ubuntu

A Russell Quant Mystery

Anthony Bidulka

INSOMNIAC PRESS

Library and Archives Canada Cataloguing in Publication

Bidulka, Anthony, 1962- ☐   Sundowner Ubuntu / Anthony Bidulka.

(A Russell Quant mystery) ISBN 978-1-897178-43-0

    I. Title. II. Series: Bidulka, Anthony, 1962- . Russell Quant mystery.
PS8553.I319S95 2007   C813'.6   C2007-904516-2

The publisher gratefully acknowledges the support of the Canada Council, the Ontario Arts Council and the Department of Canadian Heritage through the Book Publishing Industry Development Program.

Printed and bound in Canada

Insomniac Press
192 Spadina Avenue, Suite 403
Toronto, Ontario, Canada, M5T 2C2
www.insomniacpress.com

Canada

The Canada Council | Le Conseil des Arts
for the Arts | du Canada
since 1957 | depuis 1957

ONTARIO ARTS COUNCIL
CONSEIL DES ARTS DE L'ONTARIO

For our beloved Mocha & Bali

Missing you

Belly scratches and love
Tony and Herb

Acknowledgements

I am writing this late on a Friday afternoon, after a long week of work, happy to take the time to recall the many people and places, events and celebrations that are woven into the intricate patterns that make up this book. After five novels, I know that writing a book is about much more than sitting in front of a computer. It is about YOU the reader, and it is about:

The faces I see, from the first launch, the first book reading, the first book club, the first promotional appearance, to the last. I wish I could name all of you here, but I do remember you, and you are dear to me. You celebrate with me; you bolster me; you communicate so much by being there. Then you give even more: e-mails, calls, gifts, flowers, letters and cards. I am the luckiest man. From Humboldt to Houston, Swift Current to Seattle, and all the stops in between—it's been a wonderful ride and what a pleasure to have been on it with you.

Everyone knows there is nothing quite like *feeling the love* from your hometown peeps. October 26, 2006: I still fall to wordlessness when asked to describe that night. You do me a great honour by continuing to show up…no, not just show up…by being a wave of support that washes over me and buoys me and gives me the confidence to keep on going.

Once upon a time, in the magical land of Audit & Accounting, I worked for a firm called Ernst & Young. Our fearless leader was Shelley. Shelley led an incredible troupe of people, including Nikki, Karren, Bev, Rhonda, Ashley, Laurie, Donna, Lilly, Noreen, Sherri-Lynn, Trina, Cheryl, Gail, Janet, and sometimes, all the way from Regina, Ken. There are bits and pieces of our lives (and the people that go along with them) that stay with us forever, and thankfully, this is one of mine.

In a world full of news, I am especially appreciative when the women and men of print, radio, web, and TV give Russell Quant their time and attention. Be it a book review, broadcast or back slap, you have my gratitude. I hope you know that.

Special moments and people abound—did I mention how

lucky I am?—the Pacific Palisades party in Vancouver; Bouchercon in Madison; Saskatoon launch special guest Rob Harasymchuk; tableside dinner readings of my work by Lynne, Jill, Kelly, Marv, Herb, Rhonda, Shelley; Fran making it to Humboldt over skating rink roads. Britainy and Ned, thanks for the great coverage; *PlanetS* readers, thanks for putting me on your favourite author list again—I'm shooting for #1 some day! Sandra, you tingled my spine in that under-construction hotel bar; Jessica and Steve rock; Pat and Mike, *zapiastock*; Kathryn and Gerard and Judy, thanks for always showing up; Leona and Jerry, I look forward to many more great meals together; Robert, you give good Archives; Richard for much more music; I finally met Nigel—you are one special guy; Gord, Mary, Heather, Andree, Bill—avuncularly yours; Debi— loved meeting you in Seattle; hi, Pat & Jack, Dan, Judy and Jim in Seattle too—what a treat to see you there; Holly—so glad you survived the Titanic; Jo-Ann, and especially Frances and cohorts, thanks for an evening below a sky of flying pigs; Farewell, Jim. Farewell, Dick. Travelling through Texas with Caro Soles—thank you to all the terrific people who proved that Texas hospitality is alive and well: Sue for a special day at Dallas's Cathedral of Hope; Dan and Rosario for keeping Austin weird; Alex, Will and the incomparable Wayne Gunn for a fantastic night out in San Antonio; Paul for the great work you do with Saints & Sinners; Ellen—I'll dine out with you in New Orleans any time! Thanks Mom and Moo for taking on New York with such style and grace; Gio and Norm for the rock star jacket; all the entrants in the Frances Morrison Library Seniors Writing Contest for sharing your wonderful stories; book clubbers for many enjoyable nights. Presenting a Lammy is always fun—thanks Charles. Congrats Dori on your new line of SOB undergarments. Thanks to the real Roy for ferrying us safely about South Africa and keeping us well informed; thank you to all our safari guides and companions, friends of David (Hi Craig and Vicky and Pookie, thanks for the pink champagne in Cape Town!) We wish all good things for you, Kumelo. Who doesn't want to meet Arthur Drache? Thanks for supporting HRC, Steve O'Neill. Thanks to family and friends for an unbreakable circle of support.

Africa introduced us to the spirit of *ubuntu*, which we will do our best to keep with us. From that experience grew new relationships with special children who needed help, and for that we are grateful.

Author! Author! So many writers who I admire, love and learn from have given me their time and the benefit of their wisdom and friendship over the past year. From conference panels to GWR to drinks to dinners out to joint readings to quick hugs as we find time for them; let's do it all again soon.

And to the booksellers, I thank you for your hard work, dedication and creativity, for welcoming Russell Quant and for striving to keep the world of reading alive and well.

Mike, Gillian and the rest of the Insomniac gang, thanks for putting these stories between covers. Michele Karlsberg, thank you for your continued support, guidance and friendship—I hope you enjoy Aquavit.

Excerpts from an editor's letter: "Your penchant for long, often five-line sentences is getting under control...the sub-mystery is really a grand diversion...I really wasn't sure what the heck was going on...the reader is able to stay focused on the mystery storyline while you quietly follow up with past circumstances...is this an inside joke?...I did find it incongruent...I want to see what he looks at for seven hours...I'm a bit torn in terms of directing you one way or another...either I'm suffering from brain sludge or I'm being too picky...really great here, no easy answers, no easy outs...the reader is left wondering about outcomes but with some hopefulness...confident, comfortable and believable..." Thank you, Catherine, for helping to make it so. Your heart and mind are so clearly a part of this.

And Herb.

Chapter 1

Murder.

There are many reasons to commit it.

Mine? My mother asked me to.

The snow was crunchy underfoot as I approached the weathered house where he lived. Although in my head I knew it was impossible, I had a feeling in my sour gut that he knew I was coming for him. As I hesitated outside the door, I passed the knife from hand to hand, feeling its unfamiliar heft in my sweating palms, then tested the glistening blade's sharpness against my thumb.

My eyes crinkled against bright morning sun. "Quant," I muttered under frosty breath, "what the hell are you doing?"

But, disgusted as I was, I could not turn away.

The door shuddered, then made a scraping noise as I slowly pulled it open, wrecking my hope for silence so as not to announce my arrival to Mr. Crow—or anyone else—inside. Not that it mattered much; my course was set. I poked my head inside and was instantly assaulted by an acrid scent; *eau de* ammonia. Cloying warmth encircled me. As my pupils adjusted to the darkness, I heard sounds of burbling disturbance and discontent. Our eyes met. And so it began.

I quickly circled behind him, grabbing him and locking him in my arms. Surprisingly, he barely struggled as I took him outside. He knew. I splayed him on the white ground beneath my greater bulk, my knees and thighs keeping him in place, and shivered at the thought of what I was about to do. I began to entertain wild thoughts of alternative courses of action.

It was too late to turn back now.

I pulled back his head, revealing his vulnerable neck to the nippy air. Only then did he make gurgling sounds of protest. Maybe he hadn't really believed I'd be capable of this until right then, in that last, defining moment of his life. But it was too late for Mr. Crow, way too late. This had to be done.

Tightening my grip around the wooden handle of the knife, knuckles white, I pressed the sharp cutting edge of the instrument against his throat. I was surprised by the ease with which the knife did its evil duty. I was even more surprised by the amount of blood and how it spurted and spewed. The body underneath me shook with a death fury that unhinged me with its intensity. Although he was no match for me in size, I felt myself being bucked off; I fell back, slipping on an ice patch as I attempted to get a grip with my Timberland boots and pull myself up.

Dumped on my ass, the first thing I noticed was the knife, still in my hand. It looked perfectly clean, as if I'd wiped it off, yet I hadn't. The steel had been cold, the blood hot; the two did not stick together.

The second thing I noticed was the headless body of my victim rising to his feet.

My face contorted in horror as I realized that Mr. Crow was not dead.

He turned a full three-hundred-and-sixty degrees, swayed left, then right, hopped from one foot to the other, then he turned again.

I haltingly made it to my feet, the knife falling to the ground, burying itself beneath reddened snow. Mr. Crow made a jarring move towards me.

Then he charged.

I turned and ran for the hills, a scream burning in my throat.

"Dat's goot, uhuh?" my mother, Kay Quant née Wistonchuk, asked for the millionth time as I forked another heap of her home

14

cooking into my mouth.

March had come in like a lion, a roaring storm chasing me from Saskatoon to Howell as I'd headed for my mother's homestead farm for what was supposed to be a two-hour visit. That was two days ago. I'd been storm-stayed—and desperately trying to shovel my way out ever since.

"You haf no chicken?"

Damnation, she'd noticed. I thought for sure that with all the other meats—meatballs, beef slabs, veal cutlets, farmer's sausage—she wouldn't.

"You don't like de chicken, den? It's goot." She passed me the platter, heavy with deep-fried, golden pieces of Mr. Crow, and urged me with her eyes. "Have the *letka*."

"My plate's full right now, Mom," I begged off on her offer of the drumstick, the leg of the same chicken that had tried to chase me down in that bloodied field of trampled snow, even after its owner had lost his head. "Maybe later." Like never.

I just couldn't bring myself to eat it, and perhaps I will never eat chicken again. Each time I see a leg or some other readily identifiable chicken part, I picture the *Braveheart* battleground of Mr. Crow's last stand. Sure, he'd come to his execution willingly, with uncommon dignity even, but things got ugly after that. That damn Mr. Crow, named—by my mother—after his morning ritual, seemed as capable of living without a head as he was with one (at least for several, horrifyingly long minutes, and he'd made the best of them). By the end of his pursuit, during which he'd demonstrated an uncanny sense of where I was (*sans* eyes to see me with), the previously pristine landscape surrounding the henhouse—once gleaming white from the storm's snowfall—was splattered a grisly crimson, as though a game of paintball had gone dreadfully wrong. I had taken refuge atop a nearby grain seeder turned flowerpot, amongst brittle stalks of long dead delphiniums and shasta daisies and watched in utter horror as Mr. Crow danced headless to his slooooooooooooow death.

"Vell, ve go to town tomorrow, and I buy odder meat mebbe, uhuh? You tell vhat you like and I buy," my mother offered.

I finished chewing a tasty pickled beet before giving the reply

I knew she'd been dreading. "Mom, I'm going home tomorrow morning. I've been here two days, and I really have to get back to work."

"Not two days," she argued back. "You vant cream in coffee? Vhat for dessert? I heat up some *nalesnehkeh*."

"Yeah, Mom, two days."

"But de roads, not safe yet. You vait one more day, dey be much better den, uhuh."

I knew it wasn't the roads she was really worried about; it was loneliness, the result of cabin fever that commonly sets in with farm folk, particularly near the end of long winters. She wanted me to stay. She always does, as a matter of fact, winter or summer. It makes me feel wanted, for sure, but it's difficult being a detective from a desolate farmhouse, nestled in the hills that surround Howell, Saskatchewan, population too low to count.

When it comes to where I prefer to lay my head at night, I am much like my mother: stubborn. If at all possible, I want to be in my own bed, in my own house, with my dogs and things surrounding me, in the nest I've worked a lifetime to build. I want running water that is hot consistently, rather than on a whim as it is on the farm. I want it gushing from the shower head, not dribbling out between globs of rust. I want to flush the toilet with careless abandon, rather than with bitten lip in fear of the septic system acting up, as it so often does. I want Internet access and more than three channels on the TV. I want 7-Eleven and Mr. Sub and a gym to go to rather than an exercise routine that includes a few laps around the barn with a mouldy German shepherd-husky-cross nipping at my heels and looking at me as if I'm crazy for running around with nothing to chase.

I do not want to murder my supper.

She was lonely. I got that. My father had died several years earlier and Mom had decided to maintain the status quo and remain on the farm. She did what she could to keep things as they had been, which included blocking her son from returning to his life in the city every chance she got.

"The graders have gone by a couple of times," I told her. "The roads are good. I checked when I was outside earlier." While escaping the beheaded Mr. Crow.

She nodded as if not really caring, and rose to reheat that morning's coffee in an old tin pot that sat atop the stove.

"Why don't you come into the city with me for a few days?"

Some time ago we'd even talked about her moving in with me—well, into the space above my garage, so technically she would be moving in *next* to me. Mom's only sixty-seven, but I worry about her living in relative isolation. Even I get a bit creeped out being on the farm—it's *really* dark, and when the coyotes start to howl at night it sounds as if they're right at your doorstep.

What a city boy I've become.

"Vhat for? Vhat I do in city? You go. You go and take care of dose dogs. Your poor dogs, vhat's happened to dose poor dogs?"

"Carol is looking after them," I told her. By Carol I meant Errall, and by Errall I meant Sereena. When I'd called her about being stuck in the country, my neighbour Sereena had agreed to look after my pooches, Barbra and Brutus. My mother and Sereena have met, but their very essences are at such polar extremes, they've chosen to ignore the existence of one another. So that's why I told Mom that my friend, Errall—which she pronounces as Carol—was looking after the dogs.

"We can hang out, go to movies, whatever, but Mom," I said with an unpleasant lump of guilt in my stomach. "I've really got to get back."

"I know, Sonsyou, I know."

Clara Ridge was half an hour late for her appointment, which was going to make things tight; I had to be at the airport by five.

"I'm very sorry," she apologized as she lowered herself into the chair in front of my desk, pulling off black leather gloves by their fingertips. "I hate being late."

Usually a statement like that is followed by an explanation, but when it became apparent none was forthcoming I moved along. "Are you sure I can't take your coat? Would you like a coffee or something else to drink?"

She shook her head and I noticed her hair, styled to within an inch of its freshly dyed life, moved along with it, without one follicle falling out of place. "Thank you, but your receptionist already offered. I'm a little chilled, so I'll keep my coat on."

Clara Ridge was a handsome woman in her mid fifties who'd obviously gone to some trouble to appear in my office looking well-groomed. Along with the too perfect hair was a spotless makeup job and fresh manicure complete with bright red nail polish. Her coat was dark fur, real fur; don't see those around much anymore.

"I saw your ad in the Yellow Pages," she told me. "I hope that's okay. I haven't been referred or anything. You know how it is with doctors—specialists especially—if you haven't been referred by another doctor, they simply won't see you, no matter how long you're willing to wait for an appointment. Are private detectives like that? I don't know, that's why I'm asking."

I smiled. "Not this one."

In fact, I wasn't too picky at all about how my clients came to me. Being a detective in Saskatoon, a small prairie city, has its challenges. There isn't a mysterious dame (or dude) smoking a long, slim cigarette, wearing a jaunty hat low over worried eyes, silhouetted against the frosted glass of my office door at midnight, nearly often enough to keep a private dick like me in continual work. I'd been lucky of late though, working fairly regularly, usually on rather pedestrian cases, affairs of domestic or financial distress, but they pay the bills and allow me a few indulgences (nice coats and scarves in winter, bedding plants in summer, shoes and good wine always).

"How can I help you?" I asked the woman.

"I want you to find my son. Can you do that?"

Immediately my mind went to some likely scenarios: runaway, druggie, custody battle. I nodded. "I can certainly give it my best, Mrs. Ridge." I reached for a pad of paper and pen. "Let's talk about details. What is your son's name, and when did he go missing?"

"His name is Matthew and he's been missing—or rather I haven't seen him—for about twenty years."

Holy Amelia Earhart! And you're just realizing it now? Not a very observant parent. "I see," I said with little conviction. "How old was Matthew the last time you saw him?"

Mrs. Ridge was staring straight at me, eyes wide, as if waiting to be led into telling a story she didn't want to tell but knew she had to. "Sixteen."

"Can you tell me what happened?" I was betting on a runaway.

"He didn't run away from home," she said, guessing my thoughts. (Either that or I'd said it out loud and didn't know it.) "He was...taken."

For a split second I had an unsettling feeling that aliens were going to come into this story, but I brushed it off. More likely a divorce custody arrangement gone bad. "By whom?"

"The police."

Although I wrote the two words on my pad, I didn't quite comprehend the connection between the cops and a missing kid. I stayed silent.

"You see, Matthew was a good boy; he really, really was."

Uh-oh, the deluded—and usually misguided—parent's refrain. How many teachers and police constables and social workers and babysitters and detectives had heard that one before?

"He was such a beautiful boy, too; tall, with the most gorgeous blond hair, like straw, and a sweet, sweet smile. He enjoyed school, did well, loved sports and had lots of friends. And we tried our best with him, but you know how it is, you get busy with life, work and all. We had a struggling business, a corner grocery store that my husband and I ran; we had no other employees to help out. Matthew seemed so well-adjusted, and well, we just didn't realize he was having problems; he got in with the wrong kind of kids, I guess.

"By the time he was thirteen he started getting into trouble with the police. At first it was petty vandalism, bullying kids in school, that kind of thing, not serious really. Even so, my husband, Clement, would punish him, severely. We thought it helped, but I guess...well, I guess it didn't. Things got worse. By the time Matthew turned sixteen he had started stealing things, getting involved with drugs." She seemed a bit flustered and began to peel off her fur. "I'm hot now. Perhaps I will take off my coat. Could I have a glass of water, please?"

While Mrs. Ridge de-furred herself, I poured a glass of water at my office sink and found ice cubes in the bar fridge that holds up one end of my desk. She accepted the drink and downed half of it, her eyes glued to the ceiling.

"Was Matthew arrested?" I queried to get her going again. "Is that why the police took him away?" I knew at sixteen Matthew Ridge would have been a minor and subject to different laws than an adult, but even so, there was punishment available for serious crimes committed by a teenager.

She nodded. "Yes. The summer after he completed grade ten. He got caught one too many times. He had multiple charges against him, a long history with the police by that point, so they decided—and we agreed—he needed to be rehabilitated. He was sent to reform school."

I do not know a lot about reformatories, but I was pretty certain they weren't in the habit of cutting off all contact between parents and their children. So then why had the Ridges never seen their son again? "Did Matthew escape from the school?"

"No," she whispered. "I'm sorry, Mr. Quant," she said, dabbing at her upper lip with the cocktail napkin I'd given her with her drink, "this is very difficult to talk about." She dug around in her purse and pulled out a neatly folded pile of tissues, no doubt softer than the napkin. Withdrawing one from the pile, she dabbed at the area under her eyes.

"Take your time," I said, touched by her obvious torment. There was something she wasn't telling me yet, but I could almost see it on the tip of her tongue. "Can you tell me why you didn't see Matthew after he went away? Did something happen to him at the school?"

"That's not it," she said. "You see, Mr. Quant, we hadn't seen Matthew for several weeks *before* he was sent away to reform school." She wrung her leather gloves and tissue together into a twisted rope of leather and…whatever it is tissues are made of. "You see, grade ten was a difficult time for Matthew, and he got into a lot of trouble. When it continued into the summer, my husband finally got fed up. He kicked Matthew out of the house and told him never to come back. Matthew's actions were affecting our business; most of our customers were local, friends and neighbours, but no one wanted to shop in a store owned by the family of Matthew Ridge, the biggest troublemaker in the area. People knew he was into drugs, and they thought he might be a dealer—although I'm sure he wasn't—and they didn't want their children anywhere near Matthew or his bad friends.

"I know it sounds stupid, I know it," she said, her voice growing hoarse with sorrow and despair. "We should have tried to help Matthew rather than put him out on the streets, but I was powerless against my husband's wishes. I told Clement it was better to have Matthew at home where at least we could watch over him, try to teach him some sense. I begged. But there was nothing I could do. When we heard that Matthew had continued to get into trouble and had been arrested, that was just the last straw for Clement. He washed his hands of him, as if he had no son. They sent him away. Matthew never called us; we never visited him, I don't...," she sobbed, "I don't even know if he ever got out of that horrible place, if he even survived it. I don't know what became of him. Oh God, Mr. Quant, I feel so horrible. I've been a terrible mother."

And she cried.

I offered her a box of tissues even though I knew she had her own stash somewhere in her lap. She took one and gazed pleadingly at me through a curtain of tears. "Can you help me?"

I looked at her, not immediately answering, wondering what happens to a middle-class but troubled, sixteen-year-old boy abandoned by his parents and left to fend for himself in the world.

"There was nothing I could do twenty years ago, but there is now," she told me, her voice suddenly strong, belying the tears.

"Has your husband had a change of heart?" I inquired.

"In a manner of speaking," she said. "My husband had a heart attack."

"Oh," I said, surprised for some reason. "I'm sorry."

"Don't be. He's dead. Six months ago." She didn't seem too broken up about it, so I swallowed any further words of sympathy. "In his will he left me everything. And do you know what that bastard did?"

I didn't, but I had the feeling I was about to find out. Something about a wife calling her dead husband a bastard sends a guilty thrill of anticipation through me. This was going to be good.

"He left me over a million dollars."

I cocked an eyebrow. Bastard wouldn't be the first name that came to mind for someone who left me a million bucks, but okay.

"We lived like paupers all our married life," she explained, her cheeks grown pink with emoting. "Clement always led me to believe that we were on the brink of bankruptcy, that we should eat hamburger rather than steak, repair our clothes rather than buy new ones, stay home rather than go out. And that's what we did, year after year after year. No joy in life at all. None of those special treats that people need sometimes. We just need them. Don't we? Sometimes? I hope you don't think me a frivolous woman, Mr. Quant, a pleasure seeker, because I'm not. I just wanted...I wanted...something more out of life than what we had."

She readjusted herself in her seat and kept on. "But do you know what the truth was? All along, instead of improving our lives, Matthew's life, my husband was using the earnings from the grocery store to invest in real estate, mostly houses near the university. Houses. He bought and sold houses. According to the people at the bank, most of them became little gold mines and netted him big profit, so I suppose he knew what he was doing. But we could have used that money, not only for ourselves, that's not what I mean, Mr. Quant, but we could have used it to get help for Matthew; he obviously needed it. We could have been a real family. We could have gone on vacations and done things together. Instead, our poor boy, our poor little boy, just disappeared...oh God," she sobbed, "how will he ever forgive me?"

I couldn't answer that. Although I admired Clara Ridge's desire to reconnect with her son, I couldn't help but wonder what twenty years of abandonment does to a boy's mind. Then again, he wouldn't be a child any more. Assuming Matthew Ridge was still alive, we were now dealing with a thirty-six-year-old man.

"Mrs. Ridge, are you certain this is what you want to do, to find Matthew? Have you thought it through?" Her son could be anywhere; he could be anyone. He could be alive or dead. He could be the president of a company or a low-life criminal. He could be married with six kids and living a happy life he didn't want interrupted by a woman who had, for all purposes that mattered to him, given him up to the streets. Or he could be a manipulative piece of scum who'd more than welcome a millionaire mama to take advantage of. At this point, the possibilities were endless.

"I've thought of nothing else since Clement died, and certainly since I found out about the money. I want to share it with my son. He deserves it, certainly more than I do. Who knows how hard his life has been? This could really help him. I hope it can help him," she told me in a voice confident that she was doing the right thing. "But I know what you mean, Mr. Quant. I want to find him, but he may not want to be found. I've thought about that too. And that's why I want you to keep your investigation a secret. I want you to find him, but when you do, don't let him know; don't tell him anything about me. I don't want to scare him off. Just find him—tell me where he is, what his life has become, where he lives, where he works and then...well, then I'll decide what to do. Maybe...maybe I'll just send him some money anonymously. All I know for sure is that I want to know if my son is alive or dead. And if he's alive, I'm going to help him."

I finished up my business with Clara Ridge—collecting what little data she had about her son, her contact information, a signed contract and a retainer cheque to get me started—by about quarter of five. After asking Lilly to show her out the front, I dashed down the back fire-stairs like a crazy man, jumped into my Mazda and headed for John G. Diefenbaker Airport.

Downtown and Idylwyld Drive were sausage-packed with rush hour traffic, and I was running about ten minutes late when I pulled into a metered spot in front of the terminal. Lucky for me the flight was running about twenty minutes late—weather delays in Vancouver—so I was waiting next to the luggage carousels (like a dutiful boyfriend should be) when Alex Canyon walked through the security doors.

Eight months earlier, in a set of complex circumstances involving my missing neighbour Sereena, my not-so-dead Uncle Lawrence, and a killer named Jin Chau, super hunk security specialist Alex Canyon had come into my life. Originally, although we were immensely attracted to one another, things were just too complicated to consider acting on our desires. Well, to be absolutely honest, Alex had proclaimed his attraction to me, and I sloughed it off because that's just my way of doing things around devilishly attractive men. So off he flew into the wild blue yonder to a world I knew nothing about. But then, under the guise of chaperoning Sereena back to Saskatoon, he had returned. So I showed him exactly how I felt about him, and continue to show him each time he is able to pull himself away from his *Get Smart*-secret-agent-type security duties long enough to catch a plane to Saskatoon— which was working out to be about once every six weeks or so.

"We just have time for a quick shower before we're expected at Sereena's for a fundraising dinner," I told Alex on the drive home, grinning to myself at the way he'd had to scrunch his Superman-sized body into the tiny confines of my Mazda RX-7 convertible.

"You're getting a different car," he announced with a mimicking grin of his own. "What fundraiser?"

"She's calling it her Robin Hood fundraiser: taking from the rich to give to the poor."

"Couldn't we just slip a cheque for a coupla hundred bucks under the door and stay home?"

My eyes moved from the road ahead of me to the man next to me. Of everyone I knew, Alex Canyon was the person most like the Energizer Bunny, with a seemingly endless source of oomph keeping him going and going and going. So, if he was tired, I knew he must have just come from a doozy of an assignment. We had an understanding whereby I didn't question him about his work—I had no clue whether he still worked for my uncle or even if my uncle, fatally ill when I last saw him, was still alive—and he didn't interrogate me about how many times I ate bologna sandwiches while he was out of town. "Tired?" was all I asked.

He shifted in his seat, as best he could, to face me. "That's not why I want to stay home." His left arm went behind my neck and I felt his lips zoom in on the spot between my right ear and where my hairline begins—one of my erogenous zones. (He'd been extraordinarily adept at finding every one of them in surprisingly short order given our minimal time together.) His right hand began doing other stuff I was finding to be pleasurable but quite distracting. Fortunately, by this point I'd reached the turnoff into the back alley behind my house and, although it was difficult manipulating the gearshift without disturbing Alex's actions, thanks to a remote door opener, I made quick work of pulling into the garage. Within seconds I had many fewer clothes on than I'd started with, and used a lever under my seat to recline back to enjoy the rest of the ride.

After several minutes of snuffling about below my waist Alex looked up with a serious look on his face.

"Is something wrong?" I asked, concerned.

He sniffed at the air. "Not really. I just think it would be a good idea if you turned the engine off."

Chapter 2

She was once a complete mystery to me. Sereena Orion Smith, the woman who lives next door to me, reminds me of a magnificent piece of art, an oil painting perhaps, displaying her flaws with as much unabashed prominence as her beauty.

Peals of laughter rang through the frigid air of the late-March night and I realized they'd come from her. I had never heard her laugh quite that way before. I'd always imagined there was something about her life, her past in particular, that restrained her from real laughter, the hearty, happy kind that many of us love to indulge in. Her laughs—the ones I was used to—were dry and brittle, her smiles wan and enigmatic. But tonight she laughed. Maybe it was because we were alone—despite the be-suited and be-gowned crowd we could see through the balcony's French doors. Maybe it was because I now knew a great deal more about her previously unrevealed past; maybe it was because she irksomely found the tale of our near demise extremely amusing.

"Sereena," I chastised, "it isn't funny. I'm telling you this story to elicit sympathy, not thigh-slapping guffaws."

"Oh, but Russell," she said, quickly recovering her composure, "just picture it, Mr. Courageous Detective and Mr. Macho Bodyguard, caught with their pants down in their own automobile, in their own garage, dead from carbon monoxide poisoning. All because they were too horny to turn off the engine after lowering the garage door. Honestly, Russell, it's too much. Imagine the obituary. Russell Quant, intrepid Saskatoon detective found…"

"Stop right there," I warned with a slight smile.

Having already moved on, Sereena swung around with a dramatic swish of the crinoline skirts of her mighty, ebony-hued ball gown. Her back to the terrace's stone guard-wall, she rested her elbows upon its ledge and fixed her eyes on the star-clustered sky. Around her shoulders she'd thrown a white ermine wrap with black tails and next to her left elbow was a flute of Veuve Clicquot turning frosty white from the cold.

Last summer I'd learned a great deal about my neighbour: her many marriages and affairs, miscarriages and mis-steps, loves and losses, her past lives of indulgence and adventure that spanned the globe, the sweet highs and bitter lows. And when it was all over, she'd ended up next door to me.

Now, she and I are different together. We don't talk much about her days gone by, but, as I'm one of only a few who know her whole story, it takes only a look or word between us to communicate volumes and know that we see each other more clearly than we ever did before.

"They're a fine group of people."

I looked at Sereena who'd lowered her gaze from the celestial bodies in the sky to those inside her drawing-room. She'd redecorated the spacious salon for the occasion, transforming it into a grand ballroom, with sparkling crystal candlelight chandeliers, floor-to-ceiling artwork depicting refined ladies and gentlemen staring out from a gentler time, and an expansive black-and-white tiled, silkily polished floor on which guests could promenade.

"And I see Mr. Canyon is playing nice," she commented.

I followed the path of Sereena's gaze and found my inamorato standing next to the piano, surrounded by several women in gaily tinted gowns that hinted at upcoming spring, and one disgruntled-looking husband in an ill-fitting tuxedo. I smiled with an odd kind of pride.

"Are you enjoying him?" she asked as if speaking of a new car or a Rolex watch.

"I am," I told her.

"Good."

"There seem to be some absences tonight," I observed, following a healthy swig of champers. "Errall? Anthony and Jared? What time are they arriving? Are they perfecting the grand late entrance?"

"I'm afraid not," Sereena said lightly.

What? I sensed something more to this. Not only were Sereena's parties not to be missed, but Anthony and Jared were intimately involved with this same charity, and Errall had told me herself that she would be here. What gave? I regarded my companion. Sereena is not a gossip. I knew I'd have to press to get more out of her. So I did.

"Errall and her latest are…having discussions," Sereena stated, "and called to give their regrets. Anthony and Jared, well, they're simply not here."

This was unsatisfactory. "Discussions" is Sereena-talk for a battle royal. And I knew Anthony and Jared would never simply not show up. Their reputations in all social circles as gentlemen of impeccable manners would not allow it. There had to be more to it. "Did you speak to them?" I inquired.

Sereena made a show of pulling away from the balustrade, and headed for the French doors, pulling them open with a flourish *à la* Joan Crawford. She tossed a smouldering look at me over her ermine-clad shoulder and declared, "I speak with guests, not no-shows." And in she went, quickly swallowed up by swarms of ardent admirers.

I detected a slight slur in her voice when I answered the phone. "Errall, can you slow down and tell me exactly what's wrong?" Was she drunk or just half-asleep? I knew which one I was as I stole a glance at the bedside clock. It was after three-frigging-a.m!

"There is someone outside my house!" she bellowed. "Is that clear enough for you?"

Ah, sweet, gentle Errall.

"Where's Nicole?" Sereena had told me the reason Errall hadn't been at the party was because Errall and her latest girlfriend were at home, having a fight.

"Yvonne."

"Oh. What happened to Nicole?"

"There is someone outside my house, you idiot!"

My brain was now fully awake and vibrating with the sound of Errall's unhappy voice. "Are you sure? Are you alone? Have you called the police?" I was alarmed but trying to keep my voice low so as not to wake the other inhabitants of my bedroom, namely one man and two dogs.

"Yes, yes, and I'm calling you aren't I?"

"Errall, call the police," I ordered, now taking this as seriously as I would have from the start, if it wasn't for all the champagne I'd consumed at Sereena's party, followed by some rather exhausting undercover maneuvers with my boyfriend.

"Really?" She sounded uncertain. Not a trait commonly exhibited by the normally dogmatic Errall Strane. "But, but…"

"Errall, if you think there is someone out there, call now! I'll be right there."

"Okay."

She hung up before either of us could say anymore. Had I just agreed to go over there? I lolled my head to the right to see if the ringing phone and muffled conversation had woken Alex. But who was I kidding? The guy was a security expert. Did I really think he'd sleep through this? My eyes landed on his naked bulk, seeming, as it always did (even when he was fast asleep), ready to jump into action.

"Tell me," he said, his eyes intense. He knew three a.m. calls often meant bad news. My dogs, snuffling and snoring somewhere on the floor below us, weren't nearly as intrigued.

"It's Errall. She thinks there's someone skulking around outside her house."

He sat up straighter. "Let's go."

I was about to say, "No dear, you stay here. Go back to bed, and I'll call you when I know something." But then again, who did I think we were? Rock Hudson and Doris Day? Alex Canyon was ready to go and in full *Rambo*-style fatigues, weaponry fully charged, before my bare feet hit the floor.

"Where are the cops?" I asked as Errall let us into the front door of her two-storey house on Pembina Avenue. "Aren't they here yet?" I couldn't believe it. It had taken us fifteen minutes to get there from across town, surely the police could have beat us.

"I didn't call them."

Errall was wrapped up tight in a plaid housecoat that was too thin for the time of year, and her hair was a messy pile on top of her head, held there by an incongruously girly banana clip. She was barefoot, and in her slender right hand she held a mug full of dark liquid.

"Why the hell not?"

"Alex," she greeted the big guy behind me, more as a way of ignoring my questions than in any real gracious-hostess-y way. "You guys want some coffee?"

"What we want is to be curled up together in bed for several uninterrupted hours." Middle-of-the-night house calls bring out the snarky in me. And so does Errall. "But instead, how about telling us what the heck is going on? And why haven't you called the cops? I'm gonna keep asking until you tell me, so out with it! And if this is some kind of joke—"

"No joke." She turned her back to us, leading us into the big kitchen at the back of the house where we each took a seat around the kitchen island. Errall began pouring coffee for us, regardless of the fact that neither of us wanted any.

"So? Why haven—"

Errall spun around and spat at me, "Okay, okay already!"

I waited. Patiently. Tapping my fingertips on the island counter.

"What if it was her?"

Alex and I exchanged looks but said nothing.

"Yvonne," she added helpfully. "She and I had a big fight tonight. She stormed out of here."

Errall had not been finding her re-entry into the world of dating an easy one. Not that that seemed to be stopping her from re-entering it over and over and over again with many, many women of late. But mine is not to question why. Well, actually, that's not strictly true. "Errall," I said, trying to sound more sympathetic.

"Tell us everything that happened from the beginning."

"Everything isn't your business," she began in her usual obliging way. "But Yvonne and I have been having some problems, I can tell you that. We've only been going out for a few weeks and already she wants to move in. She is such a lesbian! All she wants to do is stay home and watch *Claire of the Moon* and her DVD collection of *The L Word* episodes over and over again."

"And I'd bet she knows someone who knows Jodie Foster, right?" I couldn't help it.

In the interest of staving off the degradation of the current line of discussion, Alex wisely entered the fray. "What happened after the fight?"

Errall adjusted her sitting position so that she was facing Alex and would have to crane her neck to look at me. "She ran out of here like some fifties movie heroine and that was it. I drank half a bottle of wine, sulked a bit, and fell into bed."

"Then you heard something?"

"Yes. It wasn't very loud or anything, but whatever it was was enough to wake me up. It wasn't so much a noise as just that sense you get when you know something isn't the way it should be. Somebody was outside, I just knew it. Of course I didn't really, I suppose, but I was sure I could hear the soft squish of footsteps outside my bedroom window."

Ahhhh geeeez.

"I know what you mean," Alex said.

Uhhhh...what?

"Sounds that aren't supposed to be there are sometimes louder than they really are," he said. "Especially sounds around your own home because you know it so well."

She nodded wildly, at the same time tossing me a frown. "That's exactly it!"

She was actually smiling at him. Double ah geez.

"So you didn't really hear anything or see anything?" I handily summarized. And you were drinking, and upset from a lover's quarrel, I added to myself.

She ignored me some more. "After I talked to Russell..." Said as if I weren't there. "...I was about to call the police but then I thought, if it's Yvonne out there, I don't want to embarrass her, and I knew you guys were coming over, so I decided not to."

"The police are used to this type of thing, Errall," Alex said in a soothing voice. "If you ever doubt your safety, you shouldn't hesitate for a second to call them. That's why we have them."

"Do you still think it was her?" I asked.

She shook her head. "I called her."

"I want you to come home with us," I said. No matter what it was that had really happened or what Errall thought had happened, her fear was real enough and no one should be alone at a time like that. Even big meany Errall Strane.

She gave me a strange look and said, "I'm going over to Yvonne's."

That works too.

The three of us left the house together and as we waited for Errall to lock the front door I excused myself, asking Alex to keep watch over Errall. He didn't ask why. He knew what I was going to do. He'd thought of it himself.

I made my way down the side of the house and entered the woodsy backyard through a latched gate. I didn't have a flashlight, but the moon was full and filled the area behind Errall's house with a faint, blue light that reflected off the patina of snow like in a gloomy painting or a Tim Burton movie. I know this yard well, and, unlike my own, there is no second entrance at the rear via a back alley. There is no other way in, except the way I'd just come.

I gingerly stepped forward and peered down at the ground. The snow was undisturbed. Behind me, mine were the only tracks coming into the backyard. No one had been back here tonight. Although normally I would not think of Errall as the type of person to make things up or hear or see things that weren't really there, tonight that seemed to be the case. She'd been drinking. She'd had a fight with her girlfriend. She'd fallen into an uneasy sleep and a sound, likely something wholly innocent, had awakened her and spooked her. It happens to the best of us.

Just as I was about to turn back and return to where Alex and

Errall were waiting for me, something caught my eye. In the distance, the sheen of moonlight covering the hibernating lawn like a blanket, appeared...rumpled. I focused as best I could through the dim light and saw a definite trail, like a slithering snake, cutting through the snow.

Tracks.

I was wrong. There was another way in.

I moved closer, careful not to disturb the evidence.

Indeed there was a trail in the snow, my own track matching it as I followed it first to the back edge of the yard where someone had obviously climbed over the fence and into Errall's yard, then back toward the house where the footprints stopped. Right beneath Errall's bedroom window.

Monday, four-thirty a.m., I dropped Alex off at the airport for his stupid six a.m. Northwest Airlines flight to Minneapolis and points beyond. I was back to being a bachelor. I was tired, grumpy, coffee-less, and rather sore from carpet rash and whisker burn that covered an alarming portion of my body. Even though I'd already showered with Alex, I debated going home and cuddling up with Barbra and Brutus (who'd gone back to bed before we even left the house), but instead put on a my-work-is-never-done face and headed for the YWCA for a workout and another shower. I was even grumpier finding out I had to wait until six a.m. for the gym to open.

When I walked into PWC—once known as the Professional Womyn's Centre—which houses my office along with those of Errall the lawyer, Alberta the psychic, and Beverly the psychologist, the place was still dark. It was too early even for Lilly, our cheery-as-a-robin receptionist. I was hoping Errall might be in (as she often burns the candle at both ends), but her office door was locked tighter than my mother's change purse. I wanted to ask if she'd had any more unwelcome visitors or ideas about who had been traipsing about her backyard over the weekend. When I'd told her about the tracks I'd found, she was understandably upset and more than a little pissed off that I'd needed them to prove to me she wasn't hallucinating the whole thing. She'd concluded it was likely some neighbourhood kids on a prank, or a daring burglar who changed his or her mind after seeing the ADT Security sticker on her bedroom window. I hoped she was right.

Although I rarely do it, I love getting to work before daylight, before the clamour of regular business hours begins. I seem to get more done than usual against the backdrop of pitch black windows and impenetrable silence. And so it was that morning. I had fallen behind on a number of things during my unexpected two-day holiday with my mother and weekend with Alex, but nothing urgent. Until Clara Ridge hired me, I had only had a few small matters I was working on that needed wrapping up: finding a delinquent dad late on child-support payments (he'd moved in with his own mommy and daddy) and surveillance of a pizza delivery guy who was padding the bills in his own form of taxation. I drank coffee and filed stuff and prepared bills and paid bills and went through old stacks of mail and read the *StarPhoenix*, which had been sitting against the building's front door when I'd arrived. All-in-all a good day's work, and done by nine-thirty a.m.

I skipped down the stairs to the front door, tossing the paper at a surprised Lilly as I passed by on my way out. "Top o' the mornin' to ye, lass." (A good detective is always trying out new accents for use in undercover work.)

She gave me her usual wide smile, brimful of happy, not even blinking an eye at my brogue. "You too!" she called after me as I exited.

I decided the best place to start my search for Matthew Ridge would be the place where his parents first lost track of him: his high school. Mount Royal Collegiate is a west side public school, a typical, institutional-looking building which probably hadn't appeared much cheerier on ribbon cutting day. I entered through the front doors and found the hallways echoingly empty, as they should be in the middle of a school day, I suppose. I made my way to the counter of the Support Services area, home to several secretary-types behind computer monitors, but realm of one little Ms.

Frances Frey, the school's chief secretary and keeper of all important information. She was all of four feet tall in shabby heels. She wore a thick, navy sweater over a plain, white blouse, and a skirt that had seen a great deal of duty. Her thin, brown hair was masterfully feathered over her ears and forehead, but the rest just kind of hung there—out of sight, out of mind.

For quite some time I stood at the counter, watching as Ms. Frey, hunched at a desk, typed something into the bowels of her computer, something so vitally imperative to the continued existence of the school (and possibly the world) that she soundly ignored my presence. When it appeared she might finally take a break, disaster averted, I cleared my throat and shifted from one foot to the other, hoping for some attention. I tried a dashing smile, which went resolutely unappreciated.

"I'll be with you in a moment," she said as she referred to a pile of correspondence, no doubt time-sensitive missives from the principal and maybe the Prime Minister of Canada.

Glancing at some of the other faces in the room—thinking one of them might offer me assistance—it was wholly apparent by their averted eyes that it was solely Ms. Frey's job to deal with outsiders. I scoured the pale, blank walls for something to look at and settled on a large, round clock and watched it as the seconds ticked by with irritating regularity. The phone rang and Frances Frey answered it as if its clangorous ring somehow gave it priority over me and the computer. She talked a bit into the receiver, giving the caller some rather brusque instructions on how to load a photocopier with paper. I hoped, for the sake of the caller, she wouldn't have to go over there and do it herself.

"Can I help you?" she asked once she'd hung up the phone, her tone imperious and not at all friendly.

"I'd like to inquire about a student."

She looked at me without voicing her response, which was probably something like, "I'd like to run naked through a raging surf with Tom Cruise, but so what?"

I forged ahead. "He's an ex-student actually, and I was wondering if there was any information I could obtain about his time at Mount Royal."

"Student number?"

"No, I..."

"Name." Then she added succinctly, assuming my stupidity, "Of the student, not yours."

"Matthew Ridge."

"Doesn't sound familiar," she murmured as she typed furiously at her keyboard, studying the screen in front of her with laser-like intent. "Was he a student in term one? Before Christmas?"

"Ah, nope, a little longer ago than that."

She looked up at me with incredulity as if I should have already told her that. Maybe I should have. "Year?"

"Excuse me?" I'd heard her, but something about Ms. Frey made me want to piss her off.

"In what year did Mr. Ridge graduate?"

The phone rang and she picked it up with one sharp motion, eying me the entire time, her stubby fingers at the ready above the computer's defenseless keys, the nail of her middle finger vigorously clicking that of her thumb. She began speaking in impatient, clipped tones to the same person with the paperless photocopier problem—God help him or her—and told me with sharp eyes that she still expected an answer from me, for she was quite capable of dealing with more than one irritant at a time.

"He attended school here twenty years ago," I mouthed the words to her. Let's see what she makes of that.

She arched a severely plucked eyebrow at me before focusing all her attention on dressing down her caller for their inability to follow simple instructions. When that task was dispensed with, she hung up the phone and scoured me with a particularly abrasive look. Someone really needed to get out of the school system. "Just who are you sir, and why do you wish to know about a student who attended this school twenty years ago?"

So she could read lips. "My name is Russell Quant and I'm investigating the disappearance of one of your students, Matthew Ridge, twenty years ago."

"Well, I certainly wasn't here then," she told me, as if wanting to clear up any misconception that she could possibly have had any culpability in the misplacement of a student.

I'd play it her way. "As it seems your computer records don't go back that far, can you tell me if there is anyone currently on staff who might have been here at that time, or maybe you have old paper files?"

"Unless you have a subpoena that instructs me to release that information, I'm afraid that, for you Mr. Quant, that information will not be forthcoming."

Subpoena? Oh Kee-rist. I'd gone about this the wrong way. Ms. Frey was not to be bullied or flirted with, she was to be yielded to.

"Of course," I responded. "I certainly understand, and I admire your diligence in the protection of your students' information, and I'm sure they appreciate it too. I'll certainly mention that when I speak with Principal Rudnitsky." I had noticed one or two things other than the clock while I was waiting, including a staff roster posted to a bulletin board.

I turned to leave when I heard her say, "Mr. Rudnitsky wouldn't be the one you want to talk to."

My eyes fell back upon the sovereign queen. "Oh?"

"Mr. Rudnitsky has been here for less than a decade." Damned outsider! "Mr. Slavins, he's the PE instructor. He would have been here at the time Mr. Ridge went to school here. And there's one more thing you might find useful." She bopped up from her chair (giving her not much more clearance above the reception desk counter than when she was seated) and crossed her empire to a shelving unit, returning seconds later with a thin, bound book about the size of an eight-by-ten picture frame.

"What's this?"

"The yearbook for the year in question."

Smart cookie. I was warming to Ms. Frey. "May I have this for a while, Ms. Frey?"

"Absolutely," she told me as she whipped out a receipt book from a drawer. "That'll be twenty-four dollars and ninety-five cents."

After confirming that indeed he'd been a teacher at the school during the era in question, Donald Slavins agreed to meet me in the parking lot at the rear of the school during his morning break.

"Care for a chip?" he asked, holding forth a freshly opened bag of Zesty Nacho tortilla chips.

Yes! "No, thank you," I said, abstemiously.

The PE teacher was in his fifties sliding fast into sixties, bald as a drag queen's chest, and near on three hundred pounds. After washing down the last of the zesty triangles with half a can of no-name cola, he reached into the breast pocket of his shirt and withdrew a pack of smokes. I concluded he must teach by the "do as I say, not as I do" method.

"Now what's this all about? You said you're doing some research or something?"

"Not exactly," I said, wishing I'd worn a thicker coat. I had on a grey suede number that looked rocking (according to my menswear boutique-owning friend Anthony), but did little to keep tentacles of arctic air from slipping through its thin lining to nip at my skin. It wasn't spring yet. "I'm looking for one of your ex-students, and anything you could tell me about him or where he might have gone after leaving this school would be helpful."

"Oh," he replied between deep drags of smoke, not sounding very interested. "Why's that?"

"Excuse me?"

"Why you looking for this kid? He do something wrong or something?"

"No, not at all. I've been hired by his mother. She lost track of him and would like to see him again."

"Lost track!" he guffawed. "Not much of a mother, is she?"

Rude bugger. I let my eyes do the talking.

"So who's the kid?" he asked, ignoring my eyes.

"Matthew Ridge."

"Never heard of him," he answered, stamping his feet as if the cold had finally made it through his stratum of trans fat causing him to register the sub-zero temperature.

He was lying to me. I heard the hesitation in his voice, but, thankfully, I had Ms. Frey on my side. I just happened to have the yearbook from Matthew Ridge's tenth-grade school year. I turned to a page of individual photos, mostly acne-ravaged, gawky looking boys and heavily made up girls with hair so big at times it did not entirely fit within the frame of the picture. I pointed to one of the boys, a handsome lad with hair so blond it was almost white and a dimpled smile: the unrefined beginnings of a Hollywood hunk.

"So who's that?" Slavins asked in a manner that told me why he hadn't become a drama teacher.

"That would be Matthew Ridge."

"Yeah? Don't recognize the kid. Y'know, what year is that? I might have been teaching over at Hardy that year. Moved around a bit in those days, before I ended up here."

I flipped a few pages to the teachers' photos and pointed out Mr. Slavins minus twenty years, a hundred pounds and the disillusioned attitude; it looked good on him.

He lit up a second cigarette. "Oh, yeah, well, there ya go, there I am. Guess I was here that year. Don't remember the kid though."

I paged forward to near the back of the yearbook, to the section on sports teams, and indicated a picture of the basketball team. There was Matthew Ridge, and there was Donald Slavins as team coach.

"Yeah well, he was one kid of twenty; how's a guy supposed to remember one kid, eh?" he said with a forced chuckle. "Getting old y'know. Memory is the first to go; that's what they say, right?"

I turned to the next page. Volleyball: Matthew and coach Slavins. I regarded the teacher with a questioning eye and doubting look.

Slavins dropped his cigarette into the squishy snow beneath our feet where it spit its disappointment at being extinguished before its time. The big man stepped close to me and poked a sausage finger into my chest. I reeeeeeeeeally hate when people do that. "I told you I don't know the kid, didn't I?"

After a few seconds of him breathing his nacho smoker's breath at me I guessed he wanted an answer. "That's what you said," I admitted, but not without some attitude of my own.

"Well then, that's what I meant," he told me. "And you got no right snooping into this business anyway. His mother wants to see him so much? Misses him? Well maybe she shoulda thought about that twenty years ago? Eh? Right?"

I stood my ground silently.

"I don't wanna see your face again," he told—no, warned—me, then turned on his heel and entered the school through a windowless back door.

To the untrained eye, things hadn't gone so well. But to my way of thinking, they'd gone swell. Mr. PE's resistance to telling the truth told me one thing: I had a bona fide mystery on my hands.

Chapter 3

By mid-afternoon, I had successfully tracked down two of Matthew Ridge's high school buddies—from names I'd pulled from sports team rosters in the yearbook—but with little results. Both men certainly remembered their friend, but all they could recall is that he simply never came back to school after tenth grade, and they had no idea what happened to him. I moved on to a third name that I matched to a listing in the Saskatoon phone book: Allan Dartmouth. If it was the same guy, he'd become a massage therapist with his own business, Dartmouth Wellness Clinic, located in a busy strip mall on Circle Drive.

As I searched the mall's lot for a spot to leave my car, I found myself guessing what Mr. Dartmouth would look like compared to his yearbook photo. I was finding it fascinating to view the impact of time on the people who filled Matthew Ridge's life twenty years ago. When I first met them—or rather their pictures in a high school yearbook—they were fresh-faced and smiley, anxious to tackle the world and, if I correctly recalled how the mind of a sixteen or seventeen year old works, ready to party hard and always trying to get laid. Now they were adults in their mid-thirties, deep into careers they either chose or fell into and would likely keep for the rest of their working lives. They had families or wanted none. They had gained weight or lost weight, gained wrinkles, lost hair. They were either accomplished or, if not by this point, probably never would be. A lot of life is packed into twenty years and it changes a person. I wondered how it had changed Matthew Ridge. When I found him, what would he be like?

The young man behind the reception desk at Dartmouth Wellness Clinic was a no-nonsense kind of fellow who I guessed was the real control-wielder of the place, running the business with a firm hand and efficient manner. I could tell that nothing slipped by him, except maybe a wee detective?

"Good afternoon, which practitioner do you have an appointment with?" the young man, with a name badge that said Edward on it, asked me three seconds after I'd come through the front doors of the place.

I noted a casually elegant waiting room full of clients as I approached the desk. I debated a lie, telling him I had an appointment and making a scene when he didn't have it written down, but even I didn't buy it. Just by looking at the supercilious face of Edward—he'd never, ever, forgotten to write down an appointment (or, for that matter, made any other mistake throughout his entire life. I wondered if he was related to Ms. Frances Frey.) This was obviously a thriving business with little chance of downtime, so I went with an alternate lie. "I don't have an appointment," I began, "but I'd really like to get in to see Allan—he's an old school buddy of mine. I can see he's busy, but I just need a quick rub to sort out a sports injury before tonight's game. Is there anything at all you can do?"

Edward listened to me intently, taking in all the information and all the implied meanings of every word, and then asked me to take a seat, saying he'd see what he could do. About ten minutes later, he called me up to the desk and said he'd been able to arrange a short consultation and treatment for me in twenty minutes. I thanked him profusely and returned to my seat to further study Matthew's yearbook, which was becoming as familiar to me as a family photo album.

In exactly twenty minutes, I was called up to the desk by Edward, then led into the inner sanctum of the clinic by a young woman whom he introduced to me as *his* assistant, Sasha. As we gently floated down the white-walled, white-carpeted halls of Dartmouth Wellness Clinic, I noticed engraved door plaques bestowed each treatment room with a name like Serenity Palace or Peaceful Stirrings. I was told to enter Gentle Rain, doff my clothes and lie naked on the table, tummy down with a towel over my butt (not in exactly those words).

Two minutes later, there was a knock on the door, so unobtrusive I almost did not hear it.

"Come in," I called from my prone position on the massage table.

For the next few minutes a faceless stranger who identified himself as Dr. Dartmouth—I guess he got a doctorate in…something?—went about the well-rehearsed machinations of putting me at ease, identifying my massage needs and gently beginning the treatment by working gently on my back with big hands warmed with heated oil.

"Edward tells me we went to school together," the massage doctor slipped into the sparse conversation as his magic fingers moved to my lower back. "I don't recall the name."

Of course I never attended Mount Royal Collegiate with Allan Dartmouth, but I was counting on the fact that most people don't remember half the people they went to school with. "Yeah, it's hard to remember so long ago. Can you believe it's been almost twenty years since we graduated? I think we were a year apart though. I'm a private investigator now."

"Really? Isn't that interesting?" I think so.

"I'm looking into finding one of your classmates." Dartmouth and Matthew had been on several sports teams together, so I knew they knew each other and were probably friends. "Matthew Ridge."

I felt a sudden pressure change in the hands kneading my skin.

"Oh, Matthew, yeah." I felt the words expelled above my bare back, carried on a puff of cooled breath.

Not getting off that easy, buddy. "You were his friend, right?"

He was at my thighs now and pressing hard. "That feel alright?"

"Yes." It was about then that I realized how exposed I was to this man and that it probably would be in my best interests not to push him too hard if he didn't want to talk. Why didn't you just keep your clothes on, Quant? (I'd given myself that particular advice once or twice before.) "You knew Matthew pretty well, right?" I ventured again.

"Yes. He and I knew each other. Why are you looking for him?" He was bending my right leg at the knee, lowered it, and began pulsating the pad of my foot. Hard. "You okay?"

The electrical shivers that were coursing from my toes to a spot right behind my eyeballs were telling me no, but I could tell this guy knew something but was hesitant about spilling it, so I had to stick it out. "Fine, I'm fine. Feels good."

"Gooooood. I'm glad," he said in what might have been meant to be a comforting tone, but I was hearing something else, something faintly sinister. Maybe it was my imagination.

"You have any idea what happened to Matthew after grade ten? His mom would like to find him. She hasn't heard from him since then."

"He got sent to reform school or something like that, isn't that right?"

"Yes. Did you spend time with him at all that summer, before he got into trouble?"

"Turn over now, please."

I did as he said and caught his eye as he began to work on my chest. He looked at me a little too long, judging my intent I guess, before answering. "Not really, no. We were kids though. We got into all sorts of trouble back then. No big deal. I guess Matthew got caught and was sent off."

"You ever see him after he got back?"

"Absolutely not!"

I stared at him, registering his surprisingly vehement reaction with my eyes.

"I never saw him again," he quickly added, calmer. "The summer passed; I went back to school; Matthew didn't, things changed. Our time is done now." He pulled away, turned to wash his hands at a sink then used a soft, white towel to dry off. "Do you ever see Sally Munroe?" he asked, his back still to me. "Everyone knew her, being class prez and all."

Trickster. "Sally Munroe was the vice-principal," I answered back. "Remember?"

He turned slowly and gave me a stiff smile. "You pay at the front."

This was getting to be an expensive day.

My last call of the day was to St. Paul's Hospital, on an impover-
ished, crime-ridden block of 20th Street, where, after dark, security guards with flashlights are available to escort visitors from the
front entrance of the hospital to the door of their car. But I was safe;
it was mid-March, and the sun wouldn't drop until close to seven-
thirty.

I found a spot for the Mazda on Avenue P and made my way
up a hillock, cut through a parking lot, passed by the Emergency
entrance, and walked up the sidewalk that followed the semi-cir-
cular driveway past a Jesus statue on the centre lawn area to the
front vestibule. From making a few phone calls, I knew that
Kimberly Enns was a nurse in the Palliative Care unit. I also knew
that she probably had better things to do than talk to me while she
was on shift, but at least I could make face-to-face contact and set
up another time to talk.

On the fifth floor I exited the elevator and checked the signs.
Surgical Unit to the left, Palliative Care to the right. I passed by a
large sitting area meant for patients and their guests, but today it
was mostly patients, many in wheelchairs with IV poles at their
sides and glum looks on pallid faces. My heart did a little rat-a-tat-
tat in my chest. I don't hate hospitals as many people do, but they
are the one place where I seem unable to control my emotions; a
whole host of erratic feelings float through my body like unbidden
ghosts I'm unaware of until they show themselves and surprise the
crap out of me.

I slowed my pace and locked my eyes on the swinging doors
that separate the Palliative Care Unit from the non-dying rest of
the world. I experienced a pang of sadness at how it must feel to
come to this place to visit a loved one whose life is ending, and I
was glad that today that was not the case for me. I inched open one
of the doors and was immediately embraced by the overwhelming
solemnity that lives in those halls. The place doesn't even smell or
look like any other part of the hospital; it's just…different.

On my way to the nurses' station, I passed a quiet room, a
chapel and a room that looked like everyone's grandma's sitting
room with flower-patterned couches, doily-covered tables and a
decades-old television set. Everything my eyes settled on—every

piece of furniture, artwork, coat rack, chair—had a brass plaque attached to it that read: "In memory of…." From the bedside of a patient receiving a bit of music therapy, I heard the peeping warbles of a piccolo, and I smelled the unmistakable scent of lasagna being fresh-baked in an oven. It was calm, almost pleasant…but not.

I stepped up to a counter half-way down the hallway and looked about expectantly.

"Look at this little guy," came a woman's voice from behind me.

I turned around to find a nurse—I could tell by her lavender-hued smock and name tag—holding a puppy up to my face, seven or eight weeks old at most—the dog, not the nurse—and some mixed breed of adorability.

"Oh my gosh," I enthused, rolling my fingers over the wriggler's head. "Who's this?"

"It's Darlene's dog, Petunia. It's her day off, but she brought her in for a visit."

"That's just terrific," I said, nearly overwhelmed by some of that erratic emotion I experience in hospitals. God help me if I saw a Sasktel commercial about families reaching out to each other through the magic of telecommunication.

"Can I get you something, or help you?" the nurse asked as she nuzzled with her furry charge.

"I'm looking for Kimberly Enns? I think she's working today?"

"Oh sure, she's in the kitchen having tea."

I looked at her blankly.

The nurse smiled kindly and walked me about ten steps to a doorway that led to a kitchenette and the cheesy smell of lasagna.

Kimberly Enns, noticeably pregnant, was wearing a pink smock with a happy looking scarf pinned about her neck. She was—as were all my subjects that day—in her mid-thirties. She had a kind, round face and a head full of natural brown curls. She was sipping at a mug of something hot and she was alone at a round kitchen table.

"Hi," I said in a half whisper, not knowing what the decibel protocol was in this place. "My name is Russell Quant. You're Kimberly, right?"

She gave me a nice smile and nodded. "Yes. Can I get you some hot tea or Cup-a-Soup or something?" Her left hand was resting casually over her budding stomach, in the way of many mothers-to-be.

"No, thank you. I was wondering if I could talk to you for a few minutes though. Do you have the time?"

"Sure, have a seat. I'm sorry, I don't recognize you. What family are you with?"

I lowered myself into one of the mismatched chairs around the table. "Actually, I'm not here for a patient. I came to see you. I'm a detective."

This often gets people between the eyes for a minute or two. I kind of enjoy the reaction.

"I'm sorry…what?" She let out a short laugh as if embarrassed by mishearing me.

"I'm a detective, and I'm looking for an old classmate of yours, Matthew Ridge. I believe he was your boyfriend for a while?" I got this from one of Matthew's track teammates.

Kimberly blushed a shade that matched her smock and put down her mug on the surface of the oak table donated in memory of Grace Froesal. "I…I…yes, I guess that's right. We did go out in high school, but that was, gosh, how long ago…grade nine or ten or something like that." Kimberly was now married with a couple of kids, and I knew, regardless of the circumstances, discussing an old boyfriend or girlfriend can be an awkward thing for almost anyone. "You're looking for Matthew…why?"

"I'm working for his mother. She lost touch with Matthew several years ago, but she'd really like to reconnect with her son." I was playing hard on the mother-son thing. If anything would convince a pregnant mother to help me out, this would be it. "Anything you can tell me about him would be helpful. Or if there's a better time to do this…?"

"I don't know where he is now, that's for sure," she told me.

I nodded. That would be too easy. I gave her a hopeful, near pleading look. "Anything?"

She searched my face with pretty eyes and must have decided I was okay. "We did date, for most of a school year…I think it was grade ten, yeah, I'm pretty sure. My parents were furious with me, and of course, that made it all the more exciting," she said with a chuckle, rubbing her belly. "It wasn't serious or anything, but I did feel like he was able to talk to me about things he couldn't talk about with his friends, the other guys I mean, and certainly not with his parents. He didn't get along with his parents very well. I think that was part of the reason he always got into so much trouble, to make them mad, or maybe make them notice him. Well, that and…well, I'm not sure, but I think Matthew had some demons. Not that he ever told me exactly what they were, but I could tell.

"He was inconsistent, y'know? A real conflicted soul. Like he loved team sports and hanging with his buddies, and for a while he'd go along with everybody else, play by the rules, but then he'd just go off and do something really stupid, be all rebellious."

"Like what?"

She shifted her head to one side. "There was a volleyball coach Matthew really liked. And the coach liked him too, cut him slack lots of times when he was late or didn't perform. I think he knew Matthew was a natural, that he could have been a great athlete if he'd only straighten up and focus. I remember this one time, Matthew completely lost it during a game. He stood right there, in the middle of the court, in front of everyone, and screamed at Mr. Slavins until the coach had to throw him out."

She sipped at her tea as she accessed more long forgotten memories. "He wasn't a bad guy, not really, but a lot of people thought he was. And I don't really blame them. He did do bad stuff. He could be a bully. He drank, smoked up. A bad influence my parents would say. And yeah, he had that adolescent rage, that streak of bad boy in him that so many young girls find compelling. I sure did," she said with a small smile. "I'd tell my parents he was a star athlete. But they knew better."

"Do you remember him getting into trouble with the police?"

She wrinkled her brow a bit. "I sorta do, but I wasn't around when things got really serious. I moved."

"To another school?"

"Well yes, and to another city. My father got a job in Regina and our family moved there for a few years; that's where I graduated from high school. I moved back here after that. Saskatoon was where my friends were, but Matthew was...well, I don't know where he was. We'd broken up before I moved and well, that was it. By the time I came back to Saskatoon he was gone. I really can't tell you more than that."

I handed her a card, thanked her for her time and wished her luck with her pregnancy. On my way out I stopped at the flower shop on the main floor and arranged for a single white rose to be delivered to each occupied room in the Palliative Care unit.

It was nearing seven o'clock when I returned to PWC. I knew full well my dogs would be peeved with me for not rushing home to feed them (although they are well used to it), but I'd been away from the office all day and wanted to check my messages to see if any of my queries thus far had unravelled any loose threads. Sometimes that's the way it goes in the detecting life: when you don't have much to go on, as was the case here, all you can do is start hunting for the beginning of a thread on a spool, then run with it.

The building was deserted except for Alberta's office. Alberta Lougheed is our resident psychic and all-around eccentric. She plies her trade in the second floor office next to mine and usually at the oddest hours. Although I admit to knowing little about what she does (and I like it that way), she seems to have a steady enough customer base to remain financially viable and keep her in the gaudy, fantastic, peculiar garments she favours.

Her door was half open when I passed by, but because I could hear the murmur of voices (which I assumed were all corporeal) and smell heavy incense (and maybe some weed) I didn't bother to stop in to say hello. I entered my office and closed the door, my eyes shooting to the little button on the phone console that I rely on to tell me if I have messages. It was unlit. Not only had the day netted me no leads on the Matthew Ridge case, but no one else (i.e. new clients) had tried to call me either. Sure it was disappointing, but thankfully, business had picked up since last summer and my bank had once again begun using black ink on my monthly statements. Nothing major, mind you, but a stolen parakeet here, a fraudulent poker rally there, and I was keeping busy.

I poked my nose in the direction of my in-basket and saw nothing deposited there by Lilly except for a few flyers that had arrived by mail. I picked up a colourful one from Wilson's Greenhouse that teased the reader with the upcoming gardening season and I dutifully felt stirrings of that old familiar spring fever that arrives each year with the first whiff of evaporating ground frost.

Plopping myself into the chair behind my desk, I tossed aside the brochure and opened a new Word document on my computer screen to begin reviewing the day by typing up notes from my various interviews. I was soon done and studied the words on the screen. What did I have? A bunch of people who pretended not to know Matthew Ridge, or if they did know him, couldn't seem to remember much about him. Wouldn't seem like much to the regular Joe, but I liked it. Something wasn't quite right here; there was something someone wasn't telling me. I just had to find out who and what. Simple. Yup. Uh-huh.

Ideas about what to do next began to mix with thoughts of Alex Canyon who had left on a jet plane only twelve hours before. It seemed forever ago. This thing with the burly bodyguard was turning into the longest relationship I'd had since the heady days of my early twenties. Back then I'd proclaimed myself to be looking for love with a Prince Charming who was romantic, loyal, caring, sweet, a homemaker, humorous, devilishly handsome, and with buns of steel—and nothing less would do. It hadn't seemed like an unobtainable list at the time, and I did find him—or thought I had—more than once. The first one had lasted almost a year, although I was convinced we'd grow old together—until I found him banging one of my soon-to-be-ex club buddies. The second went on for fourteen months until he found me banging his brother—tsk, tsk, tsk, Russell. The third one—I was well-rehearsed by then—lasted just shy of four years. When that one ended, I reconsidered my list of must-haves.

Some of them I didn't want anymore, some were never a good idea in the first place, and the ones I decided to keep got stored on a back shelf somewhere in my head. I decided to just live and see what happened without getting into a relationship that required the "what's your favourite colour" conversation or a first "something" anniversary present.

I'd been surprisingly content ever since.

I had to wonder, though, if this thing with Alex really counted. Sure it had been about eight months, but for most of it he'd been doing his security work everywhere but in Saskatoon, and most of our time together had been spent sweating and grunting, rather than talking or cooking or taking long walks together like other new couples do. What I *was* sure of was that I was extremely attracted to him and he was to me; there was something about his very being that turned my belly to jelly and my knees into cheese: his voice, his skin, his eyes, his smell.

I wasn't used to thinking about this kind of stuff anymore; it used to be fun (and at times gloriously torturous) to endlessly contemplate love and relationships, but now, well, there just seemed to be a lot more at stake. Another thing I know is that you can't force introspection, so I decided to go home and have a nice dinner and an early night with my dogs. I had gotten up at four a.m. after all; I couldn't be expected to solve all my woes, personal and professional, on less than five hours of sleep. Right?

Alberta's client was making some strange humming-chanting noises when I left my office, so I made my way down the stairs as furtively as I could and headed for the back door.

As soon as I stepped outside I saw him. Waiting for me.

I heard the PWC door whooshing shut and locking behind me.

Sitting cross-legged on the hood of my Mazda was some kind of bizarre, evil-looking, yoga-instructor-gone-bad guy, all in black, with a balaclava covering his face.

Chapter 4

My first thought was to wonder if the asshole was putting a dent in the hood of my car, sitting on it like he was—especially since he looked to be a good two hundred pounds when he climbed down from his perch to confront me at the back door of PWC. I took a quick glance around, but at this time of night in this part of town—with its preponderance of churches and business buildings—the neighbourhood was virtually a ghost town. No help there. Could I get Alberta's attention somehow? If she was as good a psychic as she claimed to be, couldn't she sense I was in danger? I thought about hollering my head off, but I'm not much into screaming and decided to hold off on that route until it seemed absolutely necessary.

The night had grown glacial, as it is apt to do at that time of year, and my jacket was no warmer than it had been that morning in the Mount Royal Collegiate parking lot. It struck me that I seemed to be having a lot of parking lot conversations and would have to start dressing appropriately.

"You're the guy looking for Ridge, right?" the man asked in a baritone, no doubt influenced by watching way too many *Godfather* movies.

"Who wants to know?" Sounded like a standard reply, so I used it.

"That would be none of your business, buster. I'm just here to give you a friendly little message."

If I heard anything about swimming with the fishes or cement shoes I was going to have to laugh in this guy's face. "How friendly?" I asked in all innocence.

He had the sense to hesitate, a wee bit confused (after all, I had veered from the banal). "You just stop this business, bringing up all this crap about Ridge," he barked. "Just forget about it and go on with your other business. It's old news. It's done news. It's over. Forget about it, you hear?"

Or else?...c'mon hurry up with it.

"Or else next time won't be so friendly," he finished off.

I had to give it to Saskatoon; playing out like little Chicago in the forties, complete with this mafioso-lite ruffian and all. But really, how many detectives ever get rousted like this and say: "Oh, okay, you're right, I really should keep my nose clean. Don't worry about me, Mr. Brass Knuckles, I won't give you any more trouble." Well, on second thought, maybe some, but those guys aren't in the movies.

"Soooooooo, is that it?" I asked.

Another hesitation, then the final words: "Just quit, all right?"

I was silent, flicked my eyelashes a couple of times.

"So, are ya gonna?"

I raised an inquisitive eyebrow. "Gonna...?"

The bulldog was becoming exasperated with me and not quite sure if I was just playing with him or just too dumb to know when I was being threatened. "Are ya gonna quit doing what you're doing?"

"You actually want an answer tonight?"

"Well...yeah."

"I'll have to get back to you."

"You do that!" he blasted out before thinking about what he was saying.

"Great. Well, why don't you give me your phone number and I'll call you." I was having fun now.

"What?" He wavered a bit, then, "Oh, you're a smart guy, are you? You just better pay attention to this, buster, or else next time..."

Yeah, yeah, I know, it won't be so friendly.

"Good night," I said as he jogged off into the dark, scary land of bad guys. He was probably late returning the balaclava to the rent-it store.

Thump. The delicious sound of the first rotten apple hitting the ground. I love when bush-shaking works.

I could have just stood there and let the dramatic moment play out and fade to commercial, but that isn't my style either, so I took off after him...on the sly like. There were only so many places for him to go, and I was determined to find out which was his. All in all, this had been a juvenile, high school-prank-quality job and I was betting whoever was behind it was an amateur with no idea what they were doing. Amateurs are easy to catch.

After a quick little jag down an alley, the guy skipped across 24th Street toward a parked SUV—engine running—on 6th Avenue. He ducked into the black Lincoln Navigator, on the passenger side—so he had an accomplice, probably the guy who'd hired him (or talked him into it)—and the vehicle sped off like in a *Fast & Furious* movie. I jogged back to PWC to the rhythm of the three-digit, three-letter licence plate number I was repeating in my head.

"I can't believe you won't help me on this," I near-bellowed at Constable Darren Kirsch over the phone the next morning.

I was back in my office, he was in his at the Police Department, and we were going at it a little more vociferously than usual. We're supposed to help each other out when we can. That is our unspoken deal (well, according to me anyway). There are certain things a cop can do that a detective can't and vice versa—or at least do more expediently within the confines of the sometimes irritatingly restrictive letter of the law. Kirsch and I went to the police academy together in Regina. Eventually I went my way and he went his, and I think he'd hoped that would be the last he'd ever see of me. Ever since, I've tried to make sure his wish never comes true. A real fairy-tale love story.

Although I never let on, I know Darren is a good cop, continually rising in the ranks, honest as the day is long, a little mucho on the macho side of the scale for my taste, but we've learned to work around that. He's broodingly, darkly handsome, sturdy as a pine tree and, on a few rare occasions, manages to remove the stick from his butt long enough to have a sense of humour (I take full credit for that).

"Quant, I can't believe you're asking me to open a young offender's sealed file and spill the beans to you about what's in it, like some high school Chatty Patty. Fer crissake, man, that's stupid, even for you. Didn't you learn anything when you were on the force? Jeeeeeeeeee-zzzus!"

I was quiet for a moment, wounded by the realization that he was right and I was wrong. I would get nothing out of Darren Kirsch about Matthew Ridge's adolescent scrapes with the law. But I felt a little more gleeful when I realized this just might work to my advantage when I asked him for favour number two: to trace the plate number I'd gotten off the Lincoln Navigator that carried off Balaclava Guy. He quickly agreed, I think more to get rid of me than anything else, but he wasn't done with me yet.

"How'd you like it if somebody started opening files and telling the world about all the nelly ass things you did when you were a teenager with all your b...."

The time had come, as it does in all my telephone communications with Constable Kirsch, to hang up the phone and move on. And just as I did, it rang. He couldn't be that fast. Could he?

"Hello?"

"Is this Mr. Quant?" A voice which, thankfully, didn't sound to me like it was about to continue disparaging my youthful activities.

"Yes it is. Who am I speaking to?"

"Kimberly Enns. I'm a nurse at St. Paul's. We met yesterday?"

Cha-ching. "Yes, of course, Ms. Enns. How are you?"

"I'm fine, thanks. Listen, I did some more thinking about what we were discussing yesterday, about Matthew, and I remembered one more thing."

Angels singing. "Tell me about it. Or would you rather I meet you somewhere to talk about it?"

"No, this is okay. It's nothing big, really, maybe it won't help you at all, but, well, I remembered I *did* see Matthew one more time after we broke up, after I returned to Saskatoon from living in Regina."

Yes! My investigation had stalled at high school and the summer after grade ten when he'd gotten into trouble with the police.

I needed something to move me further down the timeline. This could be it.

"After he got out of reform school?" I asked, beginning to jot down the particulars of her call on the top page of a blank pad.

"I wouldn't know about that…I guess so…it was a few years after I graduated from high school myself."

Without Kirsch's help I wasn't sure I'd ever know the real details of Matthew's incarceration. I had to pick up his scent after he was freed. "Tell me what happened. Where and when did you see him?"

"Like I said, it was a few years after graduation. I was living in Saskatoon again and taking my nursing training at SIAST, so I guess this was maybe fourteen, fifteen years ago. I was downtown shopping with a girlfriend and we'd gone into a submarine shop to grab something for lunch. And there he was, behind the counter."

"He was working there?"

"Yeah, he had the apron and everything, and he was making subs. It was busy so he didn't look up much except to take orders, so I don't think he saw me. He looked different, grown up from when I'd last seen him. He would have been twenty-one or so by then."

"Did you talk to him?"

"No. I was—gosh it sounds so silly now—but I got flustered at seeing him and I just pulled my girlfriend out of there and we went somewhere else for lunch."

I got the details about the exact location of the sub shop and asked if there was anything else she could remember.

"Just one thing," she said. "Thank you."

"Oh?" My cheeks reddened. "What for?"

"The roses, Mr. Quant."

I had instructed the florist to keep me anonymous. "How did you know?" I asked the nurse.

"You strike me as just that kind of guy."

Forecasters were calling for the first day of above-freezing temperatures for the year. But I was taking no chances; I'd worn a thick, zip-up fleece under a black leather overcoat, a scarf and black leather gloves to work that morning. I put them on as I headed out to find what there was to find at a submarine shop where someone who might have been Matthew Ridge worked over a decade ago. This case was becoming more like an archeological excavation than an investigation. Although I'm a hopeless optimist, my expectations of discovering something useful were not high.

The shop in question was on College Drive across from the U of S campus and, not surprisingly, still in business. Submarines have long been a diet staple for much of the city's university population, which descends on Saskatoon each fall like a horde of hungry locusts with a meagre meal budget. I arrived early enough so the lunch rush was still a ways off. Even so, the staff was keeping busy, prepping the mounds of shredded lettuce, slices of sweet pickles and juicy tomatoes, and piles of meat-like stuff that would be consumed throughout the day. The kids behind the counter looked at me like I was from Uranus when I asked them about a guy named Matthew who worked there fifteen years ago. I quickly moved on to the manager who just as quickly passed me on to the owner, Wanda Woo, who just happened to be in the back, punching numbers into a massive contraption that might have been the first calculator ever invented.

"What you want?" she asked with a pinched nose and mouth, her sharp eyes full of suspicion when I'd sat myself down opposite her on a stool made of splinters.

"Well," I began hesitantly, "don't laugh, but I'm looking for an employee who worked here about fourteen or fifteen years ago."

"Not funny," she accurately pointed out.

"His name was Matthew Ridge and I thi…"

"Moxley."

I stopped there because I had no idea what she'd just said. Was it something in Chinese? Was she telling me to get the hell out of her subway shop? Had she sneezed? Should I say gesundheit? Was I simply lost in translation?

"Moxley," she repeated.

"Moooooxleeeeeeeey?" I slowly repeated after her, with what I hoped was an inquisitive oriental-flavoured upturn at the end of the unfamiliar word.

"Moxley," she said with an authoritative nod. "No Ridge. Matthew Moxley. No Matthew Ridge."

Light bulb. If I understood her correctly, she was telling me that there was no Matthew Ridge who'd worked here, only some guy named Matthew Moxley, who, unfortunately, was not who I was looking for. I was immediately disappointed, but really, the chances were low I'd find my quarry in a submarine store he *might* have worked in fifteen years ago based on a *possible* sighting by an ex-girlfriend who hadn't seen him in five years. And not only that, how many Matthews might have worked at any one fast-food outlet in fifteen years? However, if I've learned anything from my dear schnauzer Barbra whenever she sees me near the treat jar, persistent mooching pays off. Sometimes.

"What about someone named Matt Ridge? Or I wond..." I stopped there because Mrs. Woo had hopped down from her seat to her full four-foot-one height, ambled over to a time-worn filing cabinet, bent at the waist to open a bottom drawer, pulled out a file without seeming to have to even search for it, and returned to her seat. She shoved the file at me with the word, "Moxley."

"But I'm lo..."

She shook her head as if disgusted with the denseness of the matter in my head. "No Ridge. No Matt. No Matthew Ridge. Moxley. Matthew Moxley."

I took the file and saw the name Matthew Moxley scrawled on the label in barely visible pencil.

"All good," Mrs. Woo assured me. "We pay him, he work. We pay his taxes. All good. No trouble."

I began to comprehend. Mrs. Woo thought I was a Canada Revenue agent checking to see if she'd properly remitted Matthew Ridge's payroll taxes, CPP and EI. I did not bother to correct her and opened the file under the topic of "What the heck." The records were immaculate and in chronological order, starting with his application form on the day he first stepped into the sub shop, to semi-regular evaluation reports and pay hike information, to his short letter of resignation a couple of years later.

"No trouble. All good. We pay. He work. He gone now."

"I see, I see," I said, getting a far out idea. I pulled out the Mount Royal yearbook and showed her a picture of Matthew Ridge. "Is this Matthew Moxley?"

She nodded so hard I worried she'd hurt her neck.

I felt that little head rush that detectives get when they unexpectedly come upon a major clue—a near erotic sensation. I had just discovered that Matthew Ridge had, for some reason, at some point, become Matthew Moxley.

I had new prey.

"May I jot a few things down?" I asked Mrs. Woo.

She pushed a nub of a pencil and scrap of paper across the child-size desk that separated us. I had my own, but to be polite I accepted and used hers to record the details in the file that I thought I could use to track down Matthew Moxley. When I was done, I thanked the submarine shop proprietor, and left with her suggestion that I try the new spicy meatball and Italian cheese sub on the way out. I was sorely tempted.

For as long as I can remember, the intersection of Broadway and Taylor has been home to a drugstore, a gas station, a Cheesetoast restaurant and, more recently, a greenhouse (open during summer months only). And a block away, on a street named William Avenue (which only people who live there know about), I found the former home of Matthew Moxley. My knock at the front door was answered by a scowling woman peering out from behind a screen. She ordered me to use the *other* door—as if I should have known better—and sure enough, when I rounded the nondescript sixties bungalow to the south side, there she was in the *other* doorway, arms akimbo, scowl in place.

"Can't you read signs?" was her less than sunny greeting.

I gave her a questioning look as I scaled the four steps of the stoop.

"There was a sign at the front door, clear as sky, telling you to use this *other* door. A sign just like that one." She pointed a reedy, sharp-nailed finger at a foolscap taped to the clapboard siding of the house, right next to the doorbell. In bold, cap letters written in thick, black ink faded with age, were the words: "RING DOOR-BELL FOR MAIN FLOOR ONLY! FOR BASEMENT TENANTS GO DOWN THE STAIRS AND KNOCK ON THE APPROPRIATE DOOR."

"The front door is for show only," she explained. "I got good carpets up there and I don't need you or anyone else tracking street dirt or snow or who knows what all over them. I'd have to hire some overpriced carpet cleaning company to come in with all their hoses and sprays and vacuums. Don't need that, do I?" She shook her head with unambiguous conviction, setting the loose skin at her neck to quivering. "So," she challenged me, "are you ringing or knocking?"

"Excuse me?"

She expelled an exasperated sigh and once again pointed at the foolscap sign with its curled-up corners. "Ringing or knocking?"

I studied the instructions a second time. "Oh, well, I guess I'm ringing. Are you the owner of this house?"

"Gladys Nussbottem. Owned this house for forty years. If you're looking for a place to rent, all the spots are taken. But if you come back in late April, I'm sure there'll be some empty then. It's when the students go, you know."

Gladys Nussbottem was a tall woman, thin on top, thicker at the bottom, closing in on seventy. Her hair was a dull grey as was her wardrobe, her face pale, her forehead wide, she sported a healthy nose and buck teeth, and a receding chin making it look as if perhaps her maker had run out of bone and cartilage by the time He got to it.

"I'm not looking for a place; I was hoping to ask you some questions about a former tenant of yours."

She looked at me for a spell, her flickering eyes giving me a lengthy once over. I must have passed muster because she invited me in with a limp flip of her wrist. I followed her up a short flight of stairs that led up from a miniscule landing from which a second set led down to a dim, dark hallway with several doors on each side leading into what I guessed were tenant quarters and perhaps shared bathroom, washer/dryer and storage facilities. Posted on the wall along the way up to the main floor were more signs in various states of fadedness, as if added through the years as Gladys Nussbottem thought up more rules to live by like: "WIPE YOUR FEET" and "NO PETS ALLOWED," and my favourite, "LEAVE CURRY FOOD OUTSIDE AND SUSHI TOO."

"You can sit there," the landlady said once we'd arrived in her kitchen, indicating a sturdy-looking chair alongside a Formica kitchenette-sized table. On one corner of the table she'd taped a small sign with the instruction: "PLEASE LAY DIRTY KNIFE IN YOUR PLATE—NOT ON THE TABLE." A quick pass over the room revealed many others just like it, including one on the fridge telling all to "KEEP DOOR CLOSED AT ALL TIMES." But then how do you get stuff out? I took my seat.

"I have tea made," she told me. "But that's all I got, unless you want some water?"

I thought it best not be become beholden to this woman for anything, besides, I'd be too nervous about making a drink ring or setting the glass down in the wrong place. "No thank you," I answered politely.

She settled herself in the chair across from mine. "So what's this all about then? And maybe you'd like to tell me who it is I'm talking to?"

"Quant, I'm Russell Quant."

"Okay then," she responded, unimpressed, taking a sip of cold tea from a chipped coffee mug.

"I'm looking for a young man who I believe was a tenant of yours several years ago."

"Oh yes." She held her cup with both hands and fingered it like a piano.

"Matthew Moxley."

"Oh yes."

"I know it was some time ago, but I was wondering if you might remember him?"

"Of course I remember him. Who do you think I am? Some doddering, forgetful, old woman?"

"Ah, no, but it was quite some time ago, I just thought..."

"Wasn't that long ago." And to prove it she proceeded to give me the exact dates he moved in and moved out. "He was a good boy. He followed all the rules. He always kept his room clean, and when he asked to have a cat and I pointed out the No Pets sign, he was fine with it. He was a hard-working boy, too. I think at one point he was working three jobs at the same time, selling shoes, bagging groceries and clerking at some submarine shop downtown. Finally, he got enough money together I suppose, or got loans maybe, or a bursary, I don't know for sure which—he started up at the university. I don't know what he was taking. He still kept a couple of his jobs, though."

I was impressed. This didn't sound at all like the same guy who got into constant trouble at school and abused alcohol and drugs. I guess he grew up. Maybe reform school really had reformed him. Maybe when Matthew Ridge became Matthew Moxley, a few other things changed as well. But, just to be certain I wasn't scurrying down the wrong rabbit hole, I showed Mrs. Nussbottem the yearbook photo.

"Yeah, yeah, that's him. Good looking fellow, I suppose. He was a little older when I knew him, but yeah, that's him."

"Did he have any friends or family visiting him that you know of?"

She shook her head. "No. Didn't have time, what with all that working and schooling, but he got a boyfriend. Don't know where he found the time to get one, but he did. Eventually, that's why he moved out. They wanted to live together and the rooms downstairs are a little small for a couple. I rent to students, not lovebirds." I supposed she should have had a sign up for that.

"You don't happen to know where Matthew is today, do you?"

"If I kept in touch with every person who's lived in this house I'd have no time for anything else. Who do you think I am, Mother Teresa?"

Certainly not. New direction. "Do you remember the name of Matthew's boyfriend?"

I was not surprised to see her nodding. "I do. A unique name it was. I remember it because he was named after my favourite tree. It's not the tallest, or showiest, or most colourful in the fall, but it's a good, strong, sturdy, disease-resistant tree made especially for prairie conditions."

Wha...? "His name was...Poplar?"

Her near-absent chin swung back and forth as she told me, "Ash. Ethan Ash."

Back at the office, I had about as much luck as a lobster in a seafood restaurant tank finding a sniff of anybody named Matthew Moxley living in Saskatoon, Regina or the surrounding areas, so I changed gears and went in search of Ethan Ash. It didn't take long to track one down who fit the general description (plus fifteen years) given to me by Gladys Nussbottem: about six feet, a little beefy, brown hair kept too long for Gladys's taste, a little-boy smile and big feet that "tracked in snow like a shovel." There were a dozen Ashes in the phonebook although no one admitting to the name Ethan—a name I kinda liked—but I did hit upon a woman who was his mother (or who I presumed was his mother). She told me her son Ethan owned, operated and lived in a private care home facility for elderly residents called Ash House. It was located on Elliott, a leafy street in Varsity View, one of the oldest parts of town near the river and handily close to the Royal University Hospital (best known in Saskatoon as RUH). I consulted my watch—it was going to be another late dinner for Barbra and Brutus—and off I went.

Within seconds of sunset, the outdoor temperature had plummeted faster than inhibitions at a shooter party, so I was hoping to find a parking spot that would keep walking distance to a minimum. After circling the block twice, I had to settle for one around the corner from Ash House. After locking the car, I steeled myself inside my coat, buried hands inside my pockets and fast-walked toward the house with its charming, hand-carved sign swinging in the chilly wind from a post in the front yard.

I was about halfway there when an odd noise attracted my attention. I stopped, glanced about, but the shadowy streets were barren, everyone happily snuggled up indoors on this refrigerated evening.

Anthony Bidulka

I kept on.

There it was again.

This time I didn't stop, but slowed my pace considerably and controlled my breathing so I could make out the sound more clearly. It was definitely coming from behind me—clump, scrrrrrape, clump, scrrrrrape, clump, scrrrrrape.

I stopped.

The noise stopped.

I started up again.

So did the noise.

There was no doubt now. I was being followed.

Chapter 5

Clump, scrrrrrape. Clump, scrrrrrape. Clump, scrrrrrape.

I stopped and swung around as menacingly as I could. I peered through the falling darkness that seemed to be following me down the street—darkness and someone with a limp. But no one was there. Or was there? Were there places someone could be hiding? Behind trees, fences, cars? Yup, lots of hiding places. Or was I being paranoid? Could be. Maybe the sound was someone shovelling their driveway, or pulling their garbage out to the curb. All I knew for certain was that I was getting colder by the minute, and I either had to start chasing my ghost in and out of every cubbyhole on Elliott Street or get indoors.

I turned and marched towards Ash House, my ears at the ready. Nothing. Either I'd imagined it, whoever it was was innocent and finished with whatever task they had been doing, or the bad guy was onto the fact that I was onto him and wisely decided to stay hidden.

Ash House was one of those enchanting properties that really stick out, like a chocolate-covered, jam-filled bismarck decorated with frilly icing, sitting in a bakery display window amongst a bunch of plain-Jane, powdered-sugar doughnuts. I could picture people walking by, wondering why their own homes and yards didn't look nearly as good. The house balanced the unusual colour combination of an earthy burgundy mixed with highlights of harvest yellow and dusk blue. Small patches of lawn were bordered by trellises and clay pots that in spring would likely explode with colourful flowers and shrubs. Benches and tables beckoned passersby to sit for a relaxing spell, amongst bird feeders and musical wind chimes. Edwardian lampposts welcomed me down a brick pathway to a rocking chair on the porch and a gaily painted front door with a big brass door knocker that looked like a lion's head.

My knock on the cheery door was answered by a lovely looking, white-haired woman wearing a bright teal outfit, matching scarf, lots of gold jewellery and a wide smile.

"Hello, young man. May I help you?" she asked, showing an abundance of bright white dentures and a bit more excitement than I'm used to eliciting on unexpected visits. "Oh my stars, it's gotten cold out there. You better come in before you catch something." She grabbed my forearm and pulled me into the foyer, closing the door and shutting out the cold behind me. "Now, who was it you were looking for?" She gave me a quick, assessing look with inquisitive eyes and asked, "Are you Frank's grandson, Ted?"

"No, I'm not," I answered.

"Good thing," she said with a twinkle in her eye. "He hasn't time for a visit tonight. It's movie night, you know."

"Oh. What are you seeing?"

She shrugged with another delightful grin. "Who cares?" She turned and invited me to follow her. "Come along, the movie crowd is in here. That's if you dare. We're a rowdy group tonight!"

I followed her into what looked like a sitting room and library with a blazing fire in the fireplace, around which three others were huddling. Including the woman who answered the door, and excluding me, the average age in the room was about eighty, but the energy level was that of a gathering of twenty year olds on the first day of spring break.

"Everyone, this is…" The woman looked at me, shocked to realize she'd invited me in without knowing anything about me, never mind my name. She burst into gales of laughter and laid a delicate, gold-and-diamondized hand on my arm to steady herself. I noticed her nail polish was fresh and the exact same shade of teal as her outfit. "Well, I have no idea who this is!"

The others, a man and two other women turned to greet me. Their names were Frank, Hortense and Edda, and Loretta was the woman who answered the door.

"Are you here to visit someone?" Frank asked.

"I thought he was your grandson," Loretta confessed with another laugh as if it was the gosh-darn-funniest thing she'd heard all day.

"I was hoping to speak with Mr. Ash," I told them.

"Ethan, oh well, you better hurry, he's warming up the van to take us for dessert and a movie," Frank said. "You don't want to make us late," he added with a decidedly bothered look on his face.

"What are you so worried about?" Loretta asked him. "You're late for everything. I wouldn't be surprised if you show up late for your own funeral."

The others tittered while Frank, a tall, distinguished looking man, coughed up some phlegm.

"Look who's talking," he finally shot back, a little off on his timing. "It takes you so long to get ready in the morning you think lunch is breakfast."

"What's going on in here?" I heard a deep voice from the archway that led into the room. "I could hear the laughing all the way from the garage. You want the neighbours to complain again?"

I turned around to face a man I was certain was the same Ethan Ash who was once Matthew Moxley's boyfriend. He'd changed only a little since Gladys Nussbottem last saw him; he was still six feet tall with long, brown hair and big feet, but the beefiness she'd talked about had been moulded into a sturdy, well-toned frame. His little-boy smile had matured into one of those confident, friendly, manly smiles that fill a face, from small crinkles around sparkling, laughing eyes to a matching set of dimples, one below each rosy cheek. I caught his eyes resting on mine for just a tad longer than was necessary before he strode up, offering a big paw of a hand.

"Oh hello, I'm Ethan. Didn't know we had company," he said as we shook. "These old folks been bothering you, sir?" he questioned me in mock seriousness.

I grinned and said, "Not yet, but I can certainly see it heading in that direction."

The oldsters tut-tutted at the suggestion and started herding Ethan Ash and me out of the room toward the back of the house.

"We don't want to be late," Frank insisted again, obviously concerned about missing a minute of his night out on the town because of me.

"This young man is here to visit you," Loretta told Ethan.

"Don't be so pushy, Franklin MacIntyre, perhaps these boys need a moment alone," intimated Edda, a near-ninety-year-old woman who used considerably less makeup and care with her wardrobe and hairstyle than Loretta, and something about her told me she probably wouldn't be caught dead with a cup of tea, knitting needles or a blanket over her knees.

"There's lotsa moments in the van, now let's go," instructed Frank, not easily deterred and not very subtly urging the women to move along.

"I don't want to be late," Hortense spoke up for the first time. She was a tall, horsey-looking woman with ruddy skin and a pageboy dyed coal black.

"We won't be late," Edda assured her. "We're going for dessert first, remember? The movie's not till nine-ten."

"It's an eight-person van, there're only five of us. This Mr. Whoever can come with us," proposed Frank, halfway down the hallway leading to, I guessed, his coat, galoshes, the back door, and a warmed-up van.

Ethan Ash and I listened to this exchange in silence and, for some unknown reason, I heard myself saying, "I can come along."

"I call shotgun!" this from a disappearing Frank.

And so I found myself in an eight-person minivan, Mary Kay pink, heading downtown. This wouldn't necessarily have been a bad thing, but I wasn't even up front with my intended interviewee, instead finding myself in the back between Edda and Hortense discussing the *Farmer's Almanac* forecast for a long, wet spring.

Eight o'clock on a Tuesday night in March at Colourful Mary's is surprisingly busy, probably because Tuesday is cheap movie night at some theatres, and with the money they were saving, other people had the same idea as the Ash House residents: pre-movie dessert and coffee. The restaurant-slash-gay-bookstore is owned by Mary Quail—who looks after the business end of things—and Marushka Yabadochka—who looks after the cuisine end of things, and judging by their longevity and popularity they do a good job of both. Marushka was in the back preparing her baba's famous *lyougoomeenah* (hot, creamy rice pudding with spiced apple and cinnamon) for the next day, and Mary had a rare evening off, so a hostess by the name of Crystal Beth showed our troop to a table for four—for Frank and the trio of women—and another for two—for me and Ethan Ash so we might have some privacy to talk.

"I'm sorry about all this," Ethan apologized with the warm laugh that seemed to simmer just below the surface of whatever he said. "For dragging you all this way. As soon as we get them into the movie theatre I can drive you back to your car."

"You're not seeing the movie with them?" I asked.

"Sometimes I do, but although I like chick flicks as much as the next gay guy, four in one month is my limit. Poor Frank doesn't know what he's gotten himself into."

I nodded in hearty agreement and accepted a chai latte from a server.

"I still can't believe they coerced you into coming with us," Ethan said, taking a sip of his own hot drink. "I know your name, but that's about it. They said you wanted to talk to me? Is there something I can do for you, Russell?"

I chuckled. "In other words, Ethan, you're very politely asking me what the heck it is I want from you?"

He dimpled up. "Yeah, that's about right."

"I'm a detective. I'm looking for an ex-boyfriend of yours."

"Ooooooooo boy," he responded quickly. "You'll have to be more specific than that, or we could be here all night."

My eyes widened with surprise until I caught the glint in his chestnut eyes and realized he was kidding me. Humph, that's usually my shtick. "Matthew Moxley," I told him.

I find that the very first reaction to any subject matter, verbal and non-verbal, is usually the most accurate one, and from Ethan

I got a small smile that told me his memories of Matthew Moxley were not bad ones. "Matthew, yeah, what do you need to know?"

"Do you know where he is?" I started with the question at the top of the heap, hoping this case was going to take a turn for the easy.

"I don't, I'm sorry. I haven't seen Matthew for several years."

Blasted beeswax! Ah well, at least I was moving along Matthew's life path. I'd gotten out of high school and into his early working and university days. Now with Ethan Ash I was nudging slowly but surely a little bit further.

"Can you tell me about when that was, and why you lost touch?"

"Oh sure. Matthew and I were together for four years. We met at the U of S. He was in Education, and I was pursuing a social work degree via a rather circuitous route we won't go into right now," he said with a self-deprecating quirk of his eyebrows. "We moved in together after knowing each other for about six months. Hey, who told you about us anyway?"

"Gladys Nussbottem," I told him.

He sniggered. "Oh yeah, she was a real hoot. I kinda liked her though; she had a lot of rules, but you always knew where you stood with her, you know, nothing left to chance. Anyway, Matthew and I moved in together. He was a nice guy, but kind of a loner. He didn't have many friends and no family to speak of…actually none at all that I knew of. He put all his energy into school and work and volunteer work."

"Volunteer work?"

"Matthew is the kind of guy who falls in love with anyone who can't help themselves, like kids or the elderly or disabled people. He volunteered for years on the pediatric ward at RUH and even helped out at Ash House whenever he could. My dad was running it then, and he just loved having Matthew around, so did the residents." He smiled with warm reminiscences. "And, of course, so did I."

I was nodding my head in wonderment as I listened to Ethan's tale of Matthew Moxley's life. This young man seemed to have completely turned himself around after a rough start in high school (once he left Matthew *Ridge* behind).

Although I couldn't be certain, between Ethan's testimony and what I'd heard from Clara Ridge, it seemed Matthew had never attempted to re-establish ties with his parents after leaving reform school, actually going to extreme lengths to avoid it by changing his surname and, really, his entire identity. It was as if he didn't want to be found. But had his parents tried? Based on what I knew about Matthew's father, I was pretty sure the answer was no.

The people from his life when he was Matthew Ridge didn't seem to know about Matthew Moxley, but I wondered if the people from his life as Matthew Moxley knew about Matthew Ridge. It was time to find out. "Were you aware, Ethan, that Matthew Moxley was not his real name?"

Ethan Ash didn't have to answer; the tale was told on his handsome face, now drawn into a stunned mask. "What are you talking about?" he finally whispered.

"Does the name Matthew Ridge mean anything to you?"

As if desperately wishing for something, anything, to steal his brain away from the altered reality I was presenting to him, he shook his head and shot a quick glance at his charges who were chortling away in a non-stop back-and-forth joke fest across the room. Yes, Ethan Ash's relationship with Matthew Moxley had been over a long time ago, but that didn't make what I was telling him any less incredible. "Are you absolutely sure we're talking about the same guy?" he volleyed back weakly.

I nodded and fought off a desire to reach across the table and lay a comforting hand on Ethan's. Instead, I looked into his troubled eyes and told him the little I knew of his ex-boyfriend's life before they'd met. Ethan listened attentively, never interrupting with a question until the very end.

"Does the trouble he was in back then have something to do with why you're looking for him now?"

"No," I answered. "His father is dead and his mother wants to find him to...well, I think she wants to find a way to make amends."

His head bobbed up and down solemnly, and I could see in his face that he was not the kind of man to judge anyone, least of all

Matthew for lying to him or even Matthew's parents for abandoning their son. I could also see a deep sadness. Ethan Ash had lost something tonight: an unblemished memory of a man he'd once loved. I'd taken it away from him, and I was sorry to have done it.

"Ethan, I need you to tell me everything you know about Matthew: when you broke up, where he went after that, the last time you saw him or heard from him or heard anything about him." Even a rumour of his whereabouts would be better than nothing at this point.

Again he checked on Frank, Loretta, Edda and Hortense before returning his attention to me. Despite the turmoil he was going through, he was remembering to be vigilant and protective of the members of his household. Ethan Ash was good at what he did.

"Well," Ethan began his story, "we had both finished university. I was taking over Ash House, sort of in training for when my dad would retire, and Matthew had gotten a job teaching a grade three/four split in Estevan. That's near the North Dakota border, a five-hour drive away. We tried, but the relationship just couldn't survive the distance. So we parted, as friends."

"Did you see each other again?"

"A couple of times we talked on the phone, saw each other maybe once or twice over the years, but the last time, gosh, was probably five or six years ago. He was doing really well out there. As far as I know, Russell, he's still in Estevan."

We talked for several more minutes when Miss Bobo Tox, one of the joint's more colourful servers delivered a note to Ethan. He gave me a questioning look, opened it up and started to chuckle.

"What's it say?" I asked, wanting in on the joke.

He crumpled up the paper and slipped it into a pocket.

"Hey!" I protested.

"You don't want to know," Ethan said casting a teddy-bear-coloured eye toward the octogenarians we'd come with. "Apparently they think we should either get a hotel room or get off our butts and get them to the movie."

I did something I rarely do. I blushed. I surveyed the table of elderly folks who were doing their ragged best to look wholly innocent and uninterested in what was going on at our table.

Frank even managed to look a little disgruntled by the whole thing (it may not have been an act).

"Listen," Ethan said under his breath, his cheeks none too pale either. "We could keep talking after we drop them off…if you need anything else from me…I could buy you a drink or something…whatever…you know…or do you…I can just drop you off at your car…or…."

It was a lovely speech and I felt a strong temptation to accept his invitation for a drink, but I did have somewhere else to be, an important meeting at home, and so, I brought my evening with Ethan Ash to a close.

I had just gotten the fire roaring in the grate of the living room fireplace when the doorbell rang. I opened the door and Barbra and Brutus greeted our guest with the customary love and licks they always have in reserve for Jared Lowe. Having the lovely quality of many dogs (but few humans), they paid no heed to the scarring Jared had suffered as a result of having acid tossed at his face by stalker-turned-murderer Jin Chau.

Jared, Anthony's long-term partner, had been a world-renowned model, jetting from fashion shows in Monte Carlo to commercial shoots in Madrid to catwalk struts in New York City. He'd been at the end of that life, having turned the corner of thirty-five, and was just beginning to find a new kind of existence for himself when he was so horribly attacked. Over the months that followed, Anthony had spared no expense getting Jared the best treatment available in the world of facial reconstruction, but sadly, the damage had simply been too severe. Jared would never look the same. Jared would never look "normal."

Many things worked in Jared's favour in terms of what happened to him, the most important being that he survived. He did not lose his sight or any other senses. But there were things that worked against him too: the exposure time, the amount and type of acid used in the attack; the dark, olive tone of his once impeccable skin. Even the best doctors could only do so much. They could never make him whole, and now, many months later, he was the best he would ever be, given existing medical knowledge and technology.

Like my pups, all I ever see when I look at Jared is the man I've always known; the stunning cat eyes are still there behind the scar tissue, as is the high watt smile, the gentle manner, and a heart as big as the prairies. But I knew it wasn't easy for him to look in the mirror each day at the multicoloured strips of skin that cover his face like permanent bandages; no, easy was not the word.

Early on in his recuperation period, in one emotion-fuelled outburst, Jared had rid his and Anthony's penthouse apartment of every photograph, framed picture and magazine cover graced with his once beautiful face. He'd travelled through every stage of grief, and now he was left to pick up the pieces of a life as unrecognizable to him as his own face.

"I smell a fire," Jared said with anticipation as he gave each dog a treat he'd smuggled from his coat pocket.

"Something to take the chill off," I said, taking his jacket and scarf and hanging them in the foyer closet before leading him into the living room. "Why don't you warm up by the fire and I'll pour us a drink. Wine? Something stronger?"

"Wine would be good, thanks."

"Red? Amarone?" I offered.

"Perfect," he murmured as he sank into one of the fireside leather couches.

I had opened a bottle of Amarone della Valpolicella earlier and left it to breathe. Now I brought it, along with a plate of ripe cheeses I'd prepared and two crystal wineglasses (the kind with nice, big bowls), over to the seating area and set everything down. I glanced out the large picture window that overlooks my front yard and saw dark branches beginning a lazy sway—the wind was picking up—and hoped the forecasters were wrong about an overnight skiff of snow. I was so over winter for the year.

We chit-chatted a bit, ate some cheese, sipped some wine, gossiped a bit—especially about Errall and her sudden turn from dedicated single girl to wanton-sleep-around (actually we used more colourful words than that), and her recent mysterious, late-night visitor. The wine was a lovely, dark garnet rather than purple—which meant it was a mature bottle—and tasted of licorice, tobacco, and fig.

"We missed you at Sereena's party over the weekend," I ventured. "Alex was in town."

"I'm sorry," Jared answered with a sincere look. "I heard Alex was here, and I would have loved to see him, but, well, you know, domestic disturbance takes priority over fundraising dinner parties."

A little bit of me froze over at the words "domestic disturbance." Jared was telling me something, in no uncertain terms. There was trouble between him and Anthony. Over the months since Jared was attacked, I had sensed something was different between them, but I shrugged it off. Of course things would be different. Jared's life had drastically changed and, as his spouse, Anthony's had to. But had something more serious transpired between the two men while I wasn't looking? I hadn't seen much of them—certainly much less than usual—as they were so often out of town, consulting specialists and undergoing surgeries and treatments, medical and other, and I had been busy focussing on renewing my relationship with Sereena.

At the same time, I had also had my own, not inconsiderable, internal demons to battle. I had come close to being raped by the same maniac who'd disfigured Jared's face. Thankfully, with a view to the grand scale of things and a healthy dose of the optimism that has always run amok in my blood, I was making good progress in putting that dreadful episode behind me. As horrible and debasing as it had been, there were people around me who had it worse. I was with one of them right now.

"Are you okay?" I asked Jared.

"Anthony doesn't know I'm here."

That was odd, and an odd thing to say. I could feel my stomach tighten.

"I want to ask for your help, Russell."

I placed my wineglass on the coffee table in front of us and turned in my spot next to Jared on the couch. Along with my full and undivided attention, I gave him my unequivocal answer. "Anything." I would do anything for a friend.

Or so I thought.

"I want you to help me leave Anthony."

Chapter 6

I'm sure there were words appropriate to the situation that I could have uttered about then, but I was finding it difficult to form letters with my bottom lip so near my chest.

Sensing the sudden tension in the room, Barbra rose from her spot near (but not too near) the roaring fireplace and snuffled her cool, wet nose under my arm. She let out a soft whine that was her way of saying, "I'm feeling a little uncomfortable with things and need some reassurance." I looked down into her dark eyes and gave her sweet head a pat. This seemed to suffice and she returned to her place after giving her less sensitive brother, Brutus, a quick shank sniff.

Jared was wearing a charcoal grey turtleneck, which he now pulled over his head, revealing a similarly coloured T and leaving his golden locks boyishly disheveled. "Getting warm in here," he commented, folding the sweater carefully—no doubt an Anthony thing—and setting it across the back of the sofa.

"Can you repeat that?" I finally got out.

He complied with little telltale emotion. "I want you to help me leave Anthony."

"B-b-but where are you going? What are you talking about?" I had the black sense that I already knew where this was going.

Jared raised his hands and placed one on each side of his jaw as if setting his face forward for display. "Take a good look, Russell. This is it. It's over. There is nothing else that can be done. What you see is what you get. I will always look like this *and*, before you start, I don't want to hear any of the polite stuff you think you should say about my face and how it doesn't matter and all the rest of that."

He'd caught me. "But it's true."

"Maybe. For you. For Anthony. But most definitely *not* for me."

"I don't understand."

"Russell, I am grotesque."

Before I could say another word, like a drawn sword, up came a finger into the air between us to silence my retort. "In *my* eyes. Okay? I'm not placing this critique in your mouth or Anthony's mouth or my mother's mouth or anyone else's mouth, but to me, I-Am-Grotesque. But you know what? I am also a strong man. I have a strong will. I want to live and have a decent future. I can live with this, Russell. I can. I know I can."

"Then why...?"

"I am not who I was when Anthony and I first met. I know our relationship went far beyond the physical. But it *was* a factor, there is no denying that. Anthony is a very handsome man. Do you know that most people refer t...*referred* to us as 'that handsome couple' or 'the best looking men we know'? People were always defining us by how we looked together. My God, Russell, I had a career based on how I looked. But I don't fit in that life anymore, not the career, and not the couple."

"Anthony does not care about that and you know it," I told him, my cheeks sizzling from the fire, from the wine, from the inflammatory words I was hearing.

"Anthony is too busy playing the role of martyr and caregiver t..."

"That is not fair!" I shouted. "You make it sound as if everything he's done he's done for himself! That's not the way it is. He's done it for you, Jared!"

"No, no, you're right," Jared quickly recanted. "I didn't mean it that way. All I meant to say is that Anthony is too busy to realize that he is in a relationship with someone who no longer exists. All I am to him anymore, all I can ever be is this..." and again he grabbed at his scarred face with his hands "...this mask. I am wearing a mask I can never take off! Never!" He reached for his wine and downed a couple of ounces as if it were water.

Now both dogs—even Brutus—looked up at us, uneasy with the unfamiliar tones in our voices, knowing something was amiss and frustrated they did not know what to do about it.

"He'll always be waiting for it to come off," Jared continued, his voice settling to normal. "And he'll feel guilty for wanting it to, and I'll feel guilty that it can't. I love him too much to put him through that."

Now he'd really lost me. "How can you say that? I think what you're doing, what you're asking of me, of Anthony, is the most selfish thing I have ever heard from you."

Jared looked at me as if I'd just struck him, his eyes flashing with the pain of it.

"I'm sorry," I whispered. "I just don't know what's going on here."

"I want a new life," Jared attempted an explanation. "And that life has to start with who I am now. Looking like this, I may never find anyone to love me, to be with me, but at least that's honest. Staying with Anthony is a charade. Can you understand that? I have to leave."

"Leave? Leave!" I was suddenly incredulous and angry and sad and scared and so many other things I could not define. "So where are you going to go? Are you just going to run away and hide like Kelly!" Kelly had been my best friend and Errall's lover for several years. A few years earlier she'd gotten cancer, lost a breast and eventually decided to break off the long relationship with Errall and move to Toronto. None of us had heard from her since. The similarity to what was happening now with Jared was eerie.

Jared was quiet, and both dogs continued to stare at us with anxious eyes. Brutus looked as if he might bark.

"I've thought a lot about Kelly recently," Jared admitted in a low voice. "About how she just left her problems behind, sloughed them off like a snake does its skin. She just let it all go, forgot about it, started a new life somewhere. How invigorating that must have been, what a relief."

I called bullshit. "Invigorating, my ass. She also left behind a lot of hurt people and unfinished business." I could feel permanent ridges forming on my brow, just about where a dull headache was beginning to build.

"Russell, you can't understand." His face carried a look I'd never seen there before; his voice was that of a stranger. "You haven't gone through what we've gone through."

Maybe not. I crossed my arms over my chest and regarded this man on whom I'd once harboured a secret crush. Right then all I wanted to do was shake him until some sense dropped into his head.

What followed was an uncomfortable silence, both of us unwavering in our stances, and at the same time hurting inside because of this chasm that was opening up between us, right before our eyes, a chasm that threatened our friendship. Which was deeper? Where could we go from here? What could either of us say or do? Jared sipped at the dregs of his wine, his face wincing as if the alcohol had gone sour. I stared into the licking flames of fire.

Finally I could take it no longer. Saying something, anything, was better than this anguished silence. "So what are you asking me to do?" I asked him. "Exactly?"

His golden-green tiger eyes latched onto mine. "I'm asking you to try to understand, and to help me convince Anthony that it is time we parted ways. Maybe not forever, but for now."

I averted my eyes once more towards the roaring fire, and I may have even let out a "humph."

"Will you help me?" he asked plainly.

In a voice so quiet I wasn't even sure he could hear it, I answered. "No."

He nodded solemnly. "I think I should go."

Getting up at five a.m. is not my favourite thing to do, but do it I did, and I was on the road with a full thermos of coffee, bottle of water, two pears and a map, and heading for Estevan by six. It was still dark out and frosty, but the radio weatherman was promising a sunny albeit cool day in the single digits. My route took me south through Dundurn, Hanley, Davidson, then on through Moose Jaw, Milestone, Weyburn and finally into Estevan, clocking in at a little closer to four-and-a-half hours than five.

It was a long drive, but it gave me time to chew on my discussion with Jared the night before. We'd left things at an uncomfortable point. I needed the time to think about my reaction to what he'd been asking me to do: to help him convince Anthony to end their relationship. Was I being short-sighted? Insensitive? Inflexible? Bullheaded? Should I have agreed to help him? But as lengthy as my trip and as strong as the coffee I drank were, my distaste for Jared's request never left my mouth. It just wasn't right.

Estevan, about ten minutes north of the North Dakota border, is nicknamed the Energy City, with 11,000 citizens and a bustling economy heavy on coal, oil and gas, farming and ranching. I found the Comprehensive School easily enough and was told I'd have to wait until noon to meet with the principal as he was busy teaching a class. So I drove around town and generally twiddled my thumbs until it was time to return to the school and meet with Mr. Thorson. I already knew from a cellphone call made on the road that Matthew Moxley was no longer a teacher at the school, and that was certainly frustrating, but I was convinced my next clue regarding his whereabouts was somewhere in Estevan.

"I'm sorry you came all this way for nothing," Principal Thorson said after the requisite handshakes and "let's have a seat in my office" and "can I get you something to drink?" were done with.

"Well, I'm hoping it wasn't for nothing. It would be a great help if you could tell me a little more about Mr. Moxley, like when he left Estevan and where he might have gone?"

The principal scrunched his round face into a sphere of flesh-coloured Plasticine as he tried to recall facts. He would have been a drab-looking guy in a drab-looking suit were it not for the life in his eyes; it was a look I'd seen before in people who were teachers (some, not all). He loved his job. The drabness was either due to bad taste or, more likely, long, thankless hours. "His last term was, oh, let's see now, five years ago last fall? Yeah, I think that's right. He was an excellent teacher; the students loved him. They were very sorry to see him leave. We all were."

"Why did he leave?"

"Love," he said simply.

I stared at the other man, surprised by his answer.

"Mr. Moxley, Matt, was really quite an extraordinary man. Every summer during school break he did the same thing. While most of us were putting up our feet at the lake or golfing every day, Matt would pack a knapsack and fly off to some Third World country to do volunteer work. It was his passion. Oh, he enjoyed teaching well enough and was damn good at it too, but he liked nothing better than to be out there in the world, experiencing other cultures, using his skills to help others. You'd see it in his face each fall when he returned for the new school year. He was like a man who'd spent the summer falling in love. The look would fade as the year progressed," he added thoughtfully, "but then June would come around again and off he'd go. I think he even spent a couple of Christmas breaks overseas as well."

I listened in appreciative silence and my mind went to Clara Ridge, and how proud she would be to meet this new son, so different from the truant, troubled teen he'd once been: a kind, giving man she did not yet know.

"Everyone benefitted," Mr. Thorson continued. "Matt brought his experiences back here to Estevan, to share with the kids, the teachers, the church, the community. He'd host slide shows and make speeches to the Chamber of Commerce; he always carried around pictures of the places he'd been and the people he'd worked with and he wasn't shy about showing them to anyone or talking up the great need for aid and assistance, even from a small city like ours. He taught us that even we could make a difference. I would make a bet with you, Mr. Quant, that half the people in this city who sponsor kids or various building projects around the world do so because of Matt's influence on them."

"So what happened? Did he just not come back one year?"

"Oh no, he'd never do that, leave us in a lurch like that. But you're right, that is where he ended up. In his last few years with us, his favourite place to go was Africa, it really...well, something about that continent really seemed to affect him deeply. Eventually he decided that that was where he was meant to be, and helping those people was what he was meant to do. He announced one fall that it would be his last year with us and that he would be leaving for Africa the following summer, for good this time. Of course we were sad to see him go, but really, it was inevitable. We all knew it was the right decision for him."

It was a lovely story, but suddenly my insides felt hollow as I realized what it meant: the bottom had just fallen out of my case. If Matt Moxley was in Africa, well, that was one big-ass continent to find someone in. "Do you keep in touch with him?" I asked, dangling from a thin thread of hope.

He shook his head as I was afraid he might, and then: "But the minister from his church might."

Calvin Hershell was the minister of a local United Church and had been instrumental in arranging Matthew Moxley's early forays into the Third World through church-sponsored programs and other charitable foundations. Principal Thorsen had contacted the man, and he responded graciously by inviting me to his home for a talk. By one-thirty we were seated at a simple kitchen table in his simple but comfortable home eating simple but delicious bologna sandwiches. Reverend Hershell, in his fifties, was a pleasant-look-ing fellow (as ministers tend to be for some reason—must be all that communing with God) with light, sandy hair that was barely thick enough to disguise a balding pate, and rimless eyewear with well-fingerprinted lenses.

"Sorry for the food," he apologized in a soft, gentle, minister-like voice. "But I actually prefer bologna to other sandwich meats."

I grinned between tasty bites. "Actually, so do I." I felt like one of those shadowy silhouettes behind the curtain on a Frosted Flakes commercial, too embarrassed to publicly admit that they think the cereal taaaaaaaaastes grrrrrrrrrrrrrrrrrrrreat!

We chewed in companionable silence for a moment then launched into it.

"Again, I want to thank you for seeing me today, and on such short notice."

He nodded as he swallowed a mouthful. "So you're looking for Matt, are you?"

"Yes, on behalf of his mother."

"That's wonderful. I have to tell you though, I'm a little surprised. Matt never spoke about any family. I assumed they were dead."

"They've been estranged for many years. And even now, his mother doesn't want him to know she's looking for him. She just wants to know where he is and how he's doing."

"That's lovely," he declared with an approving nod. More chewing, a sip of instant coffee. "Well, I hope I can help, but I'm not sure I can."

Drat! Well, I thought to myself, might as well go for the gold. "Do you know where Matt is?"

He gave me a thin-lipped smile, unaware of a crumb of white bread precariously perched on his chin. "In theory."

Theories are okay. Detectives can work with theories. Theories, speculation, good guesses, gut instinct, all part of the game. "Oh?" I urged him on.

"I am in intermittent contact with Matt, perhaps once a year. But I haven't actually spoken with him since he left Estevan and, dear me, now that I come to think about it, the last time I had word from him was Christmas before last."

Eww boy. "So you have a phone number or...?"

"No, no phone. I have an e-mail and street address for him. I've gotten the sense that Matt moves around a fair deal, going where he's needed or where he needs to be, if you know what I mean. But the address I have seems to have been a bit of a home base for him, so perhaps that might be a good start? It's in Cape Town."

I nodded, feeling a bit numb. Matthew Ridge/Moxley was in South Africa. Not exactly a road trip away.

The trek back to Saskatoon from Estevan—as with almost any trip over an hour—seemed longer than the one going to Estevan from Saskatoon. After a short session of radio singalong, I used the first couple of hours to think through what I'd learned. Both Principal Thorsen and Reverend Hershell had been very helpful in painting an even clearer picture of the man my missing person had become since his days as a troubled and rebellious teen. They moved me considerably further along the timeline of his life, which I'd slowly been uncovering over the past few days. Unfortunately the news was not good. Although it told me—and my client, Clara Ridge—roughly where her son was, that was about it. No one had actually spoken to him in over a year or knew exactly what he was doing in Africa. With only a temporary home base in Cape Town that I knew about, his exact whereabouts could only be imagined. This would be a disappointment for Mrs. Ridge. Despite what she'd told me, I guessed that her true intention was actually to meet her son again, face to face, and try for some sort of reconciliation. That didn't seem very likely now. There was little more I could do. I've travelled before on a client's dime, but this was something altogether different; my quarry had run so far away, he'd ended up in another hemisphere. There was no hopping into my car or on a short-haul Air Canada flight to check this out.

I plugged in the earphone of my cell and dialled Clara Ridge's number.

"Hello, you have reached the answering machine of Mrs. Clara Ridge. Please leave a message, time of your call, and a return phone number after the tone."

"Mrs. Ridge, it's Russell Quant, Wednesday afternoon. I'm just on my way back to Saskatoon from Estevan." I consulted my watch. "I should be back in town by about eight." I gave her a brief outline of what I'd found out so far, ending with the fact that her son was likely to be living somewhere on the African continent, working as a teacher or caregiver to children, and that we should talk about things at her earliest convenience. I left her all my numbers and hung up.

Her earliest convenience turned out to be about an hour out of Saskatoon.

"Russell Quant," I answered the ring of my cellphone.

"You found him?" Clara Ridge.

"Sort of," I answered, trying to ignore a pet peeve I have for people who simply assume you know it is them calling and don't bother to identify themselves, as if no one else would ever be calling you. "As I explained on my message, according to the minister of his church in Estevan, the last time he heard from Matt, he was in Africa."

"But you have contact information for him in Africa? You know where he is?"

I could understand Mrs. Ridge's being anxious to have news of her son's exact whereabouts after twenty years, but I did not want to raise her hopes too high. "The information I have is over a year old. And even at that, the minister thought Matt moved around a lot. I'm sorry, Mrs. Ridge, I can't guarantee Matt is still at this address."

"You're sure about this? You're sure it's him?"

I wasn't entirely clear where she was going with her line of questioning. "As I said, Mrs. Ridge, I only know what I was told by the minister and the principal at the school Matt taught at. I'm quite convinced they were telling me all they knew, and with great sincerity, but of course there is a chance Matt is no longer in Africa. And at the moment, I'm afraid I don't have many more leads to follow up on." I hesitated, and she seemed to be thinking about what I'd told her. I added, "That's not to say there aren't other leads out there. I just haven't found them yet."

"I see. Well, I need to give this some thought, Mr. Quant."

"Of course."

"I'll get back to you. Thank you."

I wondered if I'd ever hear from her again. I was glad I'd gotten a retainer cheque.

About half an hour before reaching the outskirts of Saskatoon, blackness descended upon my car like an asphalt tarp; I was listening to a Mario Frangoulis CD and felt warm and safe. I decided to call my message manager for news of the day. I was half expecting (hoping for) a message from Jared. The longer we went without talking about things, about his request for my help in ending his relationship with Anthony, the more awkward it would become, and the greater the chance of the silence between us causing irreparable damage to our own friendship. I had pretty much decided I was going to call him if he hadn't called me. But my plans went flying out the window with a sorrow-filled message I was not expecting at all. I pressed on the gas pedal before the final words were out of the caller's mouth. I needed to get to the hospital fast.

Chapter 7

I recognized three of the faces in the Royal University Hospital waiting room, a trio of women sitting with another woman and a man I did not recognize. As I approached, they turned their weepy, puffy-eyed faces up to me and Edda, the ninety year old whom I'd thought the most stoic of the Ash House residents, released a fresh deluge of tears. I crouched down next to the small group, and Loretta immediately reached for my hands and buried them within the damp-Kleenex-lined cocoon of her own.

"Thank you for calling me," I said to her.

"I hope you don't mind," she answered, dabbing at her cheeks which were streaked with failing makeup. "It's just that…well, you gave us your card, and I thought perhaps you and Ethan were friends."

The way she said "friends" left little to the imagination about what she really thought, and I found my cheeks heating up again. Why did they keep doing that?

"The others weren't so sure," she continued, shooting long-faced Hortense a look. "But your card said you were a detective, so I thought…well, I thought this was something you might want to know about regardless, seeing as it happened the same night you were at the house."

"What exactly did happen, Loretta?" I begged to know.

"It's Ethan." She began to tear up, and my insides grew cold as I felt her little hand tighten around my own. The bright gold of her many rings dug into my skin and her now-chipped, teal fingernail polish was in stark contrast against the white of the Kleenex.

"It was last night," she began again, looking at the others as if seeking agreement on the timing. But the tears were too heavy, and she pulled away to find another hanky in a purse that matched her outfit.

"We got back from the movie around eleven-thirty," dark-haired Hortense with the severe pageboy, and the most composed of the group, took over the story. "Everything seemed fine in the house. Mary-Jane and Dmytro were in bed and heard nothing strange." I was guessing Mary-Jane and Dmytro were the two elders I did not recognize, Ash House residents I hadn't met when I visited. "But that beast must have gotten into the house somehow, without them knowing. He was waiting for poor Ethan, in his bedroom, and he attacked him and almost killed him!"

My skin was twitching, and my heart was beating an irregular drum solo in my chest as I listened to the story. I had a thousand questions, details I was desperate to know, but instead I asked, "How is he?" I cringed and realized I didn't want to hear bad news about this man.

"They don't know yet, but it can't be good," Hortense reported. "He's been mostly unconscious this whole time."

"Was Ethan able to tell anyone who did it?"

She shook her head, the sturdy sheaths of her raven hair moving along with it. "I don't think so."

Damn!

"Have you seen him? Can I see him?"

Another shake. "His immediate family are the only ones allowed in right now. We've been staying here as much as we can, just in case."

"To show our support," Loretta added, having collected her wits about her. Her lovely eyes were rimmed with red, and her fine silver hair was a flattened version of the puffier coiffure she'd sported the night before. "We all love Ethan so much. This is too horrible."

I shook my head in sympathy. "How could this have happened?" And why?

Hortense's dark eyes regarded me from beneath thick eyebrows. "There is one person who could tell you."

I was back at Ash House twenty-four hours after my first visit, but this time under much worse circumstances. Frank answered my knock and invited me to join him in the sitting room where he'd been sitting by the fire reading a John Sandford novel. Except for the gentle murmur of logs being devoured behind a fireplace grate, the place was like a tomb, so different from the laughter and joviality of a day ago.

"Someone needs to be here, I guess," he told me in a subdued voice, the vitality sucked out of him like juice from an orange. "We're taking turns. Everyone thinks I should be resting up, recovering from my 'ordeal', but hell, the only one who went through an ordeal is that poor boy. Besides, someone's gotta look after the kid."

The kid?

"I can hear you," a child's voice rang out from around an unseen corner, the unexpected sound bouncing off the walls like a Ping-Pong ball.

"That's what you get for eavesdropping," Frank called back.

"I can take care of myself. And I'm not a kid."

"Says you."

This whole conversation taking place between Frank and the disembodied voice was amusing but puzzling. Who was this kid he was talking to? And why was a kid living in a retirement home?

"If you're busy listening to other people's conversations, that must mean you're done with your homework and ready for bed. Is that correct?"

The only response was the sound of speedy footfalls escaping up a set of stairs to the second storey and far away from us.

I gave Frank a questioning look.

"Simon," he said as if the name itself were explanation enough.

"Is he someone's grandson?"

"I suppose *she's* everyone's grandkid in a way, but Simon is Ethan's daughter."

"Oh." I'd thought Ethan was gay. Hadn't he said so himself? And I thought he was single. And…oh just stop it Quant. It makes no difference, and this isn't why you're here, is it? I moved on to why I was. "Frank, I understand you saw what happened? I know this may be difficult to talk about b…"

"Bollocks! Nothing difficult about it. Yeah, I saw the bastard."

My neck hairs stood up with a thrill at his words. "Have you talked to the police?"

"Sure."

"Good. Can you tell me what happened?" I suppose it wasn't really any of my business, but, once a cop, always a cop. Besides, I had been there that night, and I liked Ethan Ash. If there was anything at all I could do to help, I wanted to do it.

"I have a hard time getting to sleep until I pee, and I have a hard time peeing because of my prostrate."

Too much information.

"We came home from the movie, and everyone headed off for bed except for me. I stayed down here, right where we're sitting right now, and read this here book, waiting for my bladder and all the other internals involved to tell me it was time to pee. We have an elevator, but I like to use the stairs every so often—for the exercise—and that's what I was doing, heading up the stairs to the bathroom—couldda used the one down here but I thought I'd head for bed right after I did my business, so I might as well make one trip because my bedroom is on the second floor, see—so I was heading up, and I'd just reached the second floor when I heard something from further up the stairwell. Only thing on the third floor is Ethan's rooms, see. The noise was muffled, but I swore it sounded like someone was fighting. And I have been in fights in my life, see, so I know the sound. So, I think to myself I should go check it out, and if it's nothing, I'll have gotten even more exercise—and, to tell the truth, I was suspecting I wasn't quite ready to pee yet anyway—but if it's something, well...

"By the time I get to the door of Ethan's suite all I can hear is some grunting. You know, young man..." And here he stopped and looked at me with furry eyebrows arched high over startlingly clear blue eyes. "For a minute there, I though I might be interrupting something else."

I made some sort of sound in response; half whimper, half groan.

"But, see, I still couldn't pee, so I decided to knock anyway. All of a sudden, the sounds stopped. There was silence, and I called out

Ethan's name, to see if he was all right. Well, next thing you know, the door flies open, and I get knocked to the floor like a mop."

Here we go, now the good stuff. "Someone came out of the room and pushed you down?"

"Isn't that what I just said?"

I ignored the question and asked, "Did you see who attacked Ethan?"

"Of course I saw him. He pushed me, didn't he?"

Frank was getting ornery and maybe needed to pee, so I thought it best to move the tale along with as much haste as possible. "Were you able to give the police a description?"

"You bet. Don't know if it'll help though, I didn't see much of his face."

My heart sank. All of Frank's bluster was to cover for the fact that he really hadn't seen much of anything. I'd seen that type of reaction before in witnesses; they wished they could help and felt guilty they couldn't, so they make a big to-do about what they did see and hear, which often amounted to not much.

"But I know it was a man."

I asked a few more leading questions, but aside from the fact that the figure was definitely not a woman (or his pride would not allow it to be), it seemed Frank could provide no further details, until one last bit that set creepy-crawlers to dancing over my skin.

"If he hadn't pushed me down, I might have caught him you know," Frank said. "He wasn't that quick on account of his leg."

"His leg?"

"There was something wrong with his right leg. When he was running away and down the stairs I saw that it lagged behind him, see. He had to pull it along after himself. Maybe got hurt in a war or something? Whatever, that fella had one hell of a limp."

My mind flashed back to the night before, walking the chilly March streets from my car to Ash House. I had had a sense that I was being followed; I'd seen nothing, but I'd heard something. Someone walking behind me. Someone with a limp.

I didn't get a lot of shut-eye that night, what with all the men keeping me busy. So topsy-turvy in fact was my sleep, that eventually both Barbra and Brutus hopped off the bed in search of quieter spots (if they don't get a full eighteen hours of sleep, the next day is absolutely ruined).

Matthew, Jared and Ethan were the guys in bed with me. I could not get them out of my mind. As soon as one was banished, another would pop up. I pictured Matthew Moxley, somewhere in Africa, tending to children, far from reach. I fretted about Jared and his request to help him break up with Anthony. What was driving him to do this? It was so wrong! Would he do it with or without my help? How would Anthony react?

And then there was Ethan Ash, now lying in a hospital bed. The fact that I hadn't been able to see him made it worse; my imagination was filling in the missing image with horrible possibilities that were probably much worse than reality. I hoped.

And then, as I was finally about to slide into sleep, a fourth man entered my dreams—Alex Canyon—and the night was lost.

Because of my rough night, I was late getting to work the next morning, so I was surprised when I pulled into the PWC lot at the same time as Errall. She was driving a brand new, ice grey BMW 5-Series. I caught up with her as she hoisted a briefcase out of the swanky vehicle's trunk, which thunked shut with the impressive solidness only money can buy.

"Wow," I commented. "Nice wheels."

She seemed to be ignoring me. Nothing new there.

"Late start today?" I asked.

She pulled the couture-cut edges of her pristine black coat's collar up around her face, either to keep warmth in or to block me out. I prefer to think it was the keep warmth in thing. She answered me with a blast in the face from her two laser-blue eyes, which looked a little tired this morning (a rude and very Errall-type greeting). Her hair was pulled back into a discreet bun, which usually meant she had an important meeting or wasn't in the mood for dangling hair.

We entered through the back door of the building, and she headed straight through to the front foyer and her office while I stayed behind in the kitchen, knowing Lilly would have a fresh pot of coffee going. I poured myself a cup, sniffed it to make sure it wasn't one of those flavoured varieties that I can barely swallow (unless the flavour is rum or Bailey's), and, assured that it wasn't, sludged myself toward the stairs and my office.

As I passed by Lilly with a salute of my coffee cup in lieu of a good morning, the sight of Clara Ridge sitting in the waiting room pulled me up short. I looked at Lilly who gave me a smile, her eyes wider than usual, saying something like: "She just showed up. She wasn't in your appointment book. I tried calling you at home, but you didn't answer."

I greeted Mrs. Ridge and invited her up to my office. As we got settled, I noted that the woman looked a little less perfectly put together than on our first meeting; the wig was a little less shel-lacked, the makeup not quite right and her nails were scrubbed clear of the bright red of a few days ago. Nevertheless, she was still handsome, maybe more so without the disguising layers of cosmetics.

Before taking her seat, Clara pulled a thick envelope from the pocket of her brown fur coat and placed it in front of me on my desk. I looked at it questioningly.

"I'd like you to go to Africa."

My tongue grew dry, and I experienced unfamiliar surges somewhere in my brain as I processed the unexpected words.

"I thought about this all night," she told me. "I have the money, so why shouldn't I spend it on what I really, really want: to find my son. I can't do it. I don't know the world in that way. I've never been out of Saskatchewan. But you, you can do it, can't you?"

Oh sure. No problem. I go to Africa all the time. They have the best deals on spices and colourful bolts of fabric.

But, of course, I *could* do this.

But, should I?

"Would you be coming with me?" I asked.

She quickly shook her head. "Oh no. I don't want him to know about me. Please remember that."

"Mrs. Ridge, I...well, first of all, I have to tell you that you have taken me a bit by surprise. Please understand, I think your willingness to find a son you haven't seen in twenty years by sending a detective to Africa is...commendable. But doesn't that show you how much you *do* want to see him? I know you are nervous about it, but you obviously love your son, and miss him. Don't you think you should be there when he's found?"

She shook her head resolutely. "I can't, not yet."

I sat silent for a moment, taking it all in. Again, Mrs. Ridge had not taken off her coat, and again it looked like she was beginning to cook. "Can I take your coat?"

"N-n-no." She seemed as jittery as an earthworm in a bait shop. "I can't stay long, really. I have a friend, a travel specialist, who can arrange your trip, all the way to Cape Town—that's where Matthew lives, right?"

"That's the address I have for him," I said with a slow nod. "But I have to caution you again, Mrs. Ridge, I cannot guarantee he will still be there."

"My friend will get you to Cape Town, so you don't have to worry about that. The money," she nodded at the fat envelope on my desk, "is for everything else once you get there. I know it won't be cheap. If you think you need more, you can let me know by calling my number." She leaned in and opened the envelope and splayed out a ream of cash, thousands of colourful Canadian dollars (lots of red ones and brown ones.) Where the heck had she come up with that? I had visions of her excavating the million dollars she'd received from her husband's estate from some old shoebox in the basement or underneath the mattress they'd once shared.

"All I need you to do is to call me, every chance you get, and tell me where you are, every day if you can. Let me know what's happening, what you find. Will you do that? I want to know exactly where he is the moment you find him."

I nodded my head in agreement, but insistent doubt was demanding my attention like a flashing neon sign in my brain, doubt about whether this was the right next step to take in this case, doubt about whether I was the one best to take it. It wasn't that I didn't want an all-expense-paid trip to South Africa, but the whole thing was happening so fast and seemed so incredible (and I was pretty certain I was going to have to get shots in the bum for dengue fever or something like that).

"I wonder, Mrs. Ridge, if it would be better to arrange for a local South African detective to look into this."

"No, this is better. I don't speak the language anyway."

"I believe many South Africans speak English," I told her.

She shook her head. "This is better. I don't want to deal with someone I don't know. How could I be sure they were any good, or if they were doing what I asked them to do? They could take my money and do nothing; I'd never know the difference." I didn't bother to point out to her that I could do the same thing for all she knew, but of course I'd never do that. Maybe she just sensed that in me.

"Besides," she kept on, "I have no passport, and I want this done now. You go. You'll let me know where you are, and you'll let me know as soon as you find him." She was very intent on my staying in close and constant touch. Maybe that was how she intended to keep tabs on me.

I couldn't tell if Clara Ridge was excited at the prospect of finding her son, or perhaps a little baffled by the enormity of what she was hiring someone to do for her, or maybe just scared of what the outcome might be, but I did know that she was serious about what she was asking. There was no doubt in her mind that she wanted this done, and I was the guy to do it. What I hoped she knew was that there was a very real possibility that she could go to all this trouble and expense and I could find nothing more in Cape Town than an empty room and more dead ends. Or, if I was lucky enough to find him, her son could shun her, have no interest whatsoever in meeting or knowing about his mother, for, despite what Clara Ridge told me, I believed this was her true goal.

We talked for another half hour and then she left. When she was gone, I sat zombie-like behind my desk, a stunned expression overtaking my face like moss on a north-facing tree, disbelief oozing from my body at every pore. What had I just agreed to do?

To alleviate the stress of the unknown, I leaned into my computer, punched a few buttons and visited the first website I found about the continent of Africa. Information is power. I read through some quick facts: Africa is considered by most scientists to be the origin of mankind, a continent of fifty-three independent countries including fifteen of the world's least developed nations; a place of vast deserts, tropical rain forests, rugged mountains and fertile grasslands. Africa is the home of the Nile, Kilimanjaro and about 690 million people, seventy percent of whom survive on less than $2 a day. Disease and famine kill millions of Africans each year and even basic education is denied to a large percentage of its children; Africa is the biggest sufferer of HIV and AIDS.

I scrolled through several more pages of information, then checked out several online photo albums, the pictures gloriously stunning regardless of whether they were taken by amateurs on safari or professional photographers. There is no denying Africa is a spectacular place with some of the most dramatic vistas in the world, and still, amongst the beauty is wretched poverty and sickness and death, and it wasn't difficult to see why this continent, with all its natural wealth and splendour, was still in desperate need of aid from people like Matthew Moxley.

I don't know if it came from the movies or some long forgotten news broadcast or TV documentary, but as I surfed through the pictures, I kept hearing the same thing, like a soundtrack for my coming adventure: an ominous voice repeating a warning to all, a warning to beware the dangers of the land known as Africa…*The Daaaaaark Continent*. My skin shifted ever so slightly.

One of Sereena's most endearing qualities is her willingness to drink in the afternoon. At the end of a rather garbled telephone call, during which my tongue was still thickened with the reservations that plagued me about my agreeing to find a single man somewhere on the second largest continent in the world, Sereena offered to meet me at Earls for a late lunch and drinks. Mostly drinks.

I was already waiting in a booth with a glass of Kendall-Jackson Collage white when Sereena made her majestic entrance behind Malibu Barbie hostess, looking like she owned the place. I watched bemused as Barbie kept on having to stop and wait as my friend alighted at this table and that like a queen bee greeting her soon to be disposed of but momentarily amusing drones. Under an early-spring jacket of mint green with a splendid tartan-patterned collar of orange, dark green and purple, she wore a darker mint sweater made of something like saran wrap and a skirt with a thigh-high cut and of the same tartan as the collar. Her towering boots were sharp-toed, her jewels sparkling, her lips vivid red and her hair big. She was in a feisty mood.

Ordering a pitcher of double margaritas with the offhand comment, "When in Rome" (a reference to Earl's prodigious margarita menu), she sent away Convertible Barbie drink-server with a twiddle of her fingers and focussed on me with gem-like eyes. "You're in love," she announced.

I snorted a few drops of Semillon Chardonnay through my nose but otherwise reacted well to her out-of-the-blue observation. "Sereena, what the h…we're here to talk about Africa, and how crazy it is to be talking about Africa as if it's like going to Puerto Vallarta, and why I shouldn't consider going even though I think I just might!" I spurted out in one breath.

"Oh that."

Yoga Teacher Barbie food-server, along with Gay Ken busboy (the only Ken available), arrived to clean up my mess—which really wasn't all that bad—and asked if we'd had time to look at the menu.

"The Sweet Soy Salmon…" Sereena started, looking at me for agreement.

"…Chili Chicken…" I added, in favour of the idea of tapas rather than full entrees.

"…Baby Calamari and Tuna Lettuce Wraps…"

"…and maybe the Spinach and Artichoke Dip?"

"Too much food," Sereena decided. "Cut the chicken and keep the pitcher full." She turned to me and poured her eyes into mine with meaningful precision. "This is superb news, Russell. You will absolutely adore Africa. And really, Russell, you have to get it out of your head that the plane is going to drop you off in some baboon-infested jungle where you'll have to battle for your life and live in a tent—as delightful as that sounds. And you can just forget any Me: Tarzan, You: Jane Russell fantasies you may be conjuring up in that handsome head of yours. You're going to Cape Town for goodness sakes, one of the most stimulating and stunning and cosmopolitan cities in the world."

"Will you come with me?"

Sereena had accompanied me on work trips before; I'd do some detecting, she'd shop, and then we'd meet at day's end for dinner and cocktails. I just knew I'd feel better about going to Africa if she was with me.

"Love to but can't," she told me, and I knew I'd only get an explanation if she felt like it and apparently she didn't. Her reasons could be anything from she just didn't feel like it to she was going to be in Abu Dhabi having dinner with the crown prince of someplace or other. "But I can arrange the next best thing." Sereena hesitated, reconsidered and added: "Well, something pretty good at least. " She consulted her watch, and announced: "Perfect." She pulled a cellphone out of her purse and began pushing buttons.

I eyed my friend over the heavily salted rim of my margarita glass (having switched from wine—when with Sereena, do as Sereena does) and wondered what the heck she was up to.

"Roy," she said into the phone's receiver, and I could tell by the look on her face—not an all-out smile by any means, but a certain glow—that she had some fondness for whoever this Roy character was. What I couldn't tell was why she'd decided to have a telephone conversation with him in the middle of a perfectly good drinkfest. "How did you know?" she said. "It's a pleasure to hear your voice as well."

As I watched Sereena talk on the phone, she moved her head just so and the restaurant lighting hit her face in such a way as to momentarily highlight the gentle half-moon scar on her chin. Although I'd seen it many times, it took me somewhat by surprise. I'd thought after my clandestine meeting with Uncle Lawrence in the Arctic last year that I'd learned everything there was to know about my enigmatic neighbour. But the scar?

How and when had she gotten that scar?

A boating accident off the island of Capri? Fisticuffs with Gisele Bundchen over Leonardo DiCaprio? A lover's quarrel gone bad? A drunken misstep on the slippery steps outside a Santorini tavern? An Oktoberfest in Berlin gone *schlecht*? I made a mental note to ask her...then thought better of it. I surveyed my friend with the detachment made possible when the person you're studying doesn't know it. Suddenly something became blazingly clear to me, something I'd never allowed as a possibility before: I'd *never* know the whole of who this woman was.

In many ways, Sereena was, is, and always will be, an alluring mystery to me. And finally, I was okay with that. I did not need to know all of her. In many ways, I preferred not to: it was endlessly more interesting for me.

"I know it's late, Roy," Sereena apologized, still on the phone. "So I promise not to keep you long, darling. I'll call you again over the weekend and we can tell naughty stories."

Late? Did she say it was late? I checked my watch, worried that I'd been drinking too much for too long and didn't even know it. Nope. It wasn't even two in the afternoon.

"I have a friend coming your way, Roy, and I'd like you to take care of him. He can make his own way to Cape Town, but he may need occasional assistance once he's there, and I'd like to be able to tell him you're available to make arrangements for him. I've told him all about you and what a magician you are and now he simply refuses to go to Africa without the promise of your help."

Sereena was plying her own brand of magic. Again I consulted my watch and did some math. It would be nearing ten p.m. in South Africa. That's where it was late.

"You are a doll, Roy," Sereena told her friend. "I'll give him your information. Thank you." She listened a bit more, sipped at her drink, then rung off with a: "Pleasure" and "Goodbye." She hung up, returned her phone to her purse and announced with a tone of finality, "Roy will take care of you."

Okey-dokey. "And who, may I ask, is Roy?"

"You may. Roy Hearn is a delightful man. He runs a travel business that looks after clients for most of the important

American touring companies that send people to South Africa, anywhere in Africa actually. Anything you need or want, Roy can get it for you," she told me with absolute confidence in the man. And if Sereena trusted Roy, I trusted Roy.

Suddenly I felt better, excited actually. I could do this. I could go to Africa. I could find my way around, especially with the help of someone like Sereena's friend. The bigger question was: how lucky was I going to be at finding a Canadian needle in an African haystack?

After partaking in a particularly punishing program of high-incline, high-speed treadmill cardio, tension squats and lunges to burn off the high-carb, high-fat, high-calorie meal Sereena and I shared in order to absorb the high-alcohol afternoon, I returned to the office to check for messages. It was nearing nine p.m. and I expected the place to be deserted. It was, except for a light under the door to Errall's office. Chances were good that she had her sharp nose deep in some legal case she would no doubt win quite handily. But given recent events, I wondered if maybe she was avoiding going home, avoiding Yvonne, or both.

I rapped lightly on the door and let myself in despite no invitation to do so.

As expected, Errall was hard at work in a circle of light, the rest of the room left in shadow, as if unwanted, unneeded. Over a nearby chair she had thrown a professionally tailored, scorching orange blazer, leaving her wearing a camisole-style top that seemed flimsy over her bird-width chest. She looked up at me with a familiar irritation that long ago stopped daunting me.

"How's it going?" I asked.

She pulled off a pair of glasses she'd only just recently taken to wearing when reading, and dropped them to the desktop as if she hated them. "I want a cigarette. I own this fucking building. I think I should be the one making the rules. If I want to smoke indoors, I think I should be able to."

So there.

"It smells, Errall. Not only in here, but the whole building. We have clients to think of."

"Oh yeah, like your clients are so delicate and refined they can't stand a bit of tobacco in the air."

Yup, she was irritable all right.

"So I take it things are going okay then?" I asked sweetly.

"Just peachy." She rose and began closing books and files as if preparing to call it a night, which I thought was a good idea.

"Seeing Yvonne tonight?"

"We broke up."

Now this was a true sign that we'd made progress in our relationship. In the past, she would have prefaced that sentence with: It's none of your business, but if you really must know…

"I'm sorry to hear that." I wanted to be supportive. "I really liked her."

"You never met her."

Oh. "Still."

She gave me a curdling look that I didn't think I wholly deserved.

"Help me out with these," she said as she shouldered herself into the blazer, which I now saw had a matching skirt worn with a pair of flirty-looking heels. Errall is nothing if not a snappy dresser.

I hadn't made it up to my office yet, but I didn't think it wise to turn her down, so I hoisted a few of the books she'd referred to and waited while she collected her coat and purse and some files. We wordlessly made our way through the foyer area to the kitchen. We had only just opened the back door when we heard the thrashing of tires against gravel.

Someone was taking a powder out of our parking lot. Someone who didn't want to be seen.

"That's the car!" Errall screeched. "Go after him!"

"What are you talking about?" I asked, even as I was scrambling in the direction of my car, fumbling with keys in my pocket.

"Hurry up!" She screeched as she waited impatiently for me to unlock the driver's side door, toss in the books I was carrying, get in, and reach across to unlock the passenger door. I had no doubt she had every intention of coming with me.

As soon as Errall was seated and still struggling with her seat belt, purse, briefcase and loose files, I fishtailed out of the parking lot and turned left onto Spadina Crescent, on the tail of a dark colour, late-model Nissan.

"Who is this?" I demanded to know as I trailed the car onto the underpass that curves beneath the University Bridge and alongside the South Saskatchewan River.

"If I knew that, we wouldn't have to follow him, now would we?" she shot back.

Errall was being a little more uppity and churlish than usual, and I tried to catch her eye while keeping one of my own on the road and the vehicle we were following. Thankfully Mr. Nissan wasn't into undue velocity. "You said, 'That's the car,' Errall. So you've obviously seen this same car before, right?"

"I've been noticing it in my neighbourhood over the last couple of days. At first I thought one of my neighbours must have gotten a new car, but it has a rental sticker. I've been nervous about it for some reason. Probably because of the peeping Tom incident the other night. But now I know I'm right, I'm not paranoid; whoever is in that car is watching me."

I couldn't argue with that (unless one of Errall's neighbours was *really* into showing off).

And so, we continued at a rather gentlemanly pace (for a car chase), past the Mendel Art Gallery toward the CP Bridge, also known as the Weir Bridge.

Originally built in 1939, the CP Bridge is one in a series of bridges that span the South Saskatchewan River within city limits. The parking lot beneath the bridge overlooks a rushing torrent of water that spills over an invisible dam—the weir—in an otherwise docile Saskatchewan River. And, taking Errall and me by surprise, it was into this parking lot that the Nissan led us.

Being as it was a rather bone-chilling night out, the parking lot was empty. The Nissan pulled into a spot, fastidiously parking between the marked lines. Good stalker. I slowed the Mazda down to a baby's crawl, and Errall and I regarded each other and the car with questioning looks. Whoever was in that vehicle had lost interest in getting away, and more so, now seemed intent on a face-to-face meeting.

"Now what, Mr. Private Eye?" Errall asked, tension obvious in her voice.

"I'm kinda tired," I responded. "I think we should head home."

"I'm howling with laughter inside," she said in a way that hinted to me that she was lying.

I turned the wheel and inserted my car into the spot next to the Nissan. In unison we leaned forward and peered into our neighbour's window. It was impossible for us to make out the inhabitant of the vehicle. One of us would have to get out. Being the brave one was part of my job. *If* someone was paying me. I glanced at Errall. She screwed up her face as if to say: I'd go, but I left my gloves at home, and it's cold outside. Big surprise.

My hand reached for the door handle and I was about to make my move when something happened.

The interior light of the Nissan flicked on.

A flabbergasted breath caught in my throat. It couldn't be.

I heard a sound coming from Errall's throat, like the mewl of a newborn kitten, and all she said was a very quiet, "No."

Chapter 8

The sensation of a plane hurtling downwards, only seven hours into a fifteen-hour flight, is not a good one. The rocking of the aircraft as it descended through layers of turbulent air jostled me out of a sound sleep. I checked my watch, recalculated time changes, and verified with my startled memory banks exactly where the heck in the world I was supposed to be. We'd departed Atlanta at 10:40 a.m. Thursday morning. We were scheduled to arrive in Johannesburg at 10:30 a.m. Friday morning, including a seven-hour time change from Atlanta (eight from home). Problem was, according to my watch, it was only nine-thirty p.m. Thursday night. And we were going down.

I jerked up in my aisle seat, the sudden motion waking the passenger next to me.

"You okay?" she asked. She mustn't have been asleep because she sounded perfectly awake and lucid and looked like a million bucks. Either that or she was one of those horrid creatures who could get up from bed a fully functioning human being. "You look a little worried," she commented. "It's only a little turbulence."

I glanced over at the woman, sort of a young Kathleen Turner type, very attractive and feminine but outdoorsy too, with shiny tresses of wavy, auburn hair that flowed attractively down both shoulders. "Uh, yeah, but isn't it a little soon to be going down?" I replied, trying to sound as cavalier as I could manage, at the same time wiping sleep from my eyes.

She laughed. "We're just stopping for fuel on Sal and picking up a few passengers. Not many, I wouldn't expect."

I blinked at her.

"Sal Island," she explained. "One of the Cape Verde Islands, *Cabo Verde* in Portuguese," she said in a knowledgeable way. "It's a group of about ten or so islands that form an archipelago off the northwest coast of Africa, near Senegal and Mauritania. You really should return here for a visit sometime—I mean for longer than an hour stopover to pick up fuel—Sal Island is beautiful: large sandy beaches, turquoise water, great windsurfing, the Cape Verdeans are lovely...what's left of them."

I gave my drowsy head a shake. What was this woman talking about? I looked around and saw that most of the other passengers around us were still dead to the world after a couple of movies and wine with dinner. It was very quiet except for the gyrating sounds of the plane doing its bit to land us on some spit of sand somewhere in the Atlantic Ocean. The cabin had that otherworldly feel planes sometimes get during lengthy, overnight flights; eerily lit by an occasional view screen or overhead reading light left on, filled with the barely perceptible buzz of music and movies played through earphones, the passengers tucked motionless into seats like moths in cocoons, all of us caught in the no man's land between the world we know on the ground and the nether world of thirty-five thousand feet in the air where we're only temporary visitors.

"They have their share of problems. Prolonged droughts," the woman stated. "The harmattan wind produces these gawdawful, choking dust storms. I was nearly caught in one once. And then there's all the volcanic and seismic activity, problems with deforestation, desertification, illegal beach sand extraction, over-fishing."

The plane gave another hump that woke a few more of our fellow voyagers.

"How do you know all this stuff?" I asked the woman. "Are you from Africa?"

"No. If only. Atlanta. You?"

"Canada." I'm rarely more specific than that on first go-round.

"What part?"

"Saskatchewan; the prairies."

"Oh my. So you've already been flying a long way. When did you start out?"

"I left Saskatoon—that's the city I live in—yesterday, overnighted in Atlanta."

"How long is that flight, from your home to Atlanta?" I noticed she didn't even attempt to pronounce Saskatoon or Saskatchewan, wisely going for the easier "your home." Who could blame her?

"About three hours to Toronto, then a couple more to Atlanta."

"I love Toronto. A mini New York. What's the weather like on the prairies this time of year?" A standard Canada question.

"Actually it's been warm for March. When I left, the snow was beginning to melt." I countered with my unexpected discovery: "It sure was cold in Atlanta though."

She nodded. "Yes, unseasonably so. It could have snowed." She smiled, displaying a row of healthy white teeth, and held out a hand. "I'm Cassandra Wellness."

I shook the proffered hand, strong, tanned. "Russell Quant."

A voice came over the PA system to tell us we were going to be landing in several minutes and that we should do the usual stuff to prepare.

"What do you do in Canada?" Cassandra Wellness asked as she shoved a sack-like purse under the seat in front of her and fastened her seat belt.

I smiled a rather mischievous smile. Who needs playing cards or travel-size backgammon? One of my favourite airplane games is creating bogus life stories to try out on people I'll never see again. I don't suggest this activity for others; it can get tricky, and a believable story that isn't your own is much harder to produce than you'd expect, but I use it for purely professional reasons as rehearsal for when I go undercover. "I'm the mayor of Saskatoon," I told her offhandedly, as if it wasn't a big deal and that maybe I was a little reticent about admitting to my lofty position.

She sat back a bit and did an admirable job of hiding her surprise as she examined my face. "My, you don't look like a mayor. And you're so young. How fascinating." She was quiet for a moment then, "Is that er…full-time work?"

I had to stifle a smile. "Keeps me busy. And what about you?

How do you know all that stuff about Sal Island if you're not from Africa?"

"I spend a great deal of time in Africa. I'm a photojournalist. Freelance," she added quickly. "But I do most of my work for one Atlanta magazine; it's called *Well-Spotted*. Maybe you've heard of it?"

I shook my head and guessed that it was about leopards. I was impressed. I'd never met a photojournalist before and wondered if one of the African pictures I'd admired on the internet was taken by Cassandra Wellness.

"It's a nature and safari magazine. Have you ever been on safari, Russell?" she asked.

"No, I haven't."

"Is that why you're going to Africa then, to go on safari?"

I nodded and added vaguely. "I hope to." She was beginning to ask too many questions, and not about what it was like to be a mayor, as I'd expected.

We sat quiet for a little longer, but Cassandra wasn't a sit quiet kind of gal.

"Where are you staying in Joburg?" she asked.

"Johannesburg is just a layover for me. I'm continuing on to Cape Town."

She jumped on that with an excited smile. "Really! So am I! I adore Cape Town! Which hotel?"

This was Roy Hearn's first coup. Clara Ridge's travel agent had set me up in what I'm sure was a decent enough hotel, but Roy, upon hearing about it, quickly pooh-poohed it and used his considerable contacts to get me a hard-to-believe deal at supposedly one of the best places to stay in Cape Town. He called it his "welcome to South Africa" present for Sereena's friend.

I answered, "The Table Bay."

"You're joking! So am I!" she repeated with a husky squeal, taking the opportunity to squeeze my right hand in delight.

It was a good thing I was taking a shine to Ms. Wellness, because it looked as if we were going to be in each other's company for a good while longer; Johannesburg was still eight-and-a-half hours away and Cape Town another two hours after that.

We chatted companionably for the duration of the landing and well into the hour turnaround time on the ground at Sal Island. Cassandra Wellness had led a fascinating, adventurer's life and she loved to tell a good tale, many of which I thought were, if not Indiana Jones worthy, at least *Romancing the Stone*-like. So fascinating in fact were her sagas that my attention was diverted only once, when the Cape Verde passengers boarded the plane.

Cassandra was correct in her guess about the number of add-ons; there were only three that night. The first two were giddy, beach-blond gals who probably worked at the Sal Island Earls. The other, the last to get on the plane, was a man, so big and burly he barely had enough room to navigate down the narrow aisle of the plane, his head skimming the ceiling of the cabin, his hefty hips brushing against seats as he passed by them. He wore a decidedly non-beach wardrobe of a dark coloured suit and tie and a white shirt, and his small forehead seemed perpetually creased above beady eyes that roamed the faces of everyone aboard as he plodded to the back of the aircraft, as if looking for someone. As he approached where Cassandra and I were getting to know one another, his pill-sized, sinister eyes took a bead on me and never left my face until he moved past our row to his seat somewhere behind us. For the rest of the trip I swore I could feel his gaze burning two holes through my seat cushion and directly into the back of my skull. And I thought a plane hurtling groundwards was an uncomfortable feeling.

Lying at the foot of its most famous landmark, Table Mountain, Cape Town is situated at the southern tip of Africa, on a small peninsula that juts out into the Atlantic Ocean. The city is South Africa's premier tourist destination, enriched by a unique blend of cultures including Dutch, British and Cape Malay influences. As the massive bulk of our plane floated majestically downwards toward the international airport, Cassandra pointed out the flat-topped mountain and layer of cloud pouring over its sides which, she informed me, was often referred to as the "tablecloth."

We touched down at two-thirty p.m. to a balmy, sun-filled day and Cassandra kindly offered to share her ride—a private van she had arranged before arriving—to our common hotel. The vehicle's progress—much of which seemed to take us right down the centre of one of the largest slums I could ever have imagined—was slowed considerably by an influx of thirty-six thousand cyclists for an annual event called the Argus (which I'd never heard of, but which Cassandra was quite pumped about) and a damaged bus abandoned on the freeway. But, in due course, the little van made its way into the stunningly beautiful Victoria & Alfred Waterfront area, down Breakwater Boulevard and pulled up in jaunty fashion to the entrance of the glamorous Table Bay Hotel.

I was a little agog at the place and hoped Cassandra—who was probably paying full rack rate—never found out the deal Roy Hearn had gotten for me. Together we followed our bags down a long, fig tree-lined, one-and-a-half-storey, glassed-in tunnel into a massive foyer dominated by a huge spray of sunflowers, a welcoming sitting area and a geometric-patterned marble floor so shiny it appeared to be under a layer of crystal clear, cool water.

Cassandra and I parted ways as we approached the bustling front desk to take care of checking-in details. When I was done and preparing to head for my room, I looked around to say so-long, nice to meet you type stuff, but Cassandra Wellness was gone. Oh well, I thought to myself, it was becoming a little tedious pretending to be the mayor of Saskatoon anyway.

My bright room—a junior suite no less (I love Roy)—was actually two separate rooms—a sitting area and a bedroom—connected by two doors thrown open between them, plus a lovely bathroom. Multiple windows revealed a most astonishing view of the busy V&A Waterfront and Table Mountain beyond it. I took a seat at a small writing table in front of one of the floor-to-ceiling windows and pulled out the Visitor Guide map the front desk clerk had handed me. I quickly identified through the window Quays 5 and 6, Jetty 1, the Victoria Wharf Shopping Centre, Market Square at Quay 4, and the Nelson Mandela Gateway to Robben Island, which I understood to be about eleven kilometres out to sea.

For a moment I allowed the enormity of what I'd just been through, where I was and what I had yet to do, to wash over me in a mixed tide of exhilaration, apprehension and appreciation. Already, I could feel that inexplicable pull of Africa so many visitors claim, and I was happy to be experiencing it.

After a speedy unpack, I fell onto the plush king-size bed and shut my eyes, my body begging for sleep.

But nothing.

No way.

Each time I closed my eyes, my brain went into overdrive.

I was too wired from the long trip. And I was in Africa, for Pete's sake!

There was one more thing occupying my already overloaded mind. A thing that had been pinching and teasing and toying with the grey matter in my skull for a couple of days now: the woman in the car at the weir back in Saskatoon.

It turned out to be Kelly Doell. Errall's ex. My high school buddy. The woman who'd left Saskatoon—and Errall—and everyone else—a few years before without a backward glance. She was back.

It was a surreal and awkward moment for me—for all of us, I think—coming face-to-face again in a parking lot. I hadn't known if I should wear my detective hat or my friend hat, and in the end opted for my babbling inquisitor hat. I had asked about a million questions, each a different take on "Why are you here? Are you staying? Where have you been?" and "Why the hell didn't you call me?" I had pretty much reached the conclusion that Kelly had missed Errall—go figure—and was back to reclaim her woman (and her dog, Brutus?) when I became aware that neither woman was paying me much attention. I had been a talking head with an audience of zero.

I'd put aside my own insatiable desire for answers and explanations and let Errall and Kelly go off on their own that night; after all, they had a lot to catch up on. Errall was the spurned ex-lover. I was just the lowly spurned friend. The next morning I'd left for Africa with no time to find out more.

Still, lying in that bed, I couldn't help but volley about a few possible reasons for Kelly's unexpected reappearance. Eventually I was interrupted by a niggle from my detective's brain telling me:

"Quant, forget Kelly. Forget sleep. You're here. Now get your ass off this bed and get to work." So, after a refreshing shower and change of clothes, I did just that.

It was still very warm outside but coming onto evening, so I opted for long pants for my trip into town and, hopefully, to Matt Moxley's home. The hotel doorman did his bit and hailed me a cab and I was on my way. As I dug around in my pockets for Matt Moxley's address I directed the driver to head out of the waterfront area into the city proper. We had just passed something called the BMW Pavilion when I found the piece of paper. I handed it to the guy and sat back to enjoy the ride.

It was a short one.

The cab driver stopped with such immediate precision, the action jolted me forward in my seat and I narrowly avoided hitting my forehead on the headrest in front of me.

"Whaaaaa...?" I wisely inquired.

"No, no, no," he explained fully, thrusting the piece of paper back at me and motioning for me to get out.

"What do you mean? I don't understand," I protested.

"No, no, no," he repeated for clarity. His face was half-serious, half-friendly, as if he himself was not sure whether this was all some big joke or a big waste of his time, in which case he'd become all-serious.

I just wasn't getting what was going on. I took the paper and looked at it but it gave no clue. "Can't you take me here? I'll pay you, right?" I assumed taxis worked the same here as they did at home.

"No, no, mister. Out. You get out tonight."

I get out tonight? Did that mean he didn't want to take me to the address tonight but would be happy to oblige some other day? Or were we simply not communicating? "Out?" I asked. "You want me to get out of the cab?"

He turned away noiselessly and seemed to be studying the street in front of him with great concentration. I guessed the conversation was over. I got out. The taxi roared away.

Not an auspicious start to my South African investigation.

I stepped to the curb, at the ready to hail another taxi. I held up my right arm, puckered my lips in proper whistle formation, and scanned the oncoming traffic. I waited like this for several minutes. Then a few more. But not a single taxi appeared on the busy street. And here I'd thought the difficulty I'd have in Africa would be finding Matt Moxley. Hell, I couldn't even find a cab willing to give me a ride.

I consulted the map of the V&A, plotted a course back to the hotel, and began walking. I fully expected that eventually I'd come across the secret taxi hiding place—known only to non-tourists— and continue to my original destination. But no, no such luck.

By time I arrived at the Table Bay, I was very hot, very sweaty and very tired. And a bit crabby. I couldn't be bothered to make it up to my room, instead plopping down in one of the cushy lobby chairs to bask in the glorious air-conditioning and debate my next move: another cab, shower or beddy-bye?

I was still far from a decision when I caught sight of Cassandra Wellness as she emerged from an elevator. She saw me too and headed my way with a beatific smile. I must have looked like a half-drowned albatross compared to her perky peacock. She was resplendent in a jaunty sailor boy outfit, a look as perfect for a fine dining room as for the bow of a scow.

"Russell! Tremendous to see you. What the hell have you been up to?" she asked with an enthusiastic air, at the same time managing to show off a fair bit more cleavage than any good sailor boy would.

"You're just the person I need to talk to," I responded after standing to greet her with a peck on each cheek.

"A lot of people say so," she cracked as she lowered herself into the chair next to mine, encouraging me to follow suit.

I handed her the paper with Matt's address on it. "So here's the story: I just tried to take a cab to this location but when the driver saw where I wanted to go he threw me out on my butt."

Cassandra studied the paper quite intently before looking up at me with a solemn look on her face. "Why are you going here, Russell?"

I stumbled on that one. Why was the mayor of Saskatoon going anywhere other than a restaurant, bar, nightclub or straight to bed on his first night in Cape Town? This is one good example why the fantasy-life-on-a-plane game isn't always the best way to go. "I'm looking up an old friend," I finally got out.

"He lives here?" she asked, shifting her head to one side, scrutinizing my face as intently as she had the scrap of paper with the address on it.

"I think so. At least that's the last address I have for him."

"Who is he?"

Now wait just a minute here. This was getting to be one too many questions for my liking. I didn't really need Cassandra Wellness; I could probably get the help I required at the concierge desk. "Just a friend," I said as I reached over to retrieve the address which she gave up only after I tugged on it.

"And where did you get the taxi? That can be a very dangerous thing to do in South Africa, you know, Russell."

I did not know.

"There are still some very vicious taxi wars on certain routes."

Taxi wars? She said it as if I should know what she was talking about. I was about to ask whether they were anything like *Star Wars*, but stopped myself. It was beginning to dawn on me that Cassandra was speaking of serious things and concerned for my safety, and that these taxi wars were nothing like those at home between Blueline and United.

Cassandra tossed her hair over her shoulders, crossed her arms and sat back in her chair, regarding me like a curious specimen of flora she didn't know whether she should admire or simply ignore. She nodded at the paper in my hand. "That address, it's in Khayelitsha."

I looked down at it. "Yes, I suppose it is."

"Do you know where that is?" She knew I didn't. "Do you remember the miles and miles of shanty towns we drove by on the way here from the airport?"

I nodded.

"They're not just slums, not the way you or I think of slums or ghettos. They're townships. That was Khayelitsha, the largest one.

Do you know what a township is?"

I shook my head. I should have read my *Fodor's*.

"Township refers to residential areas for non-white peoples."

My face drained of colour. Was this why the taxi driver would not go there? Apartheid had ended over a decade ago, but here was a vivid leftover of that brutal time. One of many, I would soon discover.

"Khayelitsha means 'new home'," Cassandra continued, "and was intended by the government to provide controlled housing to legal residents. But the influx controls didn't work. Keep in mind, Russell, they planned for one hundred and twenty thousand people to live there—today Khayelitsha is home to *over half a million*. Most of them are unemployed, and many of them live without basic infrastructure services."

I remained silent. She let that sink in for a moment or two before she made a surprising offer: "I can take you there tomorrow if you like."

My eyes widened at the suggestion. I had thought she was going to tell me how foolhardy I was to even attempt a visit to this part of town; I was thinking my search for Matt was over before it even got started. "Are you serious?"

She nodded, a slight smile on her thin but nicely shaped lips. "My driver can take us. He knows the people there and where to go."

"But, but, I can't ask this of you, it's too much…" I said it weakly—I knew this was my best, and maybe only, chance to get to where I needed to go.

"Nonsense. I'm here to take pictures and I haven't been to Khayelitsha in years. Not exactly *Well-Spotted*'s cup of tea, I suppose, but there are plenty of other magazines that will love it, and so will I." She lowered her jaw and looked at me from beneath a swath of shiny brown hair that had fallen across her left eye. "But you have to promise me something."

Here it was, the rub. No such thing as a free ride. "What is it?"

"I want you to first come with me to Cape of Good Hope. I need to take some photographs there tomorrow morning, early. You have to see this place, Russell. It's fantastic. Then we can go to the townships in the afternoon. Deal?"

We shared a brisk handshake and smiles.

"Now why don't you get cleaned up, meet me down here in half an hour and I'll take you out for a drink and, if you're good, maybe some dinner as a proper welcome on your first night in South Africa."

We started the evening at a stand-up table on the narrow outdoor deck of Café Manhattan which, after a little bit of gawking around, I realized was a gay bar. When I questioned Cassandra on her choice, she laughed and said it was one of her favourite places for sightseeing. Taking a gander at the staff and several of the patrons around us, I had to agree. In particular (although carrot tops aren't usually my taste), there was a heartbreakingly handsome redhead two tables over from us. His curly locks, orange as a Hawaiian sunset, grazed the neck line of a skin-tight, chartreuse sweater pulled over a perfect V-shaped torso, and he had these amazing sparkling eyes that strayed my way every two minutes or so. It was one of those fall-in-lust-in-a-flash kind of scenes.

After a couple of strong cocktails, Cassandra's driver, Joseph, ferried us to the Africa Café on Shortmarket Street, housed in an eighteenth century Cape Georgian home and touted as the place to go for real African feasts (which immediately made me wonder if this was the Red Lobster of South Africa). We were led to a colourful room on the second floor called the Boma, with hand-painted wall murals of earthy greens, vivid yellows and sharp oranges depicting stylized flower and butterfly designs. After describing the food offerings for the night and suggesting a menu for us, our server, dressed as a Xhosa maiden, brought us several gaily painted bowls filled with our portion of that evening's communal feast. It consisted of Malawi mbatata, cheese and sim sim balls (sweet potato and cheese rolled in sesame seeds), springbok curry, mbatata (caramelized sweet potatoes), Congolese spinach, Moroccan chermoula (crispy fried fish), Zanzibar chili coconut bean stew and many small bowls of dipping sauces and chutneys. Along with the food came my first ever bottle of Pinotage, a superb, gently oaked Beyerskloof from the Stellenbosch wine region just outside of Cape Town.

Topping the evening off, about halfway through our meal, the restaurant and kitchen staff (doubling as a troupe of African vocalists and drummers) meandered through the restaurant treating guests to a vibrant, ultra-high-energy bit of entertainment. The drummers beat their instruments with great intensity, building into swelling rhythms, as singers, mostly women (wearing kerchiefs on their heads to match their long-skirted outfits), clapped their hands and threw back their heads, letting loose chorus after chorus of melodious songs sung loud with throaty voices. It was a memorable evening, my first night in Africa.

I had stripped off my shirt and was giving my face a much needed wash at the bathroom sink when I heard the knock at my door. Towelling dry, I answered it and found Cassandra waiting for me, wearing a filmy negligee and holding aloft a pink-labelled bottle of champagne and two flutes.

"Guess what hotel management left cooling in my room?" she announced as she slithered into my room like a tempestuous temptress. "There is no possibility I can finish this all by myself...before it goes flat that is," she added with a backwards glance at me, still standing at the open door (with mouth to match). "So I come seeking your assistance, Mr. Quant."

I felt my lips turn up in pleasurable anticipation, a little too high from all the cocktails and wine we'd consumed over the course of the evening to know better. I pushed the door closed and said, "You've come to the right place, Ms. Wellness."

And so she had. Over the next hour we proceeded to do our best to relieve that pink-labelled bottle of its pinkish, bubbly contents, at the same time having very high-minded conversation about the various goings-on in the worlds of art, politics and fashion. Thanks to the tutelage over the years of my worldly friends Anthony Gatt and Sereena Orion Smith, it seemed to me, and I think Cassandra too, that I was able to keep up quite well, thank you very much, even telling my new friend a thing or two she didn't know before. It was about the time I was describing for her the Antoni Gaudí creations I'd seen in Barcelona with Errall a couple of years before that she leaned in and kissed me.

Just a peck.

At the corner of my mouth. The left corner.

I leaned into her and it wasn't long before tongues and roving hands were involved.

Stupid, drunk boy.

I discovered that negligees are filmy...and flimsy...for a reason. Why don't guys have something like that? Things began to fall out of here and there, and as they did my hands were working to catch them.

Some time later I pulled my head away and forced my eyes onto hers. "Cassandra, this is great, you're beautiful, I really like you, but I think we should stop." I thought I'd just about covered the gamut of polite-nice-guy things to say at a time like that.

Her eyes began to focus too. "Oh. Okay. Why is that?"

Fair question. "I'm...attached."

She sucked in her lips and pointedly looked downwards. "You don't look...attached."

I followed her eyes to where my male anatomy was showing off beneath my trousers. Damn that! I repeat: stupid, drunk boy. I swallowed hard and said, "I'm attached, not dead, and a lot drunk."

She threw back her head and let rip a magnificent laugh.

Thank Christ.

After she'd settled down, she put her hands in safe places and asked, straight-faced, "How about if we just neck for a while?"

Neck? Neck? I had to say it. "Neck? What grade are you in? And in what decade?"

Another laugh. "I really like you, Russell."

"I like you too."

She got up, artfully rearranging her translucent outfit like a pro, so that when she was done she looked as chaste as a nun—well, a nun with issues—and said, "Okay, I gotta go sober up, and maybe spend a few minutes with an electrical appliance. God I hope I have the right outlet adaptor."

She walked to the door, stopped and shot me a look. "Tomorrow morning, right? I promise never to take advantage of you again." And then she added with a playful snigger, her dark-fringed eyes at their most mischievous, "At least not until the next time we see the bottom of a bottle of champagne together in a hotel room."

I nodded and she departed.

I really needed to sober up myself—stupid Quant—and falling into bed was not going to do it. I threw on a T and headed out for a walk around the harbour.

Despite the late hour, the waterfront was a hive of internationally flavoured activity as tourists (and maybe some locals) window-shopped at the numerous boutiques that populate the area, dined alfresco on the wharf, danced at bars and bistros, and simply soaked up the atmosphere by indulging in leisurely strolls, the kind often promoted by proximity to water and sparkling night-lights. It was exhilarating to be part of it, but eventually I began to feel the effects of my long day—travel, heat, drinking, eating, mayor-impersonating—bear down on me, and decided to head back to my room.

After checking one of those You Are Here signs, I chose the quieter East Pier Road that would lead me to the rear of the hotel. I was enjoying the sea air and solitude when, from somewhere behind me, I heard the unexpected.

Clump, scrrrrrape, clump, scrrrrrape, clump, scrrrrrape.

Limping Man was in South Africa.

Chapter 9

When you're standing there, at the south-westernmost point of the African continent, Cape of Good Hope seems like the edge of the earth. Situated at the junction of two of the earth's most contrasting water masses—the cold Benguela current of the West Coast and the warm Agulhas Current of the East Coast—this place is popularly perceived as the meeting point of the Atlantic and Indian Oceans (but geographically they actually join a little to the east at Cape Agulhas).

I found myself distracted on the southerly drive from Cape Town in the little white van that our driver, Joseph, referred to as a "combi." Cassandra didn't seem to mind, she was preoccupied with the scenery outside our windows, and attempting to capture it with a succession of increasingly expensive looking cameras with increasingly longer lenses, the greatest of which was the length of a small child's arm. I did my best to pay attention to the ostriches, elands (a kind of antelope) and collection of boks (bontebok, grey rhebok, grysbok) that wandered alongside the road, but couldn't help but dwell on the mystery of why the man with the limp (who I suspected was the same guy I almost ran into outside Ash House in Saskatoon), had turned up literally across the world in South Africa. Was it the same guy? From what Frank had seen and heard that night, it also seemed likely that this guy was responsible for the brutal attack on Ethan Ash. If that was true, who was he after now?

I had called the hospital before going to sleep the night before, and although Ethan was recovering, he was still unable to recall any details about the night he was beaten. This, I understood from my psychologist officemate Beverly, is fairly common in the early stages of recovery from this kind of trauma; the body's first priority is to take care of its physical wounds, and it would get around to confronting the mental ones when it was good and ready to do so.

The idea that what had happened to Ethan was not some random act of violence, but rather somehow directly related to my case, turned me cold. I'd first heard the peculiar, dragging sound behind me when I visited Ethan Ash for the first time. I had assumed it was either my imagination or something completely innocent or, at worst, someone following me but certainly having nothing to do with Ethan. But when I learned Ethan had been attacked by a man with a limp, my assumptions changed. It hadn't been my imagination, and it wasn't innocent, but it also hadn't been about me: it was about Ethan.

I had to admit, I knew nothing about the Ash House proprietor; the assault could have been the result of a whole host of possible scenarios playing out in his life. The assailant could have been someone whose boyfriend was cheating on him with Ethan, or someone who didn't agree with Ethan's politics, or someone Ethan had pissed off in traffic; who knew? It had seemed that Limping Man wasn't my problem. But now, the possibility that Limping Man had followed me to South Africa would link Ethan's attack directly to me or to the case I was working on.

My frustration was growing. Of late, there seemed to be an entire spate of mystery men hell-bent on interfering with my life. Who were these guys? First the guy in the balaclava who accosted me behind PWC, then Limping Man, then the refrigerator-like thug who boarded the plane at Sal Island (to be honest I wasn't sure about him; his malevolence toward me could have been a figment of my already creeped out imagination, and he didn't limp—I checked). Were one or all of them somehow tied to Matthew Ridge a.k.a. Matthew Moxley?

I threw a glance at click-happy Cassandra who seemed oblivious to my thoughtful mood. I was ever so grateful earlier that morning when, with good coffee, fresh croissants and some hair-of-the-dog Bellinis on an elaborate silver tray, Cassandra had shown up at my hotel room door and proved, without a doubt, that she was definitely the kind of gal you could have poor judgment with the night before and have no icky, residual weirdness to deal with the next morning. For her, romantic misadventures were simply an expected and accepted part of the escapade.

The van grumbled to a halt in a gravel parking lot and Cassandra jumped out with her collection of photographic equipment, letting loose one of her trademark husky honks of delight. She dashed down a short embankment and nimbly scaled a tumble of boulders against which mighty waves and near gale force winds were crashing with shocking severity. For a long time, Joseph and I watched as she stood there, not taking pictures but simply pointing her face at the sun, thrilling to the sensation of wind and water going wild around her. The noise was tremendous, and after a while I felt that same crazed buzz in my head that one gets after staying too long at a boy-band concert in the company of giggly teenage girls and non-teenage gay guys.

When Cassandra was ready, Joseph drove us as far up the seaside cliff as vehicles could go, then we boarded the Flying Dutchman funicular (named after a phantom ship said to appear off the cape during particularly bad storms, displaying its horribly smashed mast and shredded sails—I just love stories like that), which took us the rest of the way to the top. The wind was even wilder up there, so that at times, to avoid being blown right off the hill, we were forced to our knees and moved forward on our haunches, looking not unlike the aggressive Chacma baboons that roam the grounds there, amongst endemic fynbos (fine bush) plants, proteas, heaths and reeds, scavenging for food.

While Cassandra did her photographer bit, I found a comfortable and relatively windless spot alongside a knee-high stone wall that faced north. As I sat there, somewhat awed by the fact that I was gazing back at the rest of the mighty African continent, I knew that somewhere out there was Matthew Moxley, a displaced Saskatchewan boy, just like me. And, damn it, I was going to find him.

Riding through the streets of Khayelitsha, about twenty-five kilometres out of the city centre, was like no other trip I have ever
taken or will likely ever take again. Some of the roads were paved,
some were not; some of the houses were neat, some were not; most
of it looked like the worst kind of slum one can imagine. Nearly all
the structures were made of thin, battered, corrugated tin, in every
shade of dirt, with flat roofs slanting towards the rear; many were
without windows, every spare inch of yard overflowing with what
others would think of as junk but probably wasn't. There were
communal toilets, people cooking animal heads on homemade
barbecue pits, children and cats and dogs running about wild,
women wearing colour-coded head scarves to indicate wedded
state (single, married, widowed, available) and men who stared
after our vehicle with undisguised longing. Joseph smiled and
waved at everyone and, much to my surprise, everyone enthusias-
tically returned the greeting. I asked him if he knew these people.
He said "not really," so we too began to smile and wave and got
the same in return. Eventually, we turned onto a street with somewhat better houses, some even made of wood rather than tin or
scrap metal, painted yellow and red and pastel green, with windows and curtains. On each door, or somewhere in the vicinity,
were numbers, scrawled there by hand in black paint—addresses.

The combi came to a halt and Joseph laid his arm across the
seat and turned to face us. He said, "Do not give the children anything."

I gave Cassandra a questioning look.

"It will encourage them to beg," she explained.

We got out of the vehicle and began to walk very slowly down
the centre of the street with Joseph in the lead, Cassandra and me
a few steps behind. I felt a certain amount of discomfort, but all our
smiling and waving had relieved some of the tension I'd been feeling earlier, and I tried more of it as a group of teen boys passed by
us.

"*Molo*," Cassandra said to them, along with some other stuff I
didn't catch, but I took it to mean hello or good day.

The boys all said "*Molo*" back, their dark eyes on us like glue,
filled with millions of unasked questions; curious to know what

kind of people we were and what we were doing in their town. And on we went, eventually collecting a gaggle of children, all under ten, as a not-too-discreet tail.

After about five minutes, Joseph stopped at a scarred, once-white door that was the front entrance of a house no bigger than most public restrooms. There was a haphazard "79C" painted to the left of it at about eye level. I recognized it as the address I'd been given by Reverend Hershell.

Joseph knocked, and without waiting, turned the knob and opened the door and stepped inside. I heard his voice booming in the direction of inhabitants I could not see: "We were wondering if we might come in and share in your good hospitality for a while."

He must have gotten a positive reply to what I considered a rather unorthodox request, since he motioned for Cassandra and me to join him indoors.

We stepped into a single room, a combination living room and kitchen. On the right, about midway, was a doorway with a blanket pinned over the opening that likely led to a separate bedroom and bathroom. Just inside the front door were three mismatched couches arranged around a modest television set. A young black man wearing dusty jeans and a sleeveless, Coors Light T-shirt was slouched on one of the couches watching a rugby game on the set. He barely looked up as we entered. I didn't get the sense he was being rude, just not particularly interested or surprised by our arrival, as if strangers like us walked in and out of his house every day. In the cooking area, a young woman, probably the man's wife, was lowering a full chicken into a pot of boiling water. Her face was more animated than her husband's, with a toothy white smile and inquisitive eyes. She was slender and the colour of milk chocolate, her hair hidden beneath an oft-laundered blue scarf.

Joseph sat on the couch next to the man and indicated that we should also take a seat wherever we wanted. His eyes never strayed from the TV screen while he talked to our host. He said, "We thought we would come and watch your television for a while."

The man's nod was barely perceptible.

Cassandra and I took spots on opposite ends of a harvest-gold sofa, perpendicular to where the two men sat.

Joseph confirmed what he thought their names were, Piksteel and Thandile Chikosi, and that was it. We were in.

What followed was several minutes of TV watching and chicken boiling as if we were the township version of Monica-Chandler-Rachel-Ross-Phoebe-and-Joey hanging out on a lazy Saturday afternoon, until: "We were wondering if you know a man," Joseph said, the louder tone of his voice hinting that he was talking more to the woman in the kitchen than to her quiet hubby.

"What kind of man is this?" Thandile asked as she set to work scouring pots in the sink.

"A man from Canada, a white man," Joseph told her. "He is a friend of my friend here. My name is Joseph and these are my friends, Russell and Cassandra. This man is Russell's friend."

I took that as my cue to jump in. "His name is Matthew Moxley."

"He gave this house, your house, as the place where he could be found," Joseph added.

The man was paying us no attention, but I could see that the woman was nodding and considering our words carefully.

"Do you know this man?" Joseph asked as if he was doing nothing more important than asking the time of day.

"I do," she answered to my great relief and budding excitement.

I swapped a look with Cassandra and forced myself to stay seated rather than do what comes naturally at a time like this: interrogation. "Does he live here?" I asked as slowly as I could, given my level of anticipation. "Is he here?"

She laughed a bit at me then, as one might to a child who'd mistaken a hen for a rooster. "He lives here."

Hoorah!

"He lives there," she kept on, waving her sudsy, wet hand at somewhere over her rounded shoulder.

Huh?

"He sometimes lives over there," she added for good measure, pointing to some indistinct spot past the front door we'd come in through.

132

Not *molo*.

Cassandra laid a hand on my forearm and explained. "I think she means he lives in the community, not always in this exact house." She looked at the woman to seek agreement with her statement.

"But often here," the woman said, as if in boast.

"I see." I didn't really. "Do you know where he's staying tonight?"

"Oh, he's not here now," she said. "He's gone off. To make money. He needs money to teach. He's a very good man, your friend."

"Is he working in the city then?" Joseph questioned, knowing I was not getting the information I needed.

"No, no. No work for him there. He's gone to Tuli Block, like he often does, to work in English. Then he'll teach somewhere. Maybe here, maybe not."

Joseph let out a sound as if what the woman had said made perfect sense and was all he needed to hear. He turned to me for the first time since we'd entered the house and said, "He will have gone to work in the tourist industry. He speaks English and is white and knows a great deal about Africa; he would do well as a tour guide or something like that. Teachers do not make much money. He'll work in the tourist industry to supplement his income." He then looked over his shoulder at the woman. "Do you know where he works in Tuli Block?"

"*Mashatu*," she said.

I was hoping she hadn't just said "no" in Zulu.

The mugging was quick and without preamble.

It was getting dark in Khayelitsha when we left 79C that evening. We were halfway to the combi when Cassandra let out a surprised yip, and the next thing I saw was a dark blur disappearing down an alley to our left. Almost simultaneously, the ambient noise of the street erupted into loud shouting and calling, dogs whined and barked, and children cried. I made a three-hundred-and-sixty-degree swing trying to figure out what was happening, but confusion reigned supreme. The din grew louder and, as if on cue, the sky turned a murkier grey. I heard scurrying footsteps and doors slamming and shrieks of women calling their children to home and safety. What was going on?

Throwing my arms around her, I leaned in close to Cassandra to check if she was all right.

"My case!" she moaned. "He took my case! My lenses are in there!"

"Jo..." I began but was cut short by what I saw next.

I looked up to see Joseph, our guide, running away.

Oh oh.

What was going on here? Was he about to abandon us in the middle of this township with no way to get home? Was it he who ripped off the lens case? Why? Was it that valuable? Was there a camera in the case? Had Cassandra taken a photo she shouldn't have?

"Joseph! Joseph!" I called out, but it was useless. He was gone, having disappeared behind a building, followed by a trio of men.

Cassandra remained admirably calm, the only sign of tension showing on her brow, which had furrowed itself into three long rows of worry.

"It's okay," I said, keeping a protective arm over her shoulder.

I glanced about, thinking: this is not at all okay. "Was it him? Was it Joseph who took your case?"

"No," she answered as if I'd just uttered the stupidest thing. "Of course not. Joseph is like a father to me."

"So where did daddy go?" I wanted to say but didn't.

"He must have gone after the thief," she decided. "I'm sure he'll be back."

I wasn't so sure. "Let's get back to the van and wait for Joseph there," I suggested. "We'll be perfectly safe."

She laughed. "Who do you think you're talking to? I'm not some wilting southern belle; I can see what's going on."

Good, then explain it to me!

"Thanks, though," she added quickly with a quirky smile on her face. "But it's a lousy idea. The combi is locked, and Joseph has the key."

I slowly rotated on the spot, doing another three-sixty, searching for an answer, any answer, to our predicament. Night was falling around us. We'd just been robbed. We were alone in unfamiliar, possibly unfriendly territory. We weren't safe. We had to get out of there.

In the dim light of dusk, behind a slat-and-barbed-wire fence I saw a collection of children staring at us. Half a block away, a group of boisterous young men were heading into what I assumed (because of the loud music and peeling beer posters on the walls) was a *shebeen*, an illicit tavern. I'd learned that many places such as this existed as part of a township's "informal economy," along with barbershops, food stalls, and street vendors selling clothing and small household goods, businesses taken up by local residents who could find no other means to support themselves.

The air was hot and heavy with the choking smell of paraffin— used by locals to cook with—and deep fried something or other. I was about to suggest we go back to 79C and ask for help, or at least watch some rugby, when Joseph came bounding back from around the corner of a shack.

He stopped next to us, expressionless and a little out of breath, and said, "We go now."

Good idea!

Cassandra wasn't so easily convinced. She put her hands on her hips and asked in a demanding voice, "What about my lens case? I've just been robbed."

"Don't worry about that now. We go now."

I agreed.

"That is simply unacceptable; I've been robbed," she reiterated.

Whiner!

I was all for Joseph's plan. It was getting darker by the minute. We were in unknown territory (at least to me). There were criminals roving the area. This wasn't a good place for tourists to be hanging around arguing about lost possessions. But Cassandra was steadfastly intent on her missing lenses and on letting it be known how pissed off she was. I was just about willing to offer to replace her stuff myself, but Cassandra's equipment looked rather pricey, so I kept my mouth shut. Instead, with a firm hand at her elbow, I turned her in the direction of our waiting vehicle. She began squawking about how little she appreciated being manhandled as I escorted her forward. Joseph followed, a stoic look on his face.

We watched in silence as the shadowed streets of Khayelitsha passed by. After a short ride, Joseph announced that we had entered Langa, the oldest formal township in Cape Town, its name meaning "sun" but derived from the surname Langalibalele, belonging to a Hlubi chief imprisoned after inciting rebellion against the nineteenth-century British government. The combi turned down an impossibly narrow street, named Harlem Avenue, lined with neat little homes squeezed together like books on a library shelf, and eventually rolled to a stop in front of a white two-storey with multiple windows, a tiled front courtyard dotted with potted plants, and a yellow sign on which was scripted, in vertical, the word "Lelapha."

"Dinner time," Joseph announced as he exited the van.

I turned to look at Cassandra, but she'd already scampered out after him. I followed suit.

Cassandra squeezed my shoulder as I stepped up next to her in front of the eating establishment. "You're going to love this!" she enthused, our recent caper seemingly forgotten.

We marched one by one across the courtyard and entered the building through a narrow doorway. To our immediate left, in a space that looked like it had once been an intimate sitting room with a bay window, was a collection of tables set with flower-patterned linens and occupied by customers who completely ignored us from their dark setting. Further on and to our right, I could just make out in the muted lighting, a buffet table with numerous steaming pots and pans (no chafing dishes here) filled to overflowing with the night's offerings. The air was heavy with sweet and spicy smells I could not identify, and suddenly my mouth began to water and my stomach growled. But the dining room we'd just passed was full, so I guessed we'd have to go elsewhere. Instead

Joseph led us through a warren of dim hallways deeper into the building, as if pulled by a cacophony of noise and music, drumming and chatter, to an even dimmer back room filled to beyond capacity with people sitting at long, wooden tables on long, wooden benches; not an empty spot in sight.

I was prepared to turn around, but Joseph dove head first into the fracas. He shoved and cajoled and shimmied about until he found us three (well, more like two-and-a-half) spots at a table in a corner. Nearby, a foursome of hefty women in washed-out, yet still-colourful garb, were dancing with one another to the thrumming of a small band that had somehow crushed themselves and their bulky instruments into the opposite corner. It seemed impossible that all this could fit into one undersized room the size of a pantry, and still leave room for air, never mind the restaurant servers, but everything seemed to be working out just fine and everyone (with the exception of me) seemed oblivious to the cramped conditions. It was business as usual.

For the next while, the action and noise of the place was so overwhelming all we could do was sit back, enjoy the ambiance, and stuff our faces. The buffet was a veritable free-for-all of African delights: *bobotie* (ground lamb topped with egg custard with yellow rice), mealie bread, *samp* (a boiled corn dish with sugar beans), *chakalaka* (a sweet and spicy blend of cabbage and beans), *snoek* fish, and plenty of *amagwinya* (tiny balls of chewy fried bread).

Much later, when we could eat no more, Joseph suddenly disappeared. I gave Cassandra a questioning look. She returned it. We scoured the room, noting that ours were the only white faces in the crowd. No one seemed to care, so neither did we. There was no sign of our guide. Then, just as quickly as he'd gone, Joseph returned to his seat, setting Cassandra's lens case, all the lenses in place, in front of her with little fanfare.

We stared at our driver with samp drooling from our open mouths.

"H-how…?" was all Cassandra could utter.

"My friend brought it back for me," Joseph said simply, mopping up the remaining stew on his plate with some of the mealie bread.

"I don't understand."

"*Ubuntu*," he said as if that one word would satisfactorily explain everything.

Cassandra nodded with a knowing smile on her face. "Of course."

Of course? Of course? "*Ubuntu*," I repeated the word to get a feel for it on my tongue. It wasn't easy to say at first. "What does it mean?"

"It's an ancient African word," Cassandra informed me. "It means 'humanity to others' it also means 'I am what I am because of who we all are.' *Ubuntu* brought back my case."

Uhhhhmmmmm.... "Okay. But how? Why?" I wasn't getting it.

"For the same reason these people in the townships live so harmoniously together, for the same reason the children were not scared of us today, for the same reason everyone waved at you as we passed by," Joseph told me. "They know that without the community, without the care and watchfulness and help of their neighbours, they are nothing. If a man takes a thing that is not his, such as the young, foolish boy did today, he cannot get away with it. The community cannot let him get away with it. To let him keep it is to say it is okay for this boy to steal from others, and if you steal from others you can also steal from me and my brother and my cousin, because we are all the same." He looked at me hard. "Even the two of you."

"But we're not part of this community," I countered.

"But you are. You were there today. Do you realize that most visitors to our country never visit a township? They are afraid. They don't understand. You will be surprised to learn that many city people, people who live right next to us as neighbours, many Afrikaners, have never come to our townships to see what it is to live here." He downed some beer, then continued. "The people in the community know that if they see you with me, they know you are paying me to bring you, and they know the money you pay me is returned to the township and the community.

"So today when that boy stole the case, many others saw this thing happen, there are always others who see, and there are

138

always those who know who did this thing, so I simply told these men where we would be having our dinner tonight and I knew if they could find this boy, and the thing that he took, it would be returned to us, just as they would want us to do for them in return." He smiled. "*Ubuntu.*"

Ubuntu. I would not forget it.

Tuli Block is the name given to a small, rugged block of land that pokes out from the far eastern tip of Botswana. It is bordered by the great Limpopo River with geography oddly reminiscent of parts of Arizona or New Mexico (except for the herds of elephants and giraffe that roam wild there). From Tuli Block one can see South Africa to the south and Zimbabwe to the north.

Tuli Block was where Piksteel and Thandile Chikosi had told me I'd find Matthew Moxley.

Tuli Block was where I had to go.

Getting back to the hotel after experiencing *ubuntu* at Lelapha in Langa (not a sentence you hear every day), and bidding Joseph and Cassandra a fond farewell, I returned to my room to do some work. First I called Darren Kirsch. I hadn't heard back from him before I left for Africa, and I wanted to find out what he had for me on the licence plate belonging to the ninja turtle in the balaclava. But I only got as far as the constable manning the front desk phone who told me Darren was out of town at a training seminar. Hopefully he was learning about making timely responses to the requests of sexy private eyes.

Next I reached Clara Ridge's answering machine and left her a message telling her what I'd found out so far and that I was, one way or another, on my way to some place called Tuli Block in Botswana, hot on the trail of her son. Finally, I contacted Roy Hearn and asked him to perform some magic. He definitely came through, getting me a seven a.m. South African Airways flight to Johannesburg, connecting to a 12:30 flight to Tuli Block on Botswana Air, and a reservation at the main camp of the Mashatu Game Reserve in Tuli Block.

I was set. I packed my carry-on and large, soft-sided duffle, arranged a wake-up call, admired the twinkling lights of the V&A Waterfront for the last time, and fell into bed for a deep, deep sleep.

The flight to Joburg—as Johannesburg is sometimes known—was two hours long and uneventful. When I checked in for my connecting flight to Tuli Block, I was pretty pumped to see that Roy had gotten me assigned to seat 3F on the Air Botswana flight. It seemed his connections had gotten me bumped into first class and I wondered what first class, Botswana-style, would be like. I could have kissed Roy Hearn.

Eventually Flight 216 was called and, keener than I sometimes am, I was first at the gate. The woman there took my ticket and directed me through a door behind her which put me outdoors where a white-gloved man pointed me to a huge, waiting bus, the kind with an accordion extension at its back end, like one of those Slinky dogs. I figured, as at many large airports around the world (almost all of which seem to be under interminable reconstruction), the passengers for certain flights had to be ferried to their plane rather than the plane coming to them. Hoisting my bags in front of me I boarded the bus, found a seat and waited for the other passengers.

And waited.

And then the bus doors swished shut.

There were no other passengers.

Maybe they'd taken an earlier bus?

Several minutes later the bus pulled away from the terminal and began its long journey past a United Nations of planes with tails, wings and noses painted in countless patterns and colours denoting their airline or country of origin. As time passed and the bus rumbled along, the planes gradually became smaller and smaller, from jumbo jets to smaller jets to propeller planes until we finally lurched to a stop in front of a wee little white plane about the size of a dragonfly with a blue stripe and no more than seven windows down each side. At the back hatch, opened to reveal a set of Munchkin-land steps, was a young man in a white shirt with

official-looking insignia on the chest and shoulders, smiling wide-
ly and at-the-ready to hand me a bottle of water as I boarded. I did
my best to return the smile, accepted the water, scaled the steps
and crouched down to avoid hitting my head as I entered the
plane's body. Somehow I couldn't quite believe that I was about to
fly across South Africa and into Botswana in this…this…tsetse fly.

Seat 3F was not only in the back row, it *was* the back row.

I could have smacked Roy Hearn upside the head.

I generally like to fly. I like what it accomplishes for me. In a
matter of hours I can be transplanted from freezing prairie plain to
golden sandy beach. Who wouldn't love that? Sure, if I had access
to *Star Trek* technology and could be transported from place to
place without having to fly, I'd probably do that. Until that happens, I'm okay with planes but not when they weigh less than I do.
I like big planes. The bigger the better. Somehow, for me, when it
comes to aircraft, size does matter.

The captain did some kick-the-tires-check-the-windshield-
wiper-fluid type stuff and eventually squeezed himself into his
seat at the front of the plane which was, incidentally, within arm's
reach of my own. He looked back at me with a welcome aboard
nod and smile. Yeah, sure, okay, ahoy and all that, but I know
you're the same guy who was handing out water and stowing luggage a few minutes ago and I'm not happy about it. I watched as
he took off his captain's hat and regarded the instrument panel in
front of him while sipping from a half-empty bottle of Orange
Crush. I was being piloted by the Doogie Howser of Botswana Air.

It seemed as if I was to be the only passenger when, at the last
minute, through the magnifying-glass-sized window, I saw a tiny
van, not unlike Joseph's combi, pull up next to the plane with an
admirable screech. For some reason I had the feeling I was about
to see Cassandra Wellness again and a smile cracked my waxen, I-
don't-like-this-plane face.

The smile was short-lived.

A cold sweat painted my forehead as I watched a familiar figure step from the vehicle and head for the aircraft.

Chapter 10

By the time our putt-putt plane bumped to an anticlimactic halt outside the Limpopo Valley Airfield's sole, open-air, thatch-roofed building, the only things I knew for sure about the other passenger on the flight from Johannesburg to Tuli Block were that his name was Jaegar, he was German, and he was the same tree trunk of a man who'd boarded my South African Airways flight at Sal Island. In the time since that hazy, middle-of-night, middle-of-flight experience, I'd actually begun to doubt myself, considering that perhaps I'd been overly paranoid in thinking that this complete stranger was giving me the evil eye. I hadn't seen him since and really, how likely was it that some fellow on Sal Island could have anything to do with me or the case I was on? I'd been painting him with a wide brush of discrimination, thinking he was a bad guy just because he was big and muscled with beady eyes, had a mean slant to the thin line of his mouth, and a permanently disagreeable expression on his face. But now I was back to thinking maybe I hadn't been so far off base after all. What was the probability, on a continent of over eleven million square miles, that he and I would end up being the only passengers aboard Watch-Your-Head Airlines heading for Tuli Block without there being something more to it? Of course it was possible—but not bloody likely.

When we were safely harnessed into our seats and high above the scrub of the African plain, I had tried to engage him in conversation, but he had only responded with grunts or nods or shakes of his melon head in the manner of someone who does not really speak the language he is trying to use. He did say a few guttural-sounding words at the beginning of the trip, but that was about it. I suppose it could be that he only spoke German. But then how did he expect to get around this continent in which English and countless African dialects were the major languages spoken?

Once we landed, the pilot directed us to the thatch-roofed terminal. I got the distinct impression that the airport officials—of which there were only two—had been at home tending cattle or working in their fields only minutes before the plane arrived, at which time they'd slipped into their well-worn uniforms, hopped aboard whatever transportation was available, and headed for the airport to do their job. After being processed through Botswana customs by these two fellows, we were greeted by a big black man, who told us his name was Garry (even though his name tag said Ghakarhi), and had us sign a waiver (which I read very carefully and which did nothing to ease my discomfort).

Garry led us out the front of the open-air building to a waiting Land Cruiser Jeep. The uncovered vehicle looked as if it'd come from the set of *M*A*S*H*. It had two tiers of blanketed seats behind the front one and an easily accessible shotgun strapped to the dashboard. I wasn't anxious to know what that was for.

Jaegar was first to climb aboard and took the rearmost seat. The way he spread out his gear I took to mean he did not want me joining him up there, so I settled into the middle tier seat. Garry dumped his massive bulk behind the right-side steering wheel and off we went. Seconds after we took off, I noticed another, exceedingly thin, man hop up onto the back rumble seat behind Jaegar. A stowaway? An African desert pirate? I craned my head to look back at the young man. He gave me a thumbs-up sign along with a wide, gap-toothed smile. I later found out the guy's name was Tumelo, and he came with the vehicle, much like any other accessory. He was referred to as a "tracker," but his job entailed everything from vehicle maintenance to meeting the varied whims of the guests to helping Garry spot wildlife during safari.

We were told the trip from the landing strip to the main camp of the Mashatu Game Reserve would be forty-five minutes over dirt roads. The journey took us up and down deep gulleys, over dried-up riverbeds, and through an obstacle course of ring-around-the-acacia-tree-bushwillow-and-African-wattle-rosie. Although the sky was run through with high, wispy clouds, the sun was beating down on us with ferocious intensity, and I soon pulled from my knapsack the Tilley hat Anthony had convinced me to buy. It had seemed ridiculously expensive for a hat I wasn't convinced I'd really need or ever use again, but my mentor had assured me it would become my best friend in Africa, and I was beginning to see why. It also afforded me a jaunty, Great-White-Hunter-ish look that I rather fancied. I quickly forgot about the heat and Jaegar and the bumpy road when, less than ten metres from our vehicle, I spotted my first elephant!

For the balance of the trip to the camp I was transfixed and awed by the sights and sounds around me: elephants, impala, wildebeest and too-numerous-to-count varieties of birds. None of which were behind the bars of a cage. Oh my, Aunty Em, I'm definitely not in Saskatchewan anymore.

Mashatu is nicknamed the Land of the Giants because it is home to seven of Africa's giants: the African elephant, the lion, the giraffe, the baobab tree, the eland (an antelope), the ostrich, and the kori bustard (some kind of bird). It's a privately owned wildlife sanctuary of thirty-thousand hectares situated at the confluence of the Shashe and Limpopo rivers, and rich with ancient archeological sites. This is not the Africa of steamy, moist jungles, with chattering monkeys swinging overhead from leafy vines that many of us grew up seeing on TV, but rather the Africa of spectacular, wide open scenery, of blistering, dry heat and scrubby desert-like topography upon which these remarkable giants are free to roam.

The camp itself was a series of low-ceilinged buildings hugging the bushy banks of the sluggish Limpopo. It blended so seamlessly into its surroundings that when our Jeep topped a small hill (after turning left at a marking post invisible to all but the trained eye), the camp seemed to appear out of nowhere. Although it had seemed to me that Garry had been following a haphazard, round-about route to get us to Mashatu, he must have known exactly where he was going because, as promised, it took us just under forty-five minutes to get to the camp from the airfield.

The Jeep pulled up to the front of the main building (which

looked a lot like the thatched airport terminal), where awaiting us was a collection of people, some white, some black, some in uniforms, some in safari gear, everyone wearing a hat.

"Good afternoon, and welcome to Mashatu," said a tall stick of a man with a hooked nose, balding head and a surprisingly pale complexion, given where he worked. "I'm Richard Cassoum, the camp manager."

As Jaegar and I stepped off the Jeep, our knees a little jerky from the trip, a short, middle-aged woman in a nondescript uniform handed each of us a chilled champagne glass filled with cool water. Oh mama, that tasted good!

"Good trip?" Richard asked with a piercing stare and a wan smile.

"Yes," I answered.

Jaegar grunted a bit.

Although I was up for more water, we apparently didn't have time to dither.

"Garry will show you around the camp and then to your rooms," Richard told us. "Afternoon tea is served on the terrace at half-past three. Your first game drive commences precisely at four o'clock."

I looked at my watch. It was already three. They weren't kidding around here.

Garry took us on a quick tour of the place—at one end of the camp were the kitchen and staff areas, outdoor dining area, the bar, guest lounge, and lunch and breakfast terrace; at the other end were the fourteen guest cottages, with two separate suites per building. All of it was surrounded by a high fence to keep the animals out. Jaegar and I were shown to our rooms and told to unpack, get cleaned up, and make our way to the terrace for afternoon tea. Skipping tea in favour of a shower didn't seem to be an option.

"May I have the key?" I asked Garry as he was about to leave after showing me the amenities of my impressively large room.

He gave me a strange look and said in his blunt accent, "We can get you a key. You want a key?"

I didn't want to ruffle the order of things or seem like a complete safari camp virgin, but c'mon. "Oh…well…are there keys?"

"No one to take things around here," he said with a twinkle in his chocolate-covered-cherry eyes. "Someone steal something, there are only so many suspects. Just us. So no one steals."

Was this the *ubuntu* thing again? I didn't quite buy his theory. I knew Mashatu was remote, but between staff and guests in four-teen cottages, it might not be as easy to catch a thief as he thought. Maybe I'm just jaded.

"You want a key?" he asked again.

Prepared to be a good sport, I shrugged my shoulders and said, "No, that's okay. If I want one later, I'll call the front desk."

He chuckled. "No phone."

Whazzat? Where the hell was I? "No phone?" My eyes made a quick survey of the room, and indeed, there was no phone. I was guessing high-speed Internet access was out of the question too.

"No phone," he confirmed. "You get some rest and come down for tea soon, okay? We leave at four o'clock sharp, okay?"

"Okay."

When Garry left, I took another tour through the well-lit, airy rooms of my new African quarters. There were two three-quarter beds—made up with crisp, fresh, white linens and impala fur pil-lows—pushed together to make one large bed. On the wall behind the combined bed were two huge, exquisitely framed, black-and-white prints: one of a rather pensive looking lioness, the other of a powerful elephant that seemed to be debating a charge at the pho-tographer. There was a large full bathroom and, for some inexpli-cable reason, right next to it, a second, smaller half bath. Running across the full width of the front end of the space was a lounging area with cushioned rattan lounge chairs and a daybed littered with more impala fur pillows, overlooking what appeared to be a jungle of bush through a wide expanse of tinted windows. I slid open one of the sliding glass doors, prepared for the exotic and cacophonous sounds of Africa, but instead found only a heavy quiet layered with an oppressive heat that flowed through the pro-tective screen like warm syrup.

In addition to the photos over the bed, the room's other walls were covered with more art, mostly replicas of African tribal relics, and on the tile floor were rugs made out of the omnipresent impala fur. (They sure don't think much of live impala around here, I thought to myself.) Overall, the place had a warm, outdoorsy feel to it. I liked it a lot, and could easily picture myself spending hot summer afternoons in the comfort of the air-conditioned room, lazing upon the daybed, jotting down my thoughts of the day, sipping a cool citrus drink, watching wild animals pass by my window. But there was no time for that now. It was tea time!

An amber sun lolled low on the endless African horizon when Garry maneuvered our open air Jeep up Disappointment Hill (named by a filmmaker when he came upon the rare sight of a pair of mating leopards silhouetted against the rising moon—unfortunately, he was out of film). He pulled to a halt at its summit and we fell out of the vehicle, our bones rattling from two hours of rough driving. Our tracker, Tumelo, hopped from his perch in the rear like a sprightly gazelle. He pulled down the tailgate and, with a magician's flourish, withdrew a freshly pressed white tablecloth from some hidden spot next to the tool box. He spread the pristine cloth over the tailgate and proceeded to lay out a buffet of scrumptious finger foods and the makings of a fully stocked wet bar. I grinned to myself, thinking: this is safari, Russell Quant style.

My companions were an American couple from the Boston area, Gladdy and Stuart, and four Australian twenty-somethings. When we'd loaded ourselves onto the Jeep, I'd allowed them the upper tier seats, which gave me the opportunity to sit up front with Garry. I was hoping to befriend him and pump him for information. However, I'd found it difficult to do any pumping during the safari itself, what with the noise of the shaking vehicle. And when we'd finally pull to a stop, Tumelo or Garry having spotted a lion or leopard or cheetah or kudu or jackal or guinea fowl, I knew it was time to be silent and focus on the fauna. Now that we were on half-time break, however, my chance had come.

While the Australians were busy filling their stainless steel cups with wine and the Americans were taking photos of the sunset, I waited for Garry to return from a whiz in the bushes then sidled up next to him. "This is quite something," I commented, meaning both the sunset and the spectacular spread. "Does this happen every night?"

"The sundowner," he replied through chomps of biltong (salt-cured meat akin to beef jerky). "The custom of having cocktails and a bite to eat during the sunset hour." He shot me a sideways look and, with a rakish smile, added: "The only good thing the British gave to Africa."

I chuckled and looked at my watch: six-fifteen p.m. I spent the next few minutes asking safari-appropriate questions about the animals we'd seen and Garry's experiences as a guide, all the while sipping the best gin and tonic this side of a gay Summer is Here! party. I finally hit home with: "I think a friend of mine from Canada works here. His name is Matthew Moxley. Do you know him?"

"Oh well," Garry began, covering the darkening sky with searching eyes, "many people come to Mashatu. Can't remember them all."

From what I'd seen so far, there couldn't have been more than a couple dozen or so staff in the main camp. Add a handful more for the tent camp and that didn't make a ton of people to remember. Was Garry trying to stonewall me?

"Really?" I said. "So you don't know if there is someone named Matt or Matthew working here?"

"Matt?" he said as if he'd only now heard the name for the first time.

"Matt Moxley," I repeated for good measure.

"Oh no, no one here by that name, okay."

"Oh, that's funny, I'm sure he said he worked at Mashatu. Does he work in the tent camp do you think?"

Garry was acting uneasy now, shifting his weight from one foot to the other and keeping his dark eyes anywhere but on mine. "Mmmmm no, I don't think so, no Matt at tent camp." He raised his cup in the air as if to move my attention from himself to where Stuart was studying the scenery in the valley below us through a set of binoculars. "You see something, Stuart?" he called out.

Nice diversion, Garry.

"I think I see elephants," Stuart responded in a loud whisper, as if the sound of his voice would frighten off the mammoth creatures.

Garry—delighted to be away from me—joined Stuart and the others at the rim of the hilltop and glared into the dusky outcropping. "Yes, yes," he said after a moment, pointing at a mass of grey in the distance. "There they are. Well-spotted, Stuart, well-spotted. Can everyone see them?"

Garry had, quite skillfully I might add, put an end to my interrogation. For now.

Upon returning to camp under a sky of black silk, we were given fifteen minutes to clean up and make our way to the cocktail lounge (fittingly called The Gin Trap), for more drinks before the eight-thirty dinner bell. Dusty and dirty, hot and sweaty, and wretchedly road weary after four hours of continuous bumping and humping of the safari vehicle, the seven of us made for a quiet parade down the rock-lined, gravel pathway that led to the guest quarters. Nestled in the tall reeds along the way, petite, flickering ground lanterns were the only lights available to guide us. We stumbled and tripped as we trudged along, peering through the thick darkness like moles, but eventually we found our way. The cloying air smelled of dying heat and sunburnt grass.

My cabin was at the furthest end of camp, leaving me to walk the final several metres alone (and grateful for the solitude). Still a bit wary of my unfamiliar surroundings, I kept a sharp eye out for any movement in the wild flora, horror-movie-spooky in the darkness, and took some comfort in the knowledge that the fence surrounding the property was sound protection against most wildlife.

Except for monkeys.

And crocodiles.

And snakes.

I hurried my pace until I reached my door, letting myself in with a sigh of relief, blissfully unaware that I had more to worry about inside my room than out.

I didn't have to turn on the lights to know something was not right. I stood still with my back against the door and let my eyes do the walking. Someone had been in my room. Maybe still was?

My ears burned as I tried to listen for telltale sounds of an intruder. There could easily be someone in the closet area or one of the bathrooms, both of which were out of my line of sight, but my ears told me nothing. I noticed the curtains had been pulled across the windows and my bed had been turned down. Was that it? Was that all? Was it just the maid service that was setting my detective-alarm-bell to jangling? I didn't think so, yet I couldn't readily identify what it was that was bothering me.

Then I knew.

I lifted my nose in the air and stepped further into the room. Cheap cologne, so cheap I did not know its name, but I did know where I'd smelled it before. It was in another enclosed space, not so long ago: aboard Botswana Air.

Jaegar had been in my room. I sniffed again. Probably not long ago. Well, Jaegar or the pilot, and I was pretty certain the pilot had turned tail and returned to civilization as soon as he'd dropped us off.

Fortunately, I'd had no time to unpack so it didn't take me long to go through my things. Everything was there, perhaps not quite as I left it, but nothing was missing. Jaegar had done a good job of not disturbing anything. But what had he been looking for? And had he found it?

It was a few minutes after eight-thirty by the time I managed a quick sponge bath (thank goodness I'd had the sense to buzz my hair very short before this trip, so it wasn't much of a bother), slipped on a clean pair of cotton rugbys and a striped shirt and made my way to The Gin Trap. Dinner had obviously not yet begun because the cocktail lounge was still full of mingling guests and camp staff. I descended the half-dozen or so steps that led down into the cozy space with its long bar, handful of small tables, and a cushioned perch overlooking the local (animal) watering hole, situated in a deep ravine below the bar. The lighting was low with an aura of candlelight which, along with sun-kissed cheeks and free-flowing drinks, gave everyone a handsome glow. The non-stop chatter was an international mix of several languages punctuated by occasional roars and twitters of laughter and tinkles of glasses being raised in toast to the drinkers' good fortune at having spotted an elusive cheetah or family of skittish giraffe. I bellied up to the bar and ordered a tall gin and tonic.

"Sylvia Dinswoody, Scotland," a woman to my right, settled on a cushioned stool, announced with precise diction as I waited for my drink.

"Russell Quant, Canada," I answered back with a raffish smile.

Having done her bit, the woman looked at me with a baleful glare, obviously expecting me to take responsibility for driving the conversation from there on. She was tall, misshapen, maybe fifty, with an unsymmetrical face, uneven teeth, and a thick lower torso that made up the majority of her bulk.

"Did you have a good day?" I asked, not quite familiar with safari talk. Over the last few hours I'd come to realize that most of the guests at Mashatu were veteran safari-goers, many had visited Mashatu previously and all had been on safari at least once before, leaving me the evident novice.

"It was fine," she commented dryly, slurring slightly. "We did-n't spot much. I might have stayed by the pool for all we saw. Perhaps tomorrow will be better. Who was your guide today?"

"Garry," I told her.

She nodded and swallowed a healthy draft of scotch at the same time. "Garry is good; you'll tend to see things with Garry. We had Joshua." She made the motion of looking around for eaves-droppers, though I was sure she couldn't have cared less if anyone overheard her (and probably'd have preferred it that way). "Not good, Joshua. Stay with Garry if you can. We had Garry our last two visits. Infinitely better, really."

Every detective loves a gossip, and I had the feeling I'd lucked onto a good one. My drink arrived and I signaled to the barkeeper to pour the lady another couple fingers of scotch. He was about to pour, directly into her used glass, when she used a practiced, none-too-subtle finger wag to stop the pour and direct his attention to the back cabinet where sat a much more expensive bottle of Glenmorangie. The man looked at me and I quickly nodded. Sylvia's baboon-butt-red lips spread across her face in thanks, and she laid a conspiratorial hand on my forearm, "Can't stand that other rubbish, can you?"

Although I'd have bet my favourite wonderpants she'd been swilling the house brand before I'd come along, I nonetheless agreed vehemently. She smiled more. I smiled more. We understood one another.

"So you've been to Mashatu many times?" I asked her.

"Oh yes, getting to be a bore though, I must tell you," she observed through a slurp of her refreshed drink. "And the food is ghastly. But it's the elephants: I love the elephants, and there is no other place in Africa quite like Mashatu for elephants. They breed like rabbits here; not enough lion to control the population, thankfully."

"Are there any other guides you would recommend? I hear good things about Matt."

"Oh, my, yes, now there's a good man, a good guide as well. Not bad to look at, either."

I felt the hairs on my neck do a dance, the gin rose to my cheeks and the African warmth felt oh so pleasant on my skin. Finally! I had him. "Is he here tonight?" I asked lightly, trying not to betray my thrill. "I'd like to meet him."

She gave me a sharp look. "Not happy with Garry? He's very good, you know."

"He is," I quickly agreed. "But seeing as it's my first time, I thought I'd try a variety of guides. Someone like Matt sounds good."

"Russell!" a voice bellowed from somewhere behind me. It was Stuart, one of my Bostonian safari companions from that afternoon. "Good to see you!" he called from half way across the room. "Gawd it's crowded in here. We can't seem to get to the bar. Can you order us two mart..." He stopped there as he looked away and conferred with his wife, Gladdy. "Okay, just two quick chard..." More conferring. "Okay, never mind. We'll see you in there," he hollered, nodding his head toward the closed bamboo-pole doors that separated the bar from the dining area.

I waved and nodded without, hopefully, committing myself to sitting with them during dinner. As soon as the crowd swallowed them up I returned my attention to Sylvia Dinswoody.

"As I say, you should stay with Garry," she said to me as if there'd been no interruption. "Anyway, I'm afraid Matt is long gone."

My stomach churned as if suddenly full of sour gruel. "Gone?"

"Haven't seen him at all this year," she told me, enunciating mightily with Scottish verve. "Maybe not last year either. Can't quite recall the last time I saw him, actually." As I stood there trying to take in this frustrating bit of information, Sylvia smirked, dipped her misshapen head and swivelled on her stool to face a guy who'd just pulled up to the bar on her opposite side.

"Sylvia Dinswoody, Scotland," she announced to the man as she emptied her glass.

I guess I was boring her, or she wanted a refill, or both.

I excused myself as politely as I could—to the back of her head—and decided I had better fish to fry anyway: Jaegar had just arrived at The Gin Trap.

But frying fish did not come easy that night.

"Russell! Come join us for a drink!" one of the Australians called out to me from where the entire group of them were draped over one another—and a couple of other revellers I did not know—near the centre of the small lounge.

How had they managed to get so sloshed in the few minutes since we'd gotten back from safari? Sarah, the youngest of the bunch, managed to stumble closer and pulled on my sleeve, causing me to spill my drink on the head of a petite Asian woman passing by who shrieked at the sensation of G&T flattening her hairdo. I shrieked at the sensation of good G&T going to waste. The Australians began to laugh uproariously. I apologized to the woman while a uniformed server used paper napkins to dry off her head.

Once that was over, I scoured the crush of people, looking for Jaegar. Just then the bamboo dining room doors were thrown open and the bar was filled with tribal drumming, beckoning us into the boma, the dining area with its roof open to the sky. In the centre of the lala-palm enclosed area a blazing fire roared in a gigantic pit. The Gin Trap patrons poured into the enclosure like sand into the bottom half of an hourglass and I flowed along with them. As I moved with the crowd, I continued my desperate search for Jaegar, but he was nowhere to be found. Slippery bugger.

As promised, Garry knocked at my door at five-thirty the next morning and called my name until I called back with a groggy, "I'm up." The morning drive was scheduled to begin at the ungodly time of six a.m. Do people actually consider this a vacation? I needed a rest after less than twenty-four hours.

I rolled my lead-weight body out of bed even though my plans that day did not include a pre-sunrise safari. Garry was proving to be a dead-end source, as were my other safari vehicle companions, and since I'd confirmed last night that Matt had, at least at some point, worked at Mashatu, I needed to find a new source of information to move along my investigation. And I had an idea of where I'd find that source.

I joined the other guests and guides in the breakfast area on the covered terrace adjoining The Gin Trap where half-a-dozen long tables were set up across from a small buffet. The pre-safari snack consisted of fruit, tea, instant coffee and some hard, long biscuits that reminded me of biscotti. It was surprisingly chilly and most people had added a light nylon jacket or pullover to their safari wear. At six o'clock sharp, the guides and their charges trooped off for the Jeeps that awaited them at the front entrance of the camp. I followed along until we were about halfway there, then when I was certain no one was looking, I took a detour. I'd scoped out the pathway the night before, and I was pretty sure it would lead me to where I wanted to go: the camp kitchen.

The path ended at a well-used door, dirty with the telltale marks of thousands of handprints, battered by sun and time. Where the doorknob had been was a round hole—good for air circulation—so I pushed on the door which moved inward with ease. I took a hesitant step inside the surprisingly cool enclosure and found what I'd expected: a small coterie of women in various stages of breakfast cleanup and preparation for the rest of that day's meals.

"*Molo*," I called out, feeling a bit foolish doing so, realizing that given the countless combinations of dialects and languages that seemed to abound in Africa I could have been spouting gibberish rather than saying hello. Fortunately, the women were used to dealing with idiotic tourists all day, every day, and they gave me big, gracious smiles and returned the greeting. Phew, step one complete. On to step two.

"Does anyone speak English?"

A chorus of "of course," "yes sir," "How can I help you?" rang out.

I approached the nearest woman and asked if she knew someone named Matthew Moxley, a man who had worked at Mashatu sometime during the last year or two.

"Oh yes, of course," she told me, and the others noted their agreement with great enthusiasm. This was more like it. "What do you want with this man?"

"He's a friend of mine," I lied too easily. "We come from the same town in Canada."

One of the gals let out a hearty guffaw and tried for it, "Sasacowchin?" They all began to chortle and in a shamble of voices attempted to pronounce Saskatoon or Saskatchewan, none of them getting it quite right.

"Yes," I agreed, smiling my face off. "You remember him?"

"Of course. What do you want with this man?"

Persistent bunch.

"I'd like to find him. To say hello. He doesn't know I'm in Africa. I want to surprise him."

The ladies made various noises, tsk-ing sounds and oohs and ahhs and clicked their tongues as if considering the idea before one of them said in stilted words, "He no longer be working here."

"He be a schoolteacher now," another added.

"Somewhere in Botswana," established another. "But not here."

"I don't know where. Do you know where?"

"I don't know where. Do you know where?"

"I don't, mama. You?"

"Me neither. And what about you?"

"No, I do not."

This chatter continued on for a quite some time, so long that I began to wonder if they even remembered I was there or what the original question had been, until finally: "But my sister knows." Aha! Finally something I could use.

"Does she now?" asked one of the others.

"Well, she does not know this directly of course, but she works with the boyfriend."

"Kevan?" someone said. "He has a job at Chobe, doesn't he?"

"Yes, he gives massage to the white folks there."

"That must be a hard job."

"Yes, a hard job."

"Hard on the hands."

"Yes, hard on the hands."

And on and on it went, without me.

Time was a-wasting and I wanted in. "Matt has a boyfriend named Kevan who works as a masseur at someplace called Chobe?" I summed up with a hopeful look on my face.

They looked at me as if wondering if I did not speak English, or perhaps had a hearing problem, or maybe wasn't very bright.

"Of course. Didn't we just say this?"

"We did, we did just say this."

"Yes, we did."

They were clucking like the hens in *Chicken Run*.

"Is Chobe near here?" I asked hopefully.

"Oh no, not Chobe."

Groan. "How can I get there?"

Now they looked at one another as if I'd asked what was the best way to get to the moon.

"You best talk to Mr. Richard," one of the women finally suggested.

"Yes, that is a very good idea, mama."

"Yes, Mr. Richard, he would be the one to ask."

"Yes, that seems to be the right thing to do."

"Yes, it is."

They all seemed to agree heartily on my next course of action. Richard Cassoum was the camp manager. He'd been in the greeting party when I first arrived in Mashatu the day before. I gave the women another smile and said something that sounded kind of like, *knee-a-bonga-mama,* which I hoped was thank you, ma'am. They responded with something that sounded like *knee-a-bonga-baba,* and off I went in search of Mr. Richard.

I found Richard Cassoum standing behind the front desk in the dim enclosure of the front entrance building, as if in wait for me, his tall, gawky body looking rather soldier-like. There was no one else around; even the camp curio shop across the way seemed abandoned.

"Hello," he greeted me coolly with a sharp nod of his bald head.

"Richard." He'd said we could call him that. "I'm wondering if you can tell me how I could arrange a trip to somewhere called Chobe. Do you know it?"

"Is there a problem with your stay here at Mashatu?" he inquired in a formal tone.

"Oh no, not at all, it's just that I need to get to Chobe as soon as possible. Everything here has been terrific." He didn't seem convinced. "Really it has," I added after a few seconds more.

"Why, may I ask, are you going to Chobe?"

None of your damn business I wanted to say, but instead settled for a more proper response that came out like this: "Personal business." It was downright cold in the reception area and not all of it was due to the temperature. I guessed that not many people check out of Mashatu after just one night's stay, and my unusual request wasn't sitting well with the camp overseer.

"I see. Well, I'm afraid I can't help you," Richard Cassoum informed me with clipped words. "There used to be a flight from Limpopo to Kasane, which is near Chobe, but there isn't anymore. I'm afraid you'll have to return to Johannesburg and make arrangements from there."

He certainly was "afraid" a lot. "I see." This wasn't what I wanted to hear. I wondered if Roy the wonder-travel-agent could help me find a better option. "Well, could I use your telephone?"

"I think you've been told there are no telephones here for guest use." His lips were stretched tight over smallish teeth and his brow was showing signs of stress furrowing.

"Yes, I understand that, but certainly in this case..."

"I'm afraid not."

Afraid and not very helpful. If I didn't know better, I'd have guessed Mr. Manager knew exactly why I was going to Chobe, and didn't want me to get there. But nah, my suspicious nature was working overtime.

"Johannesburg is an easy five-hour drive from Mashatu," Cassoum told me. "On a tarred road," he commented like that would make a difference. "Perhaps you have a car?"

He knew damn well I didn't.

"I guess I'll have to catch a flight," I said, resigned. "Can I get a driver to take me to the airport?" Since I obviously wasn't going to be allowed to call ahead and make a reservation, I had no other choice but to get to the airport as soon as I could and take it from there.

He thought on this for a long moment then abruptly became quite amenable to the idea of getting me away from his camp. "Of course. You'll have to wait until the others are back from the morning drive—about nine-thirty. I would say—all the Jeeps are being used until then. At that time I'm sure we can arrange for one of the men to take you to the airfield."

I nodded, he nodded, and that was it.

I returned to my room to warm up from my chilly encounter with the camp manager, pack my bags, and wait for my ride.

I had to give the guy credit, for true to Cassoum's word, a short time after nine-thirty a.m. a guide I'd not met before, Zak, knocked at my door and escorted me to a waiting Jeep. As we passed by the terrace where we'd gathered that morning, I heard the boisterous noise of the other guests, freshly returned from their morning drives, preparing to sit for a proper breakfast after which they'd retire to their rooms for a well-deserved rest and to escape the scorching heat of the midday sun. It would have been a pleasure to join them, but the future held something much different in store for me than a hot breakfast, soft bed, and cool room.

An hour later, the guide named Zak pulled to a hurried stop in front of the Limpopo Valley Airfield building. I hopped off, taking my carry-on and duffle with me, and the Jeep sped away without a backwards glance from the wordless driver, leaving me staring after him as he disappeared in a cloud of African dust.

Good riddance, I thought to myself as I turned and headed for the airport building with its low-slung, thatched overhang roof. I was in desperate need of respite from the intense sun which had already turned a temperate morning into a searing hot day with negative moisture content. My hope was that my wait for the next flight out of there would be a short one. But hope turned to despair as I stepped inside.

The building was empty.

Abandoned.

Just like me.

Chapter 11

I was back at Limpopo Valley Airport, the same airport where I'd first touched down in Botswana only yesterday. But now the place was echoingly empty, not a solitary soul in sight. The areas meant for security and custom officials were locked up tighter than a drum (whatever the hell that means) with no indication of when someone might return. There was no Arrivals and Departures board blinking announcements of upcoming activity, no check-in area with lines of waiting travellers, no Air Canada Maple Leaf lounge, and, worst of all, no cocktail bar where one might get a few last ounces of courage (which I was suddenly in dire need of).

I began my vigil by setting up camp—basically me, my knapsack and my carry-on—on one of the benches that ran along the inside wall of the building. Because of the small size of the place, and the fact that it was an open air structure, from this vantage point I could keep an eye on both the parking area in front of the building (in the hope that a vehicle might arrive to save me) and the landing strip in back of the building (in the hope that a plane might arrive to save me).

I shifted my yearning gaze from the front parking lot to the back airstrip, front to back, front to back, front back, front back....

But wishful thinking does not necessarily produce results. The scene around the tiny airport remained frustratingly unchanged. Nothing. No vehicles, no people, no movement of any kind. Just endless inactivity.

The building was a simple, rustic construction but sufficient for its purposes, I supposed. The thatch roof provided shade and the only walls were those necessary to hold up the roof and create privacy required for bathrooms, the security checkpoints and a few other rooms I guessed to be offices or storage rooms. On the off-chance that I'd missed something—or someone—I did a quick tour of the place, checking both bathrooms (water turned off) and knocking loudly on every locked door. Unfortunately, my original assessment was correct. The place was a ghost town. I returned to my spot on the bench and waited.

Front back. Front back. Front back. Checked my passport. Checked my wallet. Front back.

After an hour or so, the heat intensifying with every passing minute, I moved to the spot buried deepest within a healthy slice of shade. I pulled my feet up on the bench so that I was in a lying position and, using my carry-on as a pillow, tried to doze, but my busy mind kept me from sleep. Eventually, I got up and again paced about the structure, feeling unsure, sweaty, a little sick to my stomach, fighting an unsettling nervousness.

I pulled my Tilley hat low over my eyes and ventured outdoors to see what I could see. I circled the building twice, then found a way to hoist myself up onto some scaffolding, which provided me an unimpeded view of the area. I was looking for another building or farm or village or someplace, anyplace, to go for help. Maybe I'd catch sight of a safari vehicle or a game reserve warden.

But, as far as the eye could see, all there was the same African scrubland, repeating itself over and over again for miles and miles like a house of mirrors, reflecting in on its own reflection.

I knew there were hills and gullies and riverbeds out there—somewhere—just not close by. The one thing I hadn't seen during yesterday's safari was a settlement other than the Mashatu camp. This truly was an isolated place. And I was in the middle of it.

Back to the bench. Front back. Front back. Front back. I was exhausted. I'd lost a great deal of energy and sweat during my short outdoor foray, and this time when I lay down, I did fall asleep.

I don't know how long I slept, maybe an hour. I'd have slept longer if it weren't for the clawed insect thing that scrambled across my cheek.

Mother-of-pearl! What the hell was that? Scorpion? Centipede? I jerked awake with a start, swatting away the heinous creature. It looked like a stick with legs. I hopped to my feet, checking my clothes for other bugs. There were none. I fell back on the bench, feeling weak, empty.

Front back. Front back. Front back. Nothing but shimmering heat rising up from the ground. Hotter than Hades. Front back. Front back. Front back.

By late afternoon, I realized there wasn't going to be a plane. I wasn't waiting for a ride out of Botswana anymore. I was waiting for rescue.

Afternoon slowly disappeared and with it, mercifully, so did the heat, and I began to understand that my rescue was not imminent.

The sun would be setting soon.

I'd have to ride out the night.

The few snacks I routinely store in my airplane carry-on (Pull'n'peel licorice, stale pretzels, mixed nuts) were all I had to eat and would need to be rationed. My water supply was growing dangerously low. There would be no happy sundowner gin and tonic for me tonight.

And then—eureka! Jumping to my feet with renewed determination, I marched toward the passageway with the locked offices. Why hadn't I thought of it before? Surely they kept some sort of supplies on site? Maybe I'd find a way to turn on the water in the bathrooms. Would it be safe to drink? I'd risk it. Maybe I'd even come across walkie-talkies or some other communication device. As I never go anywhere without my lock picks, I wouldn't even have to do a *Magnum, P.I.* and bust the doors down with brute force (although at that point I was more than willing).

Entrance was easy.

Luck was not.

The rooms gave me nothing. Unless I was interested in doing a little janitorial duty, or performing repairs on a dot matrix printer.

As twilight spread across the vast backdrop of African prairie that surrounded the deserted airport like an endless brown ocean, my mind began to play out the worst of all possible scenarios. Suppose there were no flights scheduled to depart Limpopo Valley Airfield for days? Suppose I ran out of water? I only had the litre bottle I'd brought with me from camp, and more than half of that was gone. Suppose locals did pass by but didn't speak English? How could I make them understand that I'd been ditched here and desperately needed to get back to Johannesburg as soon as possible? Suppose a band of ravenous lions ventured by and—accurately judging me as defenseless prey—attacked me for their evening meal? There was no one to help me. Nowhere to go. I was surrounded by nothingness. And as hours passed and day faded into night, the nothingness became bigger and wider and by its very emptiness filled my brain with nightmare imaginations of peril.

At some point, with abrupt clarity (or the onset of raving paranoia brought on by heat and fear), I came to recognize that my predicament was not some horrible mistake. Richard Cassoum had not made a grievous and unconscious error by sending me to the airport when no flights were scheduled to leave Tuli Block that day. He had somehow learned of my desire to get to Chobe to search for Matthew Moxley, and this was his way of keeping me from my goal. But why? Why wouldn't he want me to find Matthew Moxley? Had Jaegar gotten to him? What was the connection? Were they in cahoots? The idea seemed preposterous but so was the fact that here I was, marooned in the middle of this African scrubland with no obvious means of getting help, with no phone, no Internet, and no passing traffic from which to get assistance.

With the Mashatu main camp forty-five minutes away by Jeep, and no idea if there were any other settlements nearby, never mind the very real possibility of being attacked by wild animals, there was no way I could walk for help. I was stranded, shipwrecked, cut off from any world that made sense to me. If Richard Cassoum had meant to scare me, he'd done a fine job.

When night, blacker than any I've ever seen, finally dropped around the little airport building like a dark blanket, I decided there was only one thing left to do: Hide.

In almost any other situation I could conceive of, the thought that I might actually be eaten by a lion, bitten by a poisonous snake or attacked by a gang of jackals while I slept would have been ludicrous, almost laughable. But today, given my circumstances, those unthinkable prospects were not only possible but quite likely. I needed to protect myself. I gathered my meagre belongings and headed for one of the storage rooms. It was a six by six cubicle with a cement floor that hadn't seen a broom since it was laid. But it did have a door with a lock, rudimentary but certainly sophisticated enough to ward off the cleverest of non-human beast without opposable thumbs.

For the first few minutes of my self-imposed imprisonment, I sat in the dark, cross-legged on the floor, feeling a little sorry for myself. But self-pity just isn't my style, and it didn't last long. I dug around in my duffle and pulled out a pair of cargo pants and the raincoat I'd yet to use and arranged them on the floor as a makeshift bed. I balled up a light sweater into a crude pillow and lay down, taking a minute or two to find a comfortable—sort of—position.

For many minutes I stared at the ceiling and strategized about what I would do tomorrow. In Saskatchewan, if you find yourself stranded in your car in the winter, the best advice is to stay with the vehicle. Wait for help to come to you. Every year there are too many sad tales of people freezing to death trying to walk to safety. Was this situation all that different? Sure, I knew if I set out tomorrow morning in the hopes of getting to Mashatu or some other source of help, I certainly wouldn't freeze to death, but might I die of heatstroke or dehydration? (And this was assuming the local carnivores would be at home, staying cool, and not out trying to score a McCanadian for lunch.)

So what were my options? How long could I last out here? I knew my scheduled flight back to Johannesburg was in two days. If there were absolutely no other flights in or out of Tuli Block before then, could I make it? I thought about my sorry food supply. Sure, I could do without food, but not water. I tossed around a few more scenarios, none of which ranked high on my "One Hundred Things to Do before I Die" list, and my mood turned miserable.

And then I got it.

I'd set the place on fire.

Whether or not my earlier supposition that the airport workers waited until they saw a plane in the sky to come to work was true or not, the theory was good. I had to get someone's attention. And a big old fire, the local—and as far as I knew, only—airport going down in a fiery blaze would surely get someone's attention and bring 'em running. Yes, it was a drastic move, but I was a desperate man. Or at least, I would be after another day or two like this one. I wasn't about to go down without a fight. I wasn't going to be left to die in the African sun, burning up like a piece of driftwood and disappearing on a puff of wind like I was nothing. No way. If I had to, I *would* burn this place down and, hopefully, live to tell about it.

As a last resort.

Having a plan—as radical as it was—gave me comfort. Enough to allow me to close my eyes with some semblance of well-being in my head.

The blackness of that night was absolute. I could physically feel it envelop me, covering me like paint, filling my head, dulling my senses. I wondered how long it would be before the noises of nighttime Africa arrived: hoots and clicks and thrumming and yowling and roaring and screeching and slithering. But the noises never came—or if they did, I never heard them—for I quickly fell into a deep sleep with vivid, animated visions of Curious George chasing Brendan Fraser's George of the Jungle.

By noon the next day, having run out of water, I was searching for matches and wondering how soon I could expect my first, comforting mirage to materialize—something with a kidney-shaped swimming pool, chaise longues, a Cinzano umbrella, fruity drinks and a cabana boy—when a man on a bicycle arrived. He was about a thousand years old (or really needed a good facial), with a shrivelled raisin for a face above a stick-man body, and wearing tan coveralls. He smiled a crooked smile when he saw me and listened politely as I babbled to him—something about how much I loved him and that he was my ever-blessed saviour sent by Mother Africa—after which he nodded graciously and, obviously indifferent to my plight (or not understanding a word I'd said), moved off to commence his duties.

I watched dispiritedly as he began sweeping and mopping (I hoped the storage room was on his list), and given his shuffling gait, the process took an excruciatingly long time. Eventually he moved on to pushing a large baggage cart, slooooooowly, from the front of the building to the back of the building where the planes pull up. Although I would have preferred if he had pulled out a cellphone and dialled 9-1-1 (or at the very least called me a cab to go back to camp), I took the fact that he was doing stuff with baggage carts as a very good sign. Could this mean the impending arrival of an aircraft and more people?

It did.

At about one-thirty, Garry arrived from Mashatu with a Jeep full of outgoing passengers, including the four Australians, Sylvia Dinswoody, Scotland, and her heretofore unseen husband.

"How did you get here, Mr. Russell?" Garry asked me when I ran up to him as if he was a long-lost paramour whom I'd just spotted across a sun-dappled field of waving grass and graceful daisies swaying in a gentle, flower-scented breeze.

"Water? Do you have water?" I sputtered with desperation. I'd already decided that recriminations and confrontation were not my best course of action if I wanted to get out of Botswana alive.

He gave me a concerned look and told me to sit down and wait for him. In a minute he was back with a bottle of liquid gold he'd retrieved from the cooler at the back of the Jeep. He stood above me, regarding me carefully, but did not ask the question again; it would be a waste of words he'd already used. (I'd noticed that Garry spoke as if every person were allocated only so many words for a lifetime and he did not want to run short.)

"I was dropped off here yesterday afternoon," I told him between deep, satisfying slurps. "Apparently Richard was *con-*

fused..." A little sarcasm here. "...about when the next flight to Johannesburg was."

"I see," he said darkly. Garry knew exactly what I was saying. I got the feeling he knew all about what was happening here and that maybe, just maybe, he didn't agree with it. "That is unfortunate," he added.

Understatement.

"You are feeling all right now?" he asked.

I nodded.

"Give me your return ticket. I will talk to these men and tell them to make sure you are on this next flight, okay? It leaves for Johannesburg right at two o'clock, okay?"

"Garry..." I began, searching his face for some sort of sign telling me he would be willing to help me with more than my ticket.

"No," he said quickly, a hand raised in a gesture that told me to back off. "This is all I can do for you."

I handed over my ticket, happy to have him deal with the authorities (the same two guys as when I'd arrived) who'd pulled up just as the incoming plane became visible in the sky, skimming the bottom edge of a light skiff of cloud. I watched as Garry approached the men, they spoke a few seconds, then Garry stood back to allow them to unlock the door to their booth and prepare for the new arrivals and departures before addressing my request. It wasn't a bad system really, kind of like just-in-time air travel, they show up only when needed; and given the isolated location it's not as if there was any possibility of waylaid passengers needing assistance...unless someone planned it that way....

I watched as the tiny plane, the same one I'd arrived on the day before yesterday, touched down and rolled toward the terminal. The Australians, endlessly giddy with adrenaline or perhaps an early afternoon shot of something or other, were making happy noises while Sylvia sat almost motionless behind a pair of dark, round sunglasses so big they covered three-quarters of her face. Next to her, her husband looked interminably bored. This was going to be a fun trip.

Garry came back and handed me a boarding pass and another

bottle of water. "Safe trip, huh?"

"Thank you, Ghakarhi." I must have come close to pronouncing it correctly because he smiled appreciatively. He gave me a cautioning look and said, "Be careful, Mr. Russell." And with that he returned to his Jeep to await the arrival of his newest charges.

Returning to Johannesburg that Monday afternoon, I felt as if I'd been gone from civilization for a month rather than two days. Although I was beat and sore from my night on the cement floor fearing for my life, the large and noisy modern airport and the fact that Jaegar had not been on the return flight reinvigorated me. In the real world, wild animals and menacing German guys were not hunting me down, and I was safe and sound.

If only for a short while.

I had to go back. I had to return to Botswana, to a place called Chobe, where I would find Matthew Moxley's boyfriend, Kevan, and through him, Matthew himself.

Now how the heck was I going to do all that?

As I meandered down the wide, shop-and-café-lined hallways of the bustling Johannesburg airport, looking, no doubt, like some poor, lost waif, I realized: that's exactly what I am. I had no idea where I was going, or how to get there, I had nowhere to go to get cleaned up, I knew no one, except.... There was someone.

Although I was never to meet him in person, dealing only with his disembodied voice—soft, with a clipped Afrikaner accent—over the phone, I could easily have fallen in love with Roy Hearn that day. God bless Sereena Orion Smith for giving me this guardian angel, this travel guru and resourceful Africa-know-it-all, who'd been charged, by Sereena, with providing me with assistance as I needed it. And boy, did I need it. And boy, did he come through. Again.

By dinnertime that night I was in a small, inexpensive hotel not far from the airport, enjoying a bath and room service, while he was behind a computer monitor somewhere in the city, busily pulling strings to arrange transportation for me to Chobe Game Reserve. By nine o'clock he had my itinerary fully arranged and called my hotel room with the details, beginning with an 11:20 a.m. Nationwide Air flight the next morning to Livingstone, Zambia.

When I got off the phone with Roy, I calculated that it was about one p.m. in the afternoon in Saskatoon and placed a call to my client. I reached Clara Ridge's answering machine, and left a detailed message about my African adventures to date and told her that I was now heading to the northern edge of Botswana, via Zambia, where I hoped to track down a masseur named Kevan who would lead me to her son. It sounded daunting as I gave her the particulars, but hey, I bolstered myself, I'm Russell Quant, intrepid Saskatoon PI extraordinaire!

Sometimes you just have to tell yourself stuff like that.

"What a sight for sore eyes!" the familiar voice rang out from somewhere within the mess of bodies crowding around me in the thirty-two degree Celsius heat of the unairconditioned Livingstone airport.

The day had started out well enough. I had had a pleasant, leisurely breakfast at my hotel, a van arranged by Roy Hearn had taken me to the Joburg airport, and a nice big plane had ferried me quite comfortably the hour and twenty minutes from South Africa to Zambia. The aircraft was crammed with tourists, mostly elderly Brits, Americans and a handful of Canadians, on vacation and heading for Victoria Falls, one of the seven natural wonders of the world, so named after the British Queen Victoria by the famed explorer David Livingstone. The falls are situated on the border of Zimbabwe and Zambia, where the powerful Zambezi River plunges down a series of basalt gorges creating a never-ending mist that can be seen quite clearly even twenty kilometres away. When the river is in flood, the falls are the largest curtain of water in the world. Due to the current political conditions, most of the travellers on my flight were heading for resorts on the Zambian side of the falls, but some were not, swearing that, politics be damned, the view from Zimbabwe is the more stunning to behold.

Given the tourist popularity of the area (and the nice big plane), I expected the Livingstone airport to be considerably bigger and more modern than the Limpopo airfield. It was. But not by much.

We had filed off the plane into what looked to be a Customs and Immigration line-up, where a very young man in a tattered army-fatigue-green uniform made quite a production of checking names on a typed list attached to a well-worn clipboard. Whereas a number of guests ahead of me in the line were making a fuss about having to pay this guy off, Roy had warned me: regardless of whether or not my name was on the list, I would be charged ten US dollars to enter the country (even though I was not staying in Zambia and was immediately transferring to Botswana). So I was ready for this guy, I thought.

When it was my turn, the man asked me several unintelligible questions and no amount of "excuse me"s or "I don't understand"s cleared up his English. At the end I simply shrugged my shoulders and accepted a charge of *twenty-five* US dollars to get him to allow my ass into Zambia. I had the feeling I'd been taken, but it's not as if I was buying jeans at The Gap; Rule Number One when travelling in foreign countries: don't argue with profiteers who carry shotguns.

Once through, and after waiting an exceedingly long time for my bag at the luggage carousel, I had entered the melee of the main terminal. It was crowded; and it didn't help that many of the vacationers were quite elderly, moving very slowly, with countless pieces of luggage that were also elderly and moving slowly. It was hot hot hot and didn't smell too good either. It was so hot, that when I heard the voice, I thought I might be hallucinating.

"Russell Quant, how the hell are you?" came the familiar voice once again.

Roy Hearn had told me to look out for a man with a name placard who would help me with my transfer to Botswana, but I didn't think he'd be using such a familiar tone and besides, this voice definitely belonged to a woman. I scanned the bobbing heads and grinned when my eyes fell upon none other than Cassandra Wellness. She was wearing movie star sunglasses and a khaki outfit that would have been bland on anyone else but looked superb on her; nothing fancy, mind you (except for a leopard print, silk scarf artfully arranged around her neck), just perfect. Her luxuriant auburn hair fell lush and shiny about her shoulders where she'd slung the straps of her well-worn but pricey travelling bags. She was struggling to slide her way through the crush of bodies to get to me.

"Cassandra, what are you doing here?" I called out to her.

"*Mosi-oa-Tunya*," she said to me as she arrived breathless at my side.

"*Molo*?" I responded, displaying my enviable command of African languages.

Cassandra let out a raspy laugh and said, "*Mosi-oa-Tunya*; it means 'the smoke that thunders.' It's the name given Victoria Falls by the local Kololo tribe for the thundering roar of the falls. You can hear them long before you see them."

"You're visiting the falls, then?" I took a wild guess.

She nodded and lifted her ever-present camera cases. "Photos. The river level is high this year, so the magazine editor thinks there should be some wonderful shots. I suppose I could probably just send her the shots I did the last time I was here, or the time before that, or the time before that," she said with a roll of her eyes. "I'm at the Royal Livingstone Hotel," she told me with a hopeful note in her voice. "Where are you? Care to meet for drinks tonight? I hear the vervet monkeys at the Sundowner bar are particularly mischievous this year. We can throw peanuts at them and see if they attack. Now that should make for some interesting shots! Canadian mayor attacked by African monkeys!"

"Actually, I'm not staying in Livingstone," I told her as we continued being jostled about by the crowd, as though we were in a Hong Kong subway station at rush hour. "I'm off to Chobe Game Reserve."

"I'm going with you!" she announced without a second's thought, her bright eyes dancing with exuberance. "What an outstanding idea. I've never been to Chobe. I hear it's marvellous. I'm coming with you; you don't mind, do you?"

"Ah, but, er, ah," I enunciated clearly. "What about the photos of the falls?"

"The falls aren't going anywhere. I'll come back for them."

It was about then that I noticed a change in Cassandra's facial expression. And it was also about then that I felt something hard being pressed into the small of my back, and it wasn't moving.

"Let's go outside," a slithering voice filled my left ear.

My eyes never left Cassandra's, and in the reflection of her shades I saw the ugly puss of Jaegar, who suddenly knew quite well how to speak English. I could just hear his mother saying: "If you can't say something threatening, don't say anything at all."

So how the hell had he gotten from Mashatu to Livingstone? He hadn't been on my flight to Johannesburg, and it certainly wasn't as if there was a flight leaving every hour from the Limpopo airfield (I'd learned *that* the hard way). Had he driven? Had Richard Cassoum, the Mashatu camp manager, lied to me? Was there another, easier and quicker way to get here from Mashatu that he didn't want me to know about? The possibility that Richard and Jaegar were in this together seemed more and more likely; how else would Jaegar have known where I was going? But why? I still had no idea what their connection might be, but now was not the time to ask questions.

By thrusting what I was guessing was a gun against my back, Jaegar had suddenly ratcheted up the stakes a notch or two. It was a daring move, in a crowded airport, and quite possibly a stupid one. Assuming (hoping) he wouldn't murder me in front of all these people, I realized that right at that very moment might be my best and only chance of escaping him.

But what about Cassandra? I didn't want to put her in danger.

I scoured my surroundings for ideas for a heroic plan to get us away from the gun-toting Jaegar. I found what I was looking for right over Cassandra's head. There was only one way out of this.

With a sudden, sharp thrust backwards, I shoved Jaegar far enough away from me so I could whirl around—all interpretive-dance-like—and land a sharp-toed jab directly in his crotch. I twirled again (I'm hoping it didn't look as flitty as it sounds), grabbed Cassandra's arm, and dashed towards the exit. The mass of people was still thick and slow as molasses in January. I hoped the crowd cover would work to our advantage as I encouraged a rather dumbfounded Cassandra to keep her head low and crouch-run as fast as she could.

Standing unawares near one of the terminal's exit doors was a portly, mustachioed man, looking like an African version of Agatha Christie's diminutive Hercule Poirot. He was wearing a white shirt with an A&K name badge pinned to his chest, and holding aloft a handwritten sign with the name Ruseey Grant on it. That had to be me, and if it wasn't, well, I didn't give a damn; Ruseey would just have to find another ride home.

As we reached the man, I grabbed his arm as well and—looking like a mother with two unruly children—dragged the two of them, Cassandra and the A&K guy, into the sweltering heat outside the airport building and into a parking area crammed with countless, haphazardly parked buses, vans and motorized scooters.

"Where is your vehicle?" I demanded to know, my breath grown shallow and ragged.

The man looked at me as if I was deranged and I recognized how this might appear to him. Unfortunately, I didn't have a lot of time for a get-to-know-ya session. "I'm Russell Quant, your fare. You're from Abercrombie and Kent; Roy Hearn arranged this, right?"

"Yes, that's right," he said slowly, his eyes becoming slightly less alarmed. "Welcome to Zambia. My name is Johnning. I'm your guide in charge of your transfer to the Kazungula jetty. The trip will..." I could tell he was getting set to recite a well-worn welcome speech which, although I'm sure would have been fascinating, would have to wait.

"Yeah, that's great. Can you tell us in the car? Where's your car?" I spit out, yanking him along to keep us moving and, I hoped, out of Jaegar's gunsights.

"It's over there," he said, catching on to my sense of urgency and leading us to a small, blue van that was in need of a paint job. On its side was one of those magnetic logo plates that identified it as an Abercrombie and Kent vehicle.

"I'll explain on the way," I told him, checking behind us for any sign of the German hulk. "But we really need to move fast right now."

The three of us piled into the van, Johnning in the front and Cassandra and me and our bags behind him. As I stepped into the vehicle, I pulled the logo sign off the door; who knew what Jaegar knew, and there was no need to make it any easier for him to spot us. With a choking plume of blue smoke the van came to life and Johnning directed it out of the dusty, gravelled lot.

I glanced at Cassandra, but all she had for me was a what-the-hell-is-going-on look.

As Johnning droned his A&K spiel that could not be staunched, even with a gun-wielding maniac after us, Cassandra and I fell into stunned silence, alternating between staring at one another and checking the road behind us for a tail.

"What is going on?" Cassandra eventually mouthed, the words coming out at a barely audible level.

"I'm sorry, but I'm not exactly sure," I whispered back quite truthfully.

"That guy back there, he had a gun, didn't he?"

I nodded.

"Why? Who is he?"

"I'm not sure, but the first time I saw him he was getting on the plane at Sal Island."

"Sal Island!" she exclaimed, understandably bewildered.

Johnning, sensing we weren't paying him the full attention he deserved, raised the volume of his voice. He had now left town and was on a highway, driving very slowly with his hands at ten and two, eyes never leaving the pavement.

"Can we go faster, Johnning?" I asked. We'd never outrun a tortoise at this rate, never mind hare Jaegar.

"No," he answered matter-of-factly, and continued with his information seminar, pointing out the distant mist of Victoria Falls.

Cassandra and I whispered a bit more until we realized the van was coming to a stop.

"I thought you said we were going to the Kazungula jetty," I said as if I knew what a Kazungula jetty was. "Didn't you say it was seventy kilometres away?" We hadn't driven anywhere near that far.

Suddenly a horrible thought pierced my brain like a needle full of poison.

Had I been fooled?

Was Johnning in on this too, along with Jaegar and Richard Cassoum?

Maybe Jaegar had not followed us because he didn't need to; Johnning would deliver us right to him. Or had I read too many Robert Ludlum novels?

I strained to see outside the dirty window on my side of the vehicle and saw that we had pulled up alongside a dicey-looking collection of buildings, just this side of being mud huts.

"We must get out here," Johnning said as he opened his door and hopped out of the van.

Our eyes grew wide and then narrow as Cassandra and I contemplated a daring escape rather than be captured.

The side door slid open and Johnning stood there with something in his hand. It was a bottle of water. "You must be thirsty," he said handing Cassandra the bottle, then pulled another from under his arm for me.

"What's going on?" Cassandra demanded to know with a steely edge to her already brassy voice.

"As I told you," he said, not bothering to hide a near-accusatory tone at our obvious earlier lack of attention. "We must now be processed through the Zambian exit station into Botswana."

Phew.

I made a note to listen more carefully to Johnning from there on in.

Minutes later, we were back in the van and preparing to head for Kazungula jetty—whatever or wherever that was. I was beginning to feel immeasurably better about things, until I saw another van, this one the colour of used straw—kind of a musty yellow— approaching the border crossing buildings. As the vehicle came closer, I could just make out the figure behind the wheel: Jaegar. His eyes found mine and for an interminable second we stared at one another, conveying an unmistakable message of mutual dislike.

And then it began to rain.

Now where the blasted hell on this heat-soaked day of Lucifer had that come from? It always seems to rain whenever my cases aren't going well. It wasn't torrential or even pouring, just a dotty little rain that coloured the sky a fuzzy grey (like my mood).

"Johnning," I urged with desperation. "Can you please make this thing go faster? The man in the van behind us is dangerous and he is after us."

"But we are already ahead and he too must be processed by the Zambian authorities before entering the country," he told me as we started off at a leisurely pace down the highway, as if heading for a picnic in the enchanted forest with a group of friendly elves and magical fairies. "And, once on his way, he cannot go any faster than we."

Huh? I did not know if Johnning's van could not go any faster, or if *he* simply would not go any faster, but I was certain Jaegar wasn't about to pay much attention to the posted speed limits.

"Stop this thing right now," Cassandra said, somehow knowing exactly what I was thinking. "I have to pee." Her southern belle's accent had suddenly reasserted itself, becoming overbearingly insistent.

The guide must have been used to this type of request from American women as he immediately complied with the request, and helpfully pointed out a clump of trees off the side of the road. "Not to worry," he assured. "It is quite private."

But instead of Cassandra getting out of the vehicle, I did. I came around the van and yanked open the driver's side door.

"I'm sorry about this, Johnning," I said, meaning it. "But I'm going to have to drive. And you'll have to get in the back because I have no idea where we're going."

After a bit of mumbling and bumbling, Johnning—not a dumb guy and very aware of the difference in the size of our biceps—took my place in the back next to Cassandra, and I took control of the little blue van. However, once I got us rolling, although appreciably faster than Johnning speed, no matter where I put the gear shift or how hard I pushed on the gas pedal, the A&K van indeed only went so fast. Admirably hiding my frustration, I turned in my seat and asked him, "So, where do I go?"

He shrugged, "Just drive to the water."

"Water?" I knew a jetty is usually some kind of landing pier. Pier equals water; water equals boat; boat equals discomfort for Russell Quant. Oh crap.

I'd taken a Mediterranean cruise a couple of years back and learned to make friends with the water. Oh yeah, we were real friendly-like. As long as the boat was a luxury ocean liner with handsome stewards and plenty of free-flowing champagne. I somehow doubted that was the kind of boat we were about to meet at the Kazungula jetty. But maybe…

I checked the rear-view mirror for Jaegar's van, but the rain had gotten thicker, sluicing over our vehicle like clear gelatin, making it difficult to see out. The front windshield wipers were barely keeping up and there were none for the rear window. All we could do was ride hard and watch for a body of water somewhere in front of us.

It was the longest, slowest car chase I'd ever been on. The trip to Kazungula took a tension-filled hour, and although every so often I thought I could see something yellow in our rain-blurred wake, I was never sure if we were being chased by Jaegar's van or not. At least Johnning was right. Jaegar couldn't go any faster than we could—something about how the vans were manufactured I guessed, or maybe the fuel they used didn't agree with the engines—so, whoever started out in the lead, was the winner. Thankfully, that was us.

Throughout the journey, Cassandra was chomping at the bit to pelt me with questions about our bizarre and unexpected situation, whereas Johnning dealt with it by choosing to ignore it as if nothing untoward was happening—a nervous reaction I suspect—and did so by filling the time with more verbal exposition about Zambia, the local economy, politics and religious beliefs. As I had no idea what to tell Cassandra at this point anyway, I encouraged Johnning by making appropriate sounds, like "Oh really?" and "Isn't that interesting," which kept him going and gave Cassandra little opportunity to butt in.

Finally, a clump of buildings—no *Architectural Digest* candidates here—emerged in front of us through the sheath of rain.

"We have arrived," Johnning announced, all tourist-guide-like. "This is the Kazungula jetty."

"Now what?" Cassandra wanted to know.

I shot a glance at Johnning over my shoulder. Could I trust that he was on our side and wasn't about to deliver us into the hands of whomever it was that wanted to get their hands on me?

"At the river's edge," he said, unfazed by my look, "there will be a ferry boat and a speedboat. Get on the speedboat."

I decided that if I was going to have to get on water—given the circumstances (the whole escaping-a-madman-in-the-Zambian-rain thing)—I liked the sound of a speedboat versus a ferry.

"On the speedboat," Johnning continued, "will be a man. His name is Godfrey. His job is to take you across the river to Kasane."

"And then what?"

"Godfrey will tell you." He gave us each a curt nod. "My job is done."

We nodded back.

I slowed and pulled into a lot made of mud juice, allowing the van to slip to a halt against a hunk of jagged concrete that jutted up from the wet earth for no apparent reason.

Cassandra and I collected our bags, jumped out of the van and raced towards the river's edge with Johnning loudly repeating his instructions to get on the speedboat, not the ferry, and to ask for Godfrey who would take us to the Kasane side of the river.

The Kazungula jetty area was a mishmash collection of vehicles parked in no obvious order, varied groupings of rain-soaked people, and rundown buildings that must once have served an official purpose but were now largely ignored except by varmints and critters. There were tourists trying to figure out what to do, locals trying to help the tourists, business people and area residents simply trying to cross the river, and several shifty looking characters who, no doubt, had nefarious purposes in mind. But we had no time to pay attention to any of it. Jaegar could not be too far behind and if he caught us here, our options for escape were few.

"There!" Cassandra yelled breathlessly, pointing to the banks of the sluggishly moving river, the Zambezi, where a large ferry boat (circa *Huckleberry Finn*) was moored. A couple of dozen people were aboard, expectantly waiting to depart. "Next to the ferry!"

Wedged between a rickety wooden pier and the ferry, almost hidden by a thicket of wild grass and reeds, was a small boat with seating for six (very small) people. Standing next to the boat was a tall, rangy-looking fellow whose skin had turned ebony with the wet.

"That must be Godfrey!" Cassandra called to me as she galloped toward the man and his dinghy.

"Oh shit," I replied.

Cassandra glanced over her shoulder and saw what I'd just seen: two vans were turning off the main road and heading for the river. Both of them were yellow. One of them had to be Jaegar!

Hauling ass and our bags, we ran for it, never looking back. We reached the skinny guy and breathlessly told him who we were. He nodded and with frustrating carefulness arranged our bags on the boat then told us to get on, one at a time, one on each side, and not to forget to put on our life jackets. Safety-conscious or preparing for the inevitable? Didn't matter. We needed that speedboat to do its thing. Now.

I kept my eyes on the yellow vans, which had pulled up near to where Johnning's was still parked. A large figure was getting out of the first one. I said something to Godfrey about lighting a fire under it. He gave me an indulgent smile and joined us on the boat, which swooped a little with his added weight. My stomach did the same.

Godfrey started the engine.

"Russell," Cassandra's voice came out like belligerent ketchup from a bottle. "Look."

I turned away from shooting urgent stares at our captain and saw that the figure that had gotten out of the first yellow van was now leaning into the driver's side window of Johnning's van. Through the rain, and given the distance, it was impossible to see exactly what was going on. But I could make a good guess.

"Godfrey!" I cried. "We have to go now!"

Godfrey pulled down a lever and away we went.

To my great consternation, not unlike our experience with the van, the speedboat wasn't so much a speedboat as it was a chug-boat. The river was calm, which helped our progress to the Kasane jetty on the opposite shore, but the going was painfully slow. As we puttered along, Godfrey informed us that we were about to cross the exact spot in the river where four countries meet—Zambia, Botswana, Zimbabwe and Namibia. Okay, I had to admit that was very cool, just as long as it didn't also become the exact spot where Jaegar from Germany met Russell from Canada and Cassandra from the United States.

Thankfully the rain was beginning to let up. Cassandra and I kept our eyes on the retreating shoreline, monitoring our pursuer's progress. We watched as the A&K van pulled out of the parking lot (thank goodness Johnning was okay) and then, barrelling toward the river's edge like an out-of-control locomotive, came the refrigerator-like Jaegar. When he made the bank he stood there huffing and puffing in all his Ho-Ho-Ho-Green Giant glory and I swore I felt malevolence reach across the waters, right into my chest, like a fist intent on palming my heart and squishing the life out of it. But ho ho ho, no boat for him.

About then, halfway across the river, another pseudo-speed-boat chugged by us, making its crossing from the Kasane side (where we were headed) to the Kazangula side (where Jaegar was waiting for a ride). Damn! I'd been hoping he'd have to wait for the ferry—which doubtlessly would be even slower than our boat and still didn't look anywhere near ready to leave port—but now he had a better option. I knew there was no way he wouldn't be on that next speedboat after us.

Two minutes later—at roughly the same time the opposing boat had reached Kazangula and Jaegar—we were across the river and dumped at the Kasane jetty. I calculated that we had, at most, a five to eight minute lead.

Godfrey directed us to Michael, who looked like his twin brother and was waiting for us behind the wheel of an open Jeep with a canvas canopy. I turned to Cassandra. I'd made a decision.

It was time to extricate her from my danger.

"You stay here," I told her. "Catch the next boat across and get yourself back to Livingstone. You shouldn't be here. It's dangerous, and this has nothing to do with you."

She laughed. "And leave all the fun for you? Forget it *Mister Mayor*." I think my cover was blown. "Let's go!" And with that she tossed her bags into the rear of the Jeep and pulled herself up into a seat.

I glanced across the water. Jaegar was getting on the speedboat. There was no time to argue. I hoisted myself up next to her and instructed the driver to move it, politely of course, but he got the idea. Off we went, zooming into the safety of African bush country.

For about four hundred metres.

The Jeep pulled into a clearing next to a set of buildings identical to the ones at the Zambian exit station.

"Botswana Customs," Michael informed us.

Shit! Shit! Shit! Shit! Shit!

So out we got. We entered one of the buildings and showed our identification to a squat woman sitting on a creaky chair on casters behind a long, glassed-in counter. She seemed much too busy talking to another squat woman sitting on an identical chair down the counter from her to actually pay us much attention, so it didn't take long. Back outside, while Michael drove our Jeep through a shallow ditch of dirty-looking amber liquid, we were instructed to step into a metal cake pan of the same stuff and then pull out every pair of shoes from our luggage to dip the soles in the solution as well.

"Foot and mouth disease precaution," Michael explained.

Uh, yup, okay, but we're kinda trying to escape the clutches of an evil madman who wants to shoot us.

Just as Cassandra was putting a shockingly high-heeled pair of silver toed, white leather boots (she had those in a duffle bag?) through their paces, I saw a dark-coloured SUV approaching the customs area. I couldn't see the driver but something about the angry looking grille, the blacked-out windows, the roar of the engines, told me we did not want to come face-to-face with whoever was behind the wheel, and I didn't need two guesses to conclude who it was. Jaegar was catching up!

I had no time to figure out how he'd arranged for a new vehicle so fast; he'd just done it. We had to go now! We hopped into the Jeep and encouraged Michael to make like a rocket. He did his best, and we were soon beyond the customs area and back on a road that wound its way through a landscape comfortingly thick with bush.

But it was no use. My heart sank as I faced the undeniable truth: our slow, lumbering Jeep would clearly be unable to outrun the big, bad guy in the big, bad truck on our tail. Jaegar and his gun were going to catch us, and we were defenseless.

I thought about it for about two-and-a-half seconds and whispered a plan into Cassandra's ear. She gave me a surprised look, but bless her heart did not question me. She simply grabbed hold of her bags. I grabbed mine. We jumped.

We fell hard into a swath of tall grasses and rounded bushes that had looked like a soft landing spot but wasn't. Keeping low to the ground, we scrambled to concealment and, we hoped, safety, behind a collection of gnarled trees and shrubs and watched in horror as our Jeep exploded into an angry ball of fire.

Chapter 12

Scalding bits and pieces of what was once the back end of the Jeep we'd just jumped from rained down on us like a crematory shower. For impossibly long seconds we crouched there in the relative safety of a stand of trees, aghast and overwhelmed by what had just happened and what had just about happened to us.

As the incinerated vehicle rolled to an inevitable stop on its two remaining, flattened, front tires, we watched for our driver to jump from his place behind the wheel, but he did not. God, no! I immediately tossed aside the piece of luggage I was still clasping to my chest as if it were a newborn infant, and rose to run to his rescue. I felt a hand drag me back down, causing me to stumble gracelessly to the ground.

"No, Russell!" she warned me off. "Stop!"

I looked at her as if she were crazy. "I'm going to help him!"

"Russell!" she said in an urgent but hushed voice, her eyes wild. "Take a close look. There's no one in the Jeep."

I did as she suggested and saw that she was right.

"But…"

"He jumped too," she said. "Just before we did."

"Before…?"

We looked at one another and recognized in each other's face the horrifying significance of that act. This was no accident. This was attempted murder.

My gaze shifted to a dark SUV pulling to a grinding stop a safe distance back from the burning wreckage. It was the same one we had seen at the Botswana customs station, with the ominous black windows and wicked looking grille. The bad guys were here.

A minute later, another vehicle, likely containing more recent arrivals from the Kasane jetty (or maybe more bad guys for all I knew), screeched to a halt behind the truck. The inhabitant or inhabitants of the first vehicle were not yet risking getting out, but soon they would, and when it was discovered that Cassandra and I—or rather, our burning bodies—were not there, they'd come looking for us. We had to make our escape now and put as much distance as we could between us and whoever was in that truck.

"Come on," I said to Cassandra as I gathered my stuff. "We have to hurry—and keep low."

"You know what," she replied, her voice a little unsteady. "I've changed my mind. I think I do prefer boring old Victoria Falls. I'm going back."

I searched her face for any signs of jest, but saw none. Cassandra Wellness wore a tight-fitting adventurer's shell around her southern belle interior, but enough was enough; she'd reached her limit. People with guns. Escape over water. Exploding vehicles. Stuff like that can take its toll, even on the toughest nut. An acrid smoke perfumed the air around us, and the ravenous fire that was slowly devouring our Jeep crackled like a million miniature firecrackers. This was not a pleasant environment and I could understand her desire to go back to life the way it had been. I pulled a stray twig from her dishevelled hair, then took her hands in mine and met her eyes with my own. "I'm sorry, Cassandra, but it's too late."

She looked at me, aghast.

"Look," I said with as much gentle reassurance in my voice as I could muster. "I think you should go back too."

"Good," she told me. "I'm ready."

"But not from here," I burst her bubble. "And not now."

I could see her back stiffen and her eyes glaze over with steel. "I don't remember giving you permission to tell me what to do. I came on this stupid trip because I wanted to. And now I'll go back because I want to."

This was not the time or place for a discussion. Our margin of safety was narrow enough as it was, and if we didn't hightail it out of there fast, it would soon disappear. "Cassandra, you have to listen to me," I urged. "These guys are serious, and they mean to kill us. As soon as they find out they've failed, they're gonna be on our backs like mint jelly on a lamb shank. And they have an advantage; they know this terrain. They know we're together. If you try to get back to the river from here, they're going to find you, and if they don't kill you right away, they'll use you to try to find me."

She shook her head. "I won't tell them where you're going, Russell, I promise. I'll tell them I have no idea where you were heading, that you were just some guy I picked up for some fun, and now it's over." I saw a glimpse of her familiar raffish smile when she added, "And let me tell you, this is *sooooo* over."

"They won't believe you, Cassandra. They don't care about any of that. But if they think you can help them, they'll do anything to get information out of you." I gave her hands an extra squeeze. "Anything."

"You don't know that!" she argued back. "How do you know that?"

"I don't," I answered back. "But I've dealt with these kinds of people before. Think, Cassandra. You know Jaegar had a gun. You saw what they did to the Jeep. These aren't disgruntled businessmen we're dealing with here."

I saw the look in her eyes begin to change. She knew I was right.

"Look, I'm sorry I got you into this," I told her, and I meant it. "But, it's too late now. We've gotta get away from here while we still have a chance, while they think we're dead. We have to find a place to hide until they've lost our scent."

"Why do you keep on saying 'they'? Don't you mean this Jaegar guy? Do you think there's more than one person out to get you?" She stopped there, dawning realization eroding her strong but now faltering features. "What the hell have you done, Russell Quant?"

I'd been thinking about exactly the same stuff. "Cassandra, I wasn't lying when I told you I wasn't sure why Jaegar is after me. But what I am sure about is that there has to be more than just him behind all of this. Jaegar knows too much. How did he know to find me in Zambia? How did he get a vehicle so fast after he came across the river? How did he know to set the explosives on that Jeep? He has to have had help. I know it's a dreadful thought, but we have to assume there's more than just one bad guy after us."

I saw her head make a slow bobbing motion up and down as if she were finally coming to admit the horrible truth of the situation to herself. "How far is it to Chobe from here?"

"We're not going to Chobe," I told her.

"What? Why not?"

"Cassandra, if they knew we were going to be in that Jeep, then they know we're headed for Chobe. When they find out we're not dead, that's the first place they'll go looking to finish the job. We have to find someplace else to hole up."

She glanced about at the scrubby landscape, trees scarred to premature death by elephant tusks, stalagmite-like termite hills that looked like mini pyramids and, seeing no handy Four Seasons Hotel nearby, threw up her hands and eyebrows and regarded me with an "I hope you have a plan" look in her wide eyes.

I didn't. Not really. All I knew was that I had to get her—and me—out of there as soon as possible. "This way," I said with the authority of every hopelessly lost city guy traipsing through rural Saskatchewan.

"Okay." She nodded resolutely, no fading flower for long.

After grabbing her bags, Cassandra followed my *Rambo* lead through the dense cover of trees and reeds, on the way to safety.

As we snuck away, I noticed that the rain had finally stopped.

It was a going to be a beautiful evening in Botswana.

Just as remote and unspoiled as Mashatu, the Chobe area, with its not-so-bald prairie-like landscape, provided us sufficient camouflage as Cassandra and I stealthily crab-walked our way in search of a secure refuge. We kept as close to the river as we could without revealing ourselves, hoping it would lead us to some type of shelter before dark or an unwanted animal encounter. After a long and sometimes treacherous journey, it did. We were never quite sure whether the place was an impromptu settlement of seminomadic Africans or an actual village, or perhaps a camp that provided nearby game lodges with willing and cheap labour, but it didn't much matter to us. For a very reasonable price, an English-speaking lady, Masha, offered us a room, a bed, some food and, hopefully, a safe haven until we could figure out what the heck to do next.

"God, I am so tired I could sleep standing up," Cassandra announced once we were alone inside our room.

The place was tiny and dark, hot and musty-smelling, and we loved every inch of it. We were so exhausted (and relieved to be in one piece) that a used chicken coop would have seemed a paradise. Cassandra pulled off her scarf, khaki jacket and T-shirt, leaving her with only a fancy—by my inexperienced evaluation—bra on (it had lots of lace, and each cup had a patterned underbelly.)

"Don't worry," she said with a fleeting look in my direction. "I'm not going to seduce you again. I just want to clean up a bit before moss starts growing under my arms." And with that she headed for the basin of tepid water provided by our hostess.

I shrugged and pulled off my own top layer, down to a bare chest, and got in line. Despite our close quarters, the heat and humidity of the day (all of which seemed to have gathered in our room), and the inexorable sexuality that exuded from my travelling companion like scent from a sachet, I had to show her I wasn't afraid of no woman, and that I, too, considered our sexual miscommunication in Cape Town to be over and long forgotten.

Just as we were towelling off and feeling much better for it, Masha gave a half-knock and let herself into the room with a tray laden with two plates of some kind of bok stew, mealie bread and a jug of iced tea. She set everything down on a small wooden table with one leg significantly shorter than the other three and left without a word to either of us. We pulled up two rickety chairs, placed an oil-burning lamp between our dishes so we could see what we were eating and dived in, hungry as hippos.

"So how do we get out of this mess, Russell?" Cassandra asked the million-dollar question once half our meal was gone. The food was very tasty, if a bit heavy on the salt. "How do we get ourselves back to Vic Falls?"

"Things will have cooled down by tomorrow morning," I said, telling a bit of a white lie, and sounding more confident than I felt. "We'll take you back to Kasane, or maybe we'll ask Masha if she knows of another, nearby river crossing that might be safer to use."

Cassandra laid down her spoon and looked at me. "You're not coming?"

I shook my head.

"Russell, what the hell is going on? Tell me now or I'll start screaming."

I saw a now familiar crinkle at the corner of her eyes. She was teasing, but only sort of.

"It's safer if you go back alone," I told her. "They're not after you; they don't know who you are...so far. You're in danger because of me and as much as you love escapades and all that, this is over. This isn't *The African Queen* or *Romancing the Stone* or *Lara Croft: Tomb Raider*. It's time for us to part ways."

"I don't know what that means. I don't watch much television, b...."

I winced. "They're movies."

"Whatever. You didn't answer my question. Why aren't you coming with me? You didn't want me to leave on my own before."

"That was different. Danger was imminent. If you'd tried to get back to the river then, they would have caught you. By tomorrow morning...well, if we're lucky and make it through tonight, things will be different, the heat will be off. By then they'll have no idea where we are. You'll have a much better chance of getting back to Livingstone safely."

"Chance?" she said with a not-happy look on her face. "Russell, wouldn't it just be safer for me to stay with you now?"

I shook my head. "They're still looking for me. After what happened today, I don't think they're going to give up easily. You need to get away from all this."

She arched a finely shaped eyebrow. "What exactly is *this*? Why did we almost get blown to bits? Are you..." And she stopped there as if a new, uncomfortable thought had just entered her head. "Are you a fugitive? Are you running from the law? Did you do something illegal?"

I would have been offended if it wasn't that I could see how her hypothesis made perfect sense. "No, of course not," I assured her.

"All this is very un-mayor-like," she said with an unreadable glint in her eye. She took a gulp of her drink. "God, I wish we had some scotch."

For half a second I had no idea what she was talking about, then, oh yeah, I'd told her I was the mayor of Saskatoon. Yeesh. If only I were. I'd be safe at home right now, presiding over pancake breakfasts and handing out keys to the city. Well, I decided, there was no comeback for that. Although I did toy with the idea of telling her Saskatoon was considering trade relations with Botswana, and I was here to negotiate for their best *bobotie* and *braai* recipes in exchange for our Hungarian goulash, Aboriginal bannock and Ukrainian perogy secrets. "Cassandra, I am so sorry I got you into this," was all I finally said.

"Don't flatter yourself," she shot back, her candle-lit skin glistening from the heat of the night. "No one got me into anything. I'm the only one who controls what I do, who I do it with and where I do it. Now quit stalling and tell me exactly what the hell is going on. Just how stupid do you think I am? I get it, Russell; I get that you're no mayor, and I get that you might not want to tell me exactly who you are or what you're doing, but I think after just about getting my ass turned to ash I deserve something more than misplaced macho male protectionism."

She had a point. And I didn't think she was very stupid at all, quite the contrary. "You're right, about all of that. I'm not the mayor of Saskatoon. But to tell you the truth, Cassandra, I'm not exactly sure why Jaegar is after me or wh…"

"Liar."

"Cassandra, I'm telling you…"

"Okay, okay. Jaegar's the big guy with the gun we saw at the airport and who got on the plane at Sal Island?" she said to be absolutely clear.

"Yeah, that's the guy."

"And you think it was him who blew up the Jeep?"

That pulled me up short. Of course it was Jaegar. He'd been

turning up behind me like a dog's tail ever since Sal Island. He'd put a gun to my back at Livingstone airport. It had to be him...didn't it?

"It could have been anyone," Cassandra continued. "Sure, we saw him at the airport and we assume it was him following us to Kazungula."

"He was in Kazungula. I saw him."

"But we never saw him come across to Kasane."

"I saw him get on the speedboat," I countered.

"But you never saw him after that. Right?"

That was true. Once we'd reached Kasane, we'd gotten into the doomed Jeep and skedaddled out of there. The dark vehicle with the monster grille had come up pretty quickly behind us, but I never actually saw who was in it. And, to be fair (although I hated to do it), even if it was Jaegar in that truck, that wasn't proof that he'd arranged for our Jeep to explode. Still, page one-hundred-and-twelve in the detective handbook says: if it looks like a duck, swims like a duck, and quacks like a duck, chances are it's a duck. And as far as I was concerned, Jaegar had a nice big bill, webbed feet and a fine set of tail feathers.

Cassandra expelled a frustrated snort. "But it's obvious someone is after you. You're probably right; it probably is Jaegar, what with the gun in your back at the airport. Although, I have to admit, I did not see the gun in his hands, so I'm just taking your word for it."

I gave her my most sour look.

"Still, Russell, how can you not know why Jaegar—or whoever—is after you? You must be involved in something." She gave me a suspicious glare. "Are you lying to me? Because if you're lying to me I'm outta here right now, and let me tell you, mister, I won't go quietly! I'll have every border patrol guard, African warrior, gun-toting rebel and itinerant lion breathing down your neck before you can count your toes!"

I could handle all of that, except the lion. It was time to come clean (or at least a little less dirty). "Cassandra, I'm a detective." I swallowed the last of my iced tea to wash down some mealie bread stuck in my throat. "I'm in Africa trying to find a missing person. That's it. There's nothing much more complicated to it than that. But for some reason this Jaegar character wants to keep me from doing what I'm here to do."

She gave me a raised eyebrow and a theory I had not wanted to consider: "Have you considered that maybe this missing person of yours doesn't want to be found?"

Masha assured me the well-trodden dirt path she pointed out was a safe route, even in the dark, and would take me directly to the front gates of the Chobe Game Lodge, after which point it would simply be a matter of following a paved thoroughfare. It took me about half an hour to make the trip, including a few stops to listen for wild beasts which, I was thankful, never materialized.

Unlike Mashatu's rustic appearance, Chobe's architecture was Moorish elegance with a wide, sweeping roadway leading up to the main building. I found a spot in a clump of nearby bushes from where I could case out the dimly lit front entry and consider my next move. I knew from what Masha (whose son and two sisters worked there) had told me, that all the rooms in the lodge overlooked the Chobe River and adjacent Caprivi flood plain, which meant my easiest and only land access would be from this side of the building. The question was, how to do so without drawing unwanted attention. I had no idea if Jaegar—or any other bad guy—was waiting to pounce on me, and I certainly didn't want to find out.

Over the next twenty minutes I witnessed very little activity other than one or two hand-holding couples heading in the direction of their guest rooms, located in one of the two-storey arms which reached out from either end of the main structure. I crouched some more, my legs growing numb, waiting until I was absolutely convinced there was no one else around. And then, from somewhere behind me, I heard a rustling sound.

Awwwww maaaaaaaan! Jaegar? Security guard? Lion? Elephant? Godzilla?

Bit by bit I rose to my feet, coaxing blood back into them.

There it was again!

Slowly I turned on the spot and peered into the black ink around me.

More furtive shuffling, feet astir. There was definitely someone in the bushes behind me.

"Who's there?" I called out in a forceful whisper, hoping the perpetrator of the noises knew English.

No answer.

Then, I heard an unearthly grunting and the sound of running feet!

Whoever it was, was taking a run at me!

It was too dark by far to see what was happening, who was coming after me. Run? Hide? Grab a stick? But before I had time to react I saw a hideous piece of wrinkled skin and coarse hair emerge from the blackness. The thing raced toward me. I jumped back, horrified. My breath caught as my eyes made contact with two tiny, piercing, evil-looking, red orbs: The eyes of ... a warthog.

I heard a sound erupt from my open mouth and the animal sped away, disappearing as quickly as it had appeared. "Yeah, you better run, you son-of-a-bitch pig!" I cursed at the beast with ersatz bravado.

I'd had about enough of playing Marlin Perkins on *Mutual of Omaha's Wild Kingdom*. I wanted indoors. Sure I was raised on a farm—with squealing pigs and docile cows and clucking chickens and other animals around—but few of them were capable of eating me, and none of them ran around wild, with nasty-looking under bites and smelling like carrion, scaring the bejeebers out of people. (Then again, there was Mr. Crow.)

I glanced at the welcoming façade of the Chobe guest house. If I were to waltz in, who was to know I wasn't a paying guest? And if Chobe ran its morning safari drives as early as Mashatu did, chances were it was late enough by now that most guests were tucked away in bed, and the only folks hanging about would be staff; which was good for me, because that's who I wanted to talk to anyway.

I'd seen no sign of Jaegar or the dark SUV with the evil grille or anyone else untoward. So, eager to avoid any further *Hakuna Matata* moments, I took a deep breath, checked my immediate surroundings one more time for lurking malevolence, then, satisfied I was alone and unwatched, marched determinedly toward the front entrance of the lodge (my ears at the ready to detect any scampering hog hooves behind, in front or anywhere around me—damn pig).

Although it took only a moment, it seemed like an eternity before I was inside the building with its graceful high arches, barrel-vaulted ceilings, tiled floors, charming sitting areas filled with thick-cushioned rattan furniture, and walls covered in stunning tribal art. Ahhhh, much nicer than the bush.

I began to walk about. The place was quieter than a cloistered convent on Saturday karaoke night. I reached the reception desk. Unmanned. I wandered further and found that all the large public areas were completely empty. Down a hallway opposite the front desk I discovered an activities office and a curio shop, both locked up tight. Across from the office, adjacent to a narrow set of steps leading to a second floor, a sign told me that this was the way to the Chobe Lodge spa. Bingo! I'd learned from the women at Mashatu that Matthew Moxley's boyfriend, Kevan, was a masseur at Chobe. This had to be where he worked. And if not, I was definitely up for a good rub by some guy named Falcon right about then; it was a win-win situation.

I *Pink Panther*-ed my way up the stairs and into a hallway so dark I could step into oblivion and never know it. Using my hands to guide me, I slid along the wall until I finally reached a doorknob and turned it. Locked. Crap. It was obviously after hours and I'd find no Kevan here. Yet. I debated breaking in, just to find what I could find, but decided against it, thinking there'd likely be little of a personal or revealing nature in an empty spa.

I Brailled my way back downstairs, and tiptoed into the reception foyer I'd come through on my way in, but instead of turning right to leave, I turned the opposite way into the bowels of the lodge. Down two steps and to the left was a large landing with a collection of couches and chairs, and to the right a cocktail lounge, closed for business. Another two steps down was still another dimly lit sitting area that overlooked the grounds and, I guessed, the river, although I couldn't see much under the cloak of nighttime. To the right was a wide corridor that led to a dining area, also faintly lit and deserted. I slowly made my way down the walkway and entered the dining room where I caught sight of my first human: a uniformed woman setting tables for breakfast.

I approached her with a cautious hello and she looked up with an expressionless face. "Can I help you, *Rra*?" she asked with a tone that was flat but still hinted at the singsong accent that I'd come to associate with many African dialects.

"I hope so," I answered. "I'm a guest here," I began, hoping that bit of information would make her feel a bit more obliged to help me out, "and I wanted to book a massage with Kevan, but I can't find him and no one seems to be at the front desk. Do you happen to know where I might find him or what his room number is?" I was going for gold.

"Kevan, you say, *Rra*? Sure, he's here but he won't be giving no massages until tomorrow morning. It's late now; you should get some sleep."

I felt that little thing that gurgles in my stomach when I get excited. Although I'd been told Kevan worked here, I'd been sent on wild goose chases before and didn't even end up with a goose. But this woman had just confirmed that Kevan did indeed work here, and if I had Kevan, I had Matthew. "Tomorrow morning? He's here, working at the spa tomorrow morning?"

"Yes," she said breezily, as she laid out utensils around a table for six.

"So tomorrow all I have to do is go right up to the massage studio on the second floor?"

"Yeah, but it could be very busy, *Rra*. You might not get an appointment first thing. You should have booked earlier."

"That's why I was hoping to talk to him tonight." I thought I'd try for that one more time. But by the look on her face, I saw my strategy wasn't going to get me anywhere.

"You should get some sleep now, *Rra*," she suggested again.

She was right. The day had been full and long, and I was suddenly feeling every stressful minute of it. I did need rest, and the thought of returning to the small, stiflingly hot little room in the no-name village in the bush and falling into bed for a good night's rest was a welcome one. I thanked the woman and headed out of the lodge the same way I had come in. I hesitated at the entrance, studying the landscape for anyone (or anything—that means you, warthog) I might not want to run into, but saw nothing suspicious. I dashed across the paved road into the safety of the bushes and made for home.

The trip back took a little longer than the trip there, probably because my feet were dragging, and I had used up every ounce of adrenaline my body had to offer for the day. Fortunately, my five senses were not on total vacation, for I needed some of each of them (except taste) to help me locate the little settlement that had virtually disappeared into the folds of night. Not a light, not a sound, not even a warthog was stirring. I eventually reached the makeshift village and retraced my steps home as best I could, having to backtrack only once. I should have left a trail of mealie bread crumbs.

Having found the lean-to B&B we'd acquired for the night, I gently pushed open the door, hoping I wouldn't wake Cassandra. The room smelled of her perfume, remnants of our stew, and the staleness of dissipating heat. Having walked for thirty minutes in near blackout conditions, my eyes were used to the dark, but inside this windowless, cave-like dwelling, there was no moon to provide contrast between the differing shades of black, and I had to guess where the bed—barely a double—was. It was the only bed and we'd agreed to share it, rather than one of us (me), chivalrously taking to the floor. As I peeled off my shirt and socks I just hoped Cassandra wasn't the kind of gal who slept in the nude, regardless of companion and circumstance (although something told me that was exactly the kind of gal she was).

I lowered my aching, weary bulk onto the low, thin mattress, first sitting on the edge then pulling my feet up to lie down. It was much too hot to need a blanket.

I slowed my breathing and attempted to empty my mind in preparation for sleep that would not come. Something was very wrong.

I caught another scent in the air: the smell of trouble.

With tentative movements I reached for the other side of the bed.

It was empty.

I sat up with a suddenness that made the aged bed creak with complaint. I fumbled around on the bedside table for the oil lamp we'd used earlier over dinner and a box of matches. I struck a match, lit the lamp, and my breath caught in my throat.

I beheld the wretched result of unexpected treachery.

Chapter 13

Cassandra Wellness had vanished.

It was obvious from the destruction in the room that what had happened here had been against her will. The little table where we'd eaten our dinner lay overturned on the floor, the dishes and cutlery strewn about the room. Pieces of clothing, area rugs and wall hangings sat in crumpled heaps. It was amazing I hadn't tripped on any of the debris on my way to the bed in the blinding darkness when I'd first arrived from my jaunt to Chobe.

But why had this happened? Why take Cassandra? Why not wait until I returned and take me? Was this some kind of hostage thing? Was Jaegar—or whoever—going to use Cassandra to get me to do—or not do—whatever they wanted? Or was this something altogether different? Had we been two naïve fools, trusting Masha and the people of this ramshackle village, and now they'd made their foul endgame obvious? But was it obvious? Robbery, I could understand. Even murder for goods would be easier to figure out than this. But to take a human being…why?

I was mad. And confused. In the bitter-smelling, sputtering light of the oil lamp I surveyed the damage more carefully. Things—our things and things belonging to the room—had been tossed about pretty well. But nothing was destroyed, drawers weren't rifled through or searched, it was apparent they hadn't come looking for anything other than what they got—Cassandra. The mess I was seeing had been caused by a ruckus; Cassandra hadn't made it easy for her captors. That's my girl. I only hoped her actions hadn't caused her any physical damage or repercussions from her attackers.

After throwing on a shirt and shoes, and a brief rummage through the wreckage to collect and repack our things, I rushed to get out of that miserable shelter, our bags in tow. It was no longer safe there. Outside, the village was still as black as a new chalkboard, and silent as a crypt. Was everyone truly asleep? Or were they just waiting to make their next move? Or waiting for mine? Judging by the mess, it was doubtful this had happened without some noise, particularly from Cassandra. Had no one heard anything? I suppose if they were complicit in this it wouldn't much matter. Was Masha a part of this? Everyone else? I had a hard time believing it.

I thought about the people who were following me—there was Jaegar, and whoever was in the dark vehicle with the tinted windows and wicked grille, and of course the limping man, whoever he (or she?) was; and then there was the camp manager at Mashatu, Richard Cassoum, and the Jeep driver who'd escaped his vehicle before it exploded. Was everyone in Africa conspiring against me? On that grim, sombre night in the Botswana bush, it sure seemed so.

As I trudged down the grimy streets of the murky village, my eyes darted back and forth with growing suspicion, and I realized I couldn't trust anyone here. Even if someone did have a phone (which I doubted), it wouldn't be safe to ask to use it. My only chance for help was at Chobe Game Lodge.

My exhausted brain cells located a few last drops of battery juice, and I began the long voyage back. Although I was now weighed down by both my own and Cassandra's packs, I jogged most of the way, and used the time to think. I thought about what the hell I was doing out there, scurrying like a bandit through the pitch-black of a sweltering African night, slogging through a case in search of a man who perhaps was never meant to be found, barely knowing where I was, unsure whether I was about to be attacked by some unknown bad guys…or a warthog. But mostly I thought about what to do to help Cassandra Wellness. I had gotten her into this, there was no way I wasn't going to get her out of it. Or die trying.

When I reached the lodge, muscles screaming from the strenuous trip, I dropped into my by-now familiar hiding spot in the bushes just outside the front entrance. I took a moment to catch my breath and massage the most painful spots of my strained body: calves, shoulders and lower back. That done, I poked my head above a convenient frond, and checked out the situation. The place appeared as deserted as when I had left it well over an hour earlier. Coast clear. I hoisted the straps of our gear over my shoulders and traipsed across the road and into the lodge.

I knew I didn't have the time (or patience) to explain to some lodge manager who I was, what had happened to Cassandra, or why, so I quickly dismissed any ideas of finding someone in authority to ask for help. Instead, I used my lock picks to let myself into the first place I hoped would give me access to a phone (and privacy): the activities director's office I'd seen earlier, just off the front foyer.

I closed and locked the door behind me, found a desk lamp to give me some light, and gratefully unloaded the luggage onto the floor. I zipped open my duffle and pulled out a sweater and used it to line the bottom of the door to keep anyone who might pass by from seeing the light. Then I sat behind the desk and lifted the receiver. And there I stopped.

Who to call?

The cops? Where does one find cops in the northern extremity of a national game park? Did 9-1-1 work here? I tried it. Nope.

I felt appallingly exposed, and for a horrible moment I allowed the enormity of the situation to engulf me as if I were drowning in a steaming hot bowl of helpless soup.

Who could I go to for assistance? I did not know how this country worked. My normal resources were too far away to be any good to me. I was so desperate I would have swooned to hear the growling, inhospitable voice of Darren Kirsch at the other end of the phone line.

I gave my head a wild shake, told myself to buck up, to stop feeling sorry for myself and regroup. This sometimes works, sometimes doesn't, but my choices were deplorably few.

I began with my new hero, Roy Hearn in Cape Town.

I dialled the number I had memorized by now and waited as it rang, counting rings off like petals being pulled from a he-loves-me-he-loves-me-not daisy.

But understandably, given the lateness of the hour, he was not answering his phone. He was at home, fast asleep. And probably, I realized with dejection, even if I *did* know anyone else on this entire continent, they probably wouldn't get out of bed to answer their phone either.

What could I do? Cassandra needed help. I needed help to help her, and, perhaps more importantly, I needed to get someone else on her side, someone who would be aware of her situation and prepared to step in should I...well, should Jaegar or someone else make good on their threats against me.

After much trial and error, I finally reached an international operator and directory assistance for the state of Georgia in the United States. There was no listing for a Cassandra Wellness in Atlanta. There were twenty-one listings that included a C. Wellness and eighty-seven more for Wellness with other initials or names attached to them. Crikey. I'd be discovered long before I got through half of them. How could I narrow it down? I had no idea who she lived with, if she was married, nothing.

But I did know one thing about her. I knew why she was in Africa.

I found my way back to a helpful operator who gave me the number for the head offices of *Well-Spotted* magazine in Atlanta. Surely someone there would be able to contact Cassandra's family or use the magazine's contacts in Africa to bring aid to her in these grim circumstances. Surely a magazine that regularly did business in Africa would know people here who could help us. It was a long shot, I knew, but worth a try. Eventually I reached someone (thank goodness for time changes) who connected me to someone who connected me to someone else who mercifully took the time to listen to my story (excluding some of the more sensational bits).

"Oh my," the woman replied at the end of my tale. "That is horrible, sweetie, just horrible. Who did you say you were calling about?"

"Cassandra Wellness," I said with a deep sigh; just the sound of someone from my side of the world gave me relief. "She's on assignment for your magazine, here in Africa. She was scheduled to be at Victoria Falls."

"I'm sorry, hon, but that's not possible. You see, I've never heard of her."

A cold front bit the edges of my heart, but I kept on trying: "She's freelance," I told the woman, "not a full-time employee."

"Doesn't matter, hon. *Well-Spotted* is a magazine for birders. We have nothing to do with safaris or Africa or anything like that. We're all about birdwatching, here in the wonderful U-S-of-A. You interested in that, sweetie? Oh, I guess that doesn't matter to you right now, now does it?" She released a little giggle. "And you see, hon, we don't ever send freelance writers on assignment. We have a full-time staff, who all write their articles from the safety of their own little cubicle. I'm afraid you must have made a mistake."

My throat tightened, and my skin grew hot on my cheeks. "Are you certain?" I asked weakly, my mind racing to swallow the information this woman had just fed me. "Is there another magazine called *Well-Spotted* in Atlanta?"

She gave a little laugh. "I should think not," she answered. "I'm the managing editor here. If there's another magazine out there with the same name, well, they better call their lawyers, sweetie. But I'm pretty sure there isn't." She listened to my silence for a few seconds then added, "I'm sorry, hon, but there is no such person by the name of Cassandra Wellness who works for *Well-Spotted* magazine. I'm afraid someone's been pulling your leg."

She was in on it.

My God, she was in on it!

I carefully laid the phone back down on its cradle and stared at the door.

My ears pumped with the effort of listening for the someone I was certain was on the other side of it, waiting for me.

They knew I was in here.

They knew I was onto them. They knew they had to stop me. They knew they had me. I was vulnerable and alone.

My brain was a salad spinner as I considered my circumstances. Was I being irrational? Maybe, but if nothing else, my paranoia was real enough and I had to find a way to address it.

From the very start of this case, I had had the sense that something was not right about it. Some unknown forces were at work behind the scenes. First, there was the black-hooded figure waiting for me outside of PWC, then Ethan Ash being attacked in his home by the limping man, Jaegar getting on the plane at Sal Island and following me to Mashatu and Chobe, Richard Cassoum, the Mashatu Camp Manager, abandoning me at the Limpopo Airfield, the exploding truck, the seemingly innocent meeting of Cassandra Wellness and her eventual abduction. And now I found out that Cassandra had been lying to me all along. She wasn't who she said she was (of course I wasn't who I told her I was either, but that didn't count). Was all of this some type of trap? Could travel planner Roy Hearn be in on this too, somehow? Was that how Jaegar and Cassandra and the others in the cast of meanies always knew where I was?

And how did my search for Matthew Ridge/Moxley fit into all of this? Who was he really? Who had he become? Was he an innocent in all of this, or, as Cassandra had hinted at earlier, was he somehow complicit in what was going on here? Was she giving me a hint? Had I somehow stumbled into something bigger, more dangerous, than I knew? Bigger than Matthew's mother had reason to suspect?

I eyed the door again and felt a bead of perspiration dribble down my temple. I was being pushed into a corner. Either I had to find a way to escape or be crushed. Or...I could push back. I preferred the sound of that. The one thing I cannot abide is a bully.

The only way to find out what was going on, was to do exactly what I'd come here to do in the first place. I was going to talk to Kevan the masseur tomorrow morning, then I was going to find Matthew Moxley and let the cards fall where they would.

But until then? It was time to face down my paranoia.

I regarded the door once more. I rose from the desk and moved gingerly towards it, feeling an imaginary heat emanating from it, pulling me and resisting me at the same time. I stepped up to it and carefully placed my ear against the cool, wooden surface.

Dead silence.

Of course, no one knew I was here. I'd seen no one looking for me, either of the two times I'd been to Chobe that night. There was no reason to believe I'd been found out. There was no one behind the door. Paranoia be gone!

I knew I needed to get somewhere safe to spend the rest of the night, somewhere I could think, maybe get a couple of hours of shut-eye. That's what my exhausted, sleep-deprived body and mind desperately needed: safety, thinking time and sleep. With those three things, I hoped matters would become clearer in the morning, because they weren't too obvious right then. For some reason unknown to me—yet—Cassandra had set me up, faking her own abduction. She knew I'd return to the village, find her missing, and then what? Did she think I'd make for the river and try to get back to Zambia? Would they be waiting for me at Kasane? Kazungula? The Livingstone airport? Well, I wasn't going to make it that easy for them.

I gathered my things, and, reluctantly, Cassandra's as well; no need to advertise my break-in to the activities director when he or she got there in the morning. I'd take them with me and dump them somewhere less conspicuous. Then I'd use my lock picks and find myself a nice, quiet, unoccupied guest room (even a broom closet would do) to sleep in.

I switched off the light, opened the door and came face to face with the barrel end of a shotgun.

Not so paranoid after all, Quant.

Jaegar.

"Put your hands behind your head," he ordered in a deep voice.

"Uh, what about this stuff?" I hated to be pragmatic at a time like that, but really, my hands were full with knapsacks and duffle bags, mine and Cassandra's.

"Put the bags down…no…hold them."

I guess he realized that if I deposited the bags outside the activities director's office, they'd attract someone's attention sooner or later, and I suspected that that was the last thing he wanted.

"Walk forward," he barked.

I did as directed, and in case I needed further encouragement, I felt the tip of his firearm jab the middle of my back. "Where are we going?" I asked as casually as the situation allowed.

"River."

Oh shit.

Jaegar prodded me along as we marched down the deserted corridors of the lodge, through the front foyer, past the pleasant sitting areas, the bar, the dining room, then down a set of steps that took us into the darkness outside. We made our way past a pool area, landscaped lawns and gardens and finally onto a dirt path that was on a slight decline (which I took to mean we were getting close to the water's edge). I could smell dampness in the air, along with a faint pungency that might have been the scent of blood from a distant lion kill, warthog poop or just my own fear.

When we were far enough away from the lodge that it was unlikely anyone awake at that hour would see us, Jaegar lit a pocket flashlight, which did its best to illuminate the way but only revealed shadows of trees and grasses along the path, and alarmed a few night creatures that scurried out of our way. Eventually, we rounded a bend in the path and I saw a faint light, moving gently up and down, side to side. I soon recognized the source: a lantern on a boat, shifting listlessly in the water alongside a wooden pier.

"Get on," Jaegar ordered when we reached the craft, a large, flat-bottomed thing with a knee-high railing around its circumference and a slightly pitched roof held up at each corner by thin, round stems of metal. I realized this was probably one of the boats used for the lodge's water-based safaris, but somehow I didn't think this voyage was going be a pleasure ride. There was a long, narrow table at the centre of the boat, surrounded by a half dozen of the kind of white, plastic chairs you'd expect to find around a pool or barbecue pit. Huddled beneath a coarse blanket on one of the chairs was Cassandra Wellness. There was only one oil lamp burning on the boat, but it was enough for me to see the look on her face and immediately know that I'd been mistaken about her role in all of this. She was scared.

"What's going on here?" I demanded to know from Jaegar as

he urged me aboard and Cassandra and I exchanged wordless stares.

"Sit down," was his informative reply.

I did as I was told, lowering myself into a seat next to Cassandra. "Are you okay?" I asked in a shushed voice. "What's happening here?"

"This stupid asshole broke into our room; he attacked me, then brought me here," she spit out with enough venom to take down a tyrannosaurus rex.

"Yeah," I said, "I got that. But why? And why didn't the villagers help you? By the look of things you put up quite a fight."

"He had his big, fat hand over my mouth!" she explained, glaring at Jaegar.

Cassandra Wellness was pissed. And when Cassandra Wellness is pissed, everyone is going to know about it. Her eyes came back to mine. "I was so tired after you skulked off that I fell right to sleep. I didn't even know he was there until he was already on top of me. He probably wanted to rape me!" She turned to him again and hissed at his face. "Pervert!" Then back to me. "I couldn't scream, but I kicked things around pretty good."

I could appreciate Cassandra's disgust with our captor, but I needed facts. "How did he know where to find us?"

"He said he followed us," she told me. "But if I were you, I wouldn't believe a word this jerk has to say."

I frowned. "But that's impossible. We saw the truck that pulled up behind us. No one got out of it. They were still in the vehicle watching the Jeep burn when we left."

"He said he followed us," she repeated, pulling the blanket closer around her shoulders. The night had brought coolness and the water surrounding us was adding its own chill. "That's what he said; don't ask me." She was in a generally belligerent mood.

While we talked, I was also keeping a close eye on Jaegar. He had released a rope that bound the boat to the dock and was now using an oar to push the vessel back from the grassy shore with a silence that assured our departure would be unheard and probably unseen. Maybe he just wanted to get far enough away so no one could hear Cassandra calling him a pervert.

"Where are we going?" I stood and demanded to know in a forceful voice, hoping that someone, somewhere might hear me (if they hadn't already heard Cassandra's cussing) and come to see what the ruckus was all about.

"Shut the mouth," he ordered harshly. "And sit!"

He had the gun; I thought it best to comply.

Showing great dexterity with a shotgun in one hand (pointed at yours truly), and the boat's controls (the kind that faced into the boat—and at us—rather than outward from the bow) in the other, Jaegar started the motor. He kept it at a quiet idle, but that was enough to back the boat further away from shore and send it floating down the centre of the wide, listless river. I guess I was wrong earlier. This *was* becoming *The African Queen*.

We travelled this way for several minutes, Cassandra continuing to fume and me trying to get my bearings and figure out an escape plan. The water and sky were black as tar, becoming one at some indistinguishable point. The river was not so wide as to make the shore on either side invisible—in daylight—but at this time of night I could barely make out the vague impression of some unidentifiable shapes that might signify trees and bushes on good old terra firma. But it didn't matter, for I had other measuring sticks that told me we weren't travelling too far from land.

Every so often, the purplish glow of the African moonlight would catch a flash of silver—the watching eyes of night predators on the prowl for supper. The eyes of hyenas, leopards and those damn warthogs. Along with the visual evidence of the hunt came the sounds: low moans, snarls and rumbles born deep within powerful chests; and too, somewhere in the far off distance, I could hear drumming. The African villagers were beating out the traditional rhythms of a time long past but never forgotten. Under other circumstances, this ride would have been a most remarkable experience, magical, unforgettable, but tonight it was a foreboding journey, part of a sinister master plan I'd yet to figure out.

Jaegar throttled down, bringing the boat's engines to a halt. We seemed to be drifting aimlessly until the craft unceremoniously bumped up against a spit of land, a three-metre-by-three-metre island of mud chunks and tall reeds with edges so sharp they looked as if they would slice skin with the slightest pass. I knew we'd departed from Botswana and that the land mass on the opposite shore was Namibia, so that made this little piece of soggy earth in the middle of the Chobe River...up for grabs? Perhaps we'd landed here to lay claim to this desolate, sodden piece of dirt in the name of...Jaegarland?

Jaegar's steps made heavy sounds that reverberated over the calm surface of the water as he made his way to where Cassandra and I sat. With the gun's barrel level with my face, he ordered me to get up.

Dark. Deserted. Gun in my face. Not good.

"No!" Cassandra let out in a tremulous voice, her earlier brashness discarded as she gave in to the gravity of our threatening situation. "What are you doing?"

"It's okay," I lied as I stood, giving her a reassuring look followed by a "come on, you're not really going to shoot me" look for Jaegar.

"Hands up," was his disheartening response.

I did as I was told.

With the front of his gun, SpongeBob SquareHead motioned for me to walk ahead of him to the far end of the boat. I proceeded to the desired spot, my feet moving slowly but my mind racing, frenetically trying to identify ingenious "how am I going to get out of this one?" scenarios. So far all I'd come up with was a quick swim to shore, hoping he was a poor shot.

I reached the edge of the boat, the insubstantial railing the only thing between me and the water.

"If you don't agree to do what I tell you to, I will shoot you and you will fall into the water and you will die," Jaegar said with irritating succinctness. I'd never heard him speak more than a few words at once before, so he must have been practicing this soliloquy for quite some time.

"I'll probably go for the 'doing what you tell me to' thing," I replied, "but can you tell me exactly what that is first, and then I'll decide?" A smart ass to the bitter end.

"Russell, don't fool with this guy," Cassandra warned. "I think he means business."

You *think*?

I couldn't see because my back was to them, but I was hoping Cassandra was sneaking up on Jaegar with a flowerpot or something to hit him over the head with. It worked on *Three's Company*; it could work here.

"What do you want, Jaegar?" I asked. "I really want to know."

"Not what I want," he told me. "What the boss wants."

Interesting. This was beginning to sound kind of *Sopranos*-ish. Maybe Matthew Moxley hadn't changed his stripes so much after all. Maybe he'd become some kind of crime lord and Jaegar was his muscle. "Who's your boss?" I asked, not really expecting an answer. I was surprised with the one I got.

"Christian Wellness."

I slowly rotated on the spot, hands still in the air, and let my eyes move past the considerable bulk of Jaegar to Cassandra Wellness. I couldn't make out much in the muted light given off by the lamp, but I could see enough to know that my fellow prisoner was in as much shock as I was at this tasty tidbit of information. She remained motionless in her seat, then ever so slowly her eyes made for the floor.

"Relative?" I asked, sucking in my cheeks, seeing as I was too far away to bite off her head.

"My husband," she answered in a muffled voice after a moment of stunned silence.

"This is what he wants," Jaegar interrupted our lovely chat.

"Okay, spill it," I said, feeling more than a little pinch of irritability in the knotted space between my eyes.

Jaegar began. "He wants you to be so very much scared that you are going to run so fast no one will see you. And you run so far you will never see his wife again. If you don't agree to this, I will shoot you. And if the bullet doesn't get you, the hippopotamus will."

I almost laughed. It was not just the way the word hippopotamus sounded in his thick Germanic accent, but really, "The hippopotamus will get me?" I was pretty certain I could outrun or outswim a roly-poly hippo.

Jaegar must have seen the skepticism in my face and sensed

the lack of seriousness with which I was taking his threat, so he added, "Hippopotamus are the most dangerous animal in the water in Africa. Not snake. Not crocodile," he said darkly. "Hippopotamus." He smiled then, as if in respect for their reputation. "They will snap you in half with their jaws, just because they can."

"It's true, Russell," Cassandra said in a sombre voice.

I glanced over my shoulder at the black swill of water below me and rapidly changed my mind about that swim to shore.

"Who are you?" I called to Cassandra in not the friendliest of tones.

"Russell, I'm sorry," she said, moving to get up.

"Sit!" Jaegar commanded and she complied.

"My husband is...my husband is Christian Wellness, and we live in Atlanta but...but...I don't work for a magazine," she said contritely, but for me, well, it was a little too little a little too late.

I swore under my breath and reconsidered diving into the river, just to get away from these two.

"But I do love to take pictures," she added brightly. "And I do love adventure, and I do love Africa. It's just that I need to get away sometime, by myself, to be the girl I was in college instead of this stuffy, proper, southern wife of a stuffy, proper, rich, southern man." She looked at me and didn't see what she hoped for and kept going. "You have to believe me, Russell, I had no idea this big oaf worked for my husband or why he was following us. I've never seen him before in my life." She turned and gave Jaegar a disgusted look. "And I hope I never see him again after tonight." Back to me. "Christian has never done anything like this before."

"Before?" She'd obviously taken an unannounced powder from her proper, southern life on more than one occasion.

She ignored the question. "Usually when I go away, I have some fun, do some things, then I go back home. I always go back home. He yells, he forgives me, and we go on. But this time...this time..."

"He'd had enough," I concluded. I didn't disagree with him.

I looked hard at Cassandra Wellness and wondered why I'd been so attracted to her. Yes, I enjoy her type of personality: bold, brash, adventurous, a force of nature. But, I realized, I hadn't gotten involved with her because I'd foolishly been drawn to her, pursuing her like some lovestruck puppy, but rather because she had pulled me in with a leash of her own design. As I watched her wring her hands, her brows knitted with worry, I knew I liked her still, but I no longer admired her.

"I suppose so," she agreed meekly. "I told him I come to Africa because I love the country, the people, the culture, the food, the vibe of its cities, and all of that is true. But I presume he must have come to suspect that I come here for something more—to be with other men. Obviously he sent his henchman to find out for sure." She turned on Jaegar once more. "But you've made a big mistake, you goon. You have it all wrong." Then back at me. "I guess he saw us hanging around and, well, assumed the worst."

Oh really, sister? Our short-lived drunken dalliance in Cape Town flashed through my head like a dirty movie. I focused on Cassandra's face. Her lips were saying one thing, her eyes quite another. She was asking me to protect her, to lie for her, to pretend that what her husband suspected of her wasn't true, when indeed it was. Regardless of the fact that we hadn't actually had sex, the lack of touchdown had nothing to do with Cassandra's unwillingness. Christian Wellness had good reason to be distrustful of his beautiful wife. The question was, on whose side would I come down? I regarded Jaegar. I debated trying to convince the big lug that I was gay and could never want what Christian Wellness suspected I wanted from his wife. But really, what was the point? It's not as if I carry around a gay membership card to prove my preference. There was only one, efficient way out of this mess.

I shifted position and looked Jaegar in the eye. "I'm gonna do what you told me to. I'm very scared and I'm gonna run away very fast and very far." I nodded towards shore. "As soon as you get us back to dry land." I heard Cassandra give a squeak of consternation, but I didn't really care. "How about it?"

Jaegar searched my face for deception, then shifted his gaze to Cassandra. I could have jumped him at that point. But nah, I was pretty certain this was over, that I wasn't about to become hippo chow. This was all about Christian Wellness hiring a thug to scare the pants off his wife and the man she was fooling around with; this wasn't about murder. Studying the look on Jaegar's face closely for the first time, I doubted the big German was even capable of killing anyone.

That's when the shooting started.

Chapter 14

As we scrambled for cover from the spray of bullets biting the boat, we simultaneously realized there was precious little to be had. We were fully exposed on a flat, floating piece of wood (or whatever the damn thing was made of) with nothing to hide behind except the podium that housed the controls. Jaegar seemed intent on hogging that spot all to himself, and given the look of horror on his face, I was quite certain he wasn't about to give it up. Fortunately, even though bullets were zigging and zagging all over the place like in a *Dick Tracy* comic strip, the shooters were either particularly bad shots or having a hard time getting a bead on us in the dark all the way from shore.

"The lamp!" I called out to Jaegar, who was closest to it. "Extinguish the lamp!" My hope was that with no light to draw attention to our position in the water, maybe they'd give up their midnight hunt as hopeless.

But Jaegar was useless, frozen with fear into a balled up position. I was right about the guy; he really *was* just a big old teddy bear on the inside—a useless, pansy-ass, fluffy-eared, cotton-hearted teddy bear. I would have to do it. The boat wasn't that big. Jaegar and the lamp weren't that far away.

I laid a hand on Cassandra's head, which was plastered against the floor like gum to a shoe, and laid my lips against her exposed ear. "It's gonna be okay," I whispered.

She turned her head ever so slightly and gave me an "Are you insane? People are shooting at us!" look. Justified, I suppose.

"Stay here," I ordered. "And don't move a muscle."

"Don't worry," she managed through lips squashed against the bottom of the boat.

"I'm going to try to get to the lamp," I said to no one in particular.

She mumbled something that did not sound anything like, "Be careful, Russell" or "You're my hero, Russell," but I could be wrong about that.

Leaving Cassandra's side, I slithered off, as close to the ground as I could get, and alligatored my way toward Jaegar and the offending lamp. The big guy's eyes were shut tight, probably with the childish hope that if he didn't see them, they couldn't see him. Idiot. I noticed his hands were wrapped around himself. Where was the gun? Jaegar might not be in the mood to do any shooting back, but I certainly was. But the firearm was nowhere to be seen. Was he lying on it? I finally reached his side and lay next to him like a reluctant lover, waiting for cessation in gunfire before reaching up for the wick knob of the lamp, positioned on a ledge just above his head.

"How're you doing?" I asked him. I wasn't totally devoid of sympathy for the bruiser, even though he had just threatened to push me overboard.

"They're not trying to hit us," Jaegar managed to get out from between gritted teeth, his eyes opening a sliver. "If we stay down and out of the way we won't be shot."

Uh, excuse me, did you notice the bullets? "What are you talking about?"

"They are aiming for the engine. Easier to hit."

"Oh shit," I heard Cassandra proclaim.

I agreed, but wasn't quite up to snuff on the import of what he'd said.

"They want us dead in the water," Cassandra uttered, a trail of dread following her words like slime from a snail.

The phrase sounded worse than the reality. So what if our engine got knocked out? Given the choice, I'd rather the engine take one for the team than me get a hot piece of lead in my butt cheek. Or worse.

"Couldn't we just release the anchor," I suggested, "or whatever it is that's keeping us tied to this bloody island, and float away from these guys?"

"If the boat goes adrift, if we cannot use the motor and steer it away, it will float into hippopotamus territory," Jaegar explained, sounding a lot like Arnold Schwarzenegger with a particularly difficult script line to deliver.

"I thought we *were* in hippo territory," I countered, then added with a bit of sass, "Remember when you were gonna feed me to them?"

Jaegar shook his head. "I lied." He motioned with his head to somewhere up river and closer to the shoreline. "Over there is where the hippopotamus live. They are everywhere. They float below the water…"

"Did you know hippopotamus can hold their breaths for several minutes?" This helpful bit of information came from the prone body (but not so prone lips) of Cassandra. It was beginning to dawn on me what it was they were getting at, but I didn't want to let it in just yet.

"You never know they are there," Jaegar continued as if telling a scary story around a campfire. "They come up below boat. Without motor we cannot get away. If boat is small enough—a boat like this—they will capsize it, and throw us into the water. And they will attack. And we will die."

I did not particularly like this story. "So we stay here then. We won't let the boat go adrift."

"Doesn't matter," Cassandra said with resignation.

"They will come," Jaegar agreed. "The hippopotamus will come for us. Without motor, we cannot escape."

Oh dear.

"So, we can't drive this thing outta here because they'll shoot us. If we set ourselves adrift the hippos will get us. If we stay the way we are and they shoot out our engine the hippos will still get us. Do I have the situation pretty much summed up? Basically you're saying, we're damned if we do, damned if we don't? Is that about it?"

Jaegar shrugged his agreement.

"Who are these bastards who are shooting at us anyways?"

Cassandra demanded, as if one of us should know. It was obvious they weren't friends of Jaegar's. And certainly not mine. "Why are they doing this? Are they marauders of some sort?"

"Not robbers," Jaegar said. "They would want the boat, and the engine, for themselves, not destroyed by their guns."

"Then who?"

Jaegar and I exchanged looks.

"These might be the same people who blew up the Jeep," I said, knowing Jaegar had seen exactly what we had. "They want us dead. They want *me* dead. By gunfire or hippo; one way or the other."

I knew that if we were going to get out of this without ending up full of holes or as hippo chow, we needed to stop the shooting and save our engine.

"Where's the gun?" I asked Jaegar.

He didn't answer immediately, which I took to be a sign that he either didn't know or didn't want to tell me. The bullets were whizzing through the air with alarming regularity. I'd been unable to find a break in the gunfire to reach up to extinguish the lamp. I feared our time was running out. I repeated the question. "Jaegar, where is the gun? We have to defend ourselves; we have to defend the engine!"

"I don't know," was his mumbled reply.

"What do you mean? You just had it. I saw it. It was very close to my face as a matter of fact."

"It is gone."

"I'm afraid I'm going to have to ask you to be a little bit more specific than that," I said through tight lips, barely keeping my frustration in check. "I don't have to do the shooting if you don't want me to have the gun. If that's the problem, I can understand that, but somebody needs to start shooting back. Now!" Another especially vociferous volley of gunfire punctuated my point.

"It is gone," he said, "overboard."

Cassandra weighed in with an, "Oh fuck."

"It fell into water when I hit the floor," he explained.

I had to concur with Cassandra's take on the situation.

The shooting stopped momentarily. Maybe they were reloading. It was time for Plan B, which, come to think of it, was why I was spooning with this German hooligan in the first place.

Finding my mark first with my eyes, I rapidly reached up, found the lamp's knob and turned it to extinguish the flame, throwing us and the boat, mercifully, into total blackness. "Shhh," I told the others.

They shushed and we listened.

Immediately the sound of gunfire resumed, filling the air with its deadly retort, then began to peter out, and, eventually, halted.

For a moment, the echo of bullets zipping over our heads remained with us, then that too was gone. Plan B had worked. I was tentatively and quietly elated. I'm sure the others were too, but the only thing I could hear in the damp, dark air was the jagged, uneasy breathing of Jaegar and Cassandra. Mine too.

For a long time we lay there in the belly of that boat, not daring to move because there was a chance the shooters were still out there, waiting for us to show ourselves. We did not talk, afraid the sound of our voices would carry over water and act as a targeting device. We breathed. In and out. In and out.

We waited.

And waited some more.

Although my head told me it might still be too soon, my aching muscles could no longer stay in the same position. Inch by painful inch, I raised myself up until I was resting on numb forearms and elbows. My head bobbed above my shoulders, at the ready to disappear like a turtle into its shell at the first sign of gunfire. It was still black as crow out there, and scanning the horizon did little to appease my concern that we might still not be alone.

"It will be light soon," I heard Jaegar whisper from the shadows.

"He's right," this from Cassandra.

Obviously neither of them had fallen asleep either. Who could?

I slipped back down into my position as a human rug and waited for dawn.

In the end, despite the seemingly endless barrage of bullets, all of us—the engine included—came away without injury. The distance from shore to boat must have been too great for whatever type of weapons they were using, and I guessed there were probably a good number of unfortunate fish with lead in their bellies in the water below us.

In some peculiar way, our harrowing escapade had knit us together as a trio with a common goal rather than the original gun-toting maniac against two captives. With the first light of dawn, Jaegar recovered enough to get us and the boat to shore, returning to the same spot at the base of the Chobe camp where we'd left from the night before. It might not have been the wisest move, but none of us knew the river well enough to know where else to go. Jaegar's original plan was to take Cassandra and me to the little island in the middle of the Chobe River, scare me into agreeing to stop seeing Mrs. Wellness, scare Mrs. Wellness into agreeing to stop bumping bellies with me or anyone else ever again, then take us back. Nowhere in his plan was there a harried escape down the convoluted waterways of Africa. We all knew what a hard time Humphrey Bogart and Katharine Hepburn had had of it, and none of us was in the mood to try it for ourselves.

When we arrived at the shore, with barely a word shared between us during the return trip, the sun was just poking its cheery head above a gloomy horizon congested with a melancholy blue haze. The air was chill and oddly flavoured with the scent of stale mud, hickory fire and fresh coffee. The fine folks at Chobe were oblivious to the adventure in terror carried out not far from their safe bedroom suites. Back on dry, hard earth, we unanimously agreed that we did not feel safe remaining at Chobe. Obviously the gunmen—whoever they were—knew it as a place where we might be found should they want to make good on their marksmanship. We were fortunate enough to land the scow without a greeting from an unwelcome landing party with guns, but it would be plain stupidity to press our luck by hanging around.

With no other obvious choice, the three of us made the trek back to the village where Cassandra and I had planned to spend the night in the first place. As far as we knew, only Jaegar had successfully tracked us there.

"So that wasn't you in the black truck that pulled up behind the burning Jeep?" I asked as we trudged along the uneven path, having gotten far enough away from Chobe to conclude we weren't being followed and could risk making some noise other than the sound of our feet.

"No," Jaegar answered. "I have no truck when I cross the water."

That jibed with his earlier story that he was working for Cassandra's husband. He'd turned up at Livingstone airport because he was following Cassandra, not me; he'd lost my trail in Mashatu; there had been no collusion with Richard Cassoum, the camp manager. That being true, Jaegar couldn't have known where we were going, and to have a truck on the other side of the river after we left Zambia would have meant he wasn't working alone—or was a very convincing and speedy negotiator, which I doubted. He'd made it across the river on the speedboat, but then what? "So how did you find Cassandra in the village?"

"I run. I get off the boat and I run. This was my only chance to catch you."

I grunted. His chances were darn good, I thought to myself, given the lightning speed (not) at which the vehicles around this place seem to travel.

"I run to where the Jeep burns," Jaegar recounted his chase. "I saw you in bushes. Hiding. I was in bushes too."

Of course. He hadn't been in the mean-looking SUV that pulled up just after our Jeep exploded, but rather far enough behind and in the perfect position to witness our escape. We'd been too focused on trying to avoid being seen by whoever was in the black-hearted truck to notice him.

"Why Sal Island?" I questioned, now that he was in a talkative mood. "And why follow me to Mashatu when Cassandra wasn't even with me?"

"I start by following Mrs. Wellness. Until I learn about you. Then I chase you."

"But why me?"

"You were together on plane. You were together in Cape Town.

You were the one. The lover. It was you Mr. Wellness wanted me to scare off. So I chase you."

Jaegar was better at his job than I gave him credit for. Had he found some way to see into my room? Did he catch me with my hands and mouth where they shouldn't have been on that drunken night at the Table Bay Hotel? Or was he bluffing? I didn't think I'd ever learn the answer to that one. "That still doesn't explain why you got on the plane at Sal Island. If you were hired by Cassandra's husband, I assume you live in Atlanta, right? And I didn't even know Cassandra yet. You couldn't have suspected me yet."

"I take a different flight from Atlanta. I then wait for Mrs. Wellness's plane in Sal. I get on at Sal to avoid as much as possible being seen by her until I find out about the man she is meeting with. But I didn't have to wait until she get to Africa. You were already sitting with her on the plane."

That was true. It was all innocent, but I could see how he could make the mistake…well, sort of mistake.

"Would you two twerps stop talking about me as if I'm not here?" Cassandra piped up with a flip of her hair, her voice dripping with molten lava. "Or better yet, stop talking altogether. I'm sick of discussing this. Let's just get back to the room and get some sleep. I am so bloody tired, I'm about to drop on the spot and use one of you for a pillow. If I hear one more peep out of either of you, that's exactly what I'm going to do!"

The rest of the trip was spent in quiet contemplation. For some reason I was still carrying both my luggage and Cassandra's.

We spent what was left of the night (or rather, early morning) in our messed up little hovel. Cassandra was no longer in the frame of mind for sharing the bed (which was too small for all three of us anyway), leaving Jaegar and me to snuggle up on the floor at her feet (which I think she took perverse pleasure in).

Later that morning, with little protest, for she knew the jig was up and it was time to face the music, Cassandra agreed to accompany Jaegar back to Livingstone, and eventually home to Atlanta.

We were at the Kasane jetty when she hugged me goodbye for the last time.

"The only part of marriage I enjoy," she whispered into my ear as we embraced, "is escaping it."

I pulled back and looked at her in dismay.

"Take my word for it, Mayor Russell," her voice huskier than usual that morning, "never surrender adventure for the simple life."

Cassandra stepped away and allowed Jaegar to help her into the waiting speedboat. As the sputtering craft began its short voyage across the Zambezi, neither passenger looked back. I felt a murmur of sadness run through me as I watched her being taken away. Cassandra Wellness was a wild animal of Africa, captured and being returned to the cage of domesticated marriage.

Good luck with that.

I returned to the village to collect my things and tidy up the small room as best I could. I was preparing to head out when Masha came in with a bowl of fresh, sliced fruit for my breakfast. Where she got fresh fruit in the middle of that arid land, I do not know, but I ate it ravenously and with gratitude.

With renewed energy and hope for a successful day, I set out with my bags in hand and once again made the by now all-too-familiar trip back to Chobe. I had unfinished business there.

When I entered the front lobby of the main lodge building, it was busier than before, but not by much; mostly scurrying employees doing whatever scurrying employees do. Most of the guests had either gone off on morning game drives or water safaris or were lazing over a leisurely, late breakfast in the dining room.

I headed directly up the set of stairs that I knew would take me to the second level where Matthew Moxley's boyfriend worked as a masseur. The dismal break-of-day sky to which we'd awakened on the boat, seemingly forever ago, had disappeared. It was a warm, cloudless day and sunshine filled the hallway that led to

Kevan's work area. A pleasing scent of jasmine, lavender and something spicy mixed together beckoned me to the room, and I could just make out the pleasant tinkling of spa-muzak as I padded toward the open doorway of the massage room.

I stepped into a small, square room that acted as a waiting area. Empty. A door to my right was partially open and I laid a hand against it to push it inwards. This room was also empty. But I was definitely in the right place, and quite a lovely place it was. In the middle of the room, surrounded by the tools of a masseur's trade—luxurious white towels, sparkling stainless steel receptacles of various sizes for various purposes, bottles and jars of creams and lotions and oils, tissues and cotton batting and pillows and other soft things—was a massage table. Beyond the table, a set of double doors, open to an outdoor balcony brimming with potted plants and a bistro table with two chairs, invited one to sit down for a chilled glass of iced tea or lemonade. A playful breeze floated through the room, promising a hint of coolness in the typically hot climate. It was a charming, pleasant place to spend one's work day.

"Hello. Can I help you? Would you like to make an appointment?" The voice was soft and low and, like the breeze, contained a hint of coolness.

I turned to face a man who'd just come through the doorway. He was holding a cup of steaming tea in one hand and a plate of crusty lumps of dough in the other. He was a unique looking man with a long, narrow face that would have appeared feminine were it not for the strong angles of his cheekbones and flared jaw line and a generous nose and forehead. His head was shaved and by the strain of the white polo shirt across his chest and arms I could tell he was an athlete, or at least someone who paid close attention to his physical fitness. His skin darkened to near black around hooded eyes, giving him a look of mystery, offset by the warm curve of a smile which was, at the moment, only tentative as he regarded me.

"Are you Kevan?" I asked, although I was almost certain of the answer.

He nodded, suspicion washing over his face. "I am. Kevan

Badanga. And you are?"

"I am Russell Quant."

Kevan's eyes moved away from me momentarily as he looked for a place to set down his tea and biscuits. When that was done he wiped his hands against each other as if preparing to use them for...?

"I'm a..."

He cut me off. "I know who you are."

I cocked my head to the side as if it might help to figure that one out. A trick I'd learned from Barbra.

"You were in Khayelitsha," he said in explanation. "Looking for Matt."

Surprise spread over my face. And just how did he know that? I was finding out that in Africa, news travels faster than Jeeps. This certainly made things a bit easier if I didn't have to explain myself to him. "That's right. Do you know where he is?"

"You must be joking," Kevan said, a slight snarl curling his upper lip.

This man did not like me, and he was not trying to conceal it. "I don't understand."

"After what you did in Khayelitsha, you expect me to help you?" he said, his voice incredulous.

"I'm sorry, Kevan," I said, truly dumfounded. "I don't know what you're talking about. I went to Khayelitsha looking for Matt, your boyfriend. They told me he was working in Tuli Block, so here I am."

"You cleverly omitted telling them *why* you are looking for Matt," he said accusingly. "You must want to see him pretty badly, to do what you did."

I frowned. "To do what I did? All I did was ask a few questions."

"Is it your intention to do the same today?" he spit out at me. I saw his mighty arm muscles flex. "Are you going to ask me a few questions?" He said it as if the words were a euphemism for something completely different. "I warn you; I will not be as helpless a victim."

I held up both hands in a defensive gesture. "Wait, wait, wait,

Kevan, I think you have the wrong guy here. Just what is it you think happened in Khayelitsha?"

Kevan let out a humourless snort of laughter. "You did the same thing there. Pretending to be innocent. Well, let me tell you, I am not believing it."

"Believing what?" This guy was talking circles around me, and I was getting dizzy trying to figure out what was going on.

"You left the Chikosi house as if it were over," he said. "But then you came back, later, without your Afrikaner guide. And then you tried to beat the information you wanted out of them."

I stood staring at him, for the moment stunned into silence.

"Why did you do it?" he demanded to know. "They'd told you everything they knew. They had nothing left to tell you. The Chikosis are good people, kind people, yet you tortured them to get information they did not have."

My brain was whirring with this new information. Who could have done this? Jaegar? But why? Cassandra had been with me that night in Khayelitsha; there was no reason for him to attack the people whose home we visited. What about Joseph, our guide? That made even less sense. No, this was someone else. Something about this felt...hauntingly familiar.

I put a hand against the well-padded massage table to steady myself. "The Chikosis...are they...all right?"

Kevan's eyes grew narrow as he weighed the motive for my question. Was it concern? Was I being sincere? Was it possible that I was not responsible for what happened to these people? Or was I trying to trick him? He began slowly, "Piksteel, he was badly beaten." He registered the upset on my face and continued. "Thandile, less so. Her injuries were mostly due to her own attack on the man, as she attempted to protect her husband. Piksteel will lose an eye, but he will live."

I winced at the words. My God. The man would lose an eye. Had I done this? Had I somehow led this brutality and violence into the home of these innocent people? Of course I had not physically carried out the appalling deed, but if this was somehow related to my case, related to the fact that I had been in the Chikosi's home, then I did bear some responsibility.

"Your face," Kevan commented, stepping closer and staring at me.

I stared back, saying nothing.

"There are no scratches."

I shook my head, not sure what he was getting at.

"Walk," he said simply.

Another head shake, not understanding.

"Walk," he repeated.

I did as he asked, taking a stroll to the balcony doors then back to my original spot.

He released a frustrated huff of air. The features of his unusual face were drawn into those of someone trying to fit a round peg into a square hole, and knowing it was futile.

"Again."

I complied, feeling a little like a circus animal.

"You do not walk with a limp," he noted, intently assessing my legs.

My heart began to race as an ugly, rotting déjà vu invaded my insides like a fast spreading disease.

"The man who attacked these people, the only things the Chikosis could tell us about him was that he walked with a limp." He hesitated for a moment, then added, "And Thandile, she is quite certain she scratched the man's face beneath his balaclava, with her fingernails. Deep. Yet you have no scars. You do not walk with a limp."

Oh good lord. What was happening here? The Chikosis had been attacked after talking to me. Just like Ethan Ash. By a man with a limp. Just like Ethan Ash. Ethan's attack happened thousands of miles away in Saskatoon, on the other side of the world, but I knew this was no mere coincidence. I had heard someone with a limp following me in Cape Town. Could it be the same man? If it was, there were so many new questions that needed answering. Who hired him? Why? And how is what happened to the Chikosis and Ethan Ash related?

"I am surprised to see you here," Kevan said. There was something about his voice and face that made me think he was softening toward me, maybe beginning to believe I truly had not been aware of the goings on in Khayelitsha.

I was about to ask why he was surprised to see me, but as I looked him in the eye, I knew.

Ubuntu.

All of this was because of *ubuntu*: Richard Cassoum, the camp manager at Mashatu, arranging to have me abandoned at the Limpopo airfield; the men who blew up the Jeep after Cassandra and I crossed the Zambezi; the gunmen shooting at us on the Chobe River—none of it was Jaegar or local criminals or anyone else. All of these acts were perpetrated by men intent on ridding Africa of a bad man who'd visited pain and suffering upon its people. And that bad man was...Russell Quant.

It was *ubuntu* at work, from the township of Khayelitsha in South Africa to Zambia to Botswana; it was *ubuntu*. An overwhelming sense of community, humanity; *I am what I am because of who we all are.* Like the stolen camera case in Khayelitsha, no bad deed against anyone is perpetrated without consequence, otherwise all bad deeds against humanity will flourish.

"*Ubuntu,*" I said it aloud.

Kevan Badanga looked taken aback to hear the word coming from my mouth. As a native, he probably practiced *ubuntu* so thoughtlessly that he rarely connected it to his actions or the actions of those around him. His eyes warmed even further and his heavy jaw moved up and down in silent accord.

"That's just crap!" I responded, surprising him. "They almost killed us!" I protested. "Blowing up our Jeep! Shooting at us! That doesn't sound like the *ubuntu* I heard about from Joseph. The way I learned it, the spirit of *ubuntu* helped keep peace in post-apartheid years; it's not supposed to be about bloodshed and killing—it's about understanding and forgiveness and humanity towards one another. That sure as hell is not what I've been through these last few days!" I fumed. "We could have died!"

Kevan nodded sadly. "The Jeep was a grave mistake. I apologize to you," he said with humility, taking responsibility for something that very likely was far from his own doing. "It was only meant to scare you, but the charges were too strong and the men over-zealous."

My eyes grew wide, still in awe that so many people over so many miles of African countryside had joined together to thwart me. "The people in the SUV with the evil grille? The driver of the Jeep that exploded? All in on it?"

"Yes," he admitted.

"And using us for target practice last night? What about that?"

"They would not have hurt you, those men," he told me. "The guns they used were loaded with blanks, or else they were firing high in the air. They were only meaning to scare you and your friends away. The big man and the woman, we did not know who they were, but if they were with you, we knew they too were dangerous. You have to understand. You were responsible for what happened to the Chikosis. And now you were in Chobe, looking for me and for Matt. You were too close. It could not be allowed."

I stared at him, as unwilling to believe him as he had been unwilling to believe me. "But I heard them! I heard those bullets whiz by my ear." I could still hear them as I spoke.

A small smile crept onto his lips. "But were you hit? Were either of your friends or the boat hit?"

Got me there.

"But you are a determined man, Russell Quant. You do not scare easily." He came a step nearer to me, as if seeing me up close would confirm his growing notion that perhaps I was not the bad man he'd been told I was. "We are all related," he said. "When the beatings took place, the story began to pass from mouth to mouth, of how a man and woman from North America had come to the townships in search of a man many of them knew well, Matthew Moxley, and how this couple was willing to use great violence to find him. If this man and woman were willing to do such a horrible thing to the people whose home Matthew once shared, what would they do to others as they continued their search? What would they do when they finally found Matthew? It set in motion a chain of events meant to drive you away from your purpose, away from Africa.

"Over the years, Matthew lived in Khayelitsha many times. He had many friends and loved ones there. When the beating of Thandile and Piksteel was discovered—the same night you had been in their home—and they told their story, the community of Matthew's friends—his African family—banded together. Thandile had made a terrible mistake. She'd told you, the man she was certain was their attacker, that Matthew was in Mashatu. The people immediately contacted Mashatu to warn Matthew. The camp manager, Mr. Cassoum, told them not to worry, that Matthew had gone to work at Chobe, and this terrible man would not find Matthew there. Even so, they made him promise that he and his staff would do whatever they could to divert you from finding out anything about Matthew. Of course, you did find out that Matthew had gone to Chobe, and when Mr. Cassoum discovered this, he contacted me, as well as Matthew's friends in the township. The people in Khayelitsha felt the circumstances had grown dire, and they made the plan to have you stopped."

I shook my head. "I did not do this thing, Kevan, but I can't explain it either. I do not know who did this, or why." I considered telling Matthew Moxley's current boyfriend about the suspicious link to the limping man in Saskatoon who assaulted Matthew Moxley's former boyfriend, but it seemed it would only cloud matters further at this point.

"This was no random act of violence," I admitted. "And the timing could not have been better to implicate me, but…well, I don't know what else to say. What else can I tell you to convince you that I had nothing to do with the attack on the Chikosis?"

"You can tell me why you are truly here."

"I told you," I began. "I'm looking for Matthew Moxley."

"That much I know," he answered back. "That much we all know. What we do not know is why."

Was this to be a stalemate? Him not believing I was innocent, and me unable to prove my innocence in the only way he could accept. My client, Clara Ridge, did not want me to reveal her purpose in sending me to find her son, but the case had grown perilous and far beyond its original boundaries. I had a choice to make: I could keep her secret and likely leave Africa with nothing, or I could tell her son's boyfriend the truth and find what I'd come all this way to look for.

"I am a detective," I told the man.

"So what?" he said, his voice telling me how unwilling he was to suffer any more malarkey from me.

"I was sent to Africa to find Matthew Moxley."

"Sent by whom?"

"His mother."

Our eyes met somewhere in the space between us, mine asking the other man to believe me and grant my request, his searching for the something in me that would allow him to do so.

"I am sorry to say this," Kevan Badanga said in measured, hesitant words, "but you have come a long way for nothing."

Oh man! Now what African country was I going to have to hump my way to in order to track down Matthew Moxley? Tanzania? Somalia? Ghana?

"I am sorry to tell you," Kevan said, "that Matthew Moxley died seven months ago."

Chapter 15

We ran into a tempestuous storm somewhere over Bermuda, causing the aircraft to sway back and forth like Elvis Presley's hips. I
cannot sleep during turbulence—I'm usually too busy praying—
so when we reached Atlanta, instead of spending the day investigating this lovely southern city as I'd hoped, I holed up in my airport hotel room, ordered in, watched movies (both the blow-em-
up and chick flick variety) and did my best to catch up on sleep.

The next day, after what seemed like years since I'd left South
Africa and a century since I'd been home, I found myself on a
plane circling Saskatoon's John G. Diefenbaker Airport. It was a
Friday night, near midnight, late March. I watched the twinkling,
tangerine-hued lights that define the city's streets and bridges and
felt a sudden unexpected longing to be home. Was it homesick-
ness? Was I simply disappointed to have gone all the way to Africa
only to fail at my task of finding my client's son? Maybe I was feeling guilt over the poverty that I'd seen in Africa, as compared to
cozy Saskatoon.

It did seem hugely unfair that when I got off this plane, I
would go to my large, beautiful, warm, home that I shared with
not one but two dogs; I would have plenty to eat, I would feel safe,
I had money in the bank, no one I knew would have died from
AIDS or malnutrition or natural disaster or violence since I'd left
home. My African adventure had been exhausting and, I had to
wonder, had it all been for nothing?

As the aircraft pointed its nose down on final descent, I looked
around the plane's cabin at the other passengers; I studied the

faces of the people I'd shared this last leg of my journey with. I felt an inexplicable warmth towards them, a warmth I was sadly certain would vanish as soon as we found ourselves elbow-to-elbow at the luggage carousel, jostling for the best spot from which to retrieve our bags and make our getaway, probably never to see each other again. I closed my eyes and waited to land.

Looking like he might have just woken from a late evening nap—the type where it's probably best to just sleep right through to morning—Alex Canyon was cute enough to eat. He was waiting for me just outside the arrivals gate looking not unlike a little lost boy searching for a familiar face. The closer I got to him, the faster I walked, so that by the time I reached him I was almost at a full gallop. I threw my arms around him and buried my head into the soft down of the thick fleece jacket that covered his chest. It was uncharacteristic of me to do this, and I'm not sure why I did it, but it felt good and he seemed to like it too.

After several seconds I pulled away and we looked at each other. He grinned a lopsided grin and I gave him one back.

"When did you get back into town?" I asked him.

"Just yesterday," he answered, his voice low and growly and sexy. "How was the trip?"

"He's dead," I blurted out.

Jeepers, what the hell was wrong with me! That was not at all what I was thinking I'd say, which was supposed to go something like: "It was fantastic. What a beautiful country. I saw an elephant! We have to go back on safari. It is so good to see you."

"Oh Russell," Alex said, placing a comforting hand on my shoulder. "I'm sorry. What happened?"

"AIDS," I answered with a frustrated bitterness in my voice, repeating what Kevan Badanga had told me. "AIDS killed Matthew Moxley, just like it kills almost everyone in Africa, it seems."

Now what the heck happened to my oogly-googly, warmth-towards-my-fellow-man, I-love-Saskatoon, we're-so-fortunate, good mood? Instead, something had happened to me between twenty-thousand feet and the ground, something that turned me into this miserable-cynic-beneath-a-black-cloud kind of guy and, I swear to God, I felt kind of weepy too. Jeez, maybe I hadn't gotten quite enough sleep in Atlanta after all.

"Let's get your luggage and we can talk about this at home," Alex wisely suggested. "There's still snow on the ground, but the temp has been pretty mild," he added, hoping to find something to distract me and buoy my spirits.

I nodded in agreement and allowed Alex to lead me through the motions as we found ourselves elbow-to-elbow at the luggage carousel, jostling for the best spot from which to retrieve my bags and make our getaway, probably never to see my fellow travellers again.

When we got home, Alex pulled me into a hot shower for two that lasted until the water turned chilly. After a speedy rubdown with thick towels that smelled of Bounce, we dived into bed, quickly followed by Barbra and Brutus. It was certainly crowded, given that none of us would ever be considered the runt of the litter. And usually I have a strict rule about no dogs on the bed when I have company in it. But they had quite obviously missed me, and I could not resist their squeals and grunts of intense pleasure as they curled up between us and nestled their cold noses into the crook of our necks, every so often sending a darting tongue of puppy love into one of our ears. We fell asleep like that and I did not wake until a luxuriously late hour the next day. Nothing had felt so good in a long time.

Saturday dawned mild but with a pearl grey sky dizzy with early spring flurries that coated the roads and roofs of the neighbourhood like coconut icing. I would have loved nothing better than to stay in bed all day with my hunk and two pooches, but I had something else that needed doing. Something that could wait no longer.

I had to tell Clara Ridge that her son was dead.

I had debated calling her from Botswana as soon as I heard the news, but I couldn't bear to give her such devastating information over the phone. This was a job best done in person.

I pulled up in front of a little bungalow in Pleasant Hill where Avenue T begins to slope down towards Fred Mendel Park and the West Industrial Area of Saskatoon. The Mazda purred with self-satisfaction at having delivered me safely on streets grown treacherously slippery with the fresh falling snow. Through a window edged with frost on the outside and condensation on the inside, I stared at the tiny, unfenced front yard. I pictured little blond Matthew Moxley, then Matthew Ridge, playing there as a child, already feeling the effects of his harsh, uncaring father and his ineffectual mother. Is this what had driven him to trouble with the law, reform school, and ultimately, being ousted from his home and family? He'd eventually found peace and love in his life through work in developing countries, teaching children, in his relationships with Ethan Ash then Kevan Badanga, only to be struck down and killed by AIDS. I shuddered at the senselessness of it all. Now I was to be the messenger of this sad, final, chapter to his mother.

I was dreading this client visit. On the drive over, it struck me that once I told Clara Ridge about her son's death, she would truly be alone in this world. No husband, no child. I suppose she'd been alone until now anyway: she hadn't known where her son was, or if he was alive or dead. But I couldn't help think that part of her motive for hiring me to find him was reaching out, trying to resurrect what was left of her family, finding a way to end her loneliness, and Matthew's as well. The news I was about to deliver would kill that hope forever.

I stepped out of the car, locked the door, and gingerly made my way down the unshovelled walkway and up three cement steps to the front door of the house. The front picture window and half-moon of glass in the door were heavily draped and after I rang the bell, I knocked—just in case. I saw the fabric over the door window shift ever so slightly. I waited another thirty seconds, then knocked again.

The door curtain was pushed to the side and behind it I saw a prune-like face that had been around for at least ninety years. Untrusting eyes stared out at me from behind the thick lenses of the elderly gentleman's dark-rimmed glasses. Even through the filmy window I could easily make out a thin line etched across each oval of the poorly crafted bifocals. Both of the man's ears were plugged with hearing aids and supported a clear tube that delivered oxygen to a device beneath his hairy nostrils. I smiled and nodded, pretty sure the old guy wouldn't be able to hear anything I said through the thick wooden door. The face disappeared, and I was glad to hear the unmistakable sound of multiple locks being unfastened.

"What is it?" the man wheezed at me when he pushed open the front door a fraction of a crack. "You selling something? I don't need anything."

"I'm not a salesperson," I assured him. "I'm here to see Clara Ridge." I was guessing this character was her father or father-in-law, and I was grateful she would not be alone when she heard my news.

The guy shook his head and began to close the crack.

"Wait, wait, wait," I said hurriedly. "Clara Ridge," I said loudly, thinking the clods of plastic in his ears weren't working up to par and he hadn't heard me clearly. "Can you please tell Mrs. Ridge that Russell Quant is here to see her. She knows who I am."

"That could be, but I don't know her! And I don't know you," he told me in a surprisingly commanding voice. "There isn't anyone here by that name."

I felt my eyebrows pull together over my nose into a frown. I pulled out the piece of paper on which I'd written my client's address. "But it says right here…"

"Mister, how many times do I gotta tell you? I don't give a rat's ass what it says on that there paper you got. There is no one by the name you mentioned living here. Not now, nor for the last fifty years since I built this house. Someone's pulling your leg, mister, pulling it real hard."

Again.

By the time I returned to the Mazda, the little car looked like a car-shaped igloo. I got in without bothering to brush it off, and sat silently in the diffused grey gloom created by weak winter afternoon light pressing through the layers of snow coating the windows. I pulled my cellphone from my jacket pocket and dialled Clara Ridge's number. I reached the same recording I'd gotten every other time I'd called it, but something told me not to leave a message this time. I started the car, set the heater and wipers to high so I could see where I was going and sped off in a cloud of fluttering flakes.

Errall's sparkly new car was behind PWC when I slipped and slid into the parking lot, but I wasn't in the mood for one of hers, so instead of using the front door that would take me right by her office, I scaled the rickety old metal stairs that hug the rear of the building and lead directly to the second storey and my office.

Once inside I saw that my phone's message light was flashing. There was one message with one very interesting piece of information. The caller was Officer Darren Kirsch. He was back from training and had traced the licence plate number I'd memorized and given to him from the SUV that balaclava man had escaped in.

Although I hate bothering him at home on weekends—okay, not really—I dialled the number for the Kirsch residence (which for some odd reason I know by heart). I reached his wife, Treena—a much lovelier woman than he deserves—and after a bit of idle chit-chat, she told me he was at the station, catching up on paperwork that had piled up while he'd been away. I hung up and dialled again.

"Kirsch," he barked into the phone.

"Quant," I barked back.

I heard some paper shuffling noises then, "Allan Dartmouth." Kirsch, the king of expeditious communication.

So, the vehicle belonged to Allan Dartmouth, massage therapist, and Matthew Ridge's high school buddy. Huh. Interesting. And frustrating. How did he figure into all of this?

"Thanks."

"So long."

"Wait, wait, wait!" I yapped into the receiver hoping to catch him before he hung up. Usually he gives very few hints that he's about to disconnect, so I was grateful for the "so long."

"Yeah?"

"You're in a fine mood today." He really was being a little more bristly than normal, even for him.

"All this paper is driving me up the friggin' wall." A rare personal admission from the cop. What he was really saying was that he'd rather be at home with Treena and their—what was the latest count? Thirteen?—children. I'd caught him being as vulnerable as a guy like him can be. The question was: should I take advantage of it? Make fun of him? Deride him for being whipped? Nope. I wanted something from him.

"Darren," I said. Not Kirsch. Nice touch, I thought. "I was wondering if there is a home address attached to that licence number?"

He huffed. "You know damn well there is."

"You in the mood for sharing?" I reminded him of why I was after the information in the first place: Allan Dartmouth, or at least his car, was involved in the harassment of one of Saskatoon's fine citizens (moi) whom Constable Darren Kirsch, as a cop, had sworn to protect.

"Yeah, yeah, save it for your mama," he replied. Right before giving me the address.

I thanked him profusely (after he'd already hung up) and, for the moment, stored the Dartmouth info in the Red Herrings File. There was a more urgent matter to attend to.

I dove into the Ridge client folder and double-checked the address Clara Ridge had given me. I had it right. I looked up Clara Ridge in the phone book. There were other listings for Ridge, but none for a Clara. I checked the number in the reverse directory but there was no listing. I went back to the white pages. There were only three listings for Ridge. On the second I hit pay dirt.

"Oh dear, no," the sweet female voice answered when I asked for Clara. "Clara hasn't lived in Saskatoon for years. But I'm her sister-in-law, can I help you?"

Clara Ridge hadn't lived in Saskatoon for years? How now brown cow? I felt a rising tide of heat bridge my jawline and work its way up my cheeks. I gave the woman the Avenue T address.

"No, no, I don't know anyone at that address. Clara and Clement lived on Witney Avenue. But like I said, that was years ago. I hope you know that Clement passed away several years ago?"

My Clara Ridge told me her husband died only six months ago. I wondered if the million-dollar windfall was a tall tale as well. You *think*, Sherlock?

"Heart attack?" I asked, which was the story according to my Clara Ridge.

"Cancer," she told me. "Are you a friend of theirs then?" the sister-in-law asked.

Lie? Truth? Lie? Truth? Lie? Truth? "Oh my goodness, no, I did not know about Clement. I'm so sorry to hear it. I'm an old friend of theirs, just back in town for a few days, thought I'd look them up. How sad about Clement. I should give Clara a call and give her my condolences."

"Oh yes, she'd like that."

"Do you happen to have her number handy?"

"Oh, I know it by heart; we talk on the phone almost every day. My husband complains about how much we talk on the phone, how expensive it is, but we are sisters-in-law after all, and she is all alone now, you know."

I made some understanding sounds.

"Are you a married man then?" she asked with a coy twist in her voice.

I blanched, then gave the simplest answer. "Yes."

"Oh, I see. You have a pen, then?"

"Yes I do."

"It's 403-555-8191."

403? Not only did Clara Ridge not live on Avenue T or in Saskatoon, but she didn't even live in Saskatchewan. 403 is an Alberta exchange. "Um, where exactly is Clara living?"

"Airdrie. Do you know it? Just outside of Calgary."

Some vague sounds of acknowledgment from me, then, "When exactly did Clara and Clement move to Alberta?"

"Oh dear, now when was that? I'd say, well, it's been at least twenty years, you know, right after all the trouble with that son of theirs. Say, when was it you said you knew them?"

Uh-oh. "Please insert seventy-five cents to continue this call," I said in my best falsetto. "I'm sorry, Mrs. Ridge, it sounds like I'm about out of time at this pay phone...crackle, crackle, crackle...thank you for your h..." Then I hung up. It was rude and I felt bad, but a PI's gotta do what a PI's gotta do.

I looked down and saw the fingers of my right hand thrumming the top of my desk, a nervous habit I seemed to have developed since getting on the phone with Clara Ridge's sister-in-law.

The old man on Avenue T was right. Someone was pulling my leg.

My client was an imposter.

Why? Why would someone pretend to be Clara Ridge and then hire me—at great expense—to find the missing Ridge son?

Oh, oh.

Wait a sec.

My money!

I booted up my darkened computer and punched the appropriate buttons to hook up to the Internet and then my online Royal Bank account, at the same time opening the fridge beneath my desk, pulling out a beer, and then putting it back when I spotted the remains of a bottle of 2003 Villard Estate Chardonnay. I'd bought it solely because it was from Casablanca—Valley that is—in Chile. I read the back of the bottle while waiting for my bank information to load: fifty-five per cent barrel-fermented and stored in French oak barrels for eleven months...displays soft tropical fruit and vanilla aromas and flavours...excellent structure and long finish. Sheesh, who writes this stuff? Doesn't matter; I bought it, didn't I?

All I had nearby was a brandy snifter (now where did that come from?), and I filled it to near the brim with the golden liquid, nicely emptying the bottle that I stored under the desk for later recycling (much later). I took a deep sip as I clicked to the page that would show me whether or not Clara Ridge's original retainer cheque had cleared.

It had. Phew.

If it hadn't, I would have been in a heap of trouble; travelling in Africa had not been cheap, even with the envelope of cash and without having to pay for the return airfare which Clara had already covered. I took another sip of the wine. It was old, having been opened over a week ago. I wouldn't serve it to guests, but for me today, it was okay.

It was time to don my thinking cap. How could a fake Clara Ridge pass off a Clara Ridge cheque? I thought back to our financial discussions and the money she'd given me. I had noted that the cheque was not personalized—as so many are nowadays, and the signature at the bottom was illegible—as so many are nowadays; so it was possible that I was paid by someone completely other than Clara Ridge. But again, why? Why would someone do that? Was the fake Clara Ridge hired by the real Clara Ridge, too afraid or meek to do it herself for some reason? Or, was there some other, more iniquitous reason? There was only one way to find out. I dialled the Alberta number.

"Hello," said a spidery voice, which I immediately knew did not belong to the woman I'd been hired by. "Clara Ridge speaking."

Truth? Lie? Truth? Lie? "Mrs. Ridge, my name is Russell Quant. I'm a detective and I live in Saskatoon. A short while ago I was hired by a woman to find your son, Matthew Ridge. This woman told me her name was Clara Ridge."

For a while there was silence, then a short intake of breath followed by, "I'm sorry, can you repeat that?"

I did. The woman was obviously thinking over the yarn I'd just told her, which I'm certain must have sounded as incredible to her as the plot of a Harry Potter novel. I gave her a moment to digest the information before continuing. "I was wondering if I could ask you a few questions? So I can clear this up."

"Of course," she finally agreed. "What do you need to know?"

I wished I could do this in person, but somehow I sensed I didn't have the luxury of time for a trip to our next-door neighbour province. I had to find the truth; I had to find out who had really hired me and why, and soon, because if I didn't, I just knew the violence that had followed me from Saskatoon to Africa would not end there. "I take it you know nothing about this woman or her wanting to find your son?"

"No I...I don't...but, well, did you?"

"Did I what?" I was stalling. I knew what she wanted to know.

"Did you find Matthew? Oh my goodness, I never thought such a thing would be possible. I never thought about a detective. Did you? Did you find him, Mr. Quant? Did you find my son?" Suddenly her weak voice sounded stronger, infused with hope.

"I'm sorry, Mrs. Ridge. I did not." Lie. Sort of.

"Oh. I see." She was crestfallen, but not as much as she would have been, had I been able to bring myself to divulge to her the horrible truth.

"Can you tell me a little about when you last saw Matthew and why…well, why you lost track of him?" I wanted to compare the real story to the one I'd been told. Any inconsistencies might give me a hint as to the fake Mrs. Ridge's true identity. "And why did you move away from Saskatoon?"

"Matthew had a difficult time in school, Mr. Quant," she began. "He was a troubled boy. I don't know why; he just was. We tried to talk to him, his father and me, but he always seemed so distant, so angry at us, at everyone around him. The older he got the worse it got. Matthew and Clement, his father, were very close when he was a young boy, so it breaks my heart to think of what happened between them later on.

"You see, Clement couldn't understand it, why his boy, the apple of his eye, suddenly became a stranger. He had been such a sweet child, you understand, so it didn't make sense to us." A coughing spell interrupted her. She gave in to it wholeheartedly, then continued. "It was the summer after he finished grade ten when it happened. And just like that, our lives were ruined. Our name was ruined. Our reputation was dirt."

This was something new. I held my tongue and waited for the story to come out.

"Our name was in the paper every day. All you had to do was mention the name Ridge and people looked at you differently. It was as if we'd all done it, not just Matthew, as if we were all guilty of what he did." She stopped there and coughed again, a smoker's cough I guessed, at least a pack-a-day habit. "Saskatoon is too small a city to go unnoticed after something like that. There was no escaping it. We had to leave Saskatoon to get away from it." She coughed some more.

I was perplexed. Petty thievery and drugs? That was the big news story that drove the Ridges away from their home, their city, their business, their son? "I'm sorry, Mrs. Ridge, but was there something *in particular* that happened the summer after Matthew finished grade ten that caused you to leave Saskatoon?"

Another brief silence. "You don't know?"

This was going to be good, I could tell. "No, I don't think I do. The woman I talked to told me that your husband kicked Matthew out of the house when he was sixteen, and eventually Matthew was sent to reform school because of some minor problems with the law, and that you never saw him again after that."

"I suppose most of that's true, Mr. Quant, except that the last bit of trouble Matthew got into wasn't a minor problem with the law. You see, they sent Matthew away because he beat up another boy. He beat that boy so bad he almost died."

Errall Strane is a friend. There, I've said it. She's also a colleague, my lawyer, my landlord, and a regular pain in the ass but a trusted confidante when it comes to my cases. We've come a long way, she and I, from tolerating each other simply because we had a person in common whom we both loved (the newly reappeared Kelly), to tolerating each other because I rent my office space from her and work in the same building, to tolerating each other because we seem to hang out with some of the same people, to tolerating each other because…well, just because we kind of enjoy tolerating each other. Make sense? Nope. I don't think so either, but there it is.

After getting off the phone following a rather lengthy conversation with the real Clara Ridge, I found myself thumping down the staircase that leads to the first floor of PWC where Errall takes up over half the square footage with her spacious and pretentiously decorated one-woman law office. I found Errall hard at work behind the war-room sized piece of metal and glass that acts as her desk, surrounded by a collection of thick lawyer-ish tomes, file folders brimming with reams of paper, and a long empty, lipstick-stained Starbucks cup. Errall's dark hair was loose around her shoulders and looked as if it had been run through with her fingers many times over during the last few hours. Although it was a Saturday afternoon, she was still wearing one of her smart and severe business suits, but she'd given in to weekend slack by leaving her blouse unbuttoned to a rather daring low point, low enough for me to see she wasn't wearing a bra.

"So who was this kid that Matthew Ridge almost killed?" Errall asked after I dumped myself into a chair in front of her desk, declared myself immoveable, and caught her up with my baffling case of client/no client.

"Robin Haywood. He was another student at the same school Matthew attended. Apparently Matthew—along with many of the other students—decided he was gay."

"Gawd, you can just hear it, can't you, with a name like that?" Errall responded with a sympathetic tone, yanking her reading glasses off her nose and tossing them to one side of the desk top. "I'd bet you a hundred bucks they called him Robin Gaywood. 'Who'd like to suck my dick? I think Robin Gay would!'" She gave her neck a rub. "Kids are such cruel bastards."

I flicked Errall a questioning look. She seemed a bit too familiar with the activity of childhood taunting. I wouldn't have been surprised to find out she herself was a bit of a "cruel bastard" in her formative years. "Anyway," I moved us along, "Robin was a quiet kid, bookish, an easy target for a boy like Matthew. They were adversaries for years." I stopped there and reconsidered my choice of words. "Well, no. Adversaries makes it seem as if they were on equal ground, which, by the sounds of it, they certainly were not. Matthew, the big, sturdy, athletic, girl-magnet was the tormentor, and Robin was his unwilling, long-suffering victim."

"But wait a second," Errall said, as always, quick as a whip at an S&M party. "I thought you told me that during your investigation into Matthew Ridge aka Matthew Moxley, you found out that he had male lovers. So, if I remember my studies correctly, doesn't that make *him* the gay one?"

I gave her a nod. "Typical of bullies and bashers."

"He doth protest too much?"

"Exactly. It happens a lot, especially with young men who suspect they themselves might be gay. These guys hate the thought of who they are so much that all they want to do is strike out against it, destroy it, beat it to a pulp. It's either that or, if the self-loathing is strong enough, they hurt or kill themselves. Unfortunately for poor little Robin Haywood, Matthew Ridge saw in him the worst of himself and wanted to punish him for it."

"What happened?"

"It was summer," I began the account as told to me by Matthew's mother. "Matthew and his buddies came upon Robin in a neighbourhood park. They were drunk and high. They confronted Robin, and without the constraints of high school, and brave and cocky from drugs and alcohol, they began to taunt him, then jab at him, and eventually it led to an all-out bashing."

"Shit," Errall declared. "How frightened that boy must have been. The assholes!"

"According to Mrs. Ridge, upon questioning the other boys, all of them agreed that things got out of hand pretty quickly. They eventually realized Robin could get seriously hurt and decided to stop. But Matthew kept at him, yelling at him, screaming, bawling him out, and calling him names, kicking him, pummelling him. They finally got it together enough to pull Matthew off of Robin. One of them said that when they did, he was crying."

"Of course he was."

"Not Robin," I told her. "Matthew."

"Oh."

"And then they ran off."

"They just left him there?" She was rightfully incensed at the thought.

I nodded sadly. "A guy walking his dog later that night found Robin, all crumpled up. He barely survived. He spent months recovering at RUH."

Errall's eyes opened into two wide pools of blue. "Wait a minute. Wait a minute! I remember this. The names were unusual. Normally they wouldn't even release the names of minors, but it was all over the news long before criminal charges were laid. The newspapers were full of the story for months. Yeah, I remember this; they referred to him as Robin with the broken wing. I was just a teenager myself, but it was a big deal; one teenager almost killing another was huge news in Saskatoon, still would be, I suppose. I remember going back to school the fall after it happened; it was a real hot topic, out of the classroom and in."

"I guess I missed all that," I said. "We didn't read a lot of city newspapers, living on a farm. If it wasn't about Four-H or grain prices, it wasn't news."

Errall kept on as if she hadn't heard me. "I remember one story; to this day I remember it, it was that vivid. It was about those two boys—Matthew and Robin—they made it sound as if they were the closest of schoolboy chums, best buddies who grew apart, and ended up mortal enemies on a bloody battlefield, in a duel to near death. So fucking melodramatic! Can you stand it? I'm not making this up, Russell," she added when she saw my skeptical face. "I remember it like it was yesterday. I think one of the girls in my class even did an essay on the whole thing. It was a very big deal in this city for a long, long time."

I nodded, finally coming to a clearer understanding of how the Ridge family might have suffered the level of stigma Clara Ridge described to me.

"I always wondered what happened to those boys," Errall said.

"Matthew Ridge was sent to reform school," I told her, "but the other boys who took part in the incident didn't get more than a slap on the wrist." My guess was that they testified against Matthew in exchange for leniency." After Matthew got out, his parents lost track of him."

"Oh come on," Errall cried out, indignant. "No one just loses track of a kid. Unless you want to."

I had to agree, but I had nothing with which to measure the shame the elder Ridges must have felt at having to face the fact that their child perpetrated such a heinous crime. According to Clara, the Ridges had their supporters at the time—mostly religious extremists who lauded Matthew's actions as a necessary evil to help stamp out those they considered deviant, aberrations of nature—people they ended up wanting to escape just as badly as the disgrace attached to the Ridge name.

"But you still have no answers as to who it really was who hired you and why?" Errall asked.

"Actually," I said as a scheme began to take shape in my head, "I think I have a pretty good theory. And you've just given me a good idea how to confirm it."

"What? What idea? What did I say?" Errall demanded to know.

But I was already out the door and heading for my car, barely hearing her reference to intended actions to diminish my manhood should I not return immediately with an answer.

Saskatoon's main library, named after Frances Morrison, an employee for thirty-seven years (most as chief librarian), and one of the first women department heads in the city, is only a few blocks away from PWC. In no time I was microfiching my way through old *StarPhoenix* newspaper articles until I found exactly what I was looking for. Once back in my car I dialled a now-familiar phone number on my cellphone.

"Mrs. Ridge," I said in answer to the answering machine request to leave a message, "It's Russell Quant. I'm back in Saskatoon. And I have your son with me."

Chapter 16

Hospital visiting hours end at eight p.m. and I made it to Ethan Ash's room seconds under the wire. I peered into the dim space just in time to see a tall figure lean over the bed, gently push aside a swath of Ethan's brown hair and place a delicate kiss on his forehead. It was Frank, one of the octogenarians who lived in the care home run by Ethan and who, it was quite obvious to me, loved Ethan a great deal. Whether it was warm affection for a caregiver or a crush, I wasn't quite sure. I debated going in. My few interactions with Frank had revealed a rather brusque, manly character who might not be comfortable being seen in this tender light, so I turned to go but came to an abrupt halt when I spotted someone else I knew coming down the hallway toward me.

Anthony Gatt gave me a tight hug and a kiss on each cheek. "Puppy, how wonderful to see you. I wish you'd call whenever you get back from these world travels of yours. Some of us worry about you, you know. How was it?"

"It was complicated. I'm sorry I didn't call. Alex is here, and between this case I'm on, and sleeping off jet lag, I haven't had much time. But I need to talk to you." My uncomfortable meeting with Jared several days ago had been at the back of my mind ever since. It was bothering me a lot, mostly I think, because I had no idea what to do about it.

"Of course."

"But...why are you here?"

"Same reason as you, I suspect. To visit Ethan."

"You know each other?" Ridiculous question. Anthony knows

249

everyone who has ever set foot in Saskatoon.

"Of course." He threaded an arm through mine and led me back to the room. "Shall we?"

We met Frank just as he was leaving.

"Frank," Anthony greeted the man as if he'd known him forever. "How are you?"

As we shook hands, Frank eyed me warily before responding to Anthony with a slight grimace. "Well, most everything aches, and what doesn't ache doesn't work anymore."

Anthony gave him a manly slap on the shoulder and one of his Robert Redford smile-and-wink combinations. "Atta boy."

"I'm just on my way home," Frank said, blushing at the attention from Anthony. "Simon likes it when I'm there. She sure misses her father."

"How is she doing through all this?"

The older man smiled, obviously fond of the girl. "She's a pip that one. She pretends she's okay, but I know better. We all do. We're giving her lots of attention. And she gets to visit her dad every day. She'll be okay."

Anthony tilted his head toward the hospital room door. "Ethan sleeping?"

"He's dozing," Frank answered. "But you should go in. He always wants to see you." He turned to me, nodded once—just barely—then tottered off to the elevator bank.

"Is it me," I whispered to Anthony, "or does that man not like me very much?"

Anthony's eyes told me I should very well know the answer to my own question, and if I didn't he certainly wasn't about to answer it for me. He began pulling off his jacket. "Come," he said, "let's be presentable when we walk in."

Underneath Anthony's overcoat was a light V-neck sweater, in a purple so deep it might have been black, which showed off his sculpted torso to its best. I pulled off my leather bomber to reveal a boxy looking, off-white, cable knit job that had seen better days. Jeepers, why does this always happen when Anthony is around? I have nice sweaters, compliments of Anthony's store, but no, today I had to go for this comfy but moth-eaten sack. Always the embodiment of graciousness (when in public), Anthony merely fingered the ink stain on my chest and smiled indulgently.

We entered the hospital room, and for a moment I was transfixed by Ethan's face; eyes closed, innocent, peaceful, beautiful like a sleeping giant in repose. Everything about him was strong and big and husky, yet achingly helpless here in a hospital room with tubes sticking out of his thick arms. Drawn to the chair next to his bed, like the prince drawn to Sleeping Beauty, I lowered myself into it. I reached out for Ethan's hand, which sat motionless at his side, and covered it with my own. I felt comforted by the fact that it was warm and soft and pulsing with life. I watched in hope as his eyelids fluttered then slowly opened. Despite the drabness of the surroundings and paleness of his face, his dark eyes seemed to shimmer like melting chocolate. In slow motion, the corners of his mouth turned up and he opened his lips and whispered my name: "Russell."

For some reason unknown to me I was struck dumb.

"How are you today, Ethan?" Anthony asked, leaning over my left shoulder where he'd placed a hand.

Ethan's eyes moved to Anthony. "I'm good. Ready to go home," he said in a weak voice that trembled with the truth. He wasn't well yet.

"The doctor says maybe early next week. It seems the swelling in your old noggin has finally come down," Anthony said gently.

"About time."

"Frank says everything in the house is going fine. So fine in fact, they may ask you to move out when you get back."

Ethan's face broke into a wide smile that sprouted dimples in his cheeks and turned his eyes into horizontal half moons.

"Gentlemen," a voice behind us said. "It's time to go. The patient needs his rest."

"Do you need anything?" Anthony asked. "I'm going to bring by some magazines—*Vanity Fair*, *The Advocate* okay?—and a sweater to cover this god awful sackcloth they dress you sick people in. Tomorrow maybe? Or are you busy?"

That was good for another good-humoured smirk. Ethan's eyes fell back onto mine and he thanked me for visiting him. I squeezed his hand and left without saying one word the entire time we were in the room.

"What are you doing here?"

He recognized me. How sweet. Allan Dartmouth lived in Stonebridge, in a house so new the stucco was still wet. As he stood there at his door, which was painted a brazen shade of orange, I could see his eyes worrying as they surveyed me and the street behind me. In his right hand he held a delicate pair of reading glasses that had probably set him back a couple of hundred bucks, even though they didn't look much different from the $34.95 version at Shoppers Drug Mart.

"I was wondering if you own a current year Lincoln Navigator, black, licence plate number 131 KGS?"

He frowned, not quite sure what I was getting at. "What are you talking about? Why do you want to know about my Navigator?"

It was cold standing out there on his fine, new stoop, but I wasn't holding my breath until I got an invitation inside. "I was just wondering if I could get a ride from you? No? Maybe if I put on a balaclava, spoke like Sylvester Stallone, threatened a local private investigator?"

It was fascinating to watch his face. Irritation turned to confusion then to curiosity which slowly, inexorably, dissolved into fear. He knew I had him. The successful, upstanding, respected massage therapist had been caught hiring a thug to scare me off. The question was why. I think I knew the answer.

"I don't know what you're talking about." He had to try. He really did. It just wasn't a very convincing try, especially with the fine sheen of sweat now covering his expansive forehead.

"I have to tell you, Allan, you surprised me," I said (and actually meant it). "I didn't expect a mild-mannered masseur would be so ballsy as to hire a no-neck to try and scare me off from finding Matthew Ridge. But I suppose," I hesitated here for drama. "Once a bully, always a bully."

He checked over his sweatered shoulder, probably for a wife or kid, then looked back at me with hate in his eyes. But I guess a cat had his tongue because he didn't say much.

"I had to wonder why," I continued on. "Why would this guy go to such extreme lengths to convince me not to dig up the past? Had to be because he didn't want something from the past to mess up his future. That about right?"

He shook his head as if not quite believing what was happening to him on the expensive doorstep his future was meant to pay for.

"That something is named Robin Haywood, isn't it?"

Allan Darmouth had lied to me. He indeed had spent time with his buddy Matthew Ridge the summer before Matthew was sent away; specifically one horrible, alcohol-and-drug fueled night, in a neighbourhood park where Robin Haywood had the great misfortune of being at the same time as Matthew and his gang. Allan Dartmouth had been one of the posse that had beaten up the defenceless boy.

It was an event so horrific and reviled—and therefore of great interest to a public insatiably curious about such things—that it spent many months on the front pages of Saskatchewan newspapers. Allan Dartmouth had done everything he could in the intervening years to distance himself from the infamous story and his involvement in it. After all, who wanted to have the same hands that once bashed the body of a teenage boy caressing your back and shoulders?

I couldn't blame him for hoping he'd never have to face judgment from his clients—his wife? his kids?—over what happened that night. For all I knew (and hoped) he'd paid for it in other ways over the years. It was obvious to me that my stirring things up would not be a popular turn of events in Dartmouth's lily-white, new life. What wasn't obvious, however, was how far he'd go to bury the truth.

One of the things I've learned in my career, first as a policeman and then as a private detective, is never to judge a book by its cover. By all appearances, Allan Dartmouth was a nebbishy, WASPy, white-collar, clean fingernails kind of guy, who probably coached his son's hockey team and chaired a host of charity boards and committees. But there was a rigid rod of cold steel running down his spine, and at that moment, he showed me a glint of that metal through slitted eyes as he murmured, with teeth clenched tight, the well-known phrase, "Fuck you."

And then he slammed that bright orange door in my face.

"I know Jared asked you to help him convince me to end our relationship."

We were at a private table in a dark corner of a popular downtown restaurant, 2nd Avenue Grill, renowned for its martini menu, and boy did we need some of those. I was having an old favourite, a Red Apple martini, while Anthony was sticking with the classic: straight-up Bombay, sniff of vermouth, and some olives.

"He told you?" I said. "Or did Barbra and Brutus spill the beans? Damn dogs, they'll say anything for a couple of Snausages," I added with a levity that wasn't called for.

"I can't believe you spoke of this in front of the children," Anthony shot back gamely.

"I'm sorry, Anthony."

"For what?"

"This is serious. I'm sorry about what you and Jared are going through. And I'm sorry I left things with Jared the way I did. He must be pretty angry with me."

"Of course he isn't. Jared doesn't get angry. Or if he does, it lasts about as long as cheap lipstick."

Anthony was right. Jared Lowe has a sweet disposition. "I suppose none of us can know what it feels like to go through what he's had to go through since...since he had his face taken away." I swallowed a mouthful of Red Apple. "God, it makes me so sad, and mad, to think about it. What must he be feeling? And you, Anthony, this isn't easy on you either. As much as I hate it, and I know it's wrong, I can understand, a little, why Jared would think it would be best to end your relationship."

"Can you? Can you really?"

I heard something new in Anthony's voice, something I'd never heard from him before in the many years I'd known him: a mocking, acerbic lilt, as if challenging me to take him on in a verbal battle he knew he'd never allow me to win.

"I don't mean it that way, Anthony," I quickly added, flinching at the tight look on his face. "I don't know what the two of you have gone through but…"

"This is all so ridiculous, absolutely ludicrous, I can hardly believe it's happening," he shot back. As he loosened control over his usually impeccable diction, his English accent grew thicker. "I am fifty-six years old, Russell. Fifty-six!"

"Oh, but look at you, you look fant…"

"Shut up, puppy."

I was ever so glad he added the "puppy".

"Save me the platitudes. I'm fifty-six years old. Jared is thirty-two. We've been together eight years. And for eight years I have wondered almost every day when he would leave me because of the way I looked, because I'd grown too old, because the wrinkles around my eyes and on my forehead were too deep, my chest dropped too low, my belly wasn't tight enough, my ass too droopy, my hair grown too thin, my mind too slow, my joints too sore. And you know, Russell, I was ready for that. I've been preparing for it. I could understand it, accept it; it just makes sense." He sipped his drink with the finesse of a well-rehearsed martini drinker. "When he's my age now, I'll be eighty years old, for goodness sake. Yet now…now…can you believe it?…he wants to end the relationship because of how *he* looks! How dare he, the little shit!"

Anthony once again artfully raised his martini glass so that it sat just above nose level, hesitating before taking a drink, his eyes swimming across the shimmering expanse to meet mine. I knew enough not to say anything.

A dark-eyed server approached our table and asked if we needed refills. He seemed particularly taken—as many people, men and women both, are—with Anthony's screen idol good looks. Anthony did this nod thing that I guess is the international signal for "God, yes, keep them coming" and the young man strode away to fill our order.

Placing a hand over mine, a magnificent amethyst ring sparkling from his third finger, Anthony said in a voice that was half-whisper, half-throttled cry, "You're going to think this despicable—and it is despicable, hideous really—but, God forgive me,

255

Russell, I almost prefer it."

My brow lowered as I tried to comprehend what my friend was saying. "You prefer...what?"

"The way he looks now."

I recoiled at the notion. "Anthony..." And that was all I could think of to say.

"Ghastly, I know," he said. "Didn't I warn you? But it's not as it sounds, really it isn't. I would never have wished this on Jared; I would give anything, my life, I would give my life, truly, if it meant that this hadn't had to happen to him. Not only the horror and pain of the actual act—and believe me, I have spent many hours torturing myself, thinking about what he must have gone through in those moments after that...that creature threw acid in his beautiful face...God, Russell, I can sometimes hardly bear the thought of my sweet, sweet Jared in such agony—and then there's all the pain he's had to go through since, learning how to live with his deformity, learning how to live with people's reaction when they see his scarred face. It's so torturously difficult for him. So no, I'm never glad for that.

"But, but, oh how do I say this? And I'd only say it to you..." And here he stopped and regarded me with the intensity of a million pairs of eyes.

I nodded my assurance that this conversation would remain between only us, just as so many before it had.

"If it *had* to happen—regardless of anything I might do or wish or think—I...I prefer this new Jared to his former magnificence."

For a full moment there was silence between us. I looked at him. He looked at me.

"It's selfish, I know," he uttered, "but you see, it is so much easier for me."

"Easier?" I could only manage a whisper. "How can this possibly be easier, Anthony?"

"Jared and I were first attracted to one another because of how we looked. It's the truth. There's no denying that. But when you are in love with a beautiful man, although everyone around you continues to see that same intensity of beauty every time they see him, you begin to see only what is inside. The shell, that lovely wrapping paper, becomes less and less important until finally, you no longer notice it. You see, Russell, I don't need Jared's lion-cat eyes, his perfect olive skin, his golden locks, his impeccably designed body, in order to love him, not anymore. I know it must sound inexcusably corny," he said with a hard smile, "and I can't believe it is coming from these lips, but all I need is what is inside.

"Over these past months, as we've been dealing with all of this, the physical and mental repercussions of the attack, the doctors, even though there has been much distress and anger and sadness, I've been having this…this feeling, a sensation I could not for the life of me identify. Until recently. Do you know what it is, Russell?"

I shook my head.

"Relief, Russell, blessed relief. Like that of a one-thousand-pound weight being lifted from my back. I feel at ease with myself and my age and what my body is becoming. I have stopped wondering about when Jared might leave me because of how I look. And by learning this about myself, about how little exterior appearances really matter to me now, including my own, I see it in him too. The state of his current exterior means nothing to me. Does any of this make sense?"

"Anthony, can I ask you a question?"

"What is it?"

"Did you ever—knowing Jared as well as you do, loving each other as you have—*really* expect that he would wake up one day, take one look at you, and say, I'm sorry but it's over now?"

He held my gaze for nearly thirty seconds—a long time if you count it out—before finally speaking. "No. To be truthful, I always believed we'd find a way to work it out. That we'd realize what everyone the world over hopes is true, but never knows for sure until something happens to test it, that we'd find out that indeed— oh gracious, save me, Russell, but I'm about to spout even more cliché—we'd find out that love truly does conquer all."

Something, somewhere, roughly in the heart region of my innards, went "boing!". It may have been indigestion. I nodded with a smile. "I think that can be very true, Anthony. You know it now. Jared just needs a reminder."

It was rather late when I snuck into my house through the back door. Barbra and Brutus greeted me with a little more reserve than usual. I think they were concerned that we might wake Alex who'd fallen asleep on a couch in the living room, waiting for me. Following in Anthony's cliché-a-minute footsteps, I dutifully kissed the big lug lightly on the cheek and covered him with an afghan. I tiptoed back into the kitchen where I found a handwritten note: "Russell—roast and potatoes in the fridge if you're hungry—dogs and I spent the day watching the *Airplane* movies—listen to your phone messages, may be important—wake me when you get in—Alex."

Part of me felt sad I'd missed the day with Alex—we get so few together—and another part of me felt guilty for the same reason. I decided against the food and waking him up, instead choosing a glass of water to dilute my belly full of martini, and led the dogs down the dim hallway into my den at the back of the house. As I passed the desk, I activated my voice mail to recite my messages and joined Barbra and Brutus on the soft leather couch to massage spots behind furry ears.

The first message was a quick "how-ya-doing" from Ric and Ian in Victoria; the second was a chatty one from my buddy Steve O'Neill who lives in Falls Church, Virginia; the third was a succinct "Ya, hello, dis is Mom. Goodbye, den," and finally, the last on the playback list, was just what I was waiting to hear: "Mr. Quant, it's Clara Ridge. I got your message. I understand you've returned to Canada with my son? As you can imagine, I'm rather surprised at that news. I don't know if I'm ready to see him in person…just yet. But I would like to know how and where you found him and what you know about him. Can we meet tomorrow morning, Sunday, at your office? Please come alone, Mr. Quant, don't bring Matthew…not now, not yet…I hope you can understand…I need to see you, talk to you first. I hope you get this message… I…well…I'll be at your office at nine a.m. I hope to see you then."

You bet you will.

It was a crisp, cool Sunday morning when I arrived at PWC, but there was something in the air, perhaps the subtle new-growth scent of trees and foliage coming to life after a long winter hibernation that hinted, ever so alluringly, at spring and summer not far off. Even so, the ground was covered in a shellac-like coating of snow, created by the recent succession of sun-warmed, melting days followed by Jack Frost freezing nights—winter's last hoorah. I parked in back but entered through the front of the building, leaving the door unlocked in preparation for my guest.

I dashed up to my office, but only spent a minute there, checking on this and that, before returning to the main floor. I tried a few different places and finally settled on the area behind Lilly's desk as the best spot from which I could easily keep watch on both the front and rear doors without immediately being seen myself.

I didn't have long to wait. I watched as the front door knob began to turn. Slowly. Deliberately. Whoever it was didn't want to advertise their presence just yet. I crouched low behind the desk and waited.

The door swung open, inch by careful inch, letting in a growing sliver of sunlight, then finally, a figure.

As expected, my visitor was not the woman I'd met as Clara Ridge, the imposter mother of Matthew, the woman who'd left me the stilted message on my voice mail, sounding as if she were reading from a script. The phony Clara Ridge was quite likely nothing but a stooge, someone playing a role, someone being used. Just as I was being used.

Until now.

You have to get up awfully early to fool Russell Quant, PI (a second time).

I watched as the man silently closed the door behind him, then turned and faced the staircase. He'd obviously done his homework, because his eyes travelled up the steps right to the door of my office. He glanced at his watch. He was early for the appointment, on purpose, obviously intending to catch me by surprise.

I pulled back as his eyes roamed the room. I hoped he wouldn't choose the same hiding spot as I had. After a second, I risked another peek. I was in luck. He was heading up the stairs. He'd obviously decided to ambush me right in my own office. Little bugger.

"Hold it right there," I said, straightening to my full height and stepping from behind the PWC reception desk.

The man stopped, frozen between two steps.

There's no better feeling than surprising someone who was going to surprise you.

"Just so you know," I added pleasantly, "I have a gun aimed at your back. Turn around slowly and come down the stairs." I rarely use a firearm in my work—just personal style, I guess—but given the history of this case, it seemed the smart thing to do.

The figure did as he was told, revealing a tall, powerfully built man with a ruddy tan and blond hair shorn close to his scalp. His eyes were bleary and circled with dark creases, and it looked as if he hadn't shaved for several days—all in all not a bad look.

And then he asked an unexpected question. "Why are you doing this?"

I smirked the smirk of the righteous. "Why are *you* sneaking into my place of business on a Sunday morning? Why are you having someone pretend to be Clara Ridge? Why are you looking for Matthew Ridge under false pretenses? Huh? Tell me that."

"What are you talking about?"

I shook my head. "I'm the one with the gun. I think that gives my questions priority, wouldn't you say? But before you answer, there's one important thing I'd like you to tell me first." I hesitated for drama. "Who are you?"

The smirk fell off my face, and the colour drained from my cheeks into my shoes when I heard his reply: "I'm Matthew Ridge."

Chapter 17

"Prove it!" I demanded of the big man. I'd had him come down the stairs and face me with hands up at shoulder height. My gun was pointed at his gut.

"My wallet," he said. "It's in my pocket."

I approached him warily, careful to keep my pistol at the ready should he make any sudden moves. I reached into his jacket breast pocket and pulled out a waterproof wallet with a Roots insignia on it. I stepped away and opened it to reveal credit cards, an insurance card, a bank card, and a driver's licence, each with one thing in common: the name Matthew Moxley inscribed on it. And indeed, the man before me bore a striking resemblance to the picture I had of a much younger Matthew Ridge. Could this actually be him? The man whose life I'd recreated out of a few scraps of information and interviews with people who knew him a lifetime ago? The man I'd travelled fifteen thousand kilometres to find? The man who *someone*, pretending to be his mother, was desperate to find? The man who was supposed to be dead!

"I suppose you can put your hands down, but keep 'em where I can see 'em," I ordered. "No sudden moves." Like that would stop him. "I've got some questions for you."

"All right, but I don't understand why you're doing this."

"Let's start with the fact that I was told you were dead," I said.

"By Kevan," he responded with a knowing nod. "We came up with that story after what happened in Khayelitsha. It became obvious you were hunting me down, willing to do anything to find me, and heading for Botswana. Our friends weren't able to scare you away, no matter how hard they tried, so the only way we could think of to stop you was to convince you I was dead." He hesitated there and gave me a look that was hard to read. "I have to tell you, Mr. Quant," he finally said, "after everything our friends did in an effort to get rid of you, we were rather surprised when our simple falsehood worked so easily."

Interesting point. Apparently words have greater power over me than bullets and explosions. I shrugged my shoulders. "I didn't think Kevan had any reason to lie to me. But obviously he didn't believe me when I told him I was not responsible for the beatings of the Chikosis."

"Actually, he did believe you, Mr. Quant," Matthew said in his deep, placid voice. He sounded like a well-rehearsed teacher; calm, composed. It was a startling contrast to his outward appearance, like an action movie hero who'd met with hard times, but would probably clean up real good.

"And that is why I am here," he continued. "Kevan maintained the fabrication we'd planned only because he didn't know what else to do. But he sensed something about you, a sincerity in the telling of your story. After you'd gone, he told me he thought you might be telling the truth."

I nodded, silently communicating that I was relieved that he'd believed his boyfriend.

"When I heard that my mother might be looking for me, I could hardly believe it. I knew that if there was even the slightest chance that what you claimed was true, I had to come back here. Enough time has passed. I've run long enough, far enough; it's time for me to stop and face my past and make peace with it, including with my mother. How can a son deny his mother a chance to see his face one last time, to give her a chance to know me again, to give her…give each of us…a chance to forgive, forget, love each other again?"

My insides were crumbling. Matthew Moxley had come all this way based on a story I'd told his boyfriend, a story I now knew to be a fabrication. I handed him his wallet back, which he accepted and returned to his pocket.

"You're very brave," I told him.

He shook his head. "No, Mr. Quant. I'm not brave at all. A lot of me is still that young boy, running scared, afraid of what's behind him, but I know now that I cannot go forward with my life unless I stop and look back there. See what there is to see. Feel it. Deal with it. Believe me, Mr. Quant, I didn't come by this decision easily. I didn't come by it alone. I've had a lot of help and guidance, from the very country I now live in and call home, and the people who live there. They've taught me this."

"*Ubuntu*," I said.

He looked at me with a kindness that was impossible to fake (unless this man was a consummate actor). "Of course. You have been to my home, to South Africa," he said in an accent that was no longer Canadian. "Maybe you have learned this too?"

I could only nod. Although I admired and maybe aspired to it, I was very far from practicing anything close to the South African's belief in *ubuntu*, the deep sense that each of us is an integral part of the thread of humanity and that we must all take care of one another to take care of ourselves. Still, I was grateful for having had the opportunity to be exposed to it, even for a short time.

"I thought I knew what *ubuntu* was," Matthew said, almost as if he was feeding off my own doubts. "I thought I was practicing it in my own life, but I was wrong. You showed me that, Mr. Quant."

"I did?" I asked, surprised.

"Through you, my mother reached out her hand to me, from Canada all the way to Africa. You were her hand. My mother was reaching out to me, and all the while all I could think of was how to pull further away. So far away that you were told I was dead, of AIDS. I used the scourge of Africa to protect myself. It's unforgivable, such selfishness. And worse still, I shunned my mother's hand. This is not *ubuntu*.

"After you and Kevan spoke in Chobe, and he told me your story and how he believed that you were telling the truth, that you were not responsible for what happened to the Chikosis, I decided that if there was even a slight chance that my mother was truly looking for me, reaching our for me, I would look for her too. I would reach out to her. Maybe, somewhere in the middle, we would meet.

"You gave Kevan your business card, Mr. Quant. I used the information on the card to follow you here to Saskatoon. I arrived late last night, rented a car and drove to this office, the address on your card. I was willing to wait outside the building for however long it took, waiting for someone fitting your description to arrive, so that I could ask you the question I want to ask you now, Mr. Quant."

I sucked in a breath and waited for it.

"Where is my mother?"

Thunk. The sound of my heart falling flat.

I believed this guy. I believed he was who he said he was and why he was here. Now I had to tell him that his mother wasn't really looking for him. How crappy is that? I struggled to formulate the gentlest way to tell him.

Thunk.

This time the sound was not my heart.

It came from somewhere on the second floor.

A jolt of fear ripped through me like lightning through a dried up birch. In that instant I knew Matthew Moxley was in mortal danger.

My eyes flew to his. "You're not safe here, Matthew!" I warned in a hushed, urgent voice.

A look of alarm covered his face as he responded, eyes wide, "What are you talking about? Is something wrong?"

There was no time to explain that if *he* wasn't my nine a.m. appointment, then someone else was about to pay us a visit, someone desperate to find Matthew Ridge, someone vicious enough to beat up Ethan and the Chikosis, someone I had lured here with my phone call fib of producing Matthew Ridge. Little did I know I was about to make good on my phony promise.

I leapt towards Matthew, clamped my fist around his arm, and raced for the front door, all the while keeping my gun trained in the general area behind our backs. I let go only long enough to throw open the door and push him through it.

"My car's in the back!" I hollered at him.

We needed a fast getaway, but I worried that the time it would

take us to circle the building to the parking lot in broad daylight
would make us perfect targets, like two rabbits racing for a hole in
a field. I saw no other choice, though, and pulled Matthew after
me.

I felt him hesitate and yanked harder.

He must have been reading my mind because he yelled at me:
"My car's right there!"

Parked on the street in front of PWC was a shiny, new, red
Sonata with a Hertz sticker on the rear bumper.

"Keys!" I bellowed as I pushed him ahead of me toward the
car, keeping myself between him and the house. He tossed me a set
of keys, and I pushed a button and heard the comforting sound of
doors unlocking just as we reached for them, me at the driver's
side and Matthew the passenger side: all very Sonny-Crockett-
Rico-Tubbs-from-*Miami-Vice*-like.

When the motor roared to life, I slammed into Drive and
pulled away faster than a hot wax strip from a hairy back. I would
have loved nothing better than to march back into PWC and confront (and identify) the intruder, but I knew my first priority was
to get the real Matthew Ridge out of the danger he'd unwittingly
stepped into. As I roared down peaceful Spadina, careful not to
ram the back ends of Sunday drivers looking to park near one of
the cathedrals in the neighbourhood, I checked the rear-view mirror. I could see no unusual or furtive activity in or around PWC.
We'd made it! So far.

"What is going on?" Matthew asked once he sensed my stress
level had lowered enough for an impromptu Q&A. "Why am I in
danger? Who is chasing us? Where is my mother? You said something about a *pretend* Clara Ridge? Is my mother okay? Is she in
danger too? Please, you have to tell me something," he pleaded.

He was right, but I waited until we were safely over the
Broadway Bridge—alone—and heading for home before I began
the convoluted story. I gave him the high points (or low points
depending on how you look at it, I suppose) and then waited for
his reaction as we pulled up to the garage at the back of my yard.
Without the garage door opener (which was in my car), we could-
n't get in, but, although I'd seen no evidence of being tailed, I

thought it was safer to park in the back alley than on the street.

"So my mother isn't looking for me after all?" Matthew said in a subdued, melancholy voice, his already tired-looking face slipping into haggardness.

My eyes caught his, and I wished I could somehow ease the pain I saw there. But the facts of what had transpired to bring him here were what they were; I could not change that. He'd come all this way solely because he believed that his mother, whom he hadn't seen in twenty years, wanted to reunite with him. He'd felt abandoned, unwanted, unloved, and now, even after all those years, he had hope that all of those feelings could be, if not erased, at least eased. I felt awful. I couldn't begin to understand what he was going through.

I reached over and placed my hand on his forearm. "Matthew, I talked to your real mother yesterday. She *does* want to see you. Badly." I wasn't sure if I was telling the big blond man the complete truth, but I had to give him some hope. Without it he'd be lost. He'd return to Africa and bury himself so deep that he'd never be found again.

"Really?" I loved the look on his face. In many ways he still *was* that little boy who landed in trouble, was sent away, and never got to go home again.

"Matthew, we can't waste any more time right now." I didn't want to give him a chance to ask too many more questions about his real mother's intentions. "Someone is after you, and I have to find a way to protect you until I find out who they are and what they want with you."

He was still understandably perplexed. "This doesn't make any sense. Who could be doing this?"

I kept mum. The silence sat between us like a bubble full of words about to burst.

He studied my face and said, "You know who it is, don't you?"

"Come on," was my only answer, reaching for the door handle.

"Where are we going now?" he asked, uncertainty flashing in his eyes. "What is this place?" All he could see from where we were parked were the big blank doors of my garage and the high fence that surrounds my yard.

"This is my house," I told him. "I need to make some quick phone calls." Rough translation: I don't know if it's safe for you here either, so I gotta find someplace to stash you. What I did know was that if they'd found my office, they'd find my home. We were not out of the woods yet, but I hoped, at least for the next little while, we'd be okay here.

I looked at Matthew and wordlessly asked him to trust me.

"Okay," he whispered.

We got out of the car. I led Matthew around the garage and through the gate that leads into the back yard, warning him to be careful on a couple of icy spots that had yet to melt away. We had just passed the twiggy bare branches of a trio of Miss Kim lilacs when I saw the body.

I gagged.

It was Barbra.

For the briefest of seconds I almost allowed choking grief to overwhelm me. I felt the wells of my eyes fill with burning tears; my knees began to buckle; my insides became a quaking mass that seemed to want to expel itself from my body.

I never want to feel what I felt then ever again, or see what I saw ever again.

Suddenly, that mildly cool, Sunday morning in March had grown unbearably cold.

"Stop!" I hissed at Matthew, using the flat of my left hand to press him back behind the questionable protection of the lilac bushes, while at the same time pulling the gun I'd held on him earlier that morning from the waistband of my pants. I forced him down into a crouching position, with me next to him, and snuck glances around the bushes in an effort to assess the situation.

"What? What is it?" He hadn't seen my dog's still body, he didn't know how grave the situation had abruptly become, and I didn't have the time to explain. I needed to go to the side of my beloved pet, to be with her, regardless of the potential danger.

From my position I could see Barbra lying motionless on the ground, next to a metalwork bird bath, and near her mouth, burning bright red against the whiteness of the snow, were spittles of blood. I looked up at the sky, blotchy with sun dogs, and gulped at the fresh air. My girl. My best friend. I wanted to scream my outrage, my fury at whatever or whoever was responsible for this. My heart was beating so fast I thought it would surely burst. I moved a little further forward and craned my neck, hoping to catch sight of the back of the house; but it was impossible, blocked by ornamental trees, shrubs, garden benches and statuary.

To hell with it, I thought to myself. "You stay here!" I ordered Matthew. "Do not move until I come back for you. Do you understand? Do Not Move!"

He nodded his compliance and was smart enough to keep quiet as I scuttled towards Barbra's body.

Almost there, almost there, almost there, then…

Not ten metres away from where Barbra lay was a second body. I was felled by the immensity of the tragedy that had visited my home in the short hours since I'd left it that morning. It was Brutus. Brother and sister had been taken down together in an act of unfathomable brutality.

I literally dropped to my knees, halfway between the two, as if shot through the heart with an arrow. And then, more horror as I looked up and saw yet another sign of treachery. About midway between the back of the house and the spot where I was near-immobilized with grief, I could see where fresh snow had been disturbed, mushed about as if there'd been some kind of tussle, and in the centre of the rough circle of trampled snow was a darkness that I knew…even without seeing it up close, without smelling it, without touching its stickiness, I knew…it was more blood.

Alex.

In the time it took me to get up and run to the back door of the house, I managed to convince myself that although I was too late to help my dear, sweet dogs, there was still a chance I could save Alex. Whoever did this, and I was certain I knew who it was, could still be in there. I hoped he was.

Because I wanted to kill him.

I had to be smart about this. As long as the asshole hadn't seen me arrive or my discovery of Barbra and Brutus, I might have a chance—however small—to take him by surprise. I snuck up to the rear of the house and plastered myself against it, counted to ten, then dared a look through the glass of the kitchen sliding door. Nothing.

The door was unlocked. Centimetre by centimetre I eased it open until I'd created a space wide enough to get me and my gun through.

I stepped inside, anxious to help Alex, yet scared of what I might find. It was mid-morning, the room was cast in shadows, and the only sound was the hum of the refrigerator. I inched forward, pistol at the ready.

I made a dash for the kitchen island and fell into a low crouch behind it.

The room was empty. My body was reverberating with adrenaline. My right hand was clasping the handle of the gun so hard I could feel my knuckles scream with the pain of it. I had to lessen the pressure. But no, I realized, I couldn't. If I did, my hand would begin to tremble.

I considered my next move. I had one thing going for me: I knew this territory better than anyone else. To the left of the kitchen was the dining room, and off of it a hallway that led to the guest bedroom and bath; to the right was the living room, and another hallway to the den and master bedroom; either direction would eventually take me to the foyer and front door.

Which way? I had to focus my mind; I had to eradicate the refrain that echoed through it like a mantra: Alex. Where is Alex? Is Alex okay? I searched the floor for a telltale trail of blood, but saw none. I hoped that was a good sign.

Make a move, Quant, and make it a good one.

I decided on right and, rising slowly, moved in the direction of the living room, using whatever furniture was available along the way for cover and stealth.

He wasn't on the couches, by the fireplace, or near the grand piano. I crept toward the bar and peeked over the edge to see behind it.

Nothing.

Where was he? Where was he?

Maybe...maybe he wasn't here at all?

But I knew I wasn't wrong about what was going on here. Not only did I have the bodies of my two pups lying outside in the snow to prove it, but I could smell it. Evil had been here, and it reeked, like caustic poison, cooking oil gone bad, days-old garbage, death. Yes, evil had definitely been here.

A noise.

I fell back behind a bar stool, poor cover, but all I had, and listened.

Nothing. I waited. Nothing. Make another move, Quant.

I was about to slither down the length of the bar and make my way into the hallway to the rest of that side of the house, to my bedroom and den, when from the corner of my eye I saw it, through the living room's arched passageway into the foyer, a sight I'd been dreading.

A foot.

I had to remember to breathe.

It was the foot of someone who wasn't standing up.

I recognized the shoe immediately.

It belonged to Alex Canyon. Was he alone? Was he...hurt? Worse? I swallowed everything horrible that was boiling up inside me like water in an unwatched kettle and, using the piano for cover, slid closer for a look.

Closer.

Closer.

I still couldn't see anything but the foot and the lower half of a jeans-clad leg. Alex's leg.

Was it a trap? Was someone luring me into position? Time was wasting. Alex might be hurt and in need of immediate attention. I could stand it no longer. I rose to my full height and brandished my weapon ahead of me like a sword of honour (and hopefully, protection). I stepped toward the foyer, each centimetre bringing the body lying in the foyer more fully into view; Alex's foot, his legs, his waist, torso, shoulders...face.

I felt my temperature spike with a temper and rage I'd not known before.

Alex had been propped against the front door. His hands were tied behind his back, and his head had fallen to the side. His mouth was gagged, and I could see two wounds on his body from which blood had oozed, staining his clothing to saturation—one at his chest and one at his left knee. Like Barbra and Brutus, he wasn't moving. The mighty Alex Canyon, my glorious gladiator, my Goliath, had fallen.

I could hold it back no longer, and an unimaginable grief consumed me like a black plague. My whole world had collapsed that morning. Three of the best things in my life were taken from me, taken and systematically destroyed.

I felt as though I was going to pass out.

And then Alex's eyes opened.

With his mouth gagged, he could not speak, but in his eyes I saw a riotous collection of competing emotions: pain, guilt, fear, anger and finally…warning!

It was too late.

Chapter 18

"Put the gun on the floor, kick it away, and turn around very slow-ly," the voice told me.

I did as ordered.

It was Matthew Moxley I saw when I turned around.

He was standing in front of the business end of a gun being held by a man I'd never seen before. He was smaller than Matthew, compact and sturdy, with tousled dark hair and vaguely Mediterranean features. Written across his face, like an advertisement of his guilt, were two angry scratches running from the corner of his left eye to the edge of his thin-lipped mouth. Courtesy of Thandile Chikosi.

I knew who he was. The man with the limp. The man who'd followed me to Ethan Ash's house and later assaulted him. The man who'd followed me to Africa and attacked the couple in Khayelitsha. The man behind the mask of the fake Clara Ridge. The man who'd *really* hired me to find Matthew Ridge.

He was Robin Haywood, the boy Matthew Ridge had bashed, nearly to death, twenty years ago, now grown up. The "...Robin with the broken wing..." as Errall had recalled him being labelled by a *StarPhoenix* article, an article I had subsequently dug up from the library archives. According to the newspaper report I'd found, Robin Haywood had survived his beating, barely, and spent months in the hospital recuperating from his wounds. The doc-tor's prognosis was that in time he would fully recover—physical-ly—except for his right leg—the broken wing—which would leave him with a permanent limp. It seemed a small price, given the severity of the beating, but the bigger damage done to Robin Haywood—the wound that was never treated and never healed— was psychological. It was only after reading this article that I knew for sure that my theory was correct: the limping man was Robin Haywood.

"Both of you," Robin said, motioning with the gun. "On the floor next to Matthew."

Whazzat? Next to Matthew? But Matthew is right in front of you.

It struck me then. He thought Alex was Matthew…?

Immediately I understood what must have transpired in my house that morning, and why. When I left the message with the fake Clara Ridge telling her I had come back from Africa with her son, I suspected (and hoped) that a meeting would be requested. Clara Ridge wouldn't show up; the real Clara Ridge was at home in Airdrie, Alberta, and had no idea any of this was going on. Instead, the fake Clara—probably some local actress hired to play the part, or a friend or relative sympathetic to Robin's cause— would have passed my message (as she'd been doing all along) to the man behind it all: Robin Haywood. It would be Robin who showed up at my office. After finding out where Matthew was, and dealing with me, he'd finally have his confrontation with his childhood nemesis. It was what he'd wanted all along: a one-on-one faceoff. Of course, in my plan, I would be the one confronting Robin with his crimes against Ethan and the Chikosis. But all of that had gone wrong. There were two things I didn't—couldn't have anticipated: the real Matthew Ridge's showing up at my office, and the presence of Alex Canyon in my home, leading Robin Haywood to make his grievously erroneous assumption.

"He's hurt," I said to Robin, indicating Alex, hoping to delay the inevitable.

"Yeah, I know," Robin said with a sneer. "Do you think I care?"

I was guessing not.

After my last phone message to "Clara," Robin must have begun a surveillance of my home and discovered Alex, whom he mistook for Matthew. I'd done my job for him by finding his child-hood tormentor; now all he wanted was to be alone with him.

He'd never intended to meet me at the office that morning. The noise I'd heard there was nothing more than my reasonable suspicions on overdrive. Through the fake message from "Clara Ridge," Robin had lured me away from my house, leaving "Matthew" by himself and unprotected. It was payback time.

Having figured out he couldn't gain access to the house or "Matthew" without first dealing with the dogs, Robin must have waited until Alex let Barbra and Brutus out into the yard (a fairly regular occurrence), then took care of them and waited for Alex to come out to investigate why the dogs weren't returning. When he did, they had some sort of struggle in the snow, which ended up with Alex being shot. He then dragged Alex into the privacy of the house to carry out whatever his endgame was, probably beginning with a browbeating and interrogation.

"Can I take the gag off of him?" I asked.

"Shut up, or I'll put one on you too. Now get down on the floor!" Robin ordered again.

Of course, Alex would have denied being Matthew Ridge, which would only have served to fuel Robin's fury further. Robin would have known he had very little time before I eventually figured things out and returned home, so he tied Alex up, gagged him, and waited in ambush for me somewhere in the backyard.

And now here we all were.

Matthew stepped toward me, his eyes never leaving mine. It must have confused him that the guy with the gun was calling the guy on the floor by his name, but I could see that he was beginning to figure things out as well.

With deliberate movements, his hands raised, palms facing out in submission, Matthew slowly twisted around to face Robin Haywood.

Suddenly I knew what he was about to do.

"No!" I warned him off his intent.

I was too late.

"I'm Matthew Ridge," he said to Robin, the two of them now face to face. "Not him." He bobbed his head in Alex's direction. "I don't know who this other guy is, but it's me you want, not him. Let these guys go," he added. A truly selfless, heroic gesture.

Beneath his tangle of dark hair, Robin's eyes moved ever so slowly from Matthew's face to Alex's bound body then back to Matthew. Dawning recognition filled them, and I was nervous about what that would mean for the real Matthew. In that instant he recognized his arch-enemy, and knew that Matthew was telling him the truth.

"Sit down, I told you!" Robin spat out at me. Then, at the real Matthew: "Not you. Stay where you are."

I lowered myself onto the floor next to Alex, and we exchanged wordless glances that said a lot. With his rigid back to us, Matthew kept his stance still and straight, standing halfway between us and Robin, and facing the gun that was now pointed at his heaving chest.

"Let these guys go," he said again. "Or better yet, why don't you and I go somewhere. We can talk this out. Just the two of us."

"It *is* you," Robin half-whispered as if he hadn't heard Matthew's request, mesmerized, his eyes covering every inch of the other man.

After a moment, the spell was broken and an ugly sneer crept onto his face. "This other guy kept telling me he wasn't you, and I didn't believe him. He wouldn't admit what he did to me. I thought once I had Quant here, and threatened to kill him, he would own up to what he did, but..." He stared at Matthew, "...but it's *you.*"

Matthew's head moved up and down. "Yes, Robin. It's me."

Their voices were surprisingly calm and measured, as if they'd been waiting for this meeting all their lives and were well-prepared for it. The only outward sign of Matthew's true state was a slight quiver in his raised hands.

I began searching the room with my eyes, looking for a means to end this thing with as little bloodshed as possible. Alex, with his hands bound and mouth gagged, suffering from gunshot wounds, would be of little assistance. Matthew was directly threatened by Robin's gun. My own firearm was too far away for me to reach without putting both Alex and Matthew in danger of being shot before I got to it. There were no other obvious weapons nearby. Okay, Quant, that's the list of bad news items. What about good news?

I couldn't come up with any.

"Do you remember it?" Robin asked Matthew, his voice growing more intense now. "Do you remember what you did to me?"

Matthew nodded.

"Do you remember it *every day*? In vivid, blood-red detail? Do
you?"

"I do," Matthew answered penitently.

"You don't! You don't! You don't!" Robin screamed. "You have
no idea what it felt like! You can't. You weren't the one being
kicked and punched and spit on! Have you ever been spit on,
Matthew? Have you ever had someone else's spit, mixed with
your own blood, running down your face, into your eyes, into
your nose and mouth, tasting it? Have you? Have you ever been
lying on the ground, defenseless, being hit, being kicked, being
called names, being called a fag over and over again?"

He took a menacing step closer to Matthew, his face contorting
into vile loathing. He shrieked, "Fag! Fag! You big fag!" He
released a snort of laughter that was painfully sad, and added bit-
terly, "And I'm not even gay, for chrissakes!"

"Robin, I di..."

"Shut up, shut up, shut up! I'm talking now. I give the orders
now. This is *my* time!"

"Okay, okay, just settle down, will you?"

"Do you know what that did to me? What *you* did to me? Sure
they fixed my cuts and scrapes, got everything all nice and clean,
covered it with bandages and ointment...What a joke; no one ever
talked about what really happened to me, or why. Not the doctors,
or my parents. I had no friends. No one ever wanted to know if I
was okay in here!" He pointed to his temple with the nose of the
gun. "They were all so desperate to forget about it, put it behind
them, pretend like it never happened; no one wanted to deal with
it. I felt like...I felt...it was like...it was like they thought maybe it
was partly my fault...maybe I'd asked for it somehow. In the end,
they just wanted to go back to life the way it was before." Another
snort. "Yeah, like that could ever happen."

As I listened to Robin's anguished telling of his story I could-
n't help but feel compassion. And empathy. I could picture his
poor, child's body, wrecked and bleeding and left all alone out-

doors, in that dark place in the park. And then, shockingly, with everything else that was happening around me at that moment, another unbidden picture filled my brain.

Another body, lying unprotected, battered, bloodied, nearly naked, all alone, outside in the dark.

It was my body. Only months ago. Attacked by a madman who'd wanted to rape me. Almost did. I heard Robin's words:

"...desperate to forget it, put it behind them, pretend like it never happened..." Yes. That was me.

I shook my head to rid it of the memory. Now wasn't the time. But I knew I would have to make time for it, someday.

"By the time I got out of the hospital," Robin continued with his harrowing tale, "everyone had it swept under the carpet like dirt they never wanted to see again. They acted like I'd gone in for an operation, had whatever it was that was bothering me removed, and now everything was fine. The ugliness had been excised, and now I was all better. It was over."

From my spot on the floor I could see only one side of Matthew Moxley's face, but that was enough for me to know that he was feeling the story as deeply as Robin.

"You'd been sent away to some reform school or something," Robin spewed. "For them, that was enough. Out of sight, out of mind. You'd been dealt with. Dealt with! Dealt with! Dealt with! Can you believe it?" he directed this last to Alex and me. "That's all it takes to deal with someone who almost beats you to death and then leaves you in a lake of your own blood and piss and shit and vomit. Is that enough punishment? Do you think so? Do you?"

We decided not to answer.

"But for me, it had only just begun," Robin kept on, the tortured planes of his face moving in and out of shadow. "Because then came the nightmares."

"I have them too," Matthew whispered.

This stopped Robin. He gave the other man a guarded, questioning look. "You do?"

"Every night," Matthew said, his own face showing the strains of repressed memories, bubbling to the surface, as unpleasant as raw sewage. "I know I can't feel your pain, Robin, but the pain of remembering what I did to you, remembering each...and... every...time I hit you and called you a name." He stopped for a moment, to swallow a lump in his throat. "I know exactly how many times I kicked you—fourteen—how many times I punched you in the back—twice—punched you in the gut—six times—how many times I hit you in the head—twelve—how many times I spit on you—four times, Robin—how many times I called you a fuckin' faggot—eleven times. I know each time by heart. I relive them in my dreams every night. And I know..." And here he hesitated, momentarily overcome with a choking remorse. "I know how many times you yelled out for me to stop. Stop!" He cried it out as if it were him calling out for help. "Fifteen times. Fifteen! Fifteen times you pleaded with me to stop!" Then his voice became quiet. "I hear it every night. That sound. Those words. They haunt me to this day. Stop! Stop, Matthew! Stop! Stop."

"But you didn't," Robin said, implacable, his words stone hard.

"I didn't."

"Why?"

"I..." Matthew could go on no longer. He lowered his head to his chest and he began to cry. Fat tears spouted from his eyes, like droplets of water through a crack in a glass, so big that I could see them from where I sat on the floor, sliding over the hump of his cheek toward his trembling chin.

After a moment, he kept on. "I didn't stop because I wanted you dead. I wanted you dead because *I* wanted to be dead. I wanted to be dead because I knew I was gay and I didn't want to be. Every time I hit you I was imagining hitting myself, the faggy boy I saw in the mirror every day, I was trying to...trying to...trying to beat the gay out of me."

"Why didn't you just kill yourself?" Robin asked in an ugly tone. "Why did you have to do this to me? To me!"

Matthew's head came up to face Robin and he gave the simple, honest, difficult answer: "It was easier. I was angry. I was a coward."

The silence that followed this admission was long, and hard to sit through, for countless reasons.

I was nowhere nearer to finding a way to disarm Robin, to

bring this to an end, but suddenly I had hope that perhaps, just maybe, he would do it himself. Robin Haywood had needed to confront Matthew, the boy who had changed his life with an act of atrocious violence. Was this exchange between the two, twenty years after the fact, going to be enough to dissolve the animosity Robin had been cultivating and nurturing for all those years? Would this bring Matthew some semblance of inner peace, the absolution he'd denied himself for so long? Could this end well for either of these men? Could the grace of *ubuntu* exist between them? Save them?

"I've never been with a woman," Robin said flatly.

Matthew could only nod.

"Not because I'm gay," he said. "I've *never* been able to form a normal sexual relationship with *anyone*. Never. Can you comprehend that? Never. No one wants to be in bed with someone who wakes up screaming from nightmares. No one wants to be with someone who can't stand to be touched because he fears that every stroke or rub or simple kiss of affection might be followed by a fist in the gut. If any-one tries to touch me, I recoil. I'm always afraid. Always alone. And I'll always be this way, Matthew. Because of you."

Another nod.

"Because of you," he repeated the conviction.

"I'm sorry, Robin," Matthew responded. "I've never said it, and I need to. I am so sorry for what I did to you, Robin. If I could take it all back, I would. If I could change places with you, I would. If I can do anything to help you now, I will. Let me help you."

They stared at one another for a long time. Finally, it was Robin who broke the silent communion. "I know how you can help me," he said.

"Tell me," Matthew replied quickly. "Anything,"

"You can die."

Aw shit.

Robin lifted his gun so that it was in line with Matthew's heart. This was it. Do or die.

I could not let this happen. I knew there was no easy way out of this, but this was my job. My job was to save Matthew Ridge. I braced myself against the floor, steeled my muscles and prepared to spring up.

Instead, I saw a dark form flying through the air, like some giant bat, aiming for Robin Haywood's back, and with it came the most ferocious sound I had ever heard. A snarl of undiluted hatred. I could not believe my ears...or eyes.

It was Barbra.

As my beloved schnauzer landed on Robin's shoulders, I leapt across the distance between me and Matthew and knocked him off his feet and to the ground. Robin let out a blood-curdling scream as Barbra snapped and bit at his face, his neck and ears, sounding like a dinosaur eating ribs and gravy. With horror I saw that the gun was still in Robin's hand and he was waving it about wildly.

A shot rang out.

I heard a grunt.

God, no.

Alex! He'd been shot by Robin a third time.

I let out a flood of expletives that included many I'd only heard in gangster movies and never used out loud before, and I meant every one of them. I jumped to my feet. Barbra and Robin were still struggling. I pounded my heel down on Robin's exposed gun wrist, so hard it might have gone through the floor if it hadn't been covered with slate tile. Robin let out an agonized shriek, and the gun popped from his grasp like bread from a toaster. I grabbed it.

I let Barbra stay on top of him while I rushed to Alex's side to see how bad he'd been hurt. As far as I could tell, the bullet had grazed his shin but never entered his body. I yanked the gag off his mouth and looked into his eyes, which were beginning to glaze over. He was going into shock.

I looked back at Barbra who was declining assistance from Matthew. She must have sensed my gaping stare, and the fact that the blubbering man beneath her was no longer much of a threat, because she stopped her nipping and growling and looked up at me with a slobbering, lopsided grin. I had no idea how she'd risen from the dead, but at that moment I didn't care.

"I love you, Barbra. I love you, girl."

I'm sure she winked at me with a "Back at ya" look covering her beautiful face.

Constable Darren Kirsch stood near the French doors of my bedroom, looking uncomfortable as he gazed out at the sunny, spring-like day in my backyard. I wasn't exactly sure why he was there. We'd gone over everything several times at the hospital during the course of Alex's treatment for his gunshot wounds and again later in his office at the police station.

Robin Haywood admitted to using the fake Clara Ridge to hire me to find Matthew. Robin hadn't hired me himself because the mother angle seemed to be the most plausible scenario to present to a detective, and he wisely wanted no connection made to him after he carried out his intended deed: killing Matthew Ridge.

At first I was unclear about the reason for the elaborate story of Clara Ridge having all that money, but it was the only way Robin could come up with to explain how a poor widow could suddenly afford to hire a detective and spare no expense in finding her son. Robin, in spite of his physical and emotional injuries, had done quite well for himself in business and had decided to dedicate some of his considerable wealth to finding the boy/man who'd ruined his life at the age of sixteen.

After failing to find Matthew himself, Robin had decided his best bet was to hire a professional to do the legwork. His plan was to follow the detective around, and when the opportunity presented itself, carry out his revenge. With both Ethan Ash and the Chikosis, Robin jumped the gun and erroneously thought I'd found the missing link that would lead him to Matthew. He thought he'd cut out the expense of the middleman—me—and at the same time release pent-up rage by beating Matthew's whereabouts out of them.

In the case of Ethan, the arrival of oldster Frank had sent him scurrying away before he could learn anything of use, but a blinding punch, before he could be identified, had taken Ethan down. In Khayelitsha, his assault had had more dire results—not only for the Chikosis, but for me. The people in the township who knew and loved Matthew assumed the worst. They did not believe my arrival to look for Matthew and the attack on the Chikosis was a coincidence. And, in retrospect, I suppose I couldn't blame them. They set in motion the power of *ubuntu*, from South Africa to

Zambia and Botswana, to protect Matthew from me.

Now, two decades after the horrible event that first started this, I could only hope things were finally being set right. Robin Haywood would get the psychological help he needed, and Matthew Ridge/Moxley would reunite with his mother.

Indeed, Matthew was en route to Airdrie, Alberta, for his first visit in twenty years with his mother. I could hardly guess what that would be like or how it would turn out. They had a lot of ground to cover, but if anyone had the right attitude for contrition and understanding, it was Matthew. My hopes were high.

I felt Alex squeeze my hand and gave him a smile.

"How ya doing?" I asked him.

He smiled back. "Good."

He was like a king being feted by his subjects, lying on my bed amongst fluffy pillows and cozy comforters, Barbra and Brutus like furry brackets on either side of him. On the bedside table was a tray of his favourite food (sent over from Colourful Mary's by Marushka and Mary), and there were get well cards and gag gifts at his feet.

Sereena was perched beautifully on the opposite side of the bed from me. She was wearing a satiny lounging outfit, sipping at a champagne cocktail and soundly ignoring my mother who stood nearby in case Alex opened his mouth wide enough for her to drop another morsel of food into it (her own home baking, not the much less *smachneh*—according to her—provisions from Colourful Mary's). Mom was dressed in a faded pink housedress under an orange and blue striped apron, her black and steel grey hair freshly set into tight curls. She was awkwardly nursing her own champagne cocktail, which Sereena'd pressed into her hands knowing full well she'd barely drink it.

Across the room was Kelly Doell. I was still somewhat shellshocked to see her, standing in my bedroom, back in our lives, as if she'd never been gone. She was enjoying a giggling gossip session with Errall and Jared on the couch beneath the picture window. Kelly'd turned up in Saskatoon just before I went to Africa, and according to my own sources of gossip, she had spent the last few days at Errall's house (the one they had once shared as a couple) with very few dealings involving the outside world. With all that was going on, I'd yet to hear exactly why she was back, and for how long. By the looks of her and Errall together, I'd say one of the things she'd come back for was Errall. I wasn't sure how I felt about that.

Anthony was keeping my other PWC officemates, Alberta Lougheed and Beverly Chaney, enthralled with selections from his never-ending collection of colourful tales. Anthony and Jared seemed okay. For now. But who really knows what goes on beneath the public surface of any relationship? I'd been invited in, briefly, but only as a visitor, not a participant—just the way it should be.

Actually, everyone seemed okay, happy. Today was about welcoming Alex home after his ordeal. My friends and family knew that, and with typical generosity of heart and spirit, they were doing a bang-up job putting aside whatever dramas were affecting their own lives to celebrate the fact that Alex still had one, after being shot three times by Robin Haywood. They were here for Alex. For me. I looked around again at this collection of people, and the phrase I'd first heard in that South African township—"I am what I am because of who we all are,"—repeated in my head. And I knew it to be truer than ever, even here in this little house on the prairies. Saskatchewan *ubuntu*.

I needed it to be true.

I gave Alex a quick kiss on the forehead and left his side to speak with Darren Kirsch.

"Thanks for coming over," I said to the big cop. "I know Alex appreciates your being here for his coming out—of hospital—party."

Kirsch gave me one of his signature looks, the one where his nose and the left side of his mouth crumple together with only his cheesy moustache keeping them apart. Kind of cute in a Troll doll kind of way. "Quant, I know what you're really thinking. You're wondering: Why the hell is he here? I don't remember inviting him."

I cleared my throat and gave him a contrite nod. "Actually, yes, that's about right." There is precious little social politeness between Kirsch and me, which I find really rather refreshing.

"Well, you're right. I wasn't invited. And that hurts me in a way I can't tell you, Quant."

I swallowed hard. Had I somehow misjudged this guy? "Darren, I'm sorry, I guess I...."

The mocking laughter stopped my blubbering idiocy.

"Kidding, Quant, I'm kidding. Ooooo boy, you are outta practice. You're more gullible than my two year old. Whassamatter with you? C'mon!" he chided me with great, hateful mirth, and then he came clean. "I showed up at the door and your mother dragged me in here. Figures someone like you would have a party in his bedroom. When does everyone change into their jammies, Sandra Dee?"

"That's a door right behind you."

He ignored my suggestion and handed me an envelope.

"What's this?"

"It's why I came over. It's the lab results on Barbra and Brutus. Just what we thought: he fed them steak laced with sedative. Looks like Brutus ate all of his and some of Barbra's, either that or Haywood simply put more of the stuff in his steak. That's why Brutus took so much longer to come out of it."

"And the blood I saw in the snow around Barbra's mouth was from her eating the raw meat?"

He nodded. "Or she may have tried to regurgitate the poisoned material if it didn't sit well in her stomach. Dogs are good about stuff like that. That might be another reason why she was able to wake up and attack Robin Haywood before he shot Matthew Ridge. I hope you've rewarded her appropriately."

"Believe me," I told him, "Barbra is being treated like a queen around here. When Mom arrived the other day she brought more food for her than for me. Have you ever heard of doggie perogies? Instead of mashed potato or cabbage, she fills them with Purina."

"Anyway," he said, "I knew you were waiting on the results, so..." He began to move away.

I laid a hand on his beefy forearm. "Hey, wait. You came all the way over here just to give me this?" He could have mailed them. He could have told me to pick them up at the police station. He could have phoned it in.

"This is Saskatoon, Quant, not Detroit," he countered a little too quickly. "It's not like I had to spend two hours in traffic to get over here to your little pajama party."

"There's beer in the fridge if you want one," I offered in a conciliatory way (which I thought was big of me, given the pajama party remarks).

"Gotta go," he told me, keeping his eyes anywhere but on me. "Treena and the kids are waiting for me to take them to Red Lobster."

"Okay." I held out a hand. We never shake. "Thanks, eh?"

"Yup." He took my hand and gave it a quick pump. He waved at Alex as he passed by the bed and left the room.

I sidled back to my place next to Alex.

"Hey," he said, pulling me in close. "Thank you for the party. I've never had anybody do anything like this for me before."

"You are very welcome. It's the least I could do for the guy who tried to save my dogs and ended up getting shot—three times—all because of me."

His face moved even closer to mine and he whispered, "It's the least I could do for the guy I love."

Love.

Oooo.

We shared a gentle kiss, and I laid my head on his chest, letting myself be lulled by its gentle up and down motion. I buried my eyes deep into the burgeoning spring outside the bedroom window.

How had this happened, I wondered to myself.

For indeed, I too...perhaps for the first time... had fallen madly, deeply...unaccountably...in love.

With someone else.